AMERICAN NIGHTS

A MORIAH DRU/RICHARD LAKE
MYSTERY

AMERICAN NIGHTS

GERRIE FERRIS FINGER

FIVE STAR
A part of Gale, Cengage Learning

GALE
CENGAGE Learning®

Farmington Hills, Mich • San Francisco • New York • Waterville, Maine
Meriden, Conn • Mason, Ohio • Chicago

GALE
CENGAGE Learning®

LIBRARY OF CONGRESS CATALOGING-IN-PUBLICATION DATA

Names: Finger, Gerrie Ferris, author.
Title: American nights : a Moriah Dru/Richard Lake mystery / by Gerrie Ferris Finger.
Description: First edition. | Waterville, Maine : Five Star, a part of Cengage Learning,Inc. 2016.
Identifiers: LCCN 2016001571 (print) | LCCN 2016006615 (ebook) | ISBN 9781432832216 (hardback) | ISBN 1432832212 (hardcover) | ISBN 9781432832049 (ebook) | ISBN 1432832042 (ebook)
Subjects: | BISAC: FICTION / Mystery & Detective / General. | GSAFD: Mystery fiction. | Suspense fiction.
Classification: LCC PS3606.I534 A83 2016 (print) | LCC PS3606.I534 (ebook) | DDC 813/.6—dc23
LC record available at http://lccn.loc.gov/2016001571

First Edition. First Printing: August 2016
Find us on Facebook– https://www.facebook.com/FiveStarCengage
Visit our website– http://www.gale.cengage.com/fivestar/
Contact Five Star™ Publishing at FiveStar@cengage.com

To my late brother's wife, Barbara Zimmerly,
and their children—the Schoenfelds:
Dina, Eddie, Hayden, Blaine, Kelby.
May you always be as happy as you are now.

Chapter One

Portia Devon folded her hands on her desk. The tilt of her head and her scheming eyes reminded me of our young days when we planned midnight excursions to forbidden clubs. She said, "Your fame has caught the attention of a prominent person."

"You called me here to tell me that?"

"Also to explain the nature of his attention."

"And who would this prominent person be?"

"An international figure who wants you to find his daughter."

So like Portia, judge that she is, to draw out a mystery. Wriggling into the leather chair designed for the discomfort of adversaries to her chambers, I thought, *This could mean a free trip, courtesy of the Internal Revenue Service.* Atlanta was weighing on my well-being. My fame, as Portia labeled it, came about because of a horrendous case the city had offered up owing to its drug and gang wars.

I said, "I get that it's a him who wants to hire me to find his missing girl. Where internationally?"

"Starting here, in this fabulous international city." Her sarcasm illustrated she meant Atlanta, a city that was trying hard to wipe the slate of its quasi-genteel southern roots. "More precisely, his wife disappeared with their daughter."

I opened my mouth to ask a pertinent question, but she raised a hand. "I don't know much more than I'm telling you, but the trace appears to be straightforward, not much danger."

I thought about other child traces. Danger could be and often was an issue. I said, "You know I don't do heights and tight places, like jumping out of planes or diving in caves."

"There *is* a cultural element."

"Cultural in what way?"

"Ethnic customs, religious differences."

"All right, Porsh, out with it—your prominent person by name, and those of the wife and daughter."

"You are familiar with the Middle East?"

Involuntarily my shoulders drew back. *No wars or terrorists, please.* "We've worked with the state department in getting children back from fathers that . . ." I paused, because up until now I'd worked only with mothers in their quest to get their children returned from countries outside the United States.

"This is not about absconding fathers," Portia said.

Portia could be so tedious when she wanted to be. "So mama snatches the girl and brings her here? How old?"

"Four." Portia tapped her expensive ballpoint pen as she spoke the words. "I don't know where she's taken the child, but there will be no state department involved."

"Sounds like a Hague case, in reverse."

"It is not a Hague."

I considered her no-argument tone of voice in terms of Hague cases. If someone illegally kidnapped a child from American soil and fled to a partner country, the Hague Abduction Convention kicked in. A Hague application was filed and forwarded to the Foreign Central Authority in that country. That was what I was used to working with; apparently, the reverse of what Portia was presenting to me, but I was not sure how.

"The child's father is from a US partner country in the Middle East," Portia said. "The child was born in a European partner country. The mother is American."

"Where in Europe was the girl born?"

"Paris, France."

"That's unusual. If Interpol is the policing agency, they are very good at locating missing children, even well-hidden children. Children have relatives and relatives talk or can be followed. In the case you're talking about, we would work with the Federal Bureau of Investigation, or maybe Homeland Security."

"The father believes they are still in America, possibly Atlanta. Interested?"

"I'd have to know more."

My agency, Child Trace, Inc., has had many clients and much experience in all that can happen in abduction cases, but I've never had a dual-citizenship case. I've had cases where girls were brought here for the slave trade, primarily from Eastern Europe, South America and China. But no one was looking for them. Sad to say, no application needed to be filed. Portia had come across them through the sleazebags that sold the girls whenever the police arrested their captors or pimps.

Portia sat back. "If you accept the case, you will be told all you need to know, but you must understand the father insists on no FBI, no state police, no Homeland Security, no CIA."

That raised my eyebrows. What the hell could Portia, a Georgia juvenile judge, have to do with a possible CIA case?

Something in her faint frown told me she knew what I was thinking. "You may well wonder," she said. "My connection to the father goes back a ways."

When she said no more, I asked, "That's all you're going to tell me? You ever work for the CIA?" On reflection, Porsh did have a dark aspect—black hair, dark eyes, sharp nose. I made my mouth smile.

She spread her hands on her desk. "Compelling, isn't it?"

"Actually, it is. When do I get to meet the man and hear the circumstances, and how urgent is it?"

"I don't think there's a lot of urgency. They've been gone a week already."

9

I didn't hesitate to tell her. "I'll have to confide in Lake."

"No Lake."

"Then, no me."

"Come on, Moriah. You and Lake aren't joined at the belly."

"Hmmm."

"You know what I meant. Lake will be duty-bound, legally, to advise his commander."

"Not if the Atlanta Police Department isn't involved. Lake does have a private life. When can I talk to your . . . uh . . . connection?"

"When I assure him of your discretion."

I got up. "I'll see you Saturday. You *are* coming to the ball game with us, aren't you? We've got a ticket for Walker, too." Walker was her son.

"Moriah, sit your ass down and listen to me." I sat. "You are the best person for this task."

"How did your connection know about, and choose, me?"

"Although he resides in New York, he read or heard about the shoot-out in the churchyard."

"Lake was part of the shoot-out, too."

Portia sighed. "I'll relay your demand."

"Does this connection of yours have problems with the police or the government?"

"Not to my knowledge. He's a foreign national working in the US. He's been a diplomat, but I don't know if he still has that status."

"Is this man in Atlanta now?"

"Yes." She rolled back her chair and rose. "Now I shall make the phone call."

She left her chambers to go into the jury room.

I admit I was intrigued, but no way was I going to withhold details of an assignment from Lake. Even if I could, I wouldn't. From our beginning—as partners when I was with the Atlanta

American Nights

Police Department—we shared information. After we started
sharing our bodies, I resigned the shop and started my own
agency. Many times he's been a valuable asset, but that isn't the
reason I would not hold out on him. We simply share everything.
Portia knows that.

She returned to her chambers and sat with exaggerated effort. "Stubborn cuss," she mumbled. "All right. You and Lake,
but no APD. You both meet with him as soon as you can. This
evening okay?"

"What's his name?"

"Husam bin Sayed al-Saliba."

"I think"—a dark, striking male face came to mind—"he was
in the news."

"For years he's been listed as one of the most handsome
princes in the world."

"I thought that man was single, most marriageable."

"He is, by Saudi law."

I called my computer geek and research specialist, Dennis
"Webdog" Caldwell, and instructed him to find all that was
available on Prince Husam bin Sayed al-Saliba. Then I Googled
the prince. Just seeing his photograph gave me a thrill. I would
be having dinner with him this evening. So would Lake, and
Lake was due to arrive here in half an hour.

I went from mirror to mirror checking my dress—neckline
high, hemline below my calves, three-quarter sleeves—and my
face, assessing my makeup, of which I usually wore little except
for lipstick. When Lake's car pulled into the driveway, I made a
decision and ran to the bathroom and washed the foundation
from my skin to avoid being chided for making up for a prince.

Lake had let himself in while I removed eyeliner. When I
went into the kitchen he was popping the top of a beer bottle.
He looked at me with a frown smearing his face. A few inches

over six feet tall, with dark hair and eyes, he was still the best-looking man I'd ever seen. An exquisite, dark-blue suit, white shirt, and red-and-blue striped tie decorated his trim, athletic frame.

He drank and rolled his lips inward before he said, "You look well-scrubbed."

"I ought to," I said. "I just removed the grime."

"Hmmm." He reached for my face, close to an ear, and rubbed a finger across my cheek. He held up the finger. "Flesh-colored grime. Did I ever tell you, skin looks good on you?" He kissed my nose. "What if I weren't accompanying you this evening?"

"I wouldn't be going. You are going with me by sufferance. Portia's."

"Let's get on the road then, red lips." He finished his beer and put the bottle in the recycle container. "I think the prince will be pleased to see a naked face. Judging from the extreme makeup worn by rich and famous women, I doubt he sees many naked—uh—faces." As we made our way to the door, he commented, "It's nice to see you in a dress. Where are you wearing your gun?"

I patted my right leg. "Thigh holster." Since the shoot-out at the church, I've been leery of retribution from Atlanta's drug gangs, one member in particular.

We left my small house, and Lake locked the door. Walking to the unmarked squad car, I said, "I looked up the prince's photograph. He's quite handsome."

On dressy evenings out, Lake holds the passenger door for me. After he'd done so, he lifted a hand above my head, something cops do when putting a subject into a squad car.

"Don't touch my hair," I said. "I spent hours on it."

"I like the scattered result."

"It's supposed to be sexy."

The car's engine roared to life. He glanced my way. "Already, you're trying to make me jealous."

"Oh that I could. I've tried my damnedest, but you're too practical."

On the way I told Lake what I'd learned from Webdog. "Prince Husam's religion is Wahabism, an ultra-conservative branch of Sunni Islam. He's thirty-six years old, but Web said that Saudi Arabian royals have a reputation for being cagey about ages. He's unmarried, but engaged to a Saudi princess, the name I forget."

"Yet he has a daughter?" Lake said.

"Portia left that for him to explain."

"An Arab man talking about procreation to a Western woman?"

"We shall soon hear. Prince Husam bin Sayed al-Saliba attended schools in Saudi Arabia, England and DC. Apparently DC is where Portia met him, because, after she graduated from the University of Georgia, she went on to Georgetown Law."

"I see," Lake said, turning onto Peachtree Street for the ride downtown.

"Husam bin Sayed al-Saliba is an attorney. In order to qualify as a lawyer in the Kingdom of Saudi Arabia you must have a bachelor's degree in Islamic jurisprudence and a bachelor's degree in law. A student can either attend a kingdom college or a recognized foreign university within rules set down by the Saudi Ministry of Higher Education."

"Thanks for the educational requirements in case I want to major in Islamic law and practice in the kingdom."

"Web, as you know, is very thorough and literal. The prince is also affiliated with an American law firm. Web told me that last year Husam al-Saliba was voted one of the ten most handsome princes in the world. Harry of England was third and our Husam was seventh. Having Googled the prince's photo, I don't agree with the ranking."

"You don't like red-headed men. That's why I dye my hair black."

"And bleach your freckles."

"That, too."

CHAPTER TWO

The restaurant chosen by the prince was one of excessive expense and masculinity, as I might have expected. I preceded Lake off the elevator and experienced the déjà vu of power in the ambience—that rarified sensation that speaks of authority and money and laps at the feet of greed. Lake asked, "How do we address this dude?"

I grinned at the idea of a prince being a dude. I parroted what Web had told me. "The royal line is composed of close relatives of the founder, King Khalid al-Saliba, and are referred to as His, or Her, Royal Highness. Other family members who do not belong to the direct al-Saliba line are second-tier. They are simply His, or Her, Highness. These lesser lights hold high ranking positions within the Saudi government, but they are not in line to the throne. One should always address a royal by title until invited to address informally. Husam bin Sayed al-Saliba gets the full royal treatment."

"I have to say that mouthful?"

"I've encountered wannabe rappers with more syllables in their names."

We ascended the handsome staircase that led to the foyer. From the maitre d's dais we followed a tuxedoed man into the bar, a quiet room of solid, dark wood. The only occupant, seated on a bar stool with his back to us, watched our progress into the room in the polished, faux gold that backed rows of liquor.

Web had told me that we should let the prince initiate the

15

greeting as there are several ways of doing so with men and women. First off, Arabs do not bow. Westernized Saudi men—something I supposed the prince was—shake hands with other men, but some still prefer the traditional Saudi greeting, which involves clasping right hands and placing the left on the other's right shoulder, and then kissing on both cheeks.

Lake said he wanted no part in the kissing tradition.

Here was my concern. It violates Muslim tradition for a man to shake a woman's hand, especially in public. If he greets me by laying a hand across his chest, I'm not supposed to think he's being rude. But what do *I* do? Web didn't know and suggested being creative.

The prince swung the bar stool toward us and stood. Facing us, he inclined his head. His smile was worthy of a toothpaste ad. He was tall, slender, dressed in expensive, subdued designer clothes. Folding his hands in front of his chest as if in prayer, he let his smile fade a little as we approached. "Good evening," he said.

I bobbed my head and Lake said, while offering his hand, "Good evening to you, sir. I am Detective Lieutenant Richard Lake."

The two men looked like they'd been friends for years. "Detective, happy to make your acquaintance."

It was my turn. "Good evening, Your Royal Highness," I said. "I am Moriah Dru."

"Forget the RH," he said, holding out a hand to me. As he slid his fingers between mine, he said, "I'm Sammy to my American friends. I feel certain I will count you among them." His English was slightly accented as a result of his early, British education. "I have reserved us a private booth, if that is all right?"

"Sounds good," I said. "How long have your wife and daughter been missing?"

He turned to the bartender and said, "We will be in compartment four-o-one."

"Fine, sir," the bartender said.

Prince Husam walked from the bar, and we followed, to the entrance of the high-ceilinged dining room. Somewhere a piano played. The maitre d' led us up a marble walk between tables clothed in white linen, under chandeliers long and sturdy enough for jungle creatures to swing, hand-over-hand, from one to another. We were headed for the back of the large, square room where fancy screens waited to cloak privacy-seekers. I had heard about Juniper Place, but never dined here. Like all stuffy places, this one made me uncomfortable. I like to think I know my p's and q's when it comes to fork and spoon selections—Mama had seen to that, enrolling me for a session in charm school. I always wait until the host or hostess takes the first bite, never blow on hot food or commit the deadly sin of breaking bread to butter it.

Before we even sat, Lake said, "I would worry if my ex-wife and daughter disappeared."

Prince Husam said quietly, "I do worry, but we will talk of this in due time."

Lake's expression said it was due time for him. "Have they been taken? Are they in danger?"

"Reeve, my wife, left without telling me where she was taking my daughter. I do not believe at this time that they are in danger, but they have been gone for a longer period of time than usual."

In this elegant establishment it appeared all the servers were men, tuxedoed men at that. It was clearly the place where CEOs would bring clients, but not a place where lovers would meet. Once ensconced in padded chairs at the round table, a most unlikely looking waiter—judging from the others I'd spotted—pulled the screen around us, departed and returned with brass coolers of white wines. A busboy followed him carrying ice and glasses on a tray. These they sat on a buffet table against the back wall. The elegant table was already stocked like a bar. The busboy departed and the waiter stood at attention by the screen. I swear he looked like a bodyguard out of central casting, and I supposed that a prince didn't travel without one.

I thought about it, but couldn't bring myself to address Husam as Sammy. He wasn't like any Sammy I'd known. I would call him Husam. He said, "If it is all right with you, I have taken the liberty of ordering our meal and its accompanying wines. If you would prefer a cocktail of your choosing, we can make those now."

Somebody ordering for me? Not quite sure about that.

Lake shook his head against a cocktail. He probably considered himself on duty. He looked every bit the cop ready to bear down on a subject. I, too, declined my favorite cocktail.

Husam said, "Then we shall first enjoy an Americano, a favorite of mine."

There goes the Islamic injunction against alcohol, I thought, and asked, "What is in an Americano?"

At the buffet, the hulky waiter had set three rocks glasses on a tray and opened a bottle bearing a colorful label. Campari— something I'd tasted but never preferred.

While he placed ice cubes in the glass, the prince said, "Campari, sweet vermouth, Perrier and a slice of orange. Campari was originally colored with carmine dye, derived from crushed cochineal insects, and this was what gave the liqueur its distinctive red color. Alas, in two-thousand-six, Gruppo Campari ceased using carmine."

I looked at Lake and him at me. Lake looked ready to choke Husam. I smiled, meaning, *go easy.*

Husam continued, "I give you the history of one of the world's most elegant aperitifs."

"But no more bugs," I said.

He smiled prince-charmingly. "No more bugs, but one wonders what makes it red today. The mystery ingredients—of which there are said to be more than eighty—are a secret still."

By this time the waiter was setting Americanos in front of us. Husam raised his glass. Lake and I did likewise. "As you say: Cheers!" he said.

We replied in kind, and I sipped past the orange floating in my glass. Best use of Campari ever.

Lake tapped his fingers on the table and did not drink.

Husam studied Lake's drumming fingers. "Let us relax before we talk of unpleasant things."

I wondered about his apparent unconcern, and maybe he read my body language because he said, "Shara is with her mother, a woman who knows how to hide herself. It may be that Reeve has taken Shara away in order to think things through and will return—that is what I believe at this time. However, it has been seven days, and I am tired of waiting. I must act. I am nervy. I keep my cell phone charged for when she calls. I will tell you the story after we have finished dining. To tell the story first would make our meal taste less delicious than it deserves."

I looked at Lake and smiled with my lips closed.

Lake containing himself through a leisurely meal was not to be. "Has she gone away to think things through before? Is that what this is about?"

"I can only hope so," Husam said. "That is why I do not want policing agencies involved. If I thought they were in danger, I would certainly call authorities." He looked at Lake. "I have told my friend, Portia Devon, that I did not want an official investigation because when they return, and I believe they will, I would look like a foolish husband." He turned to me. "But Portia said that you, Miss Dru . . ."

"Just Dru," I said.

19

"When she said that you work with a police partner who can be discreet, I thought that was a good thing." He turned to Lake. "It is a good thing, would you agree?"

Lake considered, with a sniff of conciliation. "I want to be clear—as does Dru—on what this is about." He asked me, "Isn't that right?"

"Certainly," I answered. "I don't get involved in husband–wife domestic cases where one goes home to Mama after a quarrel."

Husam held up his arms, palms out. "It is not like that. Reeve does not run home to her parents at every cross word between us. Let me tell you something. We Saudis are descended from nomadic tribes of sheep and goat herders. We are a tough breed and maintain the traditions that made us tough. Families are sacred. We look after one another. Even today, when we are part of the global community, we hold family dear. I am worried after Reeve and little Shara. Although our careers keep us apart much of the time, it is not normal for Reeve to be gone this long without contacting me." He paused to breathe, then continued thoughtfully, "I do not know what to think, but until I know something, I am not going to instigate an official matter."

"Fair enough," Lake said.

Husam nodded as if this was all he could ask and summoned the guard-like waiter hovering near the screen. The tuxedoed man hurried to the table. "This is Salman Habibi, my friend. He saved my life in New York a couple of years ago. I was accosted by thugs who wanted my wallet and were prepared to take it at the insistence of a knife."

Salman nodded and we nodded back. Salman stepped back to the screen in what seemed to be a silent choreographing of instructions between the minds of prince and servant.

A busboy took our cocktail glasses and put wine stems in

front of us. Salman stepped in to pour white wine. Husam tasted and judged it to be fit. "Let us eat, then." We drank wine and settled the glasses on the table, even Lake, who is not fond of white wines.

Husam said, "I spoke of desert traditions that we brought to the towns and cities of today. Second to family are foods—dates, and *fatir*, which you call flat bread, fava beans, yogurt and chicken. Did I mention dates?" He grinned. "We have twenty million date palms in our country. And did I mention chicken? We are the highest consumers of chickens in the world, it is said. As strict Muslims, we do not eat pork or drink alcohol." At that he raised his glass. "Here's to being in Rome and doing what the Romans do, eh? You Americans have so many wonderful axioms. And so many drinks and foods that I have come to enjoy, like chicken nuggets, which we will eat tonight—although not those wonderful fried nuggets you are so very fond of—and we will feast on lamb that is blessed."

Chicken nuggets and blessed lamb chops. Who could ask for anything more?

The appetizer course was hummus and flat bread, dates with *haysa al-tumreya* dip—a tasteless mix of flour and olive oil—and a bowl of nuts and raisins. I waited to see what utensils our host chose. Perhaps sensing my indecision, he explained, "The food before us is scooped up in bread. First we do a ritual washing of our hands and then we eat with them. But I will adhere to your custom of using the knife and fork."

In his own country, he said, he would drink a yogurt and water mixture with this meal, but he enjoyed a fine white wine when in America.

The soup course was a mix of vegetables, mostly eggplant, carrots and peas, in a thin broth that, he said, should be slurped from a bowl, but we used spoons, and shared another bottle of white wine.

Came the chicken-nugget course. It was called *kapsa.* A chicken and rice dish spiced with cinnamon, garlic and onions. Quite delicious, actually. The waiter opened another bottle of white wine.

The salad was called *tabbouleh*—made from bulgur wheat. It was oily and minty but palatable. I'd slowed down with the wine, so I didn't need a glass to go with this course.

I was delighted to see the waiter serve food I recognized, that of rack of lamb, a blessed one as announced, surrounded by mashed potatoes and asparagus. Husam put his hands together and said, "I have acquired a taste for American-style lamb chops. I also have a fondness for garlic mashed potatoes. I will depart my injunction against talking about the business that brings us together by saying that my American girlfriend made this for me the first time we had a date."

Lake had said very little about the traditional Arabian dishes, but dug into his lamb chops as if he were starving. He also appreciated the fine, old, cabernet sauvignon.

"I see," Husam said, "that our policeman has finally found his appetite."

The slitty glint in Lake's eyes told me that, though he grinned, he was not amused.

Raspberry sorbet and ginger cookies were served as dessert. Quite refreshing and delicious but not so the spiced coffee.

CHAPTER THREE

"I would very much like an American cigarette or a Cuban cigar," Husam said and sipped from a cup of cardamom coffee. He set the cup down. "But, alas, not to be had in this restaurant. Americans worry about their health as if in doing so they will not die."

"We're in no rush to reach the pearly gates," Lake said.

I hoped he wasn't going to comment on virgins and martyrdom.

Husam said, "Everyone wants to live long and prosper, but, to your point, detective, there are those who believe that to die for one's beliefs bestows a reward in the afterlife. For me, I hope to partake like my father-in-law of a couple of *lag a'mhuilins* before I near my time."

Lake smirked like he'd said *a lot of virgins*. The botched Gaelic accent was to blame, and Lake's need to get on with the case, if there was to be one. "We're ready to listen," he said.

Husam said, "I am the black prince—like the sheep, if you will—in my family. They cannot disown me. As the eldest son of one of the king's brothers—and there are many more sons than brothers—I am in line to the kingship if all my uncles do not survive me."

Lake looked confused. I know I was.

"I see I must explain. After King Khalid al-Saliba founded the kingdom and died, his sons became kings—successive sons. He had thirty-five by several different wives and nine have

23

reigned as kings. Those successors still alive are growing old. It is some of their sons, my cousins, that beg me to return to the kingdom."

"Begging is one thing; threatening to do something if you don't is another," Lake said.

"Nothing like that. No imminent threats. Returning is impossible for me."

"Why's that?" I asked.

"I have married an infidel and sired an infidel."

"Your American girlfriend became your wife."

"In American law, yes. The king would not permit me to marry a foreign woman."

Husam explained that it is permissible for a Saudi man to marry a non-Saudi woman if the family gives permission. Being a Muslim is a point in her favor. He can register her in the kingdom as his legal wife and take her home to his family if she agrees, even going so far as to take her home to other wives. "But what Western woman would agree to that?" Husam forced a laugh. He went on to say that a Saudi man can have as many as four wives at a time, and he can divorce one and marry another easily.

"But, in my case," he said, "I was forbidden by the king to marry a foreigner. The king called me into his apartment before I began my studies in America and told me that I might avail myself of the licentious females in America, but under no circumstances could I marry one."

"What if she converted?" I asked.

"Any person can convert to Islam, but, in my case, conversion would make no difference to the king."

I recalled a big to-do about a marriage in England. "Not very long ago the grandson of the Crown Prince married an Englishwoman."

"He is not in royal succession. Were I to become king, I would have the title of Guardian of the Islamic Faith. Being married to a non-Muslim would be a hypocrisy, even though many princes do marry outside the faith and to foreigners. There are more than six thousand princes in the kingdom, but only a small percentage are in line to be crown prince and then king."

I thought his odds weren't good, especially when he'd disobeyed his king. This was like a damn fairy tale, and I was beginning to wonder how long I would stay in it.

Lake was lapsing back into aggravation. Salman began refilling our cups with the heady cardamom drink. Lake had held up his hand against another cup of the strong, eucalyptus-tasting substance. Salman filled my cup before I could stop him. All the wine and coffee, soon I'd need the ladies' room.

"Where did you meet your American wife?" I asked, noticing Lake's faint frown.

"At George Washington University. We were undergraduates taking courses in engineering. Reeve is a real rocket scientist."

Lake sat forward. "Is there a problem with her having a Saudi husband? I mean, the secrecy clearance here in the states?"

"Not at all. When we married, I applied for a resident visa and had to undergo extensive vetting. I know the CIA and FBI and Homeland Security checked into my background, everything I ever did in my entire life." He sat back as if the effort of recalling was disagreeable.

How disagreeable, I wondered? "Go on," I urged him.

"Reeve Cresley is very smart and beautiful. I confess I loved her from the day I met her in the library. She was dating other men, but I determined I would have her. Not as a wife—though I longed for her. She was in my dreams, day and night. I figured out ways to run into her, accidentally on purpose. It was so silly—in the malls, museums, coffee houses—so unsubtle of me. Soon, I suggested we share a coffee. She loves cardamom coffee and there is a snug coffee shop near the campus. We would meet there, doing our work on the computers and drinking coffee and sharing fruits and sweets. One day I suggested we go to the movies. She laughed and said, 'You mean a real date?' I tried not to be offended at her mocking laughter, and said, 'A real date, yes.' She said, 'Sammy, I have been warned about Saudi men. You fit the mold. Charming and witty, but secretive in a way.' I objected to this heartily. She said, 'I don't want to get involved with anyone right now. Education comes first.' "

He sighed. "I was stricken at the brush-off. She told me about the blogs that tell tales of Saudi men wooing American women students and then casting them aside after graduation. I could not change her mind. I was heartbroken. But I am a man and went a little crazy with other women."

He stopped like we'd say something about this. When we didn't remark, he went on. "So we graduated and I congratulated her. I went back home and applied for a visa to attend Georgetown Law School. The king thought it wise for me to get a degree in American business law. That is where I met the wonderful Portia Devon." His smile outshone the chandelier above us. "Well, then," he continued, "the king called me into his apartment again. I am to be married to a royal princess, my cousin, Aya, when I return from America. Again, he is very adamant about American women. I told him that I had fallen for a woman in undergraduate school, but that had passed with bad feelings and I could not trust an American. I meant it, and he said he looked forward to Aya's and my wedding in three years."

"Was yours an arranged marriage?"

"Yes and no. I had to marry a royal princess, and there are many cousins to choose from, but Aya was a much loved cousin, and when given a choice at age fifteen, she chose me. I was honored to be her husband and she would be my number-one wife. With royals, it is custom and law."

"We know that didn't happen," Lake said impatiently.

"No," the prince answered curtly. "I was studious and avoided campus women. There are others in Washington, DC, that I paid and found that arrangement more suitable. Then one day I walked into the café at the Smithsonian and there she was, my Reeve, having a sweet and coffee. She looked up and I could see the happiness in her blue eyes. All my dreams returned, and I walked to her. I was going to be aloof and suave. She stood and said, 'I miss you.' I put my hands on her shoulders and kissed her forehead. That would be all I would do in public. That evening we dined on salad and fruit and hummus and coffee. We talked into the night where she confessed she tracked where I had coffee and waited for me." He looked shy—feigned maybe, for one so worldly. "We made love."

Lake looked bored at this love story, but I was intrigued.

"She did the anti-birth things and we traveled around America on weekends. I found I loved the country, especially the south where Reeve is from—Atlanta, the city in which we sit and I tell this story. Two years went happily by and then we were married. A scant year later Shahrazad was born."

That's a birth name I hadn't heard. "Any talk of conversion to Islam?"

"No, that is why she pushed me away before. She is Catholic and would not give up her faith. Would I give up mine? Nay. So I understood." He shrugged eloquently. "It is how we were born and how we were taught. I respected her for that."

"Were you barred from taking her to Saudi Arabia?"

"No, but there were rules, and we only visited once. The king was very angry and insisted that I marry Aya in a year's time. He said that Reeve could be my number-two wife, if she agreed. Aya would accept another wife because it is our custom. The king decreed that Reeve must never be seen outside the compound. If she did, she would be divorced from me and deported. I would keep Shara." His eyelids drooped over his black eyes. "That being unacceptable to both of us, I did not accept his bargain. I would return to Saudi Arabia only for business. It was a difficult decision, but Reeve was everything to me. The king gave me a post as cultural attaché in the New York embassy. I am a member of the International Bar Association and the American Bar Association. My practice focuses on commercial arbitrations."

"What about criminal law?" Lake asked.

"I do not touch criminal law."

"What is the name of your firm?" I asked. "And where is it? New York?"

He hesitated a titch. "Yes, and Washington, DC. The firm is Meadows, Wessell and Zogby. Please do not involve the firm in my personal matter."

"I'll try not to." The first thing I was going to do was check out his story. "It can't always be helped, though."

He hesitated. *Maybe he was going to call the whole thing off.*

Lake said, "What is the nature of these commercial arbitrations?"

Again, Husam hesitated. Lake explained. "It's important in investigative work to know all the facts. Ninety-nine percent of the time most are irrelevant, but I wouldn't want Miss Dru blindsided by lack of information."

"I see," he said, still wary. "As a member of the International Arbitration Team, my work focuses on construction-related litigation, the energy and infrastructure of highways and rail systems."

"Pipelines?" Lake asked.

"That is a volatile subject." He drew in a deep breath. "I do not work on pipeline projects."

I leaned across the table, into him. "Shahrazad. Interesting name."

"I have always loved the stories. So, too, does Reeve." Husam sipped coffee and then said, "Succession will be messy for the first time since the kingdom was founded. I fear there could be bloodshed if an agreement on who is to become second-in-command to the crown prince is not reached before the king dies."

I wondered then how old the prince was, bearing in mind that Webdog had said that ages, when appearing on Saudi biographies, were suspect.

I asked, "Is he ill?"

"He hasn't much time."

Lake interrupted. "Why do you care about succession?"

The prince sat back and spread his arms as if abashed. "It is my country."

"But you have left it."

"For the woman that I love. But that does not mean I do not love my country and all that it has been to me."

Lake nodded in surrender rather than understanding.

The prince went on, "The progressive reforms the king put into place are under attack by possible conservative successors. Some of my cousins strictly practice Sharia law. But there is a faction in my cousins' ranks that wants me to return and become a candidate for second-in-command to the crown prince. We must keep the reforms. The kingdom's oil is being depleted. My enlightened cousins are educated and see that we must become more in touch with the entire world if we are to survive as a nation. The kingdom must not fall back into tribal division and conflict, as before. My cousins asked me two years ago to come home and marry Aya, but I refused."

"Come on, Husam," Lake said, "doesn't that worry you— what they might do to your wife and daughter to get you back?"

His black eyes stared as though in a trance; his words were measured and bleak. "I worry, yes. But I do not *know*."

29

Sitting in this beautiful restaurant, it pained me to think what a child named Shahrazad went through when two cultures collided, when the bloom was off the rose of romance. People should anticipate such a conflict before they marry.

Lake eyed Husam callously. "We've been led down a devious path, and finally comes the moment of truth. What do you want Moriah Dru to do for you?"

He wet his lips with a spontaneous action of his tongue. "Find them so my wife and I may discuss our options."

"Which are?"

"It is known, unfortunately, that my daughter does not study Islam, owing to my wife's newly professed atheism, and that is unacceptable. A Saudi princess, especially a daughter of an al-Saliba, must be a Muslim and speak, read and write in Arabic and know the kingdom's history. Try and beg as I might, I could not make Reeve understand that the pressure would be off us if she allowed Shara to study Islam."

I asked, "Do you want to rise to the top, to be second, then crown prince, then king?"

"I never wanted the title or the job. I am happy here, but I am being pressured to take my rightful place in the array of candidates."

"Have they already made attempts to pressure you?"

He seemed to be absorbing some reality within himself. "Reeve said someone tried to run her car off the road on Long Island, where we stayed temporarily. Shara was in the car. She left Long Island before I was up the next day."

Lake asked the question I was thinking. "Did she report it to police?"

"I don't know. She was in hysterics at me. When she is found, I will ask her." A suggestion of aggravation flashed across his face before he sighed. "I will also ask again what were she and my daughter doing in Montauk. It was dark and cold. We were staying in Bridgehampton."

"Were you getting along?" Lake asked.

"Yes," he answered, rather curtly.

"Once they left Long Island, did you check out Montauk?"

"We did, yes. No one there ever saw her."

CHAPTER FOUR

"Do you believe that bullshit?" Lake asked.

"It's plausible," I said.

"You must think so," Lake said, his mood somewhat foul. "You agreed to help Husam bin whatever."

"I agreed to help find his wife and daughter—for him maybe, but certainly for them."

"Where will you start?"

"From here—with Reeve's near miss on Long Island—using Webdog's computer research skills and Dirk's Detectives."

Dirk's, a full line detective service, is the best in the field. We mostly use their online services, but we've had occasion to use their human-to-human or human-to-corporate services. For those cases, we have a reciprocal license agreement.

I continued, "I'm going to see Portia. She knows him better than anyone. Then I'll go see Reeve Cresley's parents. That they live in Buckhead makes me wonder something. I knew some Cresleys from Christ the King. Could it be the same family?"

"You'll soon know," Lake said, his ill mood deepening.

We were approaching Lake's favorite watering hole on Peachtree Street, and I wasn't surprised when he said, "Let's stop at Jeremy's. I have to get that god-awful coffee taste out of my mouth. I longed for a Scotch in that stifling place. It was designed for a single-malt Scotch and fine cognacs, not bad cookies and sour coffee."

"Can't disagree, my love. I'm sure the prince would have

sprung for after-dinners."

"He didn't offer."

"What do you think the bill came to?"

"I didn't see money or a credit card, did you?"

"I think that means Prince Sammy and his bodyguard, slippery Salman, are regulars."

"I didn't buy Salman as a waiter."

"That's why, my love, you are the best detective in Atlanta, *nay,* the Southeast."

Jeremy's is the most elegant cop bar you'll ever enter. All brass and wood and circumspect lighting. Speaking of brass, Commander Haskell of Major Crimes sat at the bar, a neat Scotch in front of him.

"Commander," I said, as Lake slipped onto a stool next to Haskell.

"What's up?" Lake asked.

"I could have used you this evening," Haskell said.

"Sorry, I was dining with royalty." I gave Lake a subtle shake of my head. He had agreed not to speak of the meeting with his colleagues or bosses, until and unless the need arose.

Haskell looked at me and smiled. "Dru is queen of the realm in my book."

Lake signaled the bartender for what the keep knew was his usual evening libation. He knew mine, too. A *pinot grigio.* I don't drink heavily before going to bed. Sleep comes hard enough, and I don't want a hammer in my head in the morning.

Lake asked, "What gives, Commander? We don't see you in here often, and it's usually when you need to think things out over a Scotch."

"Another home invasion, two dead," Haskell said, and drained the drink. The bartender was there for another pour.

After the liberal stream of amber liquid halted, Haskell explained. "Look at the photos tomorrow. Happened on East Paces Ferry. Crime scene's there with Boyle and Dunn. Larry Moore is leading."

"Larry's good," Lake said. Larry was a protégé of Lake's.

Lake is the lieutenant in charge of the Homicide Unit within Major Crimes. The home-invasion murders had been investigated by the Burglary Squad—initially—when they were just simple home invasions. The first murder occurred when an elderly, wealthy man left his garage door open and died of heart failure when the invaders broke in. The case stayed with burglary until the invaders apparently got high on causing someone's death, and started a reign of terror on anyone who was at home. Homicide got the case at the same time a couple of prostitutes had been murdered and a rash of fatal drug drive-bys were happening on Metropolitan Avenue. Atlanta's murder rate was the lowest in three years, but Lake was as busy as ever.

Commander Haskell gripped Lake on his shoulder. "Burglary was happy to hand it to us and I'm happy to hand it to you."

"Thanks, Commander."

Commander Haskell and Richard Lake were mentor and protégé. After Georgia State University and having graduated from the Atlanta Police Academy, Lake was assigned to the Zone Two precinct, where I met him. A year later we were partners. I later learned that he'd asked for me to partner with him. It wasn't long that we became lovers. Despite the rumors swirling around our romance, Linda and Richard Lake were deep into their amicable divorce proceedings.

Personable and dedicated, Lake came to the attention of Major Haskell and found himself on the fast track. He was selected to join Haskell's Red Dog Unit, where he was promoted to the rank of sergeant. When you're in one of the APD's elite units, you've arrived. He served a stint in the Burglary/Robbery

Unit before being transferred to the Special Operations Section, where he made lieutenant. He went on to be reunited with Commander Haskell in Major Crimes, where he is a supervisory detective lieutenant in the Homicide Unit. He'll soon make major. Haskell's on track to be appointed deputy chief.

Haskell paid and left after saying it would be an early morning for the overworked Major Crimes Unit. The early roll call had Lake dropping me off at my place without a notion of staying over. Nights were long when he stayed.

Checking my house for intruders, then going to the door, he said, "Sweet dreams about the prince and his fairy tales. Even when we got to the nitty-gritty, he was spinning shit in a crock. There's more than he's telling us."

"Thank you," I said. "There always is."

CHAPTER FIVE

Portia was robing-up when I got to her chambers.

"Well," she said, zipping. "What did you think of Husam bin Sayed al-Saliba?"

"He's charming, obviously rich and most likely full of shit, if you consider Lake a good judge of men."

Peering over glasses sliding down her nose, she said, "Aren't all charming, rich men full of shit?"

She'd been married to one for about three weeks, just long enough to get a son by him. I defended my lover. "I don't think Lake is."

"He's not rich, except in wisdom," she said, adjusting the billowing black sleeves, and tucking a handkerchief into a long-sleeved blouse beneath the robe. Portia's the only person I know that still uses lacy hankies. She said, "Trust Lake's instincts."

"I always do. Now, tell me what you know about the prince. I got that you met him in law school."

"Big man on campus, he was not. For all his wealth, he's thrifty. Some would say cheap."

"How old was he then?"

"I think he was closer to thirty than twenty, but if he ever said his age, I didn't hear it."

I sat on a chair in front of her desk to encourage her to do the same. "How did you get to be friends?"

She stood her ground. "He fit in with the academics. That

36

was before Nine-Eleven and everyone courted Arabs as though they were Aladdin and Sinbad." She paused and smiled as if in reminiscence. "You know when you go to all-white schools, foreigners, especially tall, dark and handsome ones, are quite exotic."

"Then Nine-Eleven came along. Where was the prince in all this?"

"I didn't see him after that so I assume he was on the next flight to Saudi Arabia, like a lot of them were. I met up with him a few years later when the president of the United States allowed students from the Middle East back into academia. Sammy was determined to finish law school. By that time, I had graduated and was working as a clerk with Justice Owen's legal eagles, and still lived in DC. Sammy would consult me occasionally."

"Any notion he might have been a bin Laden ideologue, or is now?"

"I doubt it very much. The royals are a breed unto themselves. They follow dietary laws in their own country, but they travel the globe, and, when they do, they party with the glamour crowd. The Muslims that bought into bin Laden's childish fantasy have a myopic world view. Better men have wanted to rule the world and failed. The truth is Osama bin Laden was your typical ruthless villain and so are his present-day followers. Why do you ask?"

"At times he seemed confident; at others he was cagey. Did you know Reeve?"

"Nope. That was after I left DC."

My eyebrows involuntarily rose. "Did you date Husam?"

"Are you kidding me?"

"On any level, you would."

"I'm not anti-anything or anyone." She sat at her desk and folded her hands on top of it. "I once had a date with a student from the Congo. Didn't go anywhere. Mama would have died before her dotage, of course, and I'm pretty much happy hanging in my own culture, thank you very much."

Hanging in my own culture. That was about as cool as Portia ever sounded.

I said, "Prince Husam bin Sayed al-Saliba told a long, rambling tale of their meeting and marriage and what led to today's problems."

"Sounds like Sammy. He loved to spin yarns. I think that's why I came up with the Aladdin and Sinbad analogy. Even his contemporary accounts of things he did had an ethereal feel to them. Sounds like he's still a male Scheherazade, telling tales that never end."

"I like endings. Did he tell you what they named their daughter?"

"Never came up. What?"

"Shahrazad. That's how he pronounced it."

"That's the Arabic pronunciation. Spelled different, too. Its origin is Persian. Given the turmoil in that region, he'd use the Arabic."

I never have to wonder where most of the esoterica that floats in my head comes from.

Portia said, "The night I met him was at a student's house. He was telling a tale out of *Thousand and One Nights*. It was called 'Ali with the Large Member.' It was about male obsession with penis size."

"He told that in front of you?"

"He was full of himself that night, and like I said, women students partied like the men so his cultural view of American women fit right in with his male needs. Did you hear that a group of Islamic lawyers is trying to get *Arabian Nights* banned?"

"Never heard that, no."

"The bed-wetters complain that it's obscene and doesn't

reflect Islamic values, or some such nonsense. Islamic values, my skinny butt. We're talking about kings that sought out seven-year-old virgins to bed at night. Sure, some tales are romance but others are downright crude, like 'Ali with the Large Member,' or 'The Butcher's Adventure with the Lady and the Bear,' or another of Sammy's favorites, 'Harun Al-Rashid and the Two Slave Girls.' These tales were written in the Arabian Golden Age. The wonk lawyers want people to think good Muslims wouldn't do or say such things. As if all humans didn't exhibit the same base attributes, and write them down."

Portia on a rant.

I asked, "Could the prince be romanticizing his love story with Reeve Cresley?"

She thought a moment. "I suppose. I didn't hear it." She looked at her watch. "And I don't have time now. I'm already seven minutes late." She flashed a question that expected the right answer. "You did record it?"

"I did."

I got the recorder out of my backpack and handed it to her. "Tell me what you think. Oh, by the way, do you remember the Cresleys from Christ the King?"

"I recall a family by that name. Didn't know them."

"Me, neither." I went to the door and turned to look back. She was getting up, coming around her desk. I said, "It could be that the 'The Prince who wants to be King' has ended his fairy-tale marriage here, to go home and marry his princess and have many *Muslim* children."

In her black, billowing robe coming at me, it looked like a flock of blackbirds preparing to take off. She stood before me. "A girl and a woman are still missing. It took a thousand and one nights for Shahrazad to keep her head on her shoulders. Find the girl and her mother, Moriah. I don't like what's in the back of your mind that has you alluding to murder."

39

CHAPTER SIX

Web found the Cresleys' address in Killarney Grounds, a posh, gated community off of East Paces Ferry Road, and a mile down the road from where a murderous home invasion recently had taken place. There were twenty Cresleys in Atlanta, not including the suburbs, but only one Reeve. Lowell Reeve Cresley. His address was unlisted, but not a problem to discover. I drove to the guard kiosk of Killarney—as the community was called, without the "Grounds" part.

I conned the security guard at the gate and drove through the iron ornamentals.

I really hate cold calls, and, in my experience, people receiving them hate them more. A handsome, blond women in her fifties answered the door of the ultramodern house. She was well-maintained, with a tan just this side of unhealthy. Lines around her mouth told me she was or had been a smoker. Her eyes were wary and spoke of stress. She was shorter than me, as most people are. She raised her head. "How did you get through the gate? There's a sign nearby. No solicitations."

I'd seen the discreet sign on the grass, and had my ID in hand. Before she could close the door, I held it up. In large letters it said, CHILD TRACE, INC. "I'm Moriah Dru. Here about your daughter Reeve, and . . ."

Her breath caught in the back of her throat. "You found Reeve?"

Not "them."

"No," I said. "I was just hired."

"By whom?"

"Prince Husam bin Sayed al-Saliba."

"Was it he who gave you our address?"

I didn't want to lie but I didn't want to put her on alert. I bobbed my head.

"You can leave now, Miss Dru. We'll hire our own investigators, thank you."

"You can do that," I said. "But I think you should hear what I have to say, because I intend to find your daughter and *granddaughter.*"

She stood still for a long moment, her mind's wheels churning. Then she backed up. "I'll give you five minutes."

I stepped over the threshold and into the foyer. While walking to the living room, she told me she had an urgent appointment. I've used that one a time or two myself.

The long room was stark, the product of an elite, contemporary-furniture designer. I couldn't recall his name offhand, but I liked the simplicity of the lines. Quite a contrast to my cottage. The black, leather sofas had rolled arms and beneath them a loop that could have contained a barrel. I don't think the designer had a dog bed in mind, though. A Pekinese ran out and sniffed my feet. Cute little pup, but it seemed to sense the mood of its mistress. I reached down to pat its head and it bared its teeth.

"Lady is very particular," Donna Cresley said.

She motioned me to a chair and settled herself primly on a sofa. "Who got you in touch with my son-in-law?"

"A classmate of his at Georgetown who happens to be a friend of mine."

"What did he tell you?"

"He told me a story. I want the other side. Since I can't get it from your daughter, yet, I'm appealing to you, her family."

She drew in a deep breath. "So typical." She waved a hand dismissively. "One of those sheik types that likes to sweep cute, blond girls off their feet."

"Since they dated for a while and eventually married, it doesn't appear he was a love 'em and leave 'em sheik type."

"Not until something better came along."

"Like becoming king?"

"You got that right, Miss Dru."

"Just Dru is fine."

Evidently it wasn't fine with her. "Well, Miss Dru, when he married Reeve, he passed on the possibility. That's what he told us, anyway. Now he'll marry his Muslim princess and try to make up to the king, who I understand is quite ill and not of sound mind."

"From what *I understand,* there's a few steps to go before he's even in line."

The light coming through the blinds sharpened her features. "He's in love with his charm. He thinks the world is awaiting his arrival for everything to be right. But Reeve's not putting up with his bull any longer."

"Why disappear?"

"To avoid being killed." *Stated so matter-of-factly, a chill ran across my shoulders.* "His royal highness won't agree to Reeve's terms for a divorce." *Funny, Husam hadn't mentioned the word divorce.* "He would have to give up his daughter, *the princess,* and he will not do that."

"He told me Reeve thought she was purposely run off the road, and so disappeared with Shara the next day."

"I don't know about that. I do think Saliba will have Reeve killed to get his daughter. Then he will go to his dreadful country and marry his Muslim and God knows who else over there. Thank God Reeve never took his name."

"What about Shara?"

42

"What about her?"

"What's her name?"

"She is Shara Cresley al-Saliba." She stood. The interview was over.

I said, "Husam said she was named Shahrazad."

A disgusted sound came from her throat.

I asked, "Do you know where Reeve and Shara are?"

"I wouldn't tell you if I did."

I held up a hand against her walking away. "A child is missing. Society takes that very seriously and wants to know why. When I take on a job to find a child, I investigate everyone involved to his or her back teeth whether they like it or not."

Having understood the implication that she was involved to her back teeth, she blinked.

I continued, "That includes the principal who hired me. My job is to find the child, not promote one side of the family over the other. I often work through the juvenile courts. You can investigate me, if you want. Judge Portia Devon put me in touch with Husam Saliba. I know what he told me, but I don't know if everything he said is true. I will find out, though."

Donna Cresley opened her mouth. "Portia Devon? We belong to Christ the King, where a family named Devon once worshipped. I recall a girl about Reeve's age named Portia."

"That's my Portia. I went to Christ the King, too. My mother is Anna Lee Dru."

She leaned in, like she was seeing me for the first time. "Yes, I recall. It comes back now. You are the child finder who saved two kids."

"That was me, with the help of a detective named Richard Lake."

She excused herself to make a phone call, and I excused myself to go to the bathroom.

Having accomplished our goals, we met in the hall and she

said, "Call me Donna. I'll call you Dru. Let's have a cup of coffee, or tea if you prefer, and sit on the lanai."

We sat across from each other on swivel chairs with reversible linen cushions covered in daffodils and crocuses. Donna referred to her husband, Lowell Reeve Cresley, as Dr. Cresley. I said I understood where her daughter got her first name. She said, "Actually, Donna is Reeve's first name. Donna Reeve Cresley. Lowell insisted his only child take his second name and be called by it. We couldn't have any more children." I didn't see that the reason was pertinent here and always try to let some questions hang unanswered. It's an investigator's trick, and a reason to return to ask them.

Reeve's back story was pretty much what you'd expect of the only daughter of a wealthy Atlanta surgeon and his socialite wife—expensive girls' schools, dancing lessons, fencing, horseback riding, golf, proms, first dates, grade angst, college acceptance—I listened to the proud mother's story through three cups of tea, and then we started on vodka tonics.

I asked and she'd told me about places where Reeve liked to go: the beach in spring to work on her tan, boating in the summer, mountain skiing in winter. As we were in the first blush of spring, perhaps Reeve was somewhere near an ocean.

By the time her daughter had entered graduate school, Dr. Cresley returned home. That could be good or bad, depending if I could open him up like I had Donna. As rosy a picture as Donna painted of her and her daughter throughout their early years, there were a few pauses that had me wondering about her and Reeve's relationship.

Donna rose to kiss her husband on the cheek. "Lowell, darling, so good to see you so early."

Over her shoulder he looked at me through thick lashes. I easily sized him up. He was underhandedly flirty. His eyes roamed when he didn't think his wife was looking. I figure he'd gone through many nurses and medical secretaries, with more to go.

After an understanding of why I was in his home, he nodded curtly and excused himself to wash the stench of hospital and patients off himself. What was it with these people? Why weren't they worried about their daughter or granddaughter? Husam Saliba, himself, wanted a leisurely dinner before discussing their disappearance. Portia explained that he liked to spin yarns. This whole drama—I was beginning to feel like a prop in a play with bad lighting and worse acting.

I'd learned from Donna during Dr. Cresley's absence that he was a "society" heart surgeon who operated on some of Atlanta's high-profile politicians, religious leaders and sports figures. She told me of his heroic effort in resuscitating a football player who'd suffered a heart attack at practice. His specialty took him to Washington, DC, and New York, often for weeks at a time. My mind idly wondered if he had a woman in each of those cities.

Dr. Cresley returned, dressed casually in designer jeans and an open-neck, casual, lavender shirt with an expensive designer logo on the pocket. "I can't join you ladies in a cocktail. I may need to return to the hospital later this evening. Two difficult patients are in ICU. Donna, we'll need an early dinner."

He sat in a rocking recliner facing us.

Donna said, "I've spoken with Miss Dru at length this afternoon. I've also spoken with Portia Devon. Do you remember the Devons from church?"

"Of course. I know Portia Devon. She's a Superior Court judge."

Donna was taken aback as if her husband had withheld vital information from her. Cresley (he hadn't invited me to call him Lowell) stared at me and said in a tone that vibrated no-baloney,

"Reeve will return when things work themselves out. She has much to think about, so no need to go looking for her."

I said, "Her husband seems confused. He can't decide if she's at risk, or if she's thinking things through."

Gritting his teeth, Cresley said, "The man's a fraud. He wants you to flush her out. Trust me, the real danger is finding Reeve and the child, then telling that man."

These two seemed to have an aversion to using their granddaughter's name.

"Tell me something," I said. "What does Shara mean to you?"

Husband and wife looked at one another, apparently waiting for the other to speak up.

Donna said, "Well, what any grandmother thinks of her granddaughter."

Cresley looked at me. "Before you comment on that vague statement, let me tell you that we were cut out of her life until the past couple of months. After Reeve married that man, she brought him home. You'd think he owned the place. After the child was born, they lived in New York and DC until Reeve began working in Boulder, Colorado."

Donna said, "Our granddaughter has been in our presence not more than a half dozen times in her entire life."

The doctor leaned back and studied my face as if he were going to ask about my blood pressure. "I'm not a bigot. Sure, I'm a southerner, and, sure, I was raised in a caste system, if you will. The rich from the poor; the white man from the black man; the Catholic from the Protestant. But, in time, thinking people mingled and learned to get along. This tribal goon from the Middle East comes in and starts telling us what we can and cannot do. Donna was her gracious self and tried to abide by his dictates, even so much as taking off her shoes in her own home and ridding our home of bacon and ham when he was here on that rare occasion. Eventually, I got fed up and told the son-of-a-bitch to get a hotel room and find a vegan restaurant."

Despite his arrogance, I could understand the antagonism.

"Naturally, Reeve was upset," Donna said. "Maybe if we'd have reacted differently, she wouldn't have stayed away."

Cresley said, "Jesus, I wish I could have a Scotch." He rose so abruptly the recliner flopped to a halt. "Miss Dru, I hope we've persuaded you to drop your search for Reeve and Shara. Trust me; they are in a safe place, and well-protected there."

I had no choice. I gave him my card, which he studied with amusement, and I left.

Wondering if I'd learned anything of significance during the entire visit and knowing that I had somehow, I drove to my office, parked and took an elevator to the seventh floor of a high-rise building near the campus of Georgia State University. I had an hour before meeting Lake for dinner.

Webdog sat at his computer, surrounded by monitors. "Whatcha got?" I asked.

Rattling keystrokes, he had symbols and unintelligible lettering scrolling down the high-tech screen.

"Firewalls," Web said.

"Dare I ask. In whose computers are those firewalls, and are they blocking your access?"

"Not exactly blocking," Web said, his voice distracted.

I shivered in the cold room and watched the keyboard genius at work.

"Hell's bells! Real-time satellite images," Web cried, turning off the web cams.

Something was wrong. The monitors showed a bunch of crazy symbols and then dot matrices or vector patterns—I forget which—about to turn into a face. Web's face.

"Jeez," he breathed out.

"What?" I asked. "Are we being hacked?"

"Not we, me. I've accessed and gotten through a firewall and they're attacking."

"Who's 'they'?"

"I hate to say it."

"Then I hate to hear it. But I'll need a heads-up when they come for you."

I've been fearful of this since Web started working for me when he was a freshman at Georgia State University. Lake brought him to me after he'd arrested Web for hacking into the Atlanta Police Department's servers for the fun of it. Lake knows genius when he meets it, and knew that I was looking for an internet person who could help in my investigations. When I started my agency I had a little seed money, but not enough to hire accomplished web detectives.

Since Web was seventeen at the time he was arrested, he could come under the jurisdiction of the juvenile court. He could also have been charged as an adult. Portia prevailed, got him straight with the cops, and I set him up with a part-time job. Now that he's in graduate school, he can give me more hours. Has he skirted the law in my employ? Not for gain. Was it for a good cause? Absolutely. Will I go down with him if what he's done now gets him arrested? Probably.

Web said, "I didn't detect that database embed when I popped the shell."

"Embed what?"

"Alarm. The penetration tester signaled an administrator that I've accessed."

"Sounds bad." I sounded quippy, and it didn't quite match my heart rate.

"Not to panic," Web said. "I've got other back-office tools to give me full control of that administrator."

"They've got your photograph."

"Not enough to ID. They don't have my multi-layered addy.

I've constructed my own penetration tools and I cover my tracks when I leave via the back door."

"Who's 'they'?"

"You really want to know?"

"The FBI?"

"No. I would have no problem getting through their back-door ports."

That made me feel better. "Who, then?"

"The law firm of Meadows, Wessell and Zogby."

"Oh, Jeez."

As Web rattled the keys, he said, "The feds have issued new regs for law firms to tighten security. Mostly to keep the nation's currency safe, because big firms route lots of cash. But the big firms are notoriously lax in keeping up with technologies. Most of their IT guys are morons. I mean, you'd think they'd hire smart people to keep their corporate clients' info secure from attackers."

"I get it, Web."

"But not these guys. Using my own multi-tiered platform software, I can't get a back door into their database, which makes me wonder what they're hiding."

"Web, you just said . . ." I was stumped to repeat what he'd just said. "What you just said."

He hunched over the computer keyboard. "I'm close. My code's still intact."

Web's frantic keystroking mesmerized me. A buzzer sounded. ACCESS DENIED! lit the screen. Web said, "So friggin' close." He whirled his chair to me. "It's there. All the information. For the taking. What are they hiding?"

I think this was the first time I'd heard Web admit defeat.

I said, "There's always Interpol." Web once told me it's easier to crack into Interpol because their hertz is stuck in the stone age. I got up. "Send an email. Be conventional."

"Interpol it is, then."

Web has a source in the International Police. I wonder how long it will take for Paul Ardai to work off his debt. The Interpol cyber cop from Lyon was more than happy to help Web ever since Web helped him track a cracker who was stealing the identities of international travelers.

"Anything from Long Island?"

"Dirk's is on it. Their Boston investigator is heading there to get a copy of the report."

"So, she did call?"

"Yep. There was a witness."

CHAPTER SEVEN

Lake came late and in a funky frame of mind. Still on duty, he declined a martini and ordered a cabernet sauvignon, saying, "I can't eat a steak without a robust red." He grinned. "And who's to know?" He winked and looked around the restaurant as if Commander Haskell was spying from the next booth.

As it was, those seated in the bar area of the Peachtree Road Steakhouse cast curious glances at Lake. I said, "You look like a cop and act like a cop with a case weighing heavily."

"Astute," he said. "The whole goddamn world is astute."

"My poor baby."

The busy waiter opened a bottle of red wine, Lake did the legs thing and two glasses of red wine sat in front of us. I sipped and said, "You tell me yours first."

"Last night, another prostitute was knifed and died. She was eighteen years old and her family knew she worked the street. What the hell is wrong with people? She lived with her boyfriend. He says he told her to be careful. This is her boyfriend talking? Be careful? How about *don't do it*?"

"Any drug drive-bys?"

"Nope."

"Home invasions?"

"Not last night. It's early yet for tonight. They start at midnight. The girl was just a kid. Good-looking, too."

"She wouldn't be for long."

"We got a new homicide case. We're drowning in cases. A

51

forty-eight-year-old named Jose Temito picked up a young, male prostitute at the intersection of Fourteenth Street and Piedmont Park. The younger beat the older man into a coma, slit his throat and left him in a stand of young dogwoods. Hello, springtime!"

The waiter came and we ordered. Me, a filet mignon and house salad; Lake a hunk of rib eye, potatoes, mushrooms, veggies, and—oh—a peach pie wedge.

When the waiter departed, I said, "You need more detectives, or fewer murders."

"Astute, my darling. As I said when I sat, all the world's astute today."

I related the events of my day, my visit to the Cresleys and Web's attempt to hack the prince's law firm's database to access the prince's on-file information. Lake frowned. I said, "It was a passive attack, meant to gather information, not change data."

"You spend entirely too much time around Webdog."

The day out of the way, we enjoyed our meal, and after a quick kiss goodnight, I headed for my cottage in Peachtree Hills, an Atlanta neighborhood dating back to 1910. One of Atlanta's earliest suburbs, it was built on the bluffs above Peachtree Creek. Like mine, the homes are mostly craftsman cottages strung along winding, narrow streets with huge trees soaring above them. And, like mine, most of my neighbors have gardens that were coming into bloom. My azalea buds were ready to burst into pink and white blossoms.

Because of several incidents, I am careful when I come home. I have a wireless alarm system. It starts at my single-car, detached garage at the back of my lot. I pressed the numbers on my smart phone and a series of rolling numbers had the garage door sliding upward. The night was dark, just a sliver of moon. I keep my shrubs low so that no one can hide in or behind them. Walking briskly, I disarmed the house system with my keychain remote. The lights came on outside and in. A turn of the key and I was in. I looked outside a window. Yes, there was a Zone Two–police car driving by. Despite his mood and the crap on his mind, Lake hadn't forgotten to alert Zone Two–officers that I was on my way home. Once such an alert foiled a burglary up the street. A panel truck was backed up to the house, its door open, and no one around. The officers checked out the oddity and arrested two young thugs lugging electronics from the house. That neighbor waters my garden in the hot summer when I'm away.

I'd just armed the control panel, and set my cell phone, keys and handbag on the kitchen island when my landline phone rang. It was too late for social calls, and I almost didn't answer. Web or Lake would call my cell phone. I thought of my mother at the pricey nursing home. The staff called the landline, even though I'd instructed them to use my cell.

The display told me the caller was unknown. I said hello. No one answered.

"Anyone there?" I said.

No answer. But a loud banging sounded.

"Anyone there?" I repeated.

No answer. A commotion was taking place wherever the call came from. Damn prankster kids. Dial randomly and play jokes. "Good-bye."

"Don't." It was a gruff plea. A man's voice.

"Don't what?" I asked him.

"Help me."

It sounded like a door crashed open, against a wall. Then no noise, then the sounds of struggle.

I cried, "What's going on?" *Could this be the gangsters I'd last tangled with warning me?*

Grunts, as in fighting.

A gunshot.

I ran for my cell phone, holding the landline receiver, and listening.

An abrupt woman's voice sounded in my ear. "What the hell!"

I shouted into the phone, "I'm calling police!"

Another gunshot.

A scream, the woman. "No-o-o. Oh no!"

Dead air.

I punched out the emergency number on my cell.

Then, another shot. Another shot. Another shot.

Five shots, the last ones sounding a deliberate three seconds apart. Some kind of *coup de grace*.

I told the 9-1-1 operator what I'd heard, but I didn't know where the call was coming from, that the number was blocked and not displayed. I repeated it and she said officers were on the way to a scene not far from my house.

I had the most dreadful feeling and called Lake. He already knew about the shots fired. A close neighbor had called the emergency number.

Half an hour later, Lake called with the bad news. The phone number of my male caller was unlisted, but the telephone company supplied the names—who had become the victims.

Donna and Lowell Cresley.

Despite their altered, terrified voices, I'd known in my heart the man calling was Dr. Cresley and the woman screaming was Donna. I saw them in my mind sitting on their lanai, calm as root vegetables in the face of their daughter's disappearance with their unloved granddaughter, as they dismissed the occurrence and its unimaginable—to them—jeopardy.

CHAPTER EIGHT

Lake called from the Cresleys' home five or six times to keep me apprised of what was taking place at the murder scene. Donna Cresley had been shot three times. Lowell had been partially strangled—thus the gruff voice—and shot twice. The forensic team had determined that he was alone in his study drinking and sitting in his fancy wing chair watching a late-night comedian. Lake said the smell of alcohol was strong. Apparently, half in the bag, he was attacked from behind. He managed to escape and ran into a bathroom where a telephone hung on the wall by the toilet. That's when Cresley called me. Lake said my card was on Cresley's desk with my home-phone number penned on the back of it. He must have looked it up somehow, because I never give out my private, home-phone number in cases. Apparently he'd memorized it, because it lay on his desk, not the bathroom floor or furniture.

The attacker, Lake said, dragged Cresley from the bathroom and shot him. Apparently, he spotted Donna Cresley in the doorway to the study and shot her. Lake said it looked like Lowell was to be silently strangled, but his escape caused his wife to hear the commotion which led to her murder when she ran into the study.

"I want to see," I said.

"Thought so. Give it a half hour, then come on. I'll walk you through it."

★ ★ ★ ★ ★

Looking around the murder room, I shuddered at the outlines of the bodies that had been taken away. One outline was straddled across the threshold that led from Cresley's study into a small bathroom. The green phone receiver still dangled from the wall, the instrument adding to the ugliness of blood that had rusted on the floor and pale-yellow walls.

The other outline was inside the door that led from the hall into the study, not three feet from where I stood imagining Donna bleeding out. She and her husband had been shot in the chest and abdomen. Their hearts still pumped as they lay dying.

I noted the presence of Amido Black in the bloodstains. After a fixing agent is applied to the stain, a chemical is used to develop a print. "Anything useful with the Amido?" I asked.

"A couple of prints surfaced. Could be theirs."

The scratches in the blood meant it was probably theirs. They'd clawed against death.

Across the room a small outline showed where the murderer dropped one of the weapons he used in the attack. A paper tent said the weapon was a garrote.

"A garrote," I said.

"It was supposed to be a quiet kill," Lake said somberly.

"Of a man sitting in a wing chair?"

Lake said, "Forensics measured. Cresley was about my height. His head and neck would have been above the back of the chair. If I sit in the chair, so are mine."

I looked around the sleek room, and though wearing forensic booties, hesitated to take a step. People had died here, in their homes, over floors they'd trod. I get spooked by in-home crime scenes where the spirits, if one believed in them, lingered.

The requisite leather was here, but not in the comfy, overstuffed varieties you usually see in the studies of rich men. The couches were black, Italian calfskin supported by silver-plated legs. Curving book shelves had been built in a rounded corner of the room. The shelves were flanked by a steel, spiral, floating staircase. It went nearly to the fourteen-foot coffered ceiling.

The aforementioned wing chair was a black, leather sling-back—my description not the designer's—that was probably comfortable when the body reclined with feet propped on the matching footstool.

Cresley's desk was a smallish, ebony piece of furniture of plain design and costing many, many thousands. Behind it was a red swan chair, although it looked more like a red four-leaf clover. Decorators would call the room and its furnishings minimalist.

A large television hung on the wall. Someone had turned it off.

"So what happened, Sherlock?" Lake asked, having watched me survey the room.

"Well, Watson, you see that door behind the wing chair?"

"My dear Holmes, I am not yet blind."

I canted my head. "That door, with all the fingerprint powder on it, leads into a liquor closet. It hid the villain until the time was most opportune."

"That being?"

"When Dr. Cresley leaned forward from his reclining position, possibly in attempting to rise and get another Scotch."

"And what Scotch was that?"

"Like I know my ashes and my butts, I know my Scotches." I looked at the nearly empty glass on the end table and twitched my nose. It can detect odors almost as well as an olfactory-challenged search-and-rescue dog. "The doctor was left-handed, smoked cigars and drank a single malt," I said.

Lake grinned. "The cigar butt in the ash tray gave away his dark secret, but how do you know he was left-handed?"

"The end table is on his left. As to the Scotch, there are two types of whiskey. The premier is single malt. It is distilled from water and *malted* barley at a single distillery. The second tier is single-grain Scotch. That doesn't mean it's made with one grain, though it has to be distilled at a single distillery. It can be made with malted or unmalted grains, but all Scotch must have barley as an ingredient."

Lake drew in a long, complex-sounding breath. "I meant what label?"

"It's dark and I detect the peaty aroma from here. Lagavulin."

"You knew already."

"You didn't listen to the prince at dinner. What did you think *lag a'mhuilin* was?"

"Cardamom-induced gibberish."

"It's Lagavulin's Gaelic name. Means *hollow by the mill*."

"You look this stuff up—just to get one step ahead of me."

Lake went to the liquor-closet door. I followed and stood next to him and saw the bottle of Lagavulin sitting on a counter. He said, "There's only one cocktail glass. If Husam came here to share a Scotch with his father-in-law, looks like he took away his own."

"Doubt that happened," I said.

A second door was at the back of the closet. I followed Lake through it into a crystal closet, one holding every type of drinking glass imaginable. Name your poison and there was a dozen or more glasses for it. It would surprise me to learn the Cresleys entertained a lot. They were too sour to be social.

Through the crystal closet we entered a large, cool room that held refrigerated wines—at just the right temperature. Not too cold. From there we entered a hall. Turn right and we were in a bona fide library. Panels of shelves; books in leather bindings, but not a hint of murder. Outside the library, a wood and marble, double helix staircase led upstairs. Walking toward the front of the house, where the hall widened into the foyer, we passed the powder room where I'd gone when Donna Cresley called Portia to check out my bona fides. On the right side of the foyer was a formal dining room; on the left side was the living room where earlier I'd talked with the late Donna Cresley. The fingerprint people had been at the walls and furniture with various colors of print powders. Fingerprints from walls are good to have in figuring the height of the person depositing them.

Dactylography, the science of fingerprinting, is not new. Babylonians used fingerprints to sign their identity on clay tablets. The Chinese were the first to use ink prints. The reason dusting powders work is because human fingers are oily and perspire. Dusting powder sticks to the oil and reveals patterns of arches, whorls and loops. It's interesting that there are racial variations. Those of African ancestry tend to have arches, Europeans have loops and Asians, a lot of whorls.

I asked Lake if he detected the race of the murderer and he just stared at me. "How did the intruder get in?"

"Doesn't appear to be an intruder," Lake said.

I had already gleaned that, but said, "They didn't kill themselves or each other. No guns to show a spousal shootout. A guest wouldn't have had to lurk in the closet."

Lake grinned. "No broken locks, windows, doors. An invited guest could have excused himself and gone to the bathroom. There's a powder room off the hall, across from the study."

"I was in there earlier when I came to talk with Donna."

"Did you wipe it clean?"

"No."

"No prints found."

"I touched stuff. I had to leave partials, at least. On the door

59

knobs to go in and out, the toilet handle, probably the towel bar."

"No prints whatsoever."

"That tells me something."

"Sure does, Sherlock."

"So our murderer excuses him—, or her, self . . ."

"From your telephone description, and the strength and length of Dr. Cresley, I don't think it's a her."

"Let's not get gender-stuck here," I said. "For reasoning's sake. Okay?"

He shrugged, showing his good nature. "Okay."

"Our murderer goes into the guest powder room, maybe uses it and wipes it down. Did your . . ."

"Ahead of you; yes, we've got someone coming to suck up the contents of the toilet and take it apart. Not everything disappears, as you know."

"Cripes. I was maybe the last one to pee in it."

"Goes to show, and you should know. Murderers and thieves should not relieve themselves at their crime scenes even if they flush. Hair can and has gotten caught in the traps."

"I'd never use a garrote," I said. "Who would use a garrote with a gun at hand?"

"Who, indeed."

"Any prints on it?"

"Wooden handles wiped clean. The cord won't take a print."

"Was it a *la loupe*?" I asked.

"Long enough to be."

"If the victim gets his fingers on one cord, he tightens the other. So, how'd Cresley get loose?"

"Happens, when a victim is not strapped down," Lake said. "Adrenaline. Executioners used to tie their victims to chairs built for the occasion."

"So, he took away the gun but not the garrote. See, I'm with you on the him/he thing. Leaving the garrote—was that a message?"

"What's it mean to you, Holmes?"

"Well, for one thing it means he came to strangle the primary victim, but had a gun—in case."

"Go on."

"It means he had a damn good reason to murder Dr. Cresley."

Lake crossed his arms "Back to your original question. Who would use a garrote with a gun handy?"

"Military types like Special Forces use it to silent sentries and sneak up on other enemies they need to quietly kill. I know the Spanish used them as a means of execution. The French Legionnaires were particularly fond of *la loupe*."

"You do remember your lessons from the academy."

"Sure do. All the methods of killing someone with any weapon at hand; and methods of killing someone with weapons you bring. Also, defending against such weapons. But in this case—unless Cresley was in the act of making a garrote for his own sinister purposes—the murderer brought the weapon with him."

"So, you're saying that those who would kill with a garrote are military types, Spanish executioners and the French Foreign Legion. Who would you go after first?"

"I was being historical." I deliberately tightened the muscles in my face against simulated hysteria. "In our case, the garrote, being a silent method of murder—if you can control your victim—is a personal weapon. Somebody who was really pissed and wanted to feel his victim die would use a garrote, if his bare hands couldn't do the trick."

Lake said, "I don't know about the military being historical. Who do we know in this case that's in the military?"

"Lake, my dearest dunderhead, a military man, trained in

silent-kill weaponry, would not get cords around Cresley's neck and then let the man pull loose."

"Hmmm. I concede. There's the question of leverage. With Cresley sitting, the would-be strangler couldn't brace against his back or kick Cresley's back knees from under him. Bad technique all around. Under the circumstances, not a kill method a military man would use."

"Very bad execution. So, an amateur."

"Could have been a woman," he said.

"Ah!"

Lake pressed and twisted his lips in that thoughtful way he has, and then said, "Cresley escaped his attacker, and ran to the bathroom, which is seven running strides across this room from the wing chair. His attacker couldn't have been far behind, yet Cresley had time to shut and lock the door and dial you."

"Doesn't make a lot of sense, unless his attacker had some kind of problem."

"Like what?"

"Old, slow, crippled."

"So, he rips open the door, which is what you heard, and drags Cresley off the pot . . ."

"The failed executioner could have tripped and fallen over the foot stool," I said, beginning to pace as I thought and spoke. "He saw that Cresley went into the bathroom. He knew it was a bathroom. He'd been in the house before. He knew about the closets. So, no hurry, but he had to get Cresley out of there and kill him. So, he pulls his gun from wherever and crashes in the door." I paused and looked at Lake. "It wasn't a heavy, wooden door, but a privacy thing with slats."

"Easy to kick in," Lake said. "The wife hears and comes running from wherever she is."

"She had to be close by. I would guess she was in here," I said, meaning the living room where we stood. "If she was upstairs and heard the ruckus I heard over the phone, she would have called 9-1-1. She wouldn't have come down the stairs, but instead locked herself in. Most of these houses have panic rooms in the bedrooms reinforced with fiberglass and Kevlar."

Lake and I spoke simultaneously: *"There were two of them."*

Lake said, "One stayed in the living room with Donna Cresley when the other used the bathroom, or excused himself, or herself, in order to do so. The attacker then came through the wine and crystal closets to hide in the liquor closet waiting his chance to kill Cresley, who was sousing himself. Which makes you wonder why Cresley wasn't in the living room with Donna and the other guest, doesn't it?"

"I peg him as antisocial, unless it suits."

Lake continued, "When Cresley escapes the garrote, the person in the living room with Donna hears the yelling and banging, most likely because he or she was listening for it, and comes to the partner's aid. Donna, alarmed but not afraid of either person, follows."

Or the guest with Donna forced her to come along.

"Therefore, they were people the Cresleys knew," I said.

"And not intruders," Lake concluded. "People Donna Cresley would entertain, or at least have in her living room, while her husband wanted nothing to do with them."

I had to say it. "Wonder where Husam and Salman were this evening?"

Lake said, "The fingerprints on the wall show the person to be tall and having fat fingers."

"Too bad you can't tell how old they are."

"An electrical analysis possibly could, but the powder negates that. Besides, it would be challenged in court because there's no age-dated print database."

"One more question. Why didn't Dr. Cresley call 9-1-1 instead of me?"

"You must have impressed him greatly."

"Or he was implicating Saliba in his coming murder."

CHAPTER NINE

The medical examiner had finished with the Cresley bodies by the morning of the next day. It was revealed that the doctor had a small cancer in a lung that was blackened from cigarette and cigar smoke. That and his cirrhosis would have shortened his life anyway. He had ligature marks on his throat that matched the double-looped garrote, but he died from two gunshot wounds to the abdomen. Donna Cresley was a healthy woman who died because the murderer pumped three bullets into her lungs and stomach. All five bullets matched, so one gun was used. Police, led by Lake, concluded that the shooter or shooters—two people could have shot the same gun—weren't pros. Pros go for the head.

The murders had been all over the media. Still no word from Reeve Cresley.

"She has to surface," Lake said. "Surely."

"Maybe not."

"Could be she hasn't heard the news."

"If she's afraid for her own life, and her daughter's," I said, "why would she show herself when her parents have been killed?"

"You really think the prince and his pal murdered her parents to smoke her out?"

"It's a possibility."

"I thought you liked the dude."

"I've disliked more church-goes than murderers I have known."

Natural-born killers learn early in life that they have to develop charming or at least affable personalities. It's the snake-spider thing. You see something repulsive, you run from it or kill it. If evil folks looked like monsters, cops could pick them off the streets. Take charismatic Ted Bundy. There were others, like shy, amiable Eddie Gein, whose horrific deeds inspired "Silence of the Lambs."

Lake said, "Wonder why Prince Charming gave you a bum phone number?"

I wonder that, too. I had no way to get in touch with Husam now that he'd apparently returned to New York. His secretary at the law firm said that he was out of town. His cell number was the wrong number Lake referred to.

Now that the Atlanta Police Department was fully involved with the disappearance of Reeve and Shara, by way of the death of the Cresleys, they had to contend with Prince Husam bin Sayed al-Saliba and immunity issues.

Did a Saudi royal have sovereign or diplomatic immunity? Or both?

Webdog, ever the digger, laid out the difference. "The sovereign doctrine stems from the old English principle that the monarch can do no wrong. Diplomatic immunity is a different herd of llamas. Under the 1961 Vienna Convention, only bona fide diplomats qualify. The diplomat's government can waive immunity, but usually doesn't. A diplomat's son in New York raped fifteen girls. All that happened to him was he was sent back to his country. You can get away with murder if you have diplomatic immunity."

The APD chief of police had contacted the United States State Department, and, yes, His Royal Highness Husam bin Sayed al-Saliba was a member of the Diplomatic Corps at the

Kingdom Saudi Arabia Embassy in the Foggy Bottom neighborhood of Washington, DC. Officially.

The chief informed the state department that the Atlanta Police Department wanted to question the prince with regard to his in-laws, the Cresleys, who were murdered in their home. The state department spokeswoman said that they would have to inform the prince's country that he was wanted for questioning in the death of his in-laws, but that he did not have to answer questions, could not be arrested or tried and convicted, unless his country waived immunity. The chief replied back that, *whoa, we haven't started down that road yet,* that he didn't want a waiver at this time, that the APD had no reason to suspect the prince of the murders, that, in fact, he was believed to be out of the city of Atlanta at the time of the murders, but that they just wanted to gather facts and find out if he knew of anyone who might want to harm his late in-laws. The state department said they'd get back with him.

"Goddamn red tape," Commander Haskell said.

I sat across from the normally constrained man. I, too, felt like we'd fallen into a vortex.

He said, "We've gone through the computers of the couple, nothing looks dodgy. No compromising or threatening emails."

I left the unproductive meeting and called Webdog. I'd just started with instructions when he interrupted to say he'd added to the prince's resume. His sister, Princess Yasmin al-Saliba, lived in Sarasota, Florida, in a gated community where many Saudis lived. One particular couple had been investigated in the terrorist attacks on the World Trade Center, the Pentagon and a plane in Pennsylvania on September eleventh.

"The couple fled two weeks before the attacks," Web said.

"Web, don't even suggest I'm investigating a bunch of terrorists."

"It strains my credulity to believe nineteen foreigners could have pulled off those attacks without help from confederates here," he said.

"Do *not* bring Homeland Security to my door."

"Try my best."

"Get on the prince's residences."

"Prince Husam owns a condominium in the Sarasota community and belongs to the golf club."

"Got a phone number?"

"No landline. Dirk's is on the cell numbers. The prince's primary residence is in Manhattan, New York. He also owns an apartment in the Atlanta Arms—no phone number attached to it—and a townhouse in DC near the embassy. I have that landline phone number if you'd like."

"I'd have liked it if you gave it to me first." I would apologize for snarking later.

He rattled out the 202 number and said, "His apartment in New York is located across from Central Park on Fifth Avenue. The Eastonton Chase. His email address is hrhprinceHusam bin Sayed al-Saliba@ksaembassy.embassy."

"Find out when his passport was last stamped, as well as those of Donna Reeve Cresley, Shahrazad Cresley al-Saliba, Lowell Reeve Cresley and Yasmin al-Saliba. That brings another thing to mind. How many passports do they have? Reeve could have a Saudi passport and Husam might have a diplomatic US passport. Second passports aren't that hard to come by, especially with VIPs and those with lots of palm-greasing cash. Gather photos of everyone connected to this case and, as we do, add a few non-connections to keep the lookers honest."

He answered on the first ring.

I recognized his pleasant baritone, but I asked anyway, "Am I speaking to Prince Husam bin Sayed al-Saliba?"

"You are, Miss Dru. The display announced you."

"I've been waiting for your call."

"And I've been waiting for permission from my country to call you."

"It's going to be like that, is it?"

"I truly hope not. But I cannot act unless directed by my sovereign."

The monarch can do no wrong.

"I understand. I hope you understand that we need to talk to you."

"We?"

"I need to talk to you, as do the Atlanta police. Lake, representing the police, would like to ask you some questions."

"I do not think your Lake is my friend."

"Lake takes a while to make friends, Prince Husam."

"While you are more amicable."

Not necessarily, bozo. "I'd like to think I'm amicable. I'd also like to think you know you can speak to me as you've done at dinner."

"Ah, dinner. So long ago."

And so artful of you. "Have you heard from Reeve?"

"I have not. Now, Miss Dru, I will call you as soon as I can speak freely. I believe my telephone is being monitored, so I am literally and figuratively not allowed to speak freely at this time."

Sometimes it's hard to rein in sudden fury.

I said, "You have my telephone number. Please call me. I'm not working on the murders, although if I come across information the police can use in their case, I'll let them know."

"You and I cannot be confidential, can we?"

"Not like attorney-client privilege, or priestly confessions, but I hold my client's words dear until compelled by court order to divulge them."

"I knew I could trust you. I trust Portia Devon. That woman is a paragon."

Paragon of what? Right now I wished she'd never met him, or me.

★ ★ ★ ★ ★

Late in the day, a telephone interview was arranged by the KSA embassy between Lake and Prince Husam bin Sayed al-Saliba. For fifteen minutes the prince denied knowing anything about the Cresley murders, and it appeared from the APD's traces of his travels before and after the killings that he couldn't have murdered his in-laws, nor taken part unless by conspiracy. He denied any involvement, and who was surprised at that? He said that he hadn't heard from his wife and that he was sure she would get in touch once she learned of her parents' deaths.

Sure, just like he did.

CHAPTER TEN

One of the things you have to wonder when murder happens in a gated community like Killarney is how the murderer(s) got in. You want safety and privacy, so you buy a house in a gated community. You drive through a sturdy gate that rises and falls upon your pin number. You have nothing to worry about. You are secure. You are safe.

You couldn't be more wrong. You are kidding yourself. What you really wanted was a status symbol or, as some say, separation from the less desirable aspects of society. That status symbol and separation can cost you. Thieves know those living behind the gates have expensive stuff to steal, and that the homeowners have a false sense of security. They neglect their security systems. Ask any security officer, even those who aren't worth a hoot. And don't forget that the faces of security are human. They have seen expensive goods come and go through those gates— the furnishings, cars, jeweled fingers and earlobes. It's oh-so tempting. Ask any cop.

Where there are no guards in a kiosk, but instead a code-entry system, experienced thieves can have a field day, or night. The intruder hits # 9-1-1 on the code pad. The system is set to allow police to enter. Even entry-level thieves know this. Electronic wizards go so far as to program their own code using a preset master code they get from the keypad maker. Even if neighbors are vigilant about pass codes, and # 9-1-1 doesn't automatically open the gates, the more enterprising thieves know how to get past locked gates by hiding in trunks and sneaking uninvited rides in delivery vans. Where there's no guard, there's the piggybacking thing where a car comes through on the tail of another. When there's a guard in the kiosk, honest-acting thieves pretend to be real-estate buyers or deliverers of missed newspapers and food service. Guards buzz in these folks on their word. That's how I got through the gates to knock uninvited on Donna Cresley's door. Hundreds of ruses fool security people every day. Ask any cop, and if you can't fool 'em, then there's always hacksaws and chain cutters for the less grandiose perimeter fences.

All that having gone through my head, I found myself listening to Lake's second interview with the head of security at Killarney. Lake had gotten the videos of twelve hours before and after the Cresleys were murdered. I'd been in the squad room and seen them, after which I'd asked Webdog to run Carl Langford's bona fides. Carl Langford was forty-two, married, two children in public schools. Deacon in the Methodist Church. Community college. US Army. Iraq and Afghanistan. Reserves now. Good credit, salary near a hundred grand with bonuses. I couldn't help but wonder: did the Cresley murders shoot this year's bonus all to hell?

A video in question was up on a monitor.

Carl Langford, the head of security, said, "As I told you, Lieutenant, my main man was on duty until his shift change." He sat at an uncluttered computer desk, hands folded. We sat in straight chairs either side of him. Next to me was a credenza with a stack of action comic books and paperback mysteries. I noted the bindings: Child, Lehane, Connolly. Langford was a trim, fit man, like a runner, and maybe his being in the reserves kept him that way.

Langford had been cooperative with Lake, and since I spotted something odd about one entry in the security log, Lake let me tag along for the second interview and the catch.

Lake said, "In reviewing the videos, I see that your cameras aren't angled to get a good look at faces, especially of anyone wearing a hat. Your audio is not clear and your cameras don't catch all the license plates on the backs of trucks."

Shrugging, Langford said, "If trucks had a set place for the plates, we'd catch them. As it is, they can hang anywhere— right, middle, left, up or below the bumpers. The guard on duty writes the tag number on the clipboard. Our system is state of the art. The installers are still setting the angles and the audio. I have nothing to do with installation except to tell them it needs more tinkering."

"Leave it as it is for now," Lake said.

I told Langford that a guard named Sonny was on the gate the day I drove up to the kiosk to see Donna Cresley. He had asked who I was visiting and checked my driver's license for ID. "I don't recall him asking my plate number, but maybe he wrote it when I passed through. One thing he didn't do was alert Donna Cresley of my coming."

Langford wriggled his nose. "He should have called Mrs. Cresley."

Lake pointed at the screen. "Advance to the time the Cresleys were murdered, maybe two minutes before." Langford did, seeming to cringe. He knew what was coming.

Lake said, "See, the guard shack had a ten-minute period where it was empty."

"I told you, Lieutenant, the second-shift man was late and the day man had to leave." He pointed to a computer monitor next to him that showed live gate activity. "I was here, viewing it live."

"There were seven vehicles that entered in that period of time. They all used the keypad. Do you know them by vehicle?"

Langford backed up and re-ran the video for the time Lake

specified. An exercise in stalling since he'd probably seen it multiple times. "I knew four of them," he said. "Three apparently were visitors who'd been given the code."

"So, three entries with no camera on them and no license identification," Lake said. Perplexed, Langford shook his head. Lake went on. "We've canvassed the community. No one so far has admitted to having visitors that night, at that time."

"It's really unfortunate," Langford said, looking at me, away from Lake's wondering eyes.

Lake said, "We talked to the night kid, the one who was late. He's admitted to being habitually late."

"I should have fired him months ago. He's a college kid making minimum wage because traffic into here is slow on his shift. But, like I told you, I look at the video from twenty-four hours before. I check off the names and plate numbers on the clipboard."

"But there were no names because there was no clipboard entry because there was no guard on duty. The cameras were not angled to catch faces that didn't want to be caught."

"Maybe enhanced imaging would help," Langford offered. About all he could.

"The lab's working on it," Lake said, then asked, "How well did you know Prince Husam?"

Langford's lip twitched. "I didn't know the man at all. As I said before, I've seen him on the monitors. Twice in the last month. The Cresleys have only lived here for four years, but I know Doc didn't care for the man."

"How do you know that?"

"Told me a couple weeks ago. He said, 'Let me know when Husam Saliba comes through those gates, if you see him.' He gave me his private hospital number. Twice, I told him. Tried to pay me for it, but no, I'm doing my job."

Never trust a man who won't accept a tip.

It was my turn. Lake and I had rehearsed this. I consulted my notebook in deliberate fashion. "According to the video, three delivery trucks came through the day the Cresleys were killed. The day guard, Sonny, listed one driver as a substitute named E. B. White."

"I recall seeing the truck on video and reading the clipboard," Langford said.

"How many times had this substitute come through the gates?"

"Is there something wrong?"

Lake said, "Maybe not."

Langford said, "I think at least twice, but let me go see." He left and Lake and I remained quiet. Ten minutes later, he returned, looking unwell. "Three times, starting five days before the murders. Jesus." He rubbed his forehead while he read from the notebook paper he held. "Two days later, and then on that— the day of the murders. What significance is this?" He was sweating even though his office was chilly. "I got the license-plate number here." He handed Lake his handwritten notes.

Lake said, "First thing I noticed on the video about the truck is the company logo wasn't exactly right, like someone had hand painted it on."

Langford shrugged, but not with a lot of confidence. "These guys are contractors, mostly, with their own trucks."

"So you say," Lake said.

Langford was going to hate me now. I said, "E. B. White is an author and poet. He won the nineteen-seventy Laura Ingalls Wilder Medal for his children's books *Stuart Little* and *Charlotte's Web*."

He looked from me to Lake as if I'd told a joke. "No wonder he's driving a delivery truck. Poeting doesn't pay as much as delivering." But he didn't dare laugh.

"So, you assumed he was credible," Lake said.

"That delivery company sends guys twice a day. Mostly the same ones, but they have subs, too."

"Guys named E. B. White?"

He looked away like he wanted to spit. "I don't read children's books, Lieutenant."

"Who were the deliveries for?" I asked.

He breathed in. "The Fergusons. On Blossom Trail."

"The Fergusons on Blossom Trail were out of town then," Lake said. "Out of the country, and still are."

"You checked on everybody lives in here?" he asked.

"Yes," Lake replied. "All sixteen little mansions."

Langford paused as if Lake had insulted him. Lake had learned that fourteen of the sixteen residents had downsized from larger homes elsewhere like the Cresleys. None of the sixteen had a felony conviction; several had DUI's though.

Langford said, "Mr. Ferguson instructed the delivery company to leave packages under the covered back deck. He gets regular supplies from the internet."

"Then the Cresleys were murdered," Lake said.

Langford looked at the ceiling, perhaps for salvation.

"So," Lake said, "I want you to open that house and let my forensic team in. The Fergusons are still in Greece, but somebody's been holed up in their house and receiving meals on wheels."

Langford looked like his perfect career was over. "I'll need an official search warrant."

As if one wasn't official.

We waited until an officer arrived to guard the Ferguson property, then left—Lake to go round up a judge for an official search warrant, and me to my office.

"The Suffolk County constabulary gave Dirk's guy a report of the accident Reeve and Shara were involved in on Long Island

76

on Montauk Highway. The deputy reported her Lexus stopped short of going into a pond. She was heading southwest to their rental place in Bridgehampton, she said, without giving him the address, because she didn't know it. A young man, Mark Stewart, going northeast toward Montauk, stopped when he came upon the Lexus on the side of the road. He said a big Mercedes nearly crashed into him head-on as they met at a curve before he came upon the Lexus. He didn't see the actual event so he couldn't say if the Mercedes intentionally ran the Lexus off the road. His thought was that the driver was going too fast in passing the Lexus, which happened a lot. The deputy noted that many accidents had happened at that spot and there were warnings to slow down. He also noted a slight smell of alcohol on Reeve Cresley's person and gave her a roadside sobriety test. She was well within the legal limit. She refused medical help for herself and her daughter, Shara Cresley. End of report."

As Husam had wondered: *What were they doing in Montauk? They were staying in Bridgehampton. It was dark and cold.* And, I wondered, what kind of sobriety test did the deputy give Reeve? Sometimes officers will call "observation of movements" a roadside sobriety test.

"What have you found out about Reeve Cresley?" I asked Web.

"Brilliant scientist," Web said.

"I know. A rocket scientist."

"Well, yeah, that's a general term for all sorts of disciplines."

"Start with her degrees."

"George Washington for undergrad. MIT masters, PhD. Accepted as an intern by NASA; settled into the field of orbital mechanics. That's the study of two bodies moving and interacting in a gravitational field. It's determined by the science of general relativity and essential to calculate how the light bends by gravity in relation to the motion of a planet orbiting its sun."

"Web, skip the lesson in relativity. What is relative is what she did after she graduated. Where did she live? Who did she date before she returned to Washington to seek out her prince?"

"Gotcha. She was part of the Jet Propulsion Lab post-doc program, then went on to the NASA planetary geology and geophysics sciences."

"Where?"

"DC headquarters for the Planetary Science Division. She was laid off temporarily and transferred to the planet-hunting mission—part of a team that discovered twenty-seven-hundred new planets before the telescope's wheels fell off. Her last station was the Boulder lab." Web ate this stuff up. So did I, when I had time.

"So we got Pasadena, California; Washington, DC; and Boulder, Colorado. Timeline, please."

Web said that she'd spent ten years with NASA in these cities: one year in Pasadena; six-plus in DC and three in Colorado. At the time she vanished, she'd been transferred back to the jet lab but never showed. I told him to look into her friendships and activities, and if there were any dalliances while away from Husam.

"My pleasure," he said, and meant it.

"See if she has a Montauk connection his royal highness doesn't know about."

"On it."

It took Lake an hour to get a signed search warrant. The court complex is near my high-rise office so he rolled by and picked me up and we headed back down Peachtree Street to Killarney. Langford seemed surprised at the quickness of our errand.

Following Langford to the back of the Ferguson home, Lake and the officer searched the upper and lower decks. I stood with Langford, itching to ask him a few questions, but decided against it. His eyes wouldn't meet mine. Maybe he was still smarting from the E. B. White thing. I didn't blame him for being edgy. He must have figured his domain was in jeopardy should the homeowners' association decide he wasn't vigilant enough.

After walking over the small garden, Lake said to Langford, "Delivery boxes under the back deck. Some from an online store, some empty. My officer and I inspected the outside locks on doors and windows. None had the marks of burglary tools."

Langford's face distorted. This was not his day, it said, as he led us around to the front door and opened it with a skeleton key, a term meaning the skeletal structure is one that can bypass all locks. It's handy for homeowners who lose their keys or burglars and squatters who steal into homes to hang out for a while.

Inside, the home was not unlike the Cresleys' in size and structure, but there the likeness ended. The Fergusons lived in a mess, or their uninvited guests did. The major mess was in the kitchen and two bedrooms. "Won't be hard to get prints off the furniture," Lake said. "Hasn't been dusted in however long the Fergusons have been away, except that the dust has been moved around, probably by those sandwich wrappers, donut boxes and chip bags."

Lake addressed Langford. "Thanks, man, for your cooperation. If we need to ask you anything else, we know where to find you."

Having been dismissed, I heard a sigh from him as he slouched out the front door.

"Our murderers hung out here?" I asked.

"Doubt it. Our missing mother and daughter, more likely."

"That's why the Cresleys never seemed worried; their girls were right up the street."

"If that's the case," Lake said, "the debris field in here says a lot about our rocket scientist and the princess."

I walked out the door when forensics came. Lake was with me. I said, "In the fog of murder, she got out of here when the cops came and she learned her parents were dead."

Lake asked, "Will you have Webdog call the cab companies, run the license tag the guard wrote down for the step van, and tell me who was supplying Reeve and her daughter with food and the necessities of life on the run?"

"You can have your able detectives check the cabbies and tags; I'll take the supplier. I'll find E. B. White in due time."

CHAPTER ELEVEN

The outline of his body was like a silhouette cast against a multi-hued horizon. Like the pines behind him, he was unmoving. He was dressed in a western suit but wore a white *ghutra* and black *igal* on his head. I know of several styles of Middle Eastern headdress and that Arafat made the black and white check *keffiyeh* popular when he adopted it, but the Saudis wear plain white. I saw Lawrence of Arabia at least ten times, which had piqued my interest in Arab head wear.

I walked across my backyard toward a man who could have played Lawrence better than Peter O'Toole. Prince Husam looked spectacular in the traditional *ghutra* that was held in place by a double circle of braided animal hair.

He placed his hands together as if in prayer, and nodded a bow. That pleased me because royals don't bow.

"Your Royal Highness," I said. "It's . . ."

"Please, you have called me Husam before, so that will do."

"Welcome to my home—and garden. Have you been waiting long?"

"Not at all. I have been very happy here in this beautiful place. The blossoming dogwoods and the azaleas about to burst into bloom have been excellent company, plus that delightful brown cat who stalks bluebirds but shall never catch one."

"Only if they're ready to give up the ghost."

He raised expressive eyebrows. "Give up the ghost?"

"Means give up and die, or stop trying."

"Ah, I am here to keep trying."

"Would you like to come inside my house?"

"I am quite comfortable out here."

I wondered if this was because Muslim men are not to be in intimate surroundings with a woman other than a wife or sister? I said, "Let's sit on the patio. Can I get you something to drink?"

"That would be nice."

We walked side by side to the patio chairs. "I have bottles of flavored water—cranberry, coconut, blueberry."

"They all sound delicious." He sat at the umbrella table that didn't have an umbrella overhead and pulled off the *igal* and then the scarf, which was a folded triangle of exquisite material that appeared to be a linen and cotton blend. He said, "If you have it, a spot of vodka in the coconut would be fine."

Maybe partaking of vodka was why he removed his *ghutra*. In my religion it would be like taking the Lord's name in vain while holding a rosary.

"Great," I said. I disarmed the locks with my cell phone and opened the back door. When I put my handbag on the counter, I felt a strange humming along my spine and looked out the window. Prince Husam appeared at ease, his hands folded in his lap, gazing at the gaudily striped horizon. My hands shook. Why had he come here?

I prepared our drinks: his, ice, coconut water and vodka; mine, gin and tonic. Mindful that my sausage snack probably had pork in it, I put pieces of cheese between saltines, the only crackers I had in the house. When I set this small repast before him he smiled. Ten thousand watts, at least.

"Now, what brings you to my home?"

"I have been advised by my sovereign to cooperate as much as I can, but that I should not implicate myself in any way in this tragedy. I have talked via telephone with the policeman. You wanted to talk to me also."

"True," I said, and sipped at my drink. "As a lawyer, you know how not to implicate yourself."

He grinned. "I am not a fool. I will not be my own lawyer."

"Do you have one?"

"Several, but not a criminal attorney. I know of one to consult, though, should the time come."

Was I being put on notice? "As I've said, our agency doesn't promise a seal of the confessional, but we do keep confidences."

"That is fine," he said, picking up his tall glass and drinking thirstily. Placing the half-full glass on the stoneware coaster, he sat back. "First I must tell you a story."

Hmmm. My discussion with Portia came to mind. "All right."

"The *One Thousand and One Nights'* stories are continuous, you understand."

I bobbed my head yes.

"One leads into another as a cliff-hanger that Shahrazad used to entrance the king to save her life night after night."

"I've read a few, like the Sinbad stories."

"Ah, yes, Sinbad, a real person, it is believed. The tales begin when Shahryar, the king, had been betrayed by his first wife and vowed to marry a virgin every day and have her killed the next morning, thus not giving her time to form male friendships. He was sure these deaths were the only way to keep his wives faithful." He paused as if this was significant and I should understand. "That's the skeleton upon which the tales hang."

He drank off the rest of his drink, then said, "The stories often have viziers to advise the king about what happens around him. For instance, in one of the famous fables of Sinbad, a vizier tells Sinbad that, 'One ought not believe everything that a mother-in-law says.' "

Prince Husam paused and cleared an obstruction from his throat, as if an imaginary vizier might say that to me.

Husam continued, "In another story, called "The Husband

and the Parrot," a good man had a beautiful wife, whom he loved passionately. One day, when he was obliged by important business to go away from her, he went to a place where all kinds of birds are sold and bought a parrot. This parrot not only spoke well, but it had the gift of telling all that had been done in its presence. The good husband, who is also a king, brought it home in a cage, and asked his wife to put it in her room, and take great care of it while he was away. Then he departed. On his return he asked the parrot what had happened during his absence, and the parrot told him some things that made him scold his wife.

"The wife thought that one of her slaves must have been telling tales on her, but they told her it was the parrot. So she resolved to revenge herself on the parrot. When her husband next went away for one day, she told one slave to turn a hand mill under the bird's cage, and another slave to throw water down from above the cage, and a third slave to take a mirror and turn it in front of the parrot's eyes, from left to right by the light of a candle. The slaves did this all night.

"The next day when the king came back he asked the parrot what he had seen. The bird replied, 'My good master, the lightning, thunder and rain disturbed me so much all night long, that I cannot tell you what I have suffered.'

"The king, who knew that it had neither rained nor thundered in the night, was convinced that the parrot was not speaking the truth, so he took him out of the cage and threw him so roughly on the ground that he killed him. Nevertheless he was sorry afterwards, for he found that the parrot had spoken the truth and he said so to his vizier. 'Sire,' the vizier replied, 'the death of the parrot was nothing. But when it is a question of the life of a king it is better to sacrifice the innocent than save the guilty. It is no uncertain thing, however, as a physician wishes to assassinate you. My zeal prompts me to disclose this to your Majesty.'

"The vizier went on to say, 'If I am wrong, I deserve to be punished as another vizier was once punished.'

" 'What had that vizier done,' said the king, 'to merit the punishment?'

" 'I will tell your Majesty, if you will do me the honour to listen,' answered the vizier.' "

Prince Husam stopped speaking and I waited for the ending, but it was not to be. He said, "And so that leads into another tale. There are said to be a thousand before Shahrazad ran out of tales, but by that time the king had fallen in love with Shahrazad. He made her his number-one wife and sent the executioner away."

He picked up his cocktail glass, which was empty. "Hold on," I said. "I'll refill if you wish."

"That would be good."

Having replenished our cocktails, I sat and grinned at him. "You've made a couple of points with the tales."

Husam drank thirstily again, then said, "You spoke with my mother-in-law and father-in-law; is that not true?"

"I did. They called you?"

"My father-in-law accused me of hiring you to *flush out* my wife to be killed."

"They believed that."

"It is a monstrous lie, but I would not kill them for it."

"You were in New York at the time. Unless you hired a killer to do it."

"I did not do that." He sat forward. "I am one hundred percent innocent of that. That is why I have come today. I want to know what happened to my in-laws. We were not the best of friends, unhappily, and I did not trust them, but I honored them."

"I don't think I can tell you anything more than what has been reported in the media."

"I believe that you can. Are you not in the confidence of Lieutenant Lake?"

"Somewhat, but there are things discussed at the police station that stay at the police station. Cops keep secrets when they're told to."

"No pillow talk?"

There was a suggestion in his eyes that I didn't care for. "No."

"I have offended you?"

"I keep my private life private."

"That is good. I wish that I could, but I know that I am being investigated. At my office, our computers were hacked."

A nerve in my stomach twitched. "Happens often," I said.

"We have ultra-tight security measures in place. We are international and have many clients to shield from prying eyes and ears."

Did he suspect me? "I'm sure."

"Because of America's fear of terrorists, I am always under suspicion; I know that."

"I think if our security services suspected you, you'd be gone from this country."

"That is true, but whenever something happens, our community, we Muslims, are under scrutiny again."

"Let me ask you a bold question without hurting your feelings. Do you think terrorists have anything to do with Reeve's and Shara's disappearance?"

He shook his head vehemently. "No Muslim would harm a princess, or a prince's wife."

"Do you know any terrorists?" I asked. "Stupid question, I know."

He laughed. "Not stupid, actually." He drank from his

cocktail glass. "A valid question to be answered. One would not announce what he is to me. Our clients are rich and want to stay that way. We enjoy capitalism and do not want it destroyed. No. There are no terrorists in our organization."

"That you know of."

"We would know." He stared at me as if I'd suggested he wet the bed at night. "We would be ruined. We have no fanatics in our firm."

"I've investigated gangland crimes and many other evils, but so far I've avoided terrorism and want to continue to avoid it. It's a crime for the feds. If your girls are part of that, I can't help you. Call the CIA, FBI or Homeland Security."

"I can assure you my family is as far away from that as we can get."

While he finished his second drink, I sipped mine and hoped I could believe him.

He placed his glass on the coaster and sat back, relaxed. "Like our clients, we are rich capitalists, getting richer. That is why we have experts to fight cyber attacks. We are very good at repelling these attacks."

"Hacking the hackers?" I ventured.

"Indeed. The Russians, who are not nearly as brainy as the Asians, seek to steal our clients' resources and information. We have specialists to study their malware in their attempts to gather financial and business intelligence. Recently a very sophisticated hack was attempted using the Linux operating system. Soon we will identify the exact version. Two ports on the attacker's computer were open; one was the proprietary database MySQL. Do you know of what I speak?"

"Not really. Our security system is rudimentary, at best."
Apologies to Webdog.

"What do you know of programming?"

"Exactly nothing, except that it takes a programmer to write erri Finger

software and software runs the machines."

"I would think you would have an IT guy working for you?"

"We do, part time. He keeps the computers up and running, making sure the latest viruses are removed."

"I see."

"Let me ask you something off the computer topic." He frowned because he was comfortable talking about the computer. He and Web could have a discussion where they understood each other. I said, "Your father-in-law was garroted before he was shot. Your mother-in-law was shot three times when she went to his aid. Probably it was two people that came into the Killarney community to kill them. Can you think of any reason for their murders?" He was already shaking his head. "How cautious were they—locking doors, making sure they knew people before opening them? That kind of thing."

"I cannot answer those questions. I did not know them that well. They seemed suspicious, but it might have been me." He shrugged, apparently keeping to the injunction of his sovereign not to implicate himself in the murders. To that end, he said, "I have read of home invasions here in Atlanta."

I wanted to smack his face. "The Cresley murders were not home invasions. The Cresleys knew their killers. It was personal."

"I did not kill the Cresleys, nor did I hire it done. They were livid when Reeve married me. They did not come to the wedding. They were never kind to me. What grandmother never holds her grandchild? What grandfather doesn't say the name of his grandchild? I can only assume there are other people they do not like and regard as inferior. I am not inferior to them." He'd raised his voice. "I am a prince of a sovereign nation. I did not bow to them and they did not like that."

My mouth twitched at his outburst. He ruffled his shoulders like he knew better than to let loose like that.

A few moments later, I said, "You and Reeve seemed to have

88

spent a lot of time apart."

"That is true. Our work took us to different cities. Sometimes on opposite coasts."

"Who did Shara live with?"

"Her mother, in DC and Colorado. Of course we visited each other often."

"Who took care of Shara while Reeve pursued her career."

"Any number of nannies and preschools. Reeve does not trust nannies. She believes they get bored and lose interest. Shara has had many nannies. Why do you ask?"

"Anything to help me know where to look for them."

I bid the prince farewell and called Lake.

The prince was correct. Lake was not a fan. He said, "Forward son-of-a-bitch. Coming to your house like that."

"He's a prince, Lake. Not like you—one of the masses."

"This mass will kick his ass if he stalks you again."

"Now, now . . . he told me several things."

"Like 'I know where you live.' "

"That's one. He wore formal Arab headdress."

"What's that say to you?"

"Not to forget that he's a prince that *I* should bow to."

"And two?"

"That we are culturally different. He reminded me of Lawrence of Arabia, except he wore a Western suit."

"I thought maybe he wore a robe. I hear they don't wear clothes under those—whatevers."

"Dishdasha."

"Are we talking about something they eat on?"

I laughed. "Nope, it's not a plate. It's a white robe; a *bhesth* is a black one."

"I like it better when you speak Gaelic, especially when it

comes to Scotch. How about joining me for one at the Highland Tavern."

"Not Jeremy's?"

"I don't want to be near a cop. Commander Haskell is probably downing one there right now."

"Kiss, kiss. See you at Highland. Have a wine ready for me."

Highland is a nice little place not too far from where I live. It reeks of tony success and academics. I saw a guy in a pinstripe suit pull his tie knot from his shirt collar. That kind of place. Lake sat at the bar, his tie knot snug in the vee of his collar. The patrons who keep up with police cases would have taken him for an APD detective because of the spring fedora placed by his elbow. He drank Sam Adams. A chardonnay sat on the bar above an empty stool, empty until I sat on it. When the bartender saw me he signaled a waiter. I should have anticipated that Lake would order food.

I asked, "How go the cases?"

"We got the guy who slit the old man's throat. Got a lead on the Metro drive-bys. The home-invasion boys are laying low and there's a prison snitch who thinks he knows who did the prostitutes."

"He a cellmate?"

"Formerly. The doer, if it's the one the snitch is referring to, just got out of Reidsville."

The waiter came with Philly steaks and fries. It was late and I wasn't hungry so I drank wine and watched Lake eat the beef and pepper sandwich with a knife and fork. The few times I'd been in Philadelphia, I'd never eaten a Philly steak, but if they're as good as Highland's then thanks, Philly, for the addition to our traditional southern cuisine.

Wiping his lips, Lake said, "The prison snitch wants a talk."

Reidsville is a town where Georgia's major maximum-security

prison is located and where Old Sparky replaced hanging as the preferred method of execution. Georgia's retired electric chair is on display there. I've been to a lot of prisons in my career and it's never a pleasant experience. Georgia has more than thirty state prisons and they are classified from minimum security to close security, meaning maximum. Three prisons are for women. The hardest to visit is in Jackson, where death row is now located. Twenty years ago a Georgia legislator wanted to replace the Jackson electric chair with the guillotine in order to harvest the condemneds' organs. It didn't pass. Lethal injection passed a decade ago. Beats being hanged, fried or sliced—at a guess.

Lake said, "You haven't touched your food."

"I was thinking unpleasant thoughts."

"I can tell."

"Where are you on Lowell Cresley's life story?"

"Nothing outstanding so far. Undergraduate science and biology major. Medical school. Heart specialty. Interned and joined a prestigious practice. Practiced at City and at Specialty in cardiovascular and thoracic surgery. Rose to associate chief of staff. If he had any enemies, they're not talking to our guys."

I pushed my sandwich toward Lake, but snagged one of the fries. "Maybe they don't like speaking ill of the dead?" I said.

"Or getting tarred with their own words. Those in the know acknowledged he had a mistress. I guess that's what you call them these days. Name's Heidi Levine. She's an obstetrics nurse. Supposedly a knockout and totally dedicated to her work and to him."

"He didn't strike me as a man with a singular appetite."

"Heidi seems to have been the *it* girl of late—and forever, now he's gone."

Lake's cell rang, the one used for police business. That's never good when he's off duty, but a lieutenant in charge of a squad of men is always on call.

"Damn it," he said, ending the cell call. "Haskell wants me back. Another home invasion. This time in Inman Park."

"That's new territory."

"Might be copycats or a change of venue."

"Husam suggested the Cresleys might have been the victims of a home invasion."

"Didn't I already tell you he's full of bull?"

The waiter brought another glass of wine, which I hadn't ordered. Lake finished his food, rose and kissed the top of my head. "Oh, I meant to tell you sooner; the license tag on E. B. White's step van had been stolen from the car of a man living in Cobb County, Georgia."

"Cabs?"

"No results so far. It's possible she walked to a bus stop. MARTA goes everywhere."

MARTA: Metropolitan Atlanta Rapid Transit Authority—trains and buses.

CHAPTER TWELVE

I sat in a wheeled office chair next to Web. "You've been hacked."

"They're still trying."

"They know your operating system is Linux."

"Oh, sure. That's easy enough. They're using nMap to . . ."

"Excuse me. nMap?"

"Network mapper." Web stretched his skinny frame out like he does when he settles back to expound. "It scans networks for security and to map an operating system, its apps and firewalls. But they don't know everything about my operating system. Haven't I told you the internet was created by hackers?"

"Yep."

He pushed his hands deep into the pockets of his khakis.. "And yours truly contributes. Each and every kernel is different depending on the programmer."

"So, you're saying you develop your own kernel."

"And Husam's IT people will never figure it out."

"So, how come your MySQL port was open?"

Web sat up and rattled some keys on the keyboard. "I unblocked port thirty-three-o-six to access MySQL from another computer, but they won't hack me. They can't."

"But you can them."

Web explained about ports and encryptions, and totally lost me. "Go easy on the techie language," I reminded him.

"I'm considering the brute-force technique to get access," he said. "Remember our old friend John the Ripper we've used in a couple of cases?"

"Yep."

"I've customized that cracker so it can run against crypts and hashes on their servers using an algorithm based on the Enigma machine. You remember my tutorial on the Enigma machine of World War Two."

"I do. You needn't re-explain."

"Certain mathematical encryptions cannot be defeated by brute force. A one-forty character string subjected to a brute-force attack would eventually reveal every string possible, including the correct answer. But of all the answers given, there would be no way of knowing which was the correct one. Defeating it relies on mistakes like the keypads not being truly random or operators making mistakes."

I got tired of listening. "Thanks, Web. That will hold me until the next chapter."

"Final exam in a week."

Back in my own office, I finished the paperwork that goes with every case, including my expenses, which I would email to the prince.

Web stuck his head through the door frame to my office. "Hey, Paul's got an interesting take."

"Interpol?"

"That Paul."

Web turned a straight chair around and sat with his arms folded on the back. "Half the royalty of Saudi lives in other parts of the world."

"So I've heard."

"But there's been a gathering of the highnesses recently."

"Which means?"

"The king is giving out deathbed wishes, or so Paul says."

"Has Paul any idea how that relates to our missing mom and daughter?"

"Let's Skype him."

"Sure."

Web set the program and once Paul's blurry visage came onto the screen, I greeted him. "*Bonjour, Monsieur* Paul."

"*Mademoiselle,*" he said. "Good to discuss with you."

"Tell me what's going on in Saudi Arabia now."

"I think the old King wants to avoid a coup. Not an army thing, but a cousin war. He is calling for important princes in foreign lands to return to the kingdom."

"If Prince Husam doesn't want to, then . . ."

Paul said, "Word is he wants to, but he's having problems. Husam is the smartest of the royals, by far. And much more stable. Most are playboys. Husam is educated, urbane, gets along with the West in his dealings, and, to put a topper on it, the West is poised to further its independence of Saudi oil. Seems we got more than they do, taking in Canada."

"Hmmm," I mumbled. "Money. Greed. It all makes sense. I'm thinking Husam has his fingers in way more pies than just a law firm in New York—being the legal clout overseeing the structural engineering of roads and bridges."

"Interpol is looking into big American firms with international dealings. So easy to traffic in money—large money. The United States sells billions in military equipment to the Saudis—fighter jets, helicopters, radar systems, anti-aircraft and ship missles, guided bombs. Plus, American military personnel train their forces on how to use them. Naturally, the old king wants to continue the sweet deal, especially since Americans kowtow to their cultural demands."

"I know," I said. "That makes the news. Americans might not know how much commerce we have with them, but they gripe when the Saudis make American women wear scarves and veils and tell the clergy to remove their crosses."

Paul said, "If the conservative Sunni cousins get control of the throne and the government, and if they fall in line with jihadists, hell would break loose. The country is ripe for holy war with the Shiites, because the majority of young people from both sects can't find jobs."

"If you can't work, you can still fight the holy fight."

"Don't forget that bin Laden was a rich man. He just didn't like the West."

"So, where does Prince Husam fit in? And the disappearances of his wife and daughter?"

"I'm not sure. Husam is *not* mentioned by name as an heir to the position of crown prince or even his deputy. Those names currently bandied about are likely to become the crown prince."

"What chance would Husam have with an American wife?"

"She doesn't count."

"What about an American-born daughter who is not studying Islam?"

"Even though she is a female, a princess means a lot in their society. She is a valuable bargaining device on the marriage market or any market with which they barter."

"Thanks, Paul."

"Let me add one more thing. There is a rumor that a book about the king and his family is soon to be published. It's a French publication. I do not know what is in it yet, but the author is known to dig in the dirt."

CHAPTER THIRTEEN

A moat and a stucco siege wall surrounded the development's perimeter where Yasmin Saliba lived. I spotted Spanish tile rooftops above the wall as I drove over the moat—called a canal in Florida. I felt if I got too close, I'd be speared by radicals in chain mail. Now this was a fortress that defied street punks with wire cutters.

The guard had been told to expect me, gave me a pass for my windshield and raised the gate. The house of my destination was also gated. Inside, a three-story palace of pale-yellow stucco with burnt-orange columns, capitals and window casements had been built. The tile roof was a deep shade of orange. Judging by the expanse of house and fountains, I'd say twenty thousand square feet. I had been instructed to press the white button on an ornamental arm sticking out of a stone pillar. I did, and the gates opened. Driving up the pavers, beneath old, Spanish moss–draped oaks, I looked over the exotic trees where peacocks roamed.

A butler who could have been a bodyguard opened the door. I stepped into a foyer with oak floors and millwork detailed on the doors and moldings. The butler led me into a vast, square living room with expansive windows and a sliding glass door in the center of the back wall. The doors opened onto a lanai with a deep-blue swimming pool. I walked over the ashlar-patterned travertine to the sliding doors. The butler slid the golden metal of the door back and held out a hand, meaning *you're on your own from here.*

The princess Yasmin lounged on a chaise, holding a cell to her ear, and purposely ignored me. Springtime in Sarasota was much warmer than in Atlanta. My long-sleeved tunic felt warm and sticky—and her ignoring me made my skin burn beneath the collar.

She purred in Arabic—I guess that was the language—laughed a lot, which sounded phony, then ended the call.

She rose lanquidly. I was surprised at her height, around five feet, nine inches. Her build was what I would call muscular rather than fat. Given her brother's elegant slimness, her bigness was surprising. She didn't resemble him much in the face, either, but then I'd read that Saudi royalty made frequent visits to Western plastic surgeons. She wore eye makeup and plenty of it. Her too-tight white, leather pants were covered at the waist by a blue, see-through silk blouse over a white, pointed, sparkling, leather bra. Her eyes roamed me, head to foot.

After a moment of study, she said, "I have an appointment in ten minutes, but I have agreed to see you on Shara's behalf." She possessed by nature a calculating look, bold and maybe scary for some. "My brother hired you and paid you ten thousand dollars for a week of work. If you do not find Shara will you give the money back?" I'd heard that Saudis were thrifty and she was proving it. "How well are you doing?"

"Progressing. Thank you for seeing me."

"That does not tell me much." Her arms folded across her chest. "How many children have you found, child finder?"

That was rude. "Many." I let my eyes wander the pool and grounds. "You have a lovely home and garden."

She advanced, more sideways than directly, across the blue tiles. "You do not say much for yourself, do you?"

Looking past her, I saw the green of the fairway just over the bougainvillea—which I supposed hid a wrought-iron fence. "I would love to have a golf course view from my back yard," I said.

"How many cases have you had?"

I gave her my best studied stare. "A *lot.*"

"What is your success rate?"

"A hundred percent." I contemplated the pool. "Marvelous how the water in the pool matches the cerulean sky."

"Were they all found alive?"

"No, but I found them."

"That is not good news. We must find Shara alive."

"Yes. And what about Reeve?"

She waved a hand. "She is the one who took Shara."

"Are you suggesting she might kill her daughter?"

She snorted, a sound I seldom hear from a woman. "It is possible."

"Why do you say that?"

"She does not want Husam to have her."

"It could be she doesn't want him to take her to Saudi Arabia."

"Shara is his daughter. He has the right." Legally she was correct. Reeve had not been granted sole legal custody of her daughter by a court of law. There was no divorce or initial rulings in the event of divorce.

"There was an incident in New York," I said, "where a car seemed to threaten Reeve and Shara. Who would want to harm your sister-in-law and niece?"

"How would I know who would do that?" she said, waving a hand. "I fear for Shara's safety, period. She is a child; she is vulnerable."

"What was your relationship with Reeve?"

"Relationship?" She asked the question in a way that made me think she wanted to think before she answered. She shook her head. "No relationship."

"Did you like her?"

"As much as any American rich girl."

"Aren't you a rich girl?"

She tossed her head and turned away, as if admiring the green fairway. "I am not required to work and earn money. I have accounts, sure."

"Reeve is a child of wealthy parents, like you."

Facing me, she said with a sneer, "She works. She is not like me at all. I would not work. I would not like to have a father that put me to work, or a mother that worked."

"Your culture is different than ours."

"That is true, but I make my own rules. I live here because I have freedom to wear what I wish and shop where I want. Now, how are you finding Shara?"

"I will try to find out why Reeve would fear for her and her daughter's safety, if she does. I want to know if they would travel under different names. I will look into the marriage of Reeve and Husam. I'll be looking for a money trail, and talking to people like you who may have a clue where Reeve might take her. Those are the starting points."

"Did you think Reeve would come here, and bring her daughter, to live with me?"

I knew that wasn't going to happen. "I considered it possible until I perceived how much you disliked Reeve."

"I did not dislike her. She was jealous of me—my home, my life, my privilege."

"It is possible that you are jealous of her. Her academics, her work as a scientist, your brother's love for her. I have to consider these things."

She waved that away with a grimace that furrowed her brow. "I am educated."

She walked toward the sliding glass door, into the interior room, me following. There was a mirror on a wall that she went to and spoke to. "Husam bin Sayed al-Saliba must marry and have a real wife, a Saudi princess for a wife, before it is too late and he is too old, and Shara must become a Muslim and go to school." She adjusted a curl on her forehead. "That is our way. Her mother knew that when she married my brother. She wanted to change him, but he will not, he cannot." Her mirrored eyes bore into mine. "So, you must find Shara and get her to where she belongs."

She turned abruptly and made for the foyer. I had no choice but to follow her. I stepped once again onto the oak boards. "Who are your neighbors?" I asked.

"What? That is none of your business. It is none of my business, and I do not make it my business."

The heat in her voice told me something. I had to figure out what.

She called for the butler and spoke in Arabic. He disappeared, then reappeared holding binoculars. "Now," she said, "I want to show you my pets."

Pets?

The butler held the door open and we walked outside. She pointed toward a tree. "In the banyan tree, see the birds?"

My lips involuntarily parted. Two birds of paradise perched on the twisty banyan trees.

"They have come to me from the rain forests."

I knew that they didn't fly to the southeastern United States. Bird poachers brought them here illegally. One had a black head, blue wings and a long, orange tail feather. The other was brilliantly yellow with blue head plumes.

The princess held out the binoculars for me to take, then gestured to the exotic birds.

"That is Boris, such a showoff, and Mica, a lazy girl with soft eyes."

Birds of paradise are related to crows and jays, and the many species can be as small as a sparrow or as large as a raven. Boris, the male, had a heavy bill and a stout body. Mica was the smaller, brilliant-yellow bird. I felt sorry for the captives.

I handed her the binoculars and stepped away. "Thanks for seeing me. It was informative."

"It was?" she said, swaying through the open door. *Take that, Moriah Dru.* Before he closed the door I noted the butler's face—tight with anxiety or fear or worry. Maybe all three.

The concrete road was laced with pavers on the running paths, the golf-cart path crossings and walk designations at intersections. I wound around the community, passing tee boxes and greens until I came upon a man walking leisurely in the road. Why was he not on the path that ran alongside the road? He carried a long golf club, probably a three iron. He was Caucasian with a deep tan. Handsome, maybe fifty. A Floridian for sure.

I stopped. He stopped. I rolled down my window and he came up. "Can I help you?"

There was something about him, and I made up the first thing that came to mind. "Yes, I'm looking for the home of Yasmin Saliba."

His face constricted nearly imperceptibly. "You've passed it at the cul-de-sac."

"That huge . . ."

"Monstrosity?" he finished.

"I wasn't sure from the directions given me. But thanks."

He stared as though he saw through my guile. He said, "You are not from here."

"No," I answered. "Are you neighborhood watch?"

"No. We don't employ that system. We have security, of course. Very good security, considering our residents."

"Are you security?"

"I don't serve in that capacity, but I am considered a nosy neighbor by most here."

"And you are wondering why I'm here?"

Nodding, he kind of smiled. "We are the subject of reporters and investigators from on-high because of some of our residents."

This was no ordinary busybody. "I'm aware of who those residents are."

"Are you one of the reporters?"

"I'm not a reporter and I'm not here to investigate terrorists who are said to have lived here. I'll leave that to the on-highs. I'm trying to find a little Saudi-American girl."

His eyes slid away. *He knows her.* "My name's Lloyd. Let's sit over there. You can park at the rail."

He motioned toward a gazebo that overlooked a sparkling lake. I did as directed and pulled into a small slot obviously for a golf cart. My tires crunched over perfectly coiffed St. Augustine grass.

Benches lined the small, octagonal building. I sat next to Lloyd. "I'm Moriah Dru. I own Child Trace in Atlanta, Georgia. I'm a private cop."

"I don't know about a Saudi-American girl who needs to be found," he said. "The Saudis pretty much keep to themselves when it comes to the authorities. And they keep their children close by."

"She is Yasmin al-Saliba's niece."

"The prince's daughter?"

"Yes."

"And she is missing?"

"That's not for publication. The prince has asked that I conduct a quiet investigation to find the girl and her mother."

His gaze at me came from cautious eyes. "These people, from that part of the world, come and go. One never knows. We are besieged by investigators looking for connections between the Nine-Eleven hijackers and folks here. I'm relatively new to the community but there are those who say there is one man here who is connected to a family that decamped in the middle of the night. That was just before the planes went into the towers leaving behind a mess."

I thought, yes, the towers were a mess—to understate that tragedy badly—but I think he'd misplaced his modifiers. He meant the decamping Saudis left a mess.

"What about now?" I asked. "Any reason to believe there's a larger network living here?"

Shrugging, he said, "Who can tell?"

"How many Saudi homes are in here?"

"Seven families, all clustered close to one another on the other side of the golf course. They're an enclave. The princess lives this side because she thinks she's special."

"She is, from what I learned of Saudi royalty."

He shrugged and grinned from the side of his mouth. There was something that disturbed me in his hazel eyes, made amber in his tan skin.

"Does Prince Husam bin Sayed al-Saliba have a home here?"

"It's for sale or is said to be. You will not see for-sale yard signs. A lot of these places are owned by corporations with a lot of people and money to hide."

"Have you met Prince Husam bin Sayed al-Saliba?"

"Once, right here in fact." His hand swept the pond. "The little girl fed the swans. That was some months ago. He is quite cordial and his little girl is beautiful. So is his wife." An almost yearning expression appeared and just as suddenly disappeared.

"When did you last see him?"

"Let me think. Two weeks ago. I saw him leave his sister's home, and we exchanged waves. The wife and little girl were not in the car, that I could see."

"Tell me about Yasmin al-Saliba?"

"I will be truthful. I know that you visited her not fifteen minutes ago."

"Busted," I said.

"And that she drove out of the palace—that's what we all call that monstrosity—a minute, if that, later."

"And you arranged to run into me. Why?"

"Something's going on. People come and go there . . ." he grinned, ". . . but not people who look like you."

"What do I look like?"

"What you said you are, an investigator. Which has got me wondering why an investigator would seek out Saliba. She is a witch, an unreliable witch."

"She knows her mind, and speaks it."

"People come and go at all hours, but not Saudis. Druggies, I think. Peddling drugs is one way we could get rid of her. Having her arrested and the FBI confiscating her house. It's been done in other communities in Sarasota and the county. They would send her packing home."

"Drug problems in a wealthy community? Who would have thought it?" I said, not too sarcastically.

"Rich men salve their greed," he said. "Cocaine keeps ladies slim."

Yasmin didn't appear to be partaking of her slenderizing product.

I tuned into what he was saying. "There's a daily parade to her place, same people, don't stay long."

"And you decided I wasn't a likely candidate."

"I used to be an analyst in security systems. I can still spot drug users, just as I can still spot investigators. Where did you train?"

"With the Atlanta Police Department and the National FBI Academy."

"Shows."

"And you?"

"At a top-secret government agency."

"I'll have to settle for that. While you're at it, why don't you go after the importers of Yasmin's birds of paradise?"

He laughed. "To say nothing of the exotic monkeys and snakes. You can sit in your yard at times and see escaped monkeys playing in the trees. He pointed at the pond. "There are exotic snakes in that pond. Along the banks you'll see signs, 'Swim at your peril.' "

"What's your last name?"

He smiled and stood, apparently taking my question to mean the end of the conversation. "Weatherby. You'll find me in the archives easily enough."

I stood, too, and we walked to my car. "I like to say, everyone I meet in an investigation, no matter how peripheral, gets scrutinized."

"You'll wonder how come a security analyst lives in a million-dollar community."

He opened my car door. "Crossed my mind."

"My late wife, as you'll find out, was from Saudi Arabia. Magda was filthy rich from an oil family. We met at university." I got in the car and he closed the door. "And, yes, I live in the Saudi enclave. Good day."

"Yasmin put him on to me," I said to Lake via my cell.

"Why?" he asked. I could tell by his mouth sounds that he was chewing something.

"I'm going to find out. It's odd him bashing a royal princess while living amongst the tribe. I'll be here until this evening. Web is vetting Lloyd Weatherby."

"We'll look at him, too. Watch out for terrorists."

"Go straight to hell."

Lloyd Weatherby, Web discovered, was a physical security specialist with NASA before retiring two years ago. NASA policy, Web said, forbids hiring foreign nationals, but he'd found nothing about an employee married to a foreign national. "Heck," Web said, "a couple of congressmen in Washington are challenging NASA because of its hiring of contractors who can be and are foreign nationals. Weatherby is one hundred percent American, born in Colorado. Got a degree in criminal behavioral studies, then went to work for the space agency. Been there all his life. Married Magda Habibi al-Humuud after college. She died almost three years ago, ovarian cancer. One son: Ben Habibi Weatherby. Lloyd Weatherby's last work station was at the Space Research Institute in Boulder."

"All roads lead to Boulder, Colorado," I said. "Wait a sec. My mind is connecting names here. Husam's goon-Friday is named Salman Habibi and we have a Habibi in Weatherby wife's and son's name."

"Here's how it works," Web said. "The first name of a Saudi man or woman is his or her given name, thus Salman and Magda. The second name is the father's name, example Habibi. The third name is the tribal name. Lot of times it's not used. Of course, royals do. Like Husam bin Sayed al-Saliba. Could be that Magda and Salman are brother and sister, or cousins."

"Very interesting, with a Boulder connection to Reeve's last duty station."

"More interesting, maybe, is that the Humuud tribe used to be rulers before the present line. A century ago there were several Arabian rulers. There was a fight over territory. It ended with victory going to the predecessors of the al-Salibas."

I was reminded of Husam's fears of a coup between certain Saliba factions over cultural, social and economic changes in that vast country.

I told Web, "Find out what I need to do to get into the Space Research Institute."

"Do I explain that you're investigating the murder of Reeve Cresley's parents, or her and Shara's disappearance?"

"Whatever it takes to get me in. And get me Weatherby's phone number."

"Will do."

CHAPTER FOURTEEN

I tried to get back into Yasmin's compound, but the guard wouldn't let me in without Yasmin's okay, and she wasn't at home. Lloyd was the one I wanted to talk to, but he wasn't at home either, according to his houseman. I ate a burger that didn't taste good because of my mood, then perused the local newspapers in the library. In the last ten years, the Saudis in the community had behaved themselves. But a Florida congressman was demanding the FBI hand over records of their investigation into a family in the community that disappeared suddenly. The family was closely related to a financier and there were suspicions that they financed some of the 9/11 attackers. The FBI gave the newspaper a heavily redacted copy of their report that seemed to clear the fleeing family. The newspaper filed an open-records request for an un-redacted report. It would be in the courts for a while.

I called Lloyd's number again. No answer. My cell number was blocked to him, but if he was at home, he was guessing I would call again and didn't answer.

So I flew home to an empty house. Lake said he was ass-deep in murder and mayhem and because of the home invasions, home-security system sales were skyrocketing. Another prostitute had been murdered. He'd interviewed the Cresleys' maid. She barely spoke English and knew absolutely nothing useful. His detectives had gone back to the hospital, only to find that Dr. Lowell Cresley had become a saint. I wrote my report, and at three thirty, dog-tired, unshaven Lake crossed the threshold. He was asleep before his head hit the pillow. At seven when I left, he was still out to the world.

Office-bound, I sat at my desk, tapping a lead pencil. I'd been stuck in idle and realized why. I didn't know Reeve Cresley. I talked to people who knew her. There was the fellow graduate student that Web had interrupted from her spa workout. She told me that Reeve Cresley was a smart-aleck go-getter, but could be nice when she wanted to be. That didn't make me know Reeve any better. I considered that in most of my cases, I'd gotten to know the character of the dead person better than the character of the still-living Reeve Cresley. What hadn't I done?

Reeve was not dead. My bones told me that; plus, finding her hideout, which produced one of her fingerprints. Still, I had an ugly feeling she was likely to be dead before long. Not that I thought Prince Husam would personally kill her, but you never knew with money, love and the promise of power.

Social psychologists write that married people, and perhaps long-time companions, grow restive after seven years. It is also alleged that if a couple can stay together for another thirteen— what a lucky number that is, although some cultures consider seven unlucky—they will probably find a way to stay to the end of one life or the other.

It would take more than luck for a brilliant, educated woman to marry a man—handsome and charismatic as the prince was— only to endure the cultural clashes that became a part of her life. I pushed back my chair, determined to ferret out the answer to my bewilderment.

Fifteen minutes later, I felt hopeful.

Doris Thebold, Mission Director of Astrophysics at the Space Research Institute, would see me in two days—enough time for me to be vetted by security specialists at the Boulder facility.

Thrilled, I further wondered if Lloyd Weatherby's co-workers were still there, and if they could—or would—talk.

I emailed the purpose of my visit, who I was visiting, my citizenship status, contact's name, contact's badge and phone numbers, the date, time and room number where the meeting would take place. Otherwise, all I needed with a valid ID.

I'd heard from Husam twice, once sounding upset with my lack of progress and another time his voice was smug as if he'd said: *I didn't think you'd find them.*

I didn't ask about a possible relationship between his man Salman and Weatherby's wife, Magda. Web was working on that with his Interpol buddy, Paul Ardai.

While eating lunch alone—when Lake can't break for a meal, he's engaged in an epic case or cases—I decided on a course of action that would take one of my employees out of her normal duties and allow her to employ talents I'd seen but never utilized.

I got back to the office to find that Paul of Interpol wanted a Skype conference.

Once we got hooked up, Paul said that he had no information on a connection between Salman Habibi and Magda Habibi, and that the Habibi name in Saudi Arabia was like Smith in the US.

But that was not what Paul was anxious to show me via Skype. He'd come across a recent photo in *Paris Personalities* that showed Prince Husam with a stunning, black-haired woman. Paul said it had been taken three months ago in Paris at the Ritz-Carlton. The woman's identity was unknown.

Paul displayed the photo. It was grainy, of course, but I recognized Husam. The woman was certainly beautiful. I remembered Donna Cresley saying, *Now he'll marry his Muslim princess and try to make up to the king, who I understand is quite ill and not of sound mind.*

The woman in the photograph wore a little hat, a fascinator. It rode forward on her head and covered her face more than her hair. The prince's and the beauty's images were caught on the outdoor camera of the Paris Ritz-Carlton.

Paul said, "Salman Habibi, Prince Husam's companion, drove the expensive Mercedes after escorting the couple to the car."

"What did the magazine piece say about the couple?"

"There was no article," Paul said. "Just a tag line that asked who was the mystery woman in Prince Husam's life, and something about him being the most eligible royal in the world."

"Thanks, Paul," I said. "Appreciate your work. Email an invoice. The prince is paying expenses."

Paul said, "I appreciate that. I have people to pay, too. There have been no passport entries on the people you're looking at in the past year. Except one, that of Lowell Reeve Cresley to Bermuda eight months ago." *Without Donna, but not alone.* "We have found no information on secondary or multiple passports. We need more information. Exact names, identification numbers, birth dates, ethnic origin, language and so on. Husam's passport was issued in Saudi Arabia. Donna Reeve Cresley's is from the United States. Yasmin's is from Saudi Arabia. The murdered Cresleys had US passports."

"Keep up the good work, Paul, and *au revoir.*"

Once we'd disconnected, I said to Webdog, "So it would seem that Donna Cresley was correct about another woman."

"Why not just divorce Reeve?" Web asked. "All Husam has to say is 'I divorce thee' and presto it's a *fait accompli.*"

"Shara. The child."

"He can have four wives and dozens of the little buggers."

So says a man who has never even had a serious girlfriend that I know of, much less a child of his own. I'm childless, too, but Lake's daughter Susanna fills me with joy when she's with us. I wouldn't be so cavalier about anyone's child.

I said, "There's more to it. Why are the Cresleys dead? Why the initial hush-hush with finding Reeve and Shara? Of course, secrecy is no longer possible with the murders of his in-laws. And why did he act smug when I told him I had no new information?"

"Dry run," Web said.

"What's the real goal then?"

"If you can't find her, no one can."

"Which would mean Reeve's dead."

"You have to consider that, Dru."

I heaved myself out of my chair. "It's not in my bones yet."

At that moment, Pearly Sue Ellis stuck her head in Web's office. "You called, ma'am?"

Ma'am. Did I look as old as I felt? "Got a trip for you, Miss Ellis," I said.

"Great. I was getting cabin fever."

"Let's go to your office," I said.

Leaving his office, I waved at Webdog. "Good job."

"Any time," he said.

Walking down the corridor, I considered I could change my mind about deploying Pearly Sue, but I was convinced now more than ever that she was right for the job.

Pearly Sue, that irrepressible southern belle, loved to go on trips. At twenty-six and happily married with a degree in social work, she was still pretty enough to wear the crown of Miss Sorghum Pie and Miss Tractor Pull. High energy belies the slur of south Georgia in her voice. A couple of years ago, as an intern, she worked a kidnap case. The father fled, taking his kids to Saudi Arabia. She now takes personal interest in this Saudi case because of the one that got away.

She sat at her desk and folded her hands. They wouldn't stay folded for long. "That prince is after the baby." Her hands came apart. "Their stupid country won't . . ."

I sat in a comfortable armchair across from her. "That may be true or not, but let's not jump ahead of ourselves."

My eye caught a photo sitting on a bookshelf behind her. It was of Pearly Sue in snake boots, an outfit that consisted of dusty-looking pants and checkered shirt. Her tousled, blond hair hung in her eyes, and she smiled like she'd just consumed a juicy Georgia peach. She was holding out a seven-foot rattlesnake on the end of a crooked staff they poke into the ground to rile the creatures. Rattlesnake roundups are a part of my region's history that I'd like to forget, but I'm happy to report things have changed. All but a few towns have changed their image and call the poking of diamondback rattlesnakes rattlesnake festivals. They no longer pour gas into the gopher holes where the poisonous snakes gather with nonpoisonous snakes and other creatures, like the gophers themselves. As a federally protected endangered species they are no longer killed for their skin and rattles. They do serve a purpose, though. They are milked for antivenin, then released back into the wild.

Another photo on the credenza showed Pearly Sue helping in the milking of the snake, her fingers perilously close to the snake's fangs. Tip: Don't get bit by a rattler. The antivenin alone costs upwards of $60,000 per dose.

In another photo, Pearly Sue is carrying a cracked shotgun over her shoulder.

She's one of those who, once you've met them, you'll never forget them.

I told her, "I want you to go to New York."

"Wow!"

"And follow Prince Husam bin Sayed al-Saliba wherever he goes, record whoever he's with. Take my camcorder. The trimmings and extra sixteen-gig memory cards are all in the backpack." I nodded to a chair where the equipment sat. "It's got two slots for the video and audio. Remember how to use it?"

"Shore do."

"If you get spotted . . ."

"That's not going to happen," she said, waving a hand. "I got my ways."

Indeed she does, and they're natural. When people lie to her, Pearly Sue can look as mean as the snake in the photo. When she's pensive, her little nose twitches and her brow furrows. She can rub her hands together and make people nervous. On the other hand, she can be sunny and skip like a little girl. When she dresses for an evening out, she looks like a runway model; when she's in black jeans and heavy eyeliner, she's a Goth raider.

She rattled at me, "Do I fly? Can I take my gun? I got my license to carry. Where will I stay? Where does the scumbag prince live?"

"Hold it. You will fly. However, you cannot—listen up—*cannot* take a gun to New York."

"In my checked luggage . . ."

"You cannot carry it. Worst state in the world . . ."

"My instructor said the best was Alaska."

"If the prince goes to Alaska, you can buy a gun, strap it on and go wherever you want. Always remember that in any state, as a PI, you've got to check in with local law enforcement. *But you do not want to deal with the NYPD.*"

I rang for Web to come in and give Pearly Sue the rundown on where to find the prince in New York: his law firm address, his favorite hangouts and so on.

Pearly Sue was still fixated on a weapon and the New York PD. "I sure hope I don't have to deal with New York cops, but just the same I'll take my nunchucks, if that's okay with you."

"I didn't hear that."

Web said, "Prince Husam's apartment is across from Central

Park so you'll not be noticed when you walk Chop-Chop, my friend's Pekinese. My friend's name is Edward Stephens. He's in China until sometime in the summer. You'll be staying at his apartment on West Fifty-Ninth Street. He has a dog sitter who lives across town, but you'll be walking the dog at relevant times. When your assignment is over, call the sitter. His number is with the packet of information I've got together for you. If you need anything at all, ring me. You don't have to disguise yourself because people looking like you walk their dogs at all hours. However, at other places, you might want to change your, uh, costumes."

Pearly Sue was agog, that's all I can say.

Web went on, "The dossier Dirk's compiled on Prince Husam is not complete, but it's a start. It would appear he is a creature of habit. He leaves his apartment at eight thirty a.m. on the stroke of it. It's a short limo ride to the office unless traffic snarls."

Web handed Pearly Sue a batch of photos. "The top two are of Husam coming out of his apartment and his limo and driver, Salman Habibi. As you can see the apartment building is on the corner of the intersecting street and the limo is an Acura SUV. The third photo is of his office on Lexington. In the afternoon he walks around Central Park, near Turtle Pond and the ball fields, where he sometimes joins a pickup game. The fourth photo is of Husam walking by Turtle Pond. He has a personal trainer named Jason Qasim, who is Egyptian. The fifth photo is of Jason going into Husam's apartment building and the sixth is of Jason and Husam entering an Islamic men's club. Husam's companions are exclusively men as far as Dirk's has learned—names not known. The seventh photo is of Husam having lunch with his law partner, Jaul Zogby. Husam is known by colleagues and friends to be married to an American career woman, but he is not known to be in an extramarital relationship, either male or female. Husam is a theater freak and patron of various upper-crust eating establishments. He also visits discreet after-hours clubs."

Pearly Sue's eyes shone as brightly as her name—*the shows, the clubs.*

I said, "Keep your receipts. Do not go through Central Park at night by yourself. Never, ever. You are not too stupid to live— remember that. During the day, hang with people around you; there will be mothers with children, athletes, runners, bicyclists, etcetera. If Husam gets ahead of you, let it be. You can pick him up later on."

Pearly Sue rubbed her hands. "When do I leave?"

Web handed her the printout of her boarding pass. "The six-forty-five this evening. The doorman at my friend's apartment is expecting you. Take a cab from the airport. Don't forget to tip everyone generously."

I slid an envelope across the desk to her. It contained ten grand in small bills. I smiled a little at the irony of Husam's picking up the tab to have himself followed.

Pearly Sue got up—excited to leave, to pack.

Web said, "Bon voyage, Pearly Sue." He held a hand to his forehead as a salute. She headed for the door. "Oh by the way . . ." he said to the closed door, ". . . nunchucks, too, are illegal in New York."

"You got anything really pressing for this afternoon?" Lake said, settling himself in the chair across from my desk. He'd grabbed a sub sandwich at a food truck down the street from my office and was spreading the wrapper out on my desk.

"Packing for Boulder."

"Ski season's over or I'd go with you."

"Crime dry up in Atlanta?"

He ripped open a bag of chips, but looked up and twisted his lip, meaning "hell, no."

"What's up?"

"I have an interview with a woman whose husband was a patient of Dr. Cresley's. I need a second set of ears." He bit into the multi-meats, cheeses and condiments piled on the soft bun.

"Take Commander Haskell."

Lake never chews and talks at the same time. He swallowed, and said, "Haskell wants to keep his distance from my cases, and that's okay with me. He tends to micromanage."

Lake does not like to be managed, micro or otherwise.

He said, "Except by you."

"Mind reader." I let him take a few more bites, chew and swallow, then said, "You said the husband *was* a patient of Cresley's."

Picking chips from the bag, he said, "The man died."

"Leaving Dr. Lowell Cresley with a problem."

"Big one."

Jordana Lemmon lived in an older, wealthy neighborhood in south Atlanta. I got out of my car and joined Lake at the curb.

She waited for us on the verandah of her old, but magnificent, Victorian house. I love garish gables, cornices, pediments and turrets. This one was three stories tall, rather skinny like Victorians built in London, with the clapboard painted robin's-egg blue.

Walking up a path surrounded by budding azaleas, Lake muttered, "Could use a paint job."

Lake likes white houses with green or black shutters.

I shook hands with Mrs. Lemmon. So did Lake. Trays of tea and coffee and cookies and cake slices sat on a table that was surrounded by deeply padded wicker rocking chairs. Despite her grief, she wanted us to be comfortable and I instantly liked her for it.

Her mannerisms were deliberate; perhaps she wanted to avoid talking about unpleasant things on this lovely afternoon, the sun just slipping behind budding oaks and cherry trees that sheltered the streets of the fragrant neighborhood.

Lake's cup rattled in its saucer, letting me know how impatient he was; but a nod from me told him that I appreciated his restraint.

Mrs. Lemmon rocked back and began, "Garland was forty-eight when he passed sixteen months ago. He existed in a vegetative state for three weeks when the doctors removed his tubes. It was in his will and papers that no extraordinary means be made to keep him alive. I wanted them to give him more time, but . . ."

Lake rocked forward. "But what, Mrs. Lemmon?"

"Dr. Cresley was in a hurry to cover up his mistake."

"Start from the beginning, and take your time."

She took a deep breath before plunging. "Do you know what the mitral valve is?"

"A heart value, yes," Lake said.

"My husband went to see Dr. Cresley because he had breathing problems. The doctor told him that he had a valve problem. It was too flabby and blood that came into his heart was flowing backwards." Her finger crossed her chest. "Dr. Cresley told us that he would make three holes in his chest, then use a robot and a computer to operate. He assured us robotic surgery was safe and that if the valve was too damaged, he would replace it. Dr. Cresley told us Garland would have less blood loss, less pain. And, he said, infection would be minimal."

So what went wrong? This was like a story that builds to a nasty climax. And we already knew the end.

She took another deep breath. "Something went wrong and they had to replace the valve. He went into cardiac shock on the operating table. That's when Dr. Cresley stopped talking to me and our son. A member of his team was left to give us the rest of the bad news."

She sipped tea, then cleared her throat. "After a while, Garland seemed to be recovering." She paused and shivered almost imperceptibly. An onlooker might have thought it was the cooling of a dying day rather than her husband. "My husband had all kinds of issues from fluid buildup. His urine was brown from kidney failure. He had another heart attack from clots and a stroke in his brain. That's the medical part," she said. "We, the family, sued."

Lake asked gently, "They replaced the floppy valve. Did the new one malfunction, too?"

"The papillary muscles and chorda tendinea ruptured." She let her lips turn into a small smile. "The chorda tendinea are called heart strings. They are tendons that pull the valve flaps closed so blood doesn't flood the whole heart." She demonstrated with her thumb and two fingers.

If that happened to someone I loved, I would know every medical term connected to the procedure. "What caused them to rupture?" I asked.

"That was what we fought about and why the hospital and doctors gave us a million and a half dollars to keep our mouths shut. Which, as you can see, I am not doing. Dr. Cresley's death has opened mine. His was the biggest contribution, given that he was operating the machine and made the decisions."

"What excuses did the attorneys for the doctor and hospital give?"

"The hospital said it was caused by natural heart disease. In other words, Garland was born that way. They said, also, that extraordinary measures were taken to save his life." Her expression said what she thought about that.

"And what was your position?"

"The valve, muscle and tendons were punctured by the

machine operated by Dr. Cresley." She let this statement ride on the floral-scented air for a moment. "Once my husband passed away, the hospital saw no need for the medical examiner to perform an autopsy. I wouldn't let them take him to the funeral parlor and I called in my own expert, someone you've seen on television—although he doesn't want to be named. His opinion was that the tendons and muscles were healthy; and said that he saw evidence that they tried to disguise puncture wounds when they opened his chest."

"And Dr. Cresley's attorney?"

"Dr. Cresley lied to save himself. He said it wasn't his fault; that the machine malfunctioned and that the staff weren't properly trained. Our attorney went after him and the hospital. A nurse came to our side and said there was chaos in the operating room after the punctures while they tried to cover it up."

I asked and got from her the name of the nurse and her phone number. She was now a nurse at a hospice facility.

I sat back and looked at Lake. Lord, some people have incredibly tragic stories.

"I settled for less than I could have gotten," she said. "I've never had need of money. My parents left me well off; my husband was an engineer. Millions mean nothing to me, nor to Garland, Junior, our son."

"Where is he?" Lake asked.

She looked him square in the eye. "When I called you, I told you, Detective Lake. He's gone to join the terrorists in Yemen. My husband was Muslim. He converted in college. My son, Junior, is also a Muslim. He vowed to kill the man who killed his dad, and I fear that he has."

Terrorists.

Save me.

CHAPTER FIFTEEN

Lake would use Jordana Lemmon's facts as she knew them in investigating the deaths of Dr. Cresley and his wife, starting with a visit to the Lemmons' lawyer, famous for specializing in medical malpractice. I would go to Boulder. The APD would use its resources to track down the whereabouts of Garland Lemmon, Junior. Webdog would query Paul Ardai. Paul had contacts among the Yemeni nationals living in France.

Several questions present themselves regarding Garland Junior's threat. Can a young man who trained for a year to be a guerilla fighter have the expertise to murder two people? We saw pictures of him. He is a wiry young man and not very tall. Then, why would the Cresleys allow him into their home? Surely, they would recognize him. And, were he able to get inside, did he have an accomplice, as we believe the killer did?

Yet, there was the possibility—I had to admit, despite my anti-terrorist hope, that it was possible—because the murder of Cresley was botched. A terrorist still in training, accompanied by his trainer, perhaps? An accomplice who helped the kid, when Cresley broke free from the garrote, by shooting Cresley and then Donna?

I had a lot of time to think on the airplane to Denver.

When I could turn on my electronics after takeoff, I got an email from Web. Doris Thebold was born in Somerville, Massachusetts, and graduated from the California Institute of Technology. She spent time at Harvard and the Smithsonian

Center for Astrophysics. She won many prizes, but not the Nobel. She had a yen for massive, compact halo objects.

That should help me in my interview with her. Otherwise, the only thing we had in common was that I hadn't won a Nobel prize either.

Another email from Web told me that Denver International Airport was the largest airport by acreage in the United States, and that one of its runways was the longest. Made sense. After some announced turbulence due to the mountains, when we finally touched down, I sincerely hoped we were on that runway and would not run out of it before the streaking plane stopped.

The terminal, named after Elrey Jeppesen, an early aviation-safety expert, was awesome. The interior made me feel like I walked beneath rows of sails and parachutes.

Once outside and riding a shuttle bus toward the car-rental agencies, I spotted the roof of the Jeppesen terminal. The shuttle driver said that the roof was modeled after the snow-capped Rocky Mountains and dedicated to Colorado's pioneers. He said a steel-cable system, often used in building bridges, supported the fabric roof. I would have asked about the fabric in a snowstorm, but we'd arrived at the agency.

I am much happier behind the wheel of an automobile, and once on Pena Boulevard, the main airport road, I took the Boulder exit to 470 North. Using the map given by the rental agency, I passed the University of Colorado Stadium exit while admiring the gorgeous foothills of the Rockies. At 5,400 feet above sea level, *it was foothills.* To the west the imposing mountains tower over beautiful Denver. The Rocky Mountains here, my info map told me, rose 14,400 feet above sea level.

Ten minutes later I arrived at my destination—the Space Research Institute. The streets ran between two-story functional buildings. I was nervous. These were scientists. Aerospace eggheads. Small talk to create a confiding atmosphere would be difficult. I locked my car and walked inside. As expected, two security guards greeted me. They were neither pleasant nor unpleasant. I handed over my identification; they made checkmarks on a form and picked up the telephone. The elevator came shortly and I held my breath. What was I doing here in this bastion of science, about to meet a woman who didn't speak my language, nor I, hers?

That woman stepped off the elevator. She was neither heavy nor short, but of big proportions. I liked her looks instantly, like a kindly, intelligent grandmother. Her hair was silver gray, and she wore a dark-blue suit and block-heeled shoes. An American flag rode on her lapel. She reached out a hand and I took it. "Doris Thebold," she said.

"Moriah Dru. Happy to meet you, Dr. Thebold."

She had stopped the elevator and waved a hand for me to enter. "It's Doris."

"Dru."

Riding up, I was too awed to begin; words stuck in my throat.

With a kind glance, she said, "You wished to talk about Reeve Cresley?"

What I like: direct. "Yes."

"The murder of her parents shocked us all."

"Had you met them?"

"Once, when Reeve first came here; they visited." That seemed to be all she was prepared to say.

We stepped off the elevator on the second floor, and she motioned for me to precede her.

Overwhelmed doesn't adequately describe my feeling when we entered the wide, dark hall. On one side, a panorama of panels displayed heavenly bodies. Planets and stars, streaking asteroids. "How wonderful," I said, giddy like a child.

On the other wall were photographs of the Hubble telescope's unimaginable voyage.

Doris pointed to the panels and said, "Each shows its relationship to the sun in size, shape and moons' configuration."

I looked up; overhead was the night sky. "Stars and constellations," Doris said. "The kids get a kick out of watching them move with the earth's rotation."

"I'm getting a kick out of them," I said. "There's the Big Dipper."

"Indeed," she said.

"When I was a kid, I was fascinated and read all I could about it." She stopped to listen to what I was saying. Having her undivided attention, I continued, "It's also known as the Starry Plough in Ireland and England. The Alaska state flag has the Big Dipper with the North Star."

"In the folk etymology of my ancestors," she said, "it was called Karlavagnen, supposedly after Charlemagne, but the Germanic name means Men's Wagon. The Little Dipper was the women's wagon." She smiled. "Nothing's changed in Western culture."

While I marveled at the night sky, she said, "The seven stars in the Big Dipper are part of the Ursa Major swarm. Two stars at the end of the Big Dipper, Dubhe and Alkaid, are moving in the opposite direction. That will change the Dipper's shape, with the bowl opening up and the handle becoming more bent. In fifty thousand years the Big Dipper will no longer exist."

We walked from beneath the stars into a room filled with computers. In the center of the room six student desks were arranged to face the monitors. Heavenly bodies winked throughout the room. I was drawn to one. "I love it—the colors."

She said, "The Universe, taken by the Hubble telescope. It is a dynamic place where stars and planets are constantly birthing and dying and being reformed from the debris of earlier generations."

"How long do stars last?"

"Depends on the mass. High-mass stars die quickly, in terms of millions of years. Low-mass stars are long-lived, for billions of years. When they die their elements are recycled to become other stars or planets, or maybe even life."

"Sounds like reincarnation."

"It is, so to speak. From the tiniest specks to the biggest stars, there is a life cycle and it is very much the same."

"Is there life in the universe?"

She moved to a monitor that held brilliant white splotches. "These are ancient, dwarf stars in our Milky Way. Our sun is middle-aged, and it would be best if we sought out stars that would support earthly life. We know that young suns spin faster and create strong magnetic fields that prohibit life as we know it. When our sun was young, its violence made it impossible for there to be life here, but with waning age and orbiting at a safe distance, the sun is an energy supply. But," she held up a hand, "it won't last forever. On a cosmological timescale Earth's habitability is nearly over. In half a billion years the sun will become too luminous and hot for water to exist in liquid form, giving us a severely intolerable greenhouse effect."

"I'm not worried," I said. "But I love what you know. I feel like a sponge ready to soak up your knowledge."

"Alas, we must get to the reason for your visit. I have a class in twenty minutes. Time flies when I'm talking with stars in my eyes."

"Do you know where Reeve Cresley is?"

"I do not," Doris said. "She left here when we became independent of NASA."

"I didn't know you did."

"NASA originally funded our work, but with cutbacks, we're mostly on our own. Oh, we get grants, some still from NASA, but scientists on NASA's payroll went elsewhere. I thought

Reeve returned to the Jet Propulsion Lab in California. I later learned that she did not."

"Have you heard from her?"

"No."

"Were you friends?"

"As colleagues, yes."

"No lunches together?" I asked with a smile.

"We all eat together sometimes. We're a close-knit group. We have our differences as scientific theorists will, but our relationships are cordial."

"Did you know Reeve's husband?"

"I did not. I met him briefly." She'd frowned involuntarily as she'd done when talking about Reeve's parents.

"Did you notice any change in her personality in the last few months?"

"Hmmm." She paused to consider, or maybe form the right words. "The last few months here were trying for her, it seemed to me."

"Her marriage?"

"One assumes. She was distracted. Her papers did not reflect the crisp style we were used to in her exposition."

"She'd lost interest?"

"One might think that, but no. Her interest was still high, but there was something else on her mind. As I say, a distraction."

"What did you think of her?"

"That might be an unfair question, depending on why you're asking."

"Fair enough. She and her daughter went missing before her parents were murdered."

"We've followed the news. There was speculation, of course."

"What kind?"

"Again, I must be circumspect and ask the reason for your question."

"I will tell you, and trust you'll keep my confidence as I will yours." She gave an *of course* nod. "I was hired by Prince Husam to find Reeve and Shara a short time before the Cresleys were murdered. Reeve apparently felt threatened in New York after an incident where someone may have tried to run her and her daughter off a road." I paused. She was listening intently. "Reeve and Shara disappeared the next day. Husam says he has no idea why she left other than the car incident, or where she could have gone. He didn't say so in so many words, but I believe he'd like to return to Saudi Arabia. I must tell you that the Cresleys did not trust him, and didn't want me to continue looking for Reeve and her daughter. Also, according to Reeve's mother, there was talk of divorce. Reeve wouldn't agree to Husam's terms, which involved their daughter, Shara."

She blinked several times. "Oh dear, that would explain Reeve's temperament change. She once said she would never live in Saudi Arabia, that she wouldn't be welcome if she wanted to."

There was much more I could have told her, but didn't.

She said, "Reeve is a strong woman. She wasn't one to run and hide. But if she felt she could lose her child, she would do what she had to."

"Who was Reeve close to here?"

"Well, her lab partner. He . . ." Her abrupt pause told me as much as her next words. "The *person* wants to remain anonymous."

She'd told me the *person*'s gender inadvertently and I had to take advantage of it, loathe that I must. "Did they have an affair?"

Bluntly, she said, "No."

I had to press. "Did she have affairs here? I know her husband was on the east coast while she was here."

She took a deep breath while she considered. "Would my

answer help you find her?"

"It could."

"Maybe her parents were right. If you found her for her husband, he may kidnap the little girl and flee to Saudi Arabia."

"I think the opposite. Finding her would spotlight what's going on. I believe she needs help in solving her situation. If Husam is serious about finding his daughter, and I know he is, he will find them."

"Do you think he killed the parents?"

"Not himself. He was out of town."

She put her thumb to her chin and pressed it. "Reeve and her lab partner went to undergraduate school together, so their long-time association was intimate. How intimate, I couldn't say."

"Is he still here?"

She hesitated. "He's on leave. Now that's all there is to be told about him." She rushed on as if to change the subject. "There was a physical security specialist with whom I thought she might have had an affair. I didn't witness anything, but the rumors flew. Colleagues reported seeing them at restaurants."

"What is his name?"

"He's no longer here, and I'm not naming names." The determined set of her mouth told me she wasn't to be indiscreet again. "I hope you understand."

Weatherby? "Was he married?"

"No, his wife had died. His wife was Saudi Arabian, so having Saudi spouses could be why they spent so much time together."

She had told me enough, purposely, that I could find out who he was. Little did she know, I'd already met the man.

"Look, Miss Dru, if you're going to be in town long, we can talk further, but I don't see how much more I can contribute to your knowledge or your search."

We left the classroom office, and headed down the hall of stars. I said, "We could discuss Sagittarius."

"Your sun sign?"

"No, that of the man I love."

"Nice cluster of stars." She pointed to a packed area of the sky, but I could not make out the starry archer.

She said, "The Milky Way is very dense near Sagittarius. It lies at the galaxy's galactic center. The New Horizon space craft is headed toward that cluster, but the batteries will long be dead before it gets there a thousand years from now."

And all this will be a brilliant blotch in the universe when our old sun dies.

CHAPTER SIXTEEN

Web had no problem isolating Reeve's lab partner from the lab's fifteen men, nor running down an address for him. Dr.— the PhD type of doctor—Thomas Page lived in Breckenridge, Colorado, more than an hour's drive up the mountain from Boulder.

I wound my way back to I-470 and then onto I-70 toward Grand Junction, heading for Breckenridge and a road called Silver Heel Pass. About a mile down the road I came to the home of Thomas Page. I could make out the red roof of the house through the aspens and ponderosas. A rustic sign hung from a long, wooden gate. I pulled into the drive and stopped at the gate of Page Ranch. A man on a patient horse stood just inside the gate. He nudged the horse with his heels and came up to me, him on one side of the fence, me on the other.

He looked down. "I see you decided to come here."

"Good morning, Dr. Page."

"Despite what I told you on the telephone, you came anyway."

His face was shaded by a brown Stetson. It was chilly up here this spring morning and he wore a vest over his work shirt. Wish I had a vest. "I wanted you to tell me face-to-face that you won't help me find Reeve Cresley and her daughter."

"Face-to-face, I'm telling you, when Reeve wants to be found, she will let you find her without any help from me, or anyone else."

"Are you protecting her?"

The horse had subtly turned, having intuited his master's ire, ready to bolt home when given the go-ahead.

Page glanced back. "She doesn't need my protection."

"But if she asked, you would, wouldn't you? I know you and she attended the university together."

"I don't appreciate your intrusion into my life."

"Intrusion happens when I try to find someone. If you know anything . . ."

"I have a public resume that isn't too hard to find, so intrude away."

"She left you for the prince, didn't she?" This was low, but I had to penetrate his protective shell.

He got off the horse and placed the reins over its shoulders. The animal lowered its head to munch on grass. The man looked like he could strangle me.

Up close, he didn't look like an astrophysicist. First off, the Stetson had a rattlesnake band with the rattle sticking from the fold. Tall, blue-eyed, slim, growing a beard, he looked like a rugged mountain man—a mean, rugged mountain man. I resisted the urge to step back. Web had told me that he was a native Coloradan, a champion fly fisherman, an avid bush-whacker and skier.

He continued to stare until I thought I would have to say something, anything, to get those blues off my face. "I'm sorry if I've . . ."

"No, you're not sorry. You threw that to make me mad, and you have succeeded. My relationship with Reeve while we were in college and afterward is none of your business. Since you have violated my privacy, I'll say this. If you threaten my life, my job or my reputation, I will sue you until I have spent every cent I have."

A flash came from across the road. We were standing in the shade with the sun rising in the east over the ponderosa pines and the glorious aspens. I reached out, across the fence rails, and knocked his shoulder sideways as the bullet snicked past where his head had been. We both hit the dirt. The horse whinnied, whirled and took off up the road. Another bullet struck the *P* in Page Ranch. I got behind the red trunk of a ponderosa.

"What the hell!" I heard Page yell.

I rolled under the rail fence, arriving next to him. We both crawled to the safety of old, fat tree trunks. Breathing heavily, neither of us said much for several seconds. He had lost his hat and his thick, brown hair fell over his forehead. I said, "Looks like I brought trouble to you. Sorry."

He looked ready to strike as if the snakeskin on his hat came to life. "Somebody trying to kill you?"

"Or you?"

"I didn't have any trouble until you showed up."

I got to my knees and, still protected by the tree, looked around it to where my rental car stood. "If I make it to the car and my cell phone without getting shot, I'll call the police."

"You'll do no such thing. You'll get in your car and take your butt out of here and never come back."

"Somebody tried to kill one of us, or both. The police . . ."

"No." Getting up, he picked up his hat and planted it on his head. He turned and jogged through the woods for a short stint, keeping trees between himself and gunfire, before running flat out up the road the horse had taken. I ran after him. We came to a dark brown, two-story house. He got into a Jeep parked at the side of the house. His determined face told me he intended to go after whoever shot at us.

Ripping open the passenger door, I said, "I'm coming."

He looked at me like I wore Dorothy's red shoes. "You get yourself back to wherever you came from."

"It's important that I go with you."

Time was wasting; he had to give in or knock me off the running board. "Then get in." He started the Jeep—I'd hardly sat before he got the Jeep turned around and heading down the lane. He pressed a button on the visor. The rail gate slid open and he roared through it, made a left and careened onto Silver Heel Pass.

He said, "Only one way he could get a shot off like that." A quarter of a mile up and on the other side of the road, he turned onto a dirt road hidden by aspens. He came to a ridge with a wide spot and a creek bubbling beneath it. He stopped. "Bastard didn't come out. Must have climbed the snake."

"Snake?"

"A mountain road that turns back on itself."

It was then that he focused on me, as if realizing he'd let an enemy into his vehicle, and his life.

I asked, "Where does the snake go?"

"Other side of the ridge. Comes out on Highway 9." He made a right, breeched the ponderosas and put the Jeep into first gear. It ground up the hill until we reached the top of the ridge. I looked over the landscape. This was a good place to set up a long-range rifle stand. I knew with certainty then that I hadn't brought the sniper to his house.

As if echoing my thought, he said, "The shooter knows the territory."

The Jeep continued to grind and climb, the road coming back in on itself, exactly like the snake. "Why would anyone shoot you?"

"I didn't know anyone wanted to until you came along asking questions."

"Don't you see? Anyone Reeve knew is in danger. Her parents. My God . . ."

He drove on, grim-faced, the hat now back on his head, the rattlesnake skin portending.

He said, "I knew them. Used to come to the campus and

take us to dinner. Bastards who killed them . . ." His chest expanded and contracted. "How'd you know to knock into me?"

"I saw the sun flash off metal. If it wasn't a gun, you couldn't have hated me any more."

"I don't hate, but I like my privacy."

"Privacy is going to be harder to come by until we find out who is stalking Reeve and you."

"Reeve and me?"

"You're protecting her, aren't you?"

"No, but you're right, I would."

"Someone thinks you are."

"Bastard she married." He lapsed into thought with a grunt. "How did things get so screwed up?"

"You tell me."

He shook his head and leaned into the steering wheel as we came to the summit of the rise. We were going down. "I never had any money, and I don't know why she saw anything in me."

I did. He was good-looking and probably very nice when he was fly-fishing or studying the planets.

He said, "Rich girl. Had everything. She wanted to be different. She met this man from another country. Hell, he could have been from Tanzania or India or another planet; she had to have someone different. I understood, still understand, Reeve."

I held on for dear life as we descended down a one-track, rocky road. How, I thought, would a driver know when someone came around one of those snakes head-on, to run you off the narrow skirt of the road?

He looked at me, holding on, and let loose a laugh. "You listen. You'd hear someone grinding up the road. There's enough of a pullover."

"Anyone ever gone off?" I said, looking down through aspens into the sheer, boulder-strewn drop-off.

"Happened a few years back."

"Reeve came back to you after she met the prince, didn't she?"

"She came back to her old shoe. And then she left again. Next thing I knew she was having a kid with the slick-ass Saudi bastard."

"How did you both get back to the research lab?"

"I put in for it. She came to see me and asked to relocate from DC."

"She came back to you again, after the marriage and the baby?"

"Yes."

We had reached Highway 9. Page pulled over and heaved a heavy sigh. He looked at me. "You got me talking in spite of myself."

"The shooter did that. You now know you've been pulled into this and you know why."

He grinned. It was kind of crooked. "You a mind reader? So, mind telling me why?"

"She came back to you."

"She would have left again. We'd about run the gamut again."

"What about Weatherby?"

He laughed. "That was her cover, she said. Old Thebold wouldn't suspect us if she pretended a thing for the security man."

I wouldn't tell him that I found it odd that she picked a man for cover who was married to a Saudi and that maybe she knew there was a family relationship between Salman, her husband's bodyguard, and Weatherby's wife. "Did Reeve tell you she suspected her husband was having an affair?"

"She never told me." He thought before he spoke. "I don't believe that she did suspect him of an affair. She tolerated his having prostitutes because of their being apart all the time. I'll tell you this though. She went to New York over the Christmas holidays. Well, you know the Muslims have nothing to do with that holiday. She didn't usually celebrate Christian holidays but she wanted to take Shara to New York to see the displays. As far as I know, that was okay with Husam, but she came back a different person. Moody. Hell—that doesn't near get to the tenth power of her personality change. She became a bitch, firing off insults and then crying she was sorry."

"Dr. Thebold told me she had a strong personality."

"Strong is one thing; unpredictable was another. Reeve was normally as predictable as the universe."

"What did you think caused it?"

"She was getting ready to leave me. I think she was back with Husam, but she couldn't go to Saudi Arabia with him because of her status, which was no status at all. Reeve, if she could, would have stormed into the palace and demanded everyone accept her. But she'd reached her limit with her prince."

He sounded like it served her right.

"So, you thought she was going to leave you for her husband."

"That's about it." He got out and looked at the earth. I stood next to him peering at the dirt. "Think our shooter started here on a horse."

I saw little indentations in the solid soil but would never have identified them as hoofprints. I looked at him again. Maybe he had Indian blood; the high cheekbones and eyes that narrowed at the corners.

He said, "Son-of-a-bitch is probably up in the hills, hiding."

Someone who knew where to hide.

He looked at me like he didn't quite know what to do with me. "Now that we've made acquaintance, let's have some lunch, with no interrogative side dishes."

"Can't. I have to get back to Denver. I have a stop to make and a plane to catch."

"Leaving so soon?" His tone was amusingly sarcastic as if he were really saying, *giving up so soon*?

"I've another lead to follow."

"I'll have to scold Dr. Thebold for ratting me out."

"She didn't. I have an investigator who has rat in his DNA."

He laughed. "Get in. We could go back by the main road, but I want to check out a few paths."

At least my side was hugging the rock side of the cliff road. On the way down, at the flats, comparatively speaking, he stopped twice to investigate wide spots that led into the aspens and pines. "Son-of-a-bitch hid in there," he said after the last inspection. He shifted into gear like a man planning a mission.

"You know who, don't you?"

He stared at me, his eyes bright with knowledge. "No."

CHAPTER SEVENTEEN

"It's tiny," Pearly Sue trilled through my cell phone. "His whole apartment could fit in my kitchen." Pearly Sue loved to cook—southern, lots of flavor and calories. "But," she continued, "the dog Chop-Chop is soooo cute."

I drove Highway 9 out of the lovely towns of Breckenridge and Frisco and called Pearly Sue. The call went to voice mail. The girl isn't one to be constantly connected to her electronics. She called back when I was on Interstate 70, heading east toward Denver and my last interview with the phone-chatty security guard, Rufus Gillibrand.

"This city," Pearly Sue began, "is incredible. Everybody rushes around and . . ."

"Pearly Sue," I said, "I only have another hour to Denver so make it quick."

"Oh, well, sure. I figured out a routine, starting yesterday. I got up extra early. It was still dark. Chop-Chop and me, we had a long walk up and down side streets, so when it was time for the prince to come out—because the time was right and the limo was parked in front—I had me and Chop-Chop walking by the entrance to his apartment building."

"And . . . ?"

"He knows Chop-Chop."

"Hmmm . . ."

"Surprised me that Web didn't know that, or didn't tell me. But, anyway, the prince reaches down and pats his little head.

Those Pekes are soooo cute. The prince said he's a dog lover and if he ever got a dog, I could walk him."

"Okay, and . . . ?"

"He wanted to know how long I'd be in New York, and why I'd come. I told him that Edward Stephens was my cousin and that he was overseas in China and that his dog walker had gotten a bug, and since I wanted to come to New York he paid my way so I could fill in for the dog walker."

"And . . . ?"

"He asked when my cousin would be back from China."

Should I worry about sending her to the big city?

Pearly Sue went on. "I said I didn't know when my cousin would be back; I was just in New York to sit his dog and apartment and see the sights."

Pearly Sue having wound down, I had time to get in a question. "He bought it?"

"Why not?" Pearly Sue's voice sounded inflexible. "He thinks I'm a stupid southern girl."

"He cottoned onto the accent."

"He said he likes southern girls, that his late wife was a southern girl from Atlanta."

"*Late* wife?"

"He was flirting with me, so he wouldn't be talking about a live wife, now would he? He *is* as charming as you said."

"Has he gone anywhere else?"

"So far he goes to work and comes home. He has a thick briefcase like he's taking work home. I've seen the personal trainer come and go, though."

"Have you checked for other exits?"

"The back exit goes into a gated courtyard that leads around the building to the side street, which I keep an eye on, but he could hop the six-foot brick wall at the back."

"What was the flirting about?"

She giggled as if nuzzling something warm. "He said I should walk Chop-Chop by Turtle Pond and the ball fields in the afternoon because that's where the dog walker walked him. I figure he wants to meet up with me there and maybe go to dinner or something."

Or something. "Pearly Sue, you've been made."

"No ma'am. I don't think so."

My mind conjured up a snatch and grab. "Stay another day, and watch yourself. And prepare to come home."

"I didn't tell you the best part."

"I can only hope for better."

"He's being followed by someone else."

"Ah . . ."

"I see this man that looks homeless across the street, a little up the way, on a bench. Sometimes he's standing beneath a tree or sitting on grass, but I think that a particular bench is his. Did you know that homeless people stake out territories. The prince's doorman says they can cause a lot of trouble if an intruder takes their spots."

"You're saying a person watching Husam is a homeless man?"

"Well, I don't know really, but he pays a lot of attention to the prince when I'm on the street, and I get the feeling I'm being watched, too."

"Then you are. Be careful."

Rufus Gillibrand lived on Peal Street in a duplex. I rang and knocked until my knuckles were barked. He'd stood me up. No wonder he'd sounded so cheerful. "Sure, come on by. I knew Weatherby. Odd duck, but okay. Takes a certain kind to marry a foreigner, ask me."

That was all I was getting from Rufus, unless I came back and grabbed him by the scruff, but I suspected that wasn't going to be necessary.

CHAPTER EIGHTEEN

The airport rooftop, looking like several flying nuns in formation, came into view. I filled the rental with gasoline and returned it. The shuttle took me to the check-in, and I was on the concourse awaiting my flight back to Atlanta.

I stood in line to board, and, on doing so, greeted the flight crew. Placing my bag in the overhead compartment, I sat in the aisle seat below. I'm not fond of flying so the window seat is not for me. I had my laptop out and was making notes when I looked up. Who should be walking up the aisle toward me but Dr. Thomas Page, Stetson and all. He stopped, removed his hat and said, "It's important that I come with you," thus echoing my words at his Jeep.

I stood and moved into the aisle. "You'll have to sit by the window."

"I like the window." He sat and looked out at the tarmac. "Gives me a view of the firmament."

"Dr. Page, how did you get a seat on this plane?"

"Call me Tom," he said, rubbing his fingers against his thumb. "Money."

This was an airline where you paid extra to go to the head of the line, but I knew the flight to Atlanta was overbooked, because a few passengers-to-be were awaiting last minute cancellations at check-in. "You paid for someone to take a later flight?"

"A student. They're always looking for extra bucks."

A stewardess stopped by our seats. "Everything all right, Dr. Page?"

"Everything's fine, Miss Connor."

"Ah, a known entity," I said.

Why had I thought in physics even though I know nothing about physics except matter can be solids, liquids and gases.

"Quantum entanglement," he said.

"The physics in physical."

"The quantum realm means that everything is connected. It's called quantum entanglement. If two quantum entities are ever in contact, they are forever connected, no matter how far apart they may become. In terms of information exchange, entangled particles act as a single system, not two separate entities—*known* or otherwise. Einstein called it spooky action at a distance."

"I forgot I was talking to a physicist. Was this your erudite way of saying that you and the stewardess are entangled?"

"Past tense."

"Have you ever married?"

"I consider myself married to Reeve Cresley, and she, me. Call us spooky action at a distance."

"Einstein would be proud his theories work in viable life."

"Unlike the great doctor, we're not all quarks and photons. Speaking of doctors, I spoke with Dr. Thebold. She is very upset with you."

"Tough."

"You are tough, that's undeniable. What came of your discussion with Gillibrand?"

"Nothing. He stood me up."

"Gillibrand didn't report for his shift. These things upset the doctors there."

"Oh, no. I hope . . ." I replayed the gunfire episode in my head.

Tom asked, "Did you get to talk to Rufus at all?"

"Only by phone."

"What did he tell you?"

"Nothing useful. I asked about Weatherby, whom I've met in Sarasota under rather unusual circumstances."

"Unusual characterizes the man. But he was an excellent guard with an excellent mind for security. So is Rufus."

"You want an expert on how to catch a burglar or guard against him, consult a successful burglar."

"A successful burglar might be hard to find."

"You might apply your quantum entanglement to that."

"We can call burglars or guards particles here. If entangled, they cannot be considered separately. They remain entangled until they decohere through interaction with the environment. In the case of our burglar, he's jailed, or our guard, he's no longer living."

"That's tough to think of."

"Then let's think of other things. I would like for you to tell me how your case began. You are a digger, I'll say that. So start from the beginning."

So, I began with Husam al-Saliba's story.

As I knew he would, Tom interrupted me several times. "Husam actually called Reeve an infidel and his daughter, too?"

"Yes, he did."

"Saudi Arabia was not in Reeve's future," Tom assured me. "She told me so. Nonetheless, she married the man knowing his parameters. She had a faith that she could change all things, all minds."

I said, "He married her knowing his restrictions, too. The women he married had to be of royal blood and Muslim, should he become the Guardian of the Islamic Faith."

That set Tom off. "Guardian of the Islamic faith! The slime. Reeve said he never sets foot in a mosque."

I said, "Did you know that there are more than six thousand

princes in the kingdom?"

"And she had to meet up with that one." He looked out the window. "Reeve was my girl." He sighed. "Those were odd times for this old boy of solid American ideas and values. Foreign students populated universities across the United States because they could afford the exorbitant tuition and accompanying costs. After Nine-Eleven the CIA and FBI pointed fingers at each other for laxities in vetting these students, some of whom turned out to be our enemies."

"Are you suggesting Husam al-Saliba is a—Jeez, I hate to say it—a terrorist?"

"Actually, no reason to think so. He might soil his *keffiyeh.*"

"You just don't like him."

"No."

"Did you have much to do with Husam in those years?"

"I was at a few parties. He liked to tell old Arabian stories and basically show off. He never impressed me much, but Reeve . . ." He looked out the window as if studying the firmament. Then his head came around. "We were involved, very involved. I hoped to marry her. I warned her against the bastard. She told me not to worry; she was just having fun with him."

I hated to rub it in, but I wanted a reaction, so I said, "Then one day Reeve walked into the café at the Smithsonian knowing that he would be there."

Tom said, "That was after a bad time with us. She was at MIT and I was at Caltech but we commuted; mostly Reeve commuted because she had the money. I was concerned about the physical distance and her distant attitude. She told me she was just tired. I, too, was tired." He sounded very tired now.

He said, "I chalked it up to ambitions with both of us. Things would, I hoped, smooth out between us."

I told Tom for what it was worth that a very smart lieutenant with the Atlanta Police Department thought Husam's story to be bullshit. "It might not be *Arabian Nights,* of which Husam is so fond, but since he resides here, Husam is stuck with the American Nights version, the parables of which are not so poetic."

Tom leaned his head back on the headrest.

"Husam," I said, "seemed to blame Reeve's religion for her unwillingness to convert to Islam."

Tom rolled his head to glance at me. "She was and still is an atheist."

"Have you spoken to her in the last two weeks?"

"Don't go thinking Reeve would have an epiphany in any time frame. She is a scientist."

"Scientist, atheist, Catholic—whatever—she's at the center of a terrible crime. Two people are dead. Rufus might be dead and you and I were targets."

"So, okay, Digger, dig deeper."

"I am and will continue to, but why are *you* telling me to?"

He looked out the window like he was making up his mind. He breathed in and looked at me. "After she came back from the Christmas holiday in New York, she wasn't the same. I tried to get her to tell me what happened. She said, and I quote, 'It was all for naught, Tom. The whole fucking mess.' "

Tom fell asleep or pretended to and I mulled over Reeve's words on coming back from New York. *It was all for naught.* Was she speaking of her husband or for herself? Start at the beginning. She went there for Christmas. An atheist doing that? What is an atheist? A simple nonbeliever? She told Husam she wanted Shara to see the holiday displays, something most atheists shun. Was she physically defying Husam's desire for Shara to learn Islamic beliefs? Beliefs. What does an atheist believe? I'd never thought about it in any substantive way, but I would think they need a belief system. Isn't that why some cultural scientists conjecture that there is an evolutionary reason our brains are so receptive to religious experiences? Early humans, it is said by experts, needed to explain the world around them. That's how we got all manner of religious beliefs and practices handed down to us. A scientist like Reeve knows a lot more about the composition of solar systems and scientific methods of explaining the world, but she was raised, like me, Christian, a Catholic. Was it likely that her high degree of education and understanding of culture and human nature eradicated religion from her mind? In one sense, it made sense. But in another—her going to see Christmas on display—it didn't. It flies in the face of my reasoning. I don't go to church much, but I consider myself religious, culturally and supernaturally. I'm like the early human. I feel the need to believe in a supernatural entity to explain my being.

The pilot had dropped the plane's landing gear. I looked at my crossed fingers and asked myself: am I seeking the help of something stronger than me to save my life?

I uncrossed my fingers and reached down for my carry-on bag. In doing so I said aloud, "My brain on culture." I looked at Tom, who was rousing, and wondered why I was so preoccupied that an atheist went to see a celebration of a holiday she'd turned her back on. One thing about my developing brain: things must make sense.

The seatbelt light went off and passengers started down the aisles. We stayed in our seats—saying little except that I would ride into downtown with him in a rental car. When the last passenger went by, I stood and got my overhead bag. Then my cell played Bach. Tom murmured something about sounding ominous. I said that Bach wove differing melodic lines in subject and answer form that were often complex and lugubrious. "Like this case."

He nodded agreement.

My caller was Lake. Because of my musings, I had forgotten that I was to call and let him know when to fetch me at the airport. Walking down the wide concourse, I called Lake and left a message that I had a ride and would meet him at Peachtree Road Steak House in forty minutes. I didn't tell him about Tom. Too much information to put into a message.

After the crowded train ride, and dodging people with rolling luggage, we got to the car-rental agency. Once in the rental, I drove, because it would be too confusing for a highly intelligent man to navigate Atlanta's highways. It just takes fortified nerves and a scatological vocabulary.

We were on Interstate I-285 when Tom seemed to shake himself out of his lethargy. "You know the story of *Appointment in Samarra*?"

"The book by John O'Hara?"

"I'm speaking of its origins."

"Besides W. Somerset Maugham and O'Hara? No. I once assumed it was from *Arabian Nights*, but learned that it was not."

Tom said, "I've always been fascinated by the little story on the harsh reality of death. Death herself tells the story about a merchant in Baghdad who sent his servant to the bazaar. The servant comes back and tells the master that he was stared at by a woman and he recognized her as Death. He tells his master that Death looked threatening. He wants his master's horse to ride to Samarra where Death won't find him. The master gives him the horse and then he goes to the market to find Death. He sees her and wants to know why she threatened his servant. Death says that she wasn't threatening his servant, that she was just surprised to see him in Baghdad since she has an appointment with him tonight in Samarra."

I said, "What is frightening is how death is so matter-of-fact."

"Like life and our inability to escape what's coming to us—the irony of the inevitable."

"I bet you know the origins of the tale."

"There are several. It's a tale much like the Noah's Ark stories. Many cultures in the Middle East have flood stories. The tale of Gilgamesh is a variation."

"I'm familiar with the legend of Gilgamesh."

"Most sources attribute the Samarra story to a version that is over a thousand years old and is titled 'When Death Came to Baghdad.' It is part of a collection put together by Idries Shah, who gathered material from oral sources and codified them in 'Tales of the Dervishes.' "

With that, we pulled up to the steak house next to Lake's unmarked squad car.

It was then that I got an uneasy feeling. *Speaking of inevitability.* I should have called Lake again and told him about Tom. *My appointment here is loaded with irony.*

Immediately upon walking into the restaurant, my eyes met Lake's. His then went to Tom with a quizzical look. I rushed forward as if to mitigate my anxiety, when instinct told me I needed a fast horse out of here.

Lake stood. My mouth missed his by a full cheek and I got his ear. I turned to Tom. "Dr. Thomas Page, this is Detective Lieutenant Richard Lake of the Atlanta Police Department."

"Ah," said Tom, "the policeman in the American Nights version. Very pleased to meet you."

Lake said, "Likewise." He slid back into the booth, taking up the middle, so I had no choice but to sit opposite him, next to Tom. Awkward and edgy, I could see the tension in Lake's jaws and felt Tom's stiff arm elbow mine.

I said, "Dr. Page—"

"It's Tom," he said, interrupting me.

Lake said nothing.

I leaned over the table. "Tom is an astrophysicist at the Boulder facility where Reeve Cresley last worked." Lake nodded. "Her last duty station," I said, uncomfortably and need-lessly.

The waitress came and took our orders. I went for a martini. *What the hell.* Tom had a bourbon on the rocks and Lake stayed with beer.

Lake raised his chin at me. "Have you eaten?"

"Yeah," I said, "right before I got shot at." *Take that, Lake-of-the-sullen-eyes. Go ahead and be jealous. All the times you've flirted with waitresses and eyed other women on the street.*

"Shot at?" Lake said. "You were shot at?"

"*We* were shot at," Tom said. "I think the rounds were meant for me. The setup was arranged well before Miss Dru came to see me."

"You both survived," Lake said, his eyes shifting between Tom and me.

"Look, I can eat at my hotel," Tom said. "I've been in Atlanta many times and know my way around Buckhead."

"Have you eaten here before?" Lake asked, his tone suddenly appeasing.

"Yes, I have," Tom answered. "But I'm not in the mood for beef."

"Great salmon here," Lake said.

"That's okay; I'll grab a bite on the way to the hotel."

"Where are you staying?" Lake asked. "If your being shot at has anything to do with my murder case, I'll need to hear your account."

"I'm at the Buckhead Ritz. My account is that Miss Dru here learned that I was Reeve Cresley's lab partner and came to speak to me regarding Reeve's whereabouts. I don't know where she is. We are friends and sometime lovers, but she didn't tell me that she wasn't going to report to the Jet Propulsion Lab in California. It was my intent to transfer there myself to be with her. Then this . . ."

Lake shook his head. When he looks abashed, he's usually adorable. Now he was offensive.

Tom rose, never having taken a sip of his bourbon-rocks. He drew a ten from a wallet he'd taken from his back pocket. "Miss Dru can give you the details. I've a feeling she has learned more about me than I remember about myself. Now, if you'll excuse me, I'll take myself off." With polite deference, he laid the ten on the table.

I watched Lake watch him leave.

"Satisfied?"

"Fair warning would have been nice," Lake said, staring. I said nothing. "A phone call explaining you'd brought a subject from Colorado." Roll-tapping the fingers of his right hand, he continued to stare. "Better than a curt message saying you got a ride and didn't need me."

"I didn't."

"So you come in with someone you picked up . . ."

"Picked up? We were shot at while he was throwing me off his property."

"How'd he end up coming back with you?"

I stood. "Being shot at, he thought it was important to take Reeve's disappearance seriously."

"You mean not as a lovers' spat, like we're doing."

"Like your being an ass." I put ten dollars down for a cocktail that I didn't drink. "I, too, will take myself off."

"You don't have a ride."

"There's always a cab outside."

"Dru . . ."

CHAPTER NINETEEN

Next morning, like I knew he would, Lake rang the doorbell at seven o'clock, hands carrying two cups of strong coffee from the famous coffee house down the street and a bag containing a blueberry muffin for him and a sticky bun for me. I opened the door and walked away to finish dressing. He went to the kitchen, calling, "Truce?" He knew better than say, "You might as well get over it now; you know you will eventually."

"No truce," I said, holding an earring. I went for the coffee and put the sweet in the freezer for later. If I was really angry, I'd have stuffed it down the garbage disposal. Knowing I'd get over my displeasure, I took my coffee into the dining room and set my handbag on the table.

Because I wore a skirt, I would lug a purse specially designed for concealed carry. It was a brown, cobbled-leather handbag, twelve inches in length and seven inches high. Plenty of room for my backup gun. At a little over six inches in length and four inches in height, my BUG held ten rounds, was 26 ounces loaded and fit very snugly into the side of the bag. There was a lock for the compartment, but if I needed the gun, I wouldn't want to be fooling around with a lock and key.

Lake sipped coffee and watched while I loaded it and secured it in the bag. He didn't even flinch or say something cute. I picked up my coffee. "Thanks," I said to him and held up the Styrofoam cup.

"Where are you going today?" he asked.

"His Royal Highness called last night. He's arriving in Atlanta. Services for the Cresleys today."

"I'm going. You, too?"

"Plan on it."

"Where's Pearly Sue?"

"Still in New York. She thinks the prince is ready to make a move on her."

"Pearly Sue has an inbred sense of these things, like any good southern girl."

I slung the purse over my shoulder and moved into the kitchen to exit the back door and make for the garage.

"We've got lots of time before the service," Lake said, moving behind me.

"I'm off to the office. Web's got info."

"Come with me, you can talk to Web on the way. That's what cells are for."

"I want to go to my office."

"You need to talk to me."

"About what?"

"Dr. Cresley's problems."

"He was sued; he lost; he paid."

"And not just once. Leaving some very angry people out there."

"What's the second . . . ?"

"Listen, I want us to get back on track."

"I'm on track."

"With me. I want you on track with me. I don't like this."

I set the house alarm and locked the door. I turned to him. "You usually don't shoot first and ask questions later." Feeling snooty, I turned on my heel. "Very unlike Atlanta's top cop."

"I'm . . ."

I looked back. Waited. He hates the word sorry.

"Look I am—I really am—I apologize for being an ass." He

looked like I was supposed to smile and say, *Apology accepted.*

But I didn't.

"Look, Dru, you know if I came into a restaurant, like you did last night, with a good-looking woman in tow, you would have huffed the place down."

Open-mouthed, I stared at him.

He went on. "You came in with a funny look on your face. You know what I think?" He started to raise a pointing finger, but thought better of it. "You knew, you absolutely friggin' knew, that I would react like I did, because you would have re-acted the same if the circumstances were turned around. If I dragged a woman into a bar, and if you had no clue that we were involved in a near-fatal incident together, you would im-mediately have gotten your Irish up and given us both the cold shoulder."

"Would you like to characterize what you and this fantasy woman of yours might have gotten yourselves into together?"

"Shot at like you and Page, traffic accident, any number . . ."

"Most likely by her enraged husband while you're climbing out the bedroom window and she's throwing on clothes."

He paused; blinked. "You're kidding."

Straight-faced, I said, "I never kid about you and your ador-ing public."

"God, you are impossible!"

"Am I following you, and, to where?"

"The cop house. I need some old and gritty coffee."

I've said it before: it warms the cockles of my heart to walk into a room full of cops. I looked up that idiom and learned two things: first, a cockle is a mollusk; second, mollusks are content when opening their cockleshells to the warmth of the sun. Who knows these things? Who studies them?

Commander Haskell came to the desk I'd borrowed from the

duty officer. "What's up, kid?"

"Thinking about the heart."

"That Cresley was a real artist. Like Houdini, he could get out of anything. Maybe it helps to booze with the city's elite."

"What about the young terrorist, Garland Lemmon, Junior?"

"No re-entry into the United States, according to the state department. Believed to be in Yemen still."

That's what Webdog had told me on the ride here. "Glad that thread is tied up. Too many in this case."

"Ain't that the truth. We have some prints from the Cresley house that don't match any on file. The lab found oil and ash in the ridges."

"Left hand or right?"

"There's a shadow print of the palm that shows the print came from the left hand. More telling, perhaps, is the ash in the ridges. Some cultures have strange hygiene habits. They use mud or ash to wash their hands. And then oil is used in ritual hand-washing. It's even known in this country, when poor people can't afford toilet paper or soap."

"Maybe some of Lemmon, Junior's terrorist buddies came over from Yemen to kill Cresley for him?"

"It could happen," Haskell said. "In turn, he'll be called upon to kill someone for them."

"The terrorist version of *Strangers on a Train*."

Stopping in front of us, Lake said, "Could be."

I asked, "What about the delivery driver calling himself E. B. White?"

Lake said, "We believe it could have been a friend bringing in food for Reeve and the girl."

"But who? She and Shara were holed up just down the street from her parents' house."

"Reeve and the Cresleys may have feared being watched."

"If they knew their daughter and granddaughter were hiding

out down the road, why weren't they more careful about letting strangers into their home?"

"Their killers weren't strangers."

This was looking too circular.

Lake gestured toward Haskell's hand. In it was a file. Lake said, "Commander, tell Dru about Dr. Cresley's second botched surgery and his penance."

Haskell read from a report. "Last year, seven-year-old Astryd Petion, a native of Haiti, came to the United States because of a life-threatening heart condition. She died as a result of receiving a heart–lung transplant from a donor who had type-A blood. Petion had type-O. Dr. Cresley led the medical team. No one checked the compatibility of blood types before surgery. When Petion showed signs of brain damage, they pumped her full of the right blood type, but it was too late."

"Jeez," I said.

"The hospital, Cresley and the surgical staff individually were reported to the American Medical Association. They were fined—the amounts differing according to their salaries—and suspended for six months." He closed the file and slapped it against the side of his leg.

"For a life? *A seven-year-old life?*"

"Petion's uncle vowed revenge."

"Strike two," Lake said.

Haskell drew in a breath. "When Cresley got his credentials back, he became associated with a medical center in DeKalb County, where he performed stent surgery. He failed to notice a blocked artery and the patient died. This patient was seventy-eight years old and had no complaining relatives. The hospital claimed the patient was in failing health and the overlooked blockage did not cause his later demise."

"How much later?"

"Six minutes."

"Strike three," Lake said.

Haskell said, "So far that's all we know. Now that the Lemmon kid's still in Yemen, we've got one suspect. The Haitian uncle looks best for it now. Haiti's a poor country. The uncle worked in the landscaping business."

"Could be where someone would pick up ash," I said. "Soils are sometimes enriched with ash for a pH balance."

"Find out if they use oils on their skin and hair," Haskell said to Lake.

"Already got someone on it," Lake said.

"Where is the uncle now?" I asked.

Lake said, "He's Janjak Petion. Lives in Lilburn, off Beaver Ruin Road. He's staying with a religious wacko."

I crossed my arms. "Excuse me. Is this your usual disdain for the sacred and the holy, or do you have more information for us?"

"Giles Petion, Janjak's uncle, is a voodoo priest. He's also a pillar of the neighborhood community, which is also served by a Catholic church, which, as you would know, does not sanction the rites that go on in the mostly Haitian neighborhood. The parish priest said many of the voodoo practitioners attend his church."

Haskell pointed a finger at Lake, saying, "You go see Janjak Petion yourself, Lieutenant."

Raising my hand, I mocked, "Can I go, too, please, please?"

Not in the mood, Haskell waved at me.

Lake said, "Delighted to go see the voodoo folks, right after I go to the hospital to talk to the victims of last night's home invasion."

I hadn't heard about last night's home invasion. After I'd left him sitting at his steak-house supper, he'd had to face more violence.

Haskell paused, wrinkled his brow in thought and said, "The

Cresley murders are higher on our priority list. Moore and Dunn will take the home invasion's victims."

Putting on his fedora, Lake said, "They'll be delighted to give up their day off."

Lifting my purse from the desk, I said, "Invasions and terrorists. Lord save us from both."

"Interesting to see who shows at the Cresleys' funeral," Haskell said.

Cops still liked to go to funerals to see if the murderer shows up. From my experience, it only happens in the movies.

"Go," Haskell said, shooing us out.

At the elevator, Lake said, "The Ritz is on the way to the cemetery. Want to run by and hear me soothe the brow of your Dr. Thomas Page?"

I ignored the *your.* "Might as well; we have hours."

On the way to the Ritz, Lake explained his visit to Dr. Cresley's tort attorney. The attorney did not divulge much about the malpractice charge and resulting lawsuit, but he did tell Lake that the doctor had been under a lot of stress at the time of the Lemmon surgery and was drinking too much. He did not represent Cresley in his second botch job, but he knew the Cresleys socially, and could see that the doctor was still stressed. He wouldn't venture a guess for the reason, but said that Cresley once told him, seriously, that there was a lot to be said for withdrawing from the rat race to a place in the country. Except that Donna Cresley would have none of it.

Donna Cresley, the APD had learned, was Atlanta born and bred, and a devout Catholic from a socialite background. She was also involved in many charities. She had a brother who was killed five years ago in a skydiving accident and a sister who was a drug addict, currently in a Florida rehab facility. Neighbors and friends told of good works and kind attentions—casseroles or cards whenever someone fell ill or lost a loved one. A shining example of rectitude.

"Shining examples make me suspicious," Lake said. "As if they're working off guilt."

I said, "I suspect neighbors and friends could tell us a lot more, but don't want to be involved, especially the socialite types."

Lake grumbled. "Don't I know socialite types and their misguided sense of straightforwardness." His ex-wife, Linda Lake, is a socialite.

Dr. Thomas Page had not checked in to the hotel, we were told. Since the community of Buckhead was in our patrol zone when we worked together—a lifetime ago for both of us—we knew the staff at the Ritz. The desk man said, "Happy to help, Lieutenant Lake. Being on days, I wasn't here, but I know we never had a walk-in last night. Wouldn't do him any good. We are booked all this week with the National Builders Convention in town."

"Where would you recommend a late walk-in go?"

"No need this week with the convention. Everything's booked. Of course, he could have gone downtown. I'll check."

The downtown Atlanta Ritz did not have a guest by the name of Dr. Thomas Page.

We walked outside. "Let's bet dinner," I said.

Lake grinned. "I've fallen for that one before. Who gets the information first, Web the tech guru, or the non-techies at the APD?"

"I'll give you a head start."

"No fair. The APD experts have to go through channels."

"Web lives in the channels."

"It's early, so let's stop for a cup of coffee and head out to Lilburn."

★ ★ ★ ★ ★

I was into my second cup of coffee and biting into a piece of Lake's muffin when Web called.

"I won," I mouthed to Lake.

Web found that Thomas Page boarded a Delta flight at 10:45 p.m. to arrive at 12:37 p.m. at JFK Airport in New York. He had no problem hacking into the airlines' reservation system, something organized for and maintained by the federal government. Page rented a car from Hertz. He had paid for the flight and rental with a credit card.

I told Web to keep on tracking Page's spending, and get me all he could on his bio, particularly what's in New York for him.

Lake said, "Renting a car means he was putting some miles between him and the city. Otherwise he'd grab a cab."

Or he wanted to keep his whereabouts out of a cab-company's logs.

Page's flight led me to think about Reeve and their relationship. Doris Thebold hadn't said how long he'd been on leave, but he might have come to Atlanta and as E. B. White to aid Reeve and Shara in their hiding from—*whatever they feared.* It made sense that it was Husam. Maybe Reeve drove to New York once her parents had been killed. That would mean she and Page were in contact, some way, somehow.

Watching Lake start on his third cinnamon roll, I outlined my thoughts.

"Into the city where her husband and his pals live?" Lake said. "I was thinking Reeve and E. B. White could be the killers."

I hadn't yet begun to suspect Reeve. "What about Uncle Petion from Haiti?"

"Donna and the Doc knew their killers."

"I'm thinking how easy it is to get into that gated community. Uncle Petion and a family member, a partner, could have got-

160

ten in as landscapers. They come and go. I watched a truck of day-laborers go in that day I talked to Donna."

"Okay."

"Think of this. The Petions pretend to work until they find a door conveniently open. Perhaps when Donna or the Doc drive into the garage, they slip in. Uncle waits in the liquor closet, while the partner hides in the powder room. We don't know that the other guest was in the living room with Donna."

"Farfetched, even for you."

"Let me finish. Uncle brings out his garrote and tries to strangle Cresley. Uncle's not adept with the garrote and Cresley cries out and escapes. Donna and the partner come rushing in. Uncle brings out his gun and shoots both Cresleys."

"There's so many holes in that, I can't begin to count them."

The Lilburn police, in cooperation with the APD, had Janjak Petion under surveillance and reported that he hadn't left the house.

Once we got on I-85, I opened my notebook computer to do a little research. Lake was lost in thought, observably and intently, as he drove.

"Listen to this, Lake."

"Hmmm."

"In *Vodou*—" I spelled it for him, "there's no praying directly to God, who is called *Bondye*. Instead, Vodouisants mingle with the *loas*—spirits, sort of like angels. African slaves brought the *loas* to the islands. Ogoun is a warrior god. Good to have a warrior god in the pantheon. Also, there's Erzulie, the goddess of love. These two are often depicted as Catholic saints. Erzulie becomes the Virgin Mary. Yikes. Bet the Vatican loves that.

"And then there are the minor spirits—ghosts of the dead, demons, snakes. Oh, and this is interesting: there are other manifestations of Erzulie. One is a lover of luxury and beauty,

161

and another is an avenging protector of children. A regular Joan of Arc. There's a song by Steely Dan called, "Two Against Nature" where the lyrics describe Erzulie as a succubus who bangs you silly but leaves a nasty bite."

"Enough," Lake said.

"I'm educating you here," I said, going on. "Let's see, it says here that a male Vodou priest is called a *houngan* and a female is a *mambo*. They are chosen by dead ancestors who make them divine when they are possessed. And, hear this, they often use their supernatural power to kill people. Then there's the *bokor*, a sorcerer of darker things."

"A *bokor*, huh?"

"In Vodou, one who is possessed is known as a *cheval*, a horse. The *houngan* and *mambo* bring those in a trance back to safety."

"I don't need to know anything more," Lake said.

I closed the notebook. We arrived on the pocked asphalt street of the down-at-the-heels neighborhood where lawns were green and flower pots lined the window ledges of colorful homes. I'd never seen a purple and turquoise house before. Spirit-lifting you might say. Oddly, I heard a succession of rooster crows echoing through the neighborhood.

Lake said, "I heard nothing in the lit-*tra*-ture you so ably supplied me about cock sacrifices."

"I thought cocks only crowed at dawn."

"Nah," Lake said. "They cock-a-doodle whenever they take a notion. We had one across the street—in the old days you could keep chickens in your backyards before the neighborhood associations started popping up. Anyway, this old bird would crow all damned day, starting with sunup and going until sundown. He became sort of a pet, and when I heard that some delinquent dirt bags were out to kill the old bird, I rounded up friends, took one of my daddy's guns, unloaded of course, since he kept his bullets hidden, and we went after the sons-a-bitches. They had hold of this huge, red bird that was fighting for its life. I slugged the nearest I came to. Blood squirted like a fountain from the blood vessels in his nose, spattering the other bastards, who let go of the bird and turned on us. The bird, by the way, joined in and kept running at and scratching the bastard who'd taken him. When the would-be rooster killers saw the gun in my hand, the wussies fled. Ol' Red and I had an understanding after that. No loud crowing on Saturday morning after sunup."

"That was before the War Between the States, wasn't it?"

Lake pulled into the driveway behind a relatively old red pickup—just the color to go with the bright blue and pink house.

He patted the purse lying beside me. "Glad to have you with me again, partner. Take my back."

"You think?"

"Never know."

I grasped my hand around the butt of the gun residing inside the carry bag. A Lilburn PD squad car pulled in behind us. An officer got out. *My* backup.

The door opened before we reached the first porch step. An elderly, black-skinned man in a dark suit and cravat tie stepped out. "Who are you?"

"Atlanta Police Department." Lake held up his shield. "Here to talk to Janjak Petion. Can I ask your name?"

The man didn't answer and the Lilburn policeman produced his credentials.

"You want to talk to my Janjak?" the man said to Lake. "What for?"

"In the matter of Astryd Petion's death."

The Lilburn cop said, "Mr. Giles, it would be well if you spoke to these folks and let them inside to talk to Mr. Janjak."

Giles's mouth turned down; his eyes glistened at Lake. "Our spirits are healing from that, Mister. Please, leave us be." His deep-throated, singsong patois was mesmerizing.

"Won't take but a few minutes," Lake said.

"My Janjak is grieving." He repeated, "Leave us be."

'I don't have a warrant so I can't force my way into your home, but I can get one and come back. It would be easier if I could come in and speak to you and Mr. Janjak Petion, and then we'll be on our way."

"It is not right," he said. "The grieving must grieve in peace." But he stepped back, and we entered the house. Lake removed his hat.

Sitting on a tatty sofa was a large black man in his forties, I would guess.

Sullen and sad, he glared at us. "I got nothing to say." His was a mumbling patois.

An older, straight-backed, small brown woman came into the room and stood against the wall. Lake said, "Morning, ma'am." She didn't respond.

Lake looked at the man on the sofa. "Are you Janjak Petion?" The man nodded. Lake said, "This won't take long."

Giles said, "Our spirits are sore, Officer."

Lake addressed Janjak. "Mr. Petion, are you aware of the homicide of Dr. Lowell Cresley, the man who operated on your niece, Astryd Petion?"

"I know what he did."

"Dr. Cresley was murdered along with his wife."

"I saw it on the television, yes."

"After the death of your niece, did you speak to Dr. Cresley?"

"I—I tried." His low voice quavered. "He would not talk to me. He went to his lawyer. And he lied."

"I am sorry for your and your family's loss," Lake said, also nodding at the woman standing by the wall, and Giles.

Janjak Petion stood, his intensity rising in his gestures. "The devil never bothered to check her blood type. What is she to him, some poor girl from Haiti that he was given to operate on?" He raised a powerful fist. "It was his wife who brought Astryd to him. Her and her good works." He shook the fist at us. "He killed her heart and brain and then tried to hide what he did. And it is never on the news, what he did. How he killed our Astryd."

Speaking of news, this was news to me. So Donna's charity work got her husband a patient that he killed. Hearing Janjak speak good English, I wondered how long he'd been in the United States and what his connection was to the Cresleys.

"Mr. Petion," Lake said, his voice meant to soothe risen passions. "I have been assigned to investigate the murders of Dr. Cresley and his wife, and I must ask you questions you may find offensive."

"I am already offended, Officer. Ask me."

Lake said, "Hospital personnel and the lawyers involved in the hearing reported that you threatened Dr. Cresley."

"I was upset, yes. I wanted to kill them all, yes. I did not kill him. I would not kill. I was upset." He started to walk away.

"So you didn't vow revenge?"

"Yes, sir, I did. I will get revenge." He lumbered from the room, saying, "Good-bye, sir."

CHAPTER TWENTY

You would think that a big-shot doctor like Cresley would have a funeral fit for a big-shot doctor. I didn't see a notice that the mass and burial were a private affair, but you'd have thought it was. There was a scattering of folks dressed in black, sitting and standing beneath the tent set up in the old St. Michael Cemetery near Northside Drive. Most were women. There was one I pegged as Heidi Levine, a striking blond whose smoky eyes and vanilla skin played well with her black, lace hat. She stood at the back of the tent, a certain defiance in her bearing. Well-dressed matrons—of charitable pedigree and functions, perhaps—and young women I assumed were nurses, dabbed their eyes and looked sorrowfully at the two coffins sitting on straps tied to brass bars. Oddly, beneath the coffins the ground had not been cut into graves. Puzzled, I looked over the heads of the priests and saw the small mausoleum. No earth to earth for Lowell and Donna Cresley.

Two priests officiated at the ceremony that got under way just as it began to rain. The newspaper had sent a photographer, as had the cable-news network. Even though the doctor's errors hadn't been publicized, they were known. It would appear, in death, those who once curried favor with Dr. Cresley and his socialite wife had abandoned them. I whispered as much to Lake.

Lake said, "Cresley was a media hound. The good doctor contributed to the money chests of the politicians they loved, and the charities they promoted. He fixed up athletes the media adores, backed their advertisers, contributed to favored municipal projects, went to court as an expert for star attorneys—so why would the media write or air bad stories about him? Christ, he only made three mistakes."

The first priest spoke of the mercy given by God to the souls of the faithful. He asked that God send angels to guard them and free their sins.

The second priest asked a merciful God to hear prayers and console those who grieve.

After the Amen, I heard rustling in the rows of black-clad folks and turned to see who caused the stir. From the lane, through the tombstones, came Prince Husam Saliba and Yasmin Saliba. Behind them was an older man I recognized but didn't know, and Salman Habibi. The air vibrated. It was hardly a collective gasp, yet I felt the murmur roll through me.

Husam's eyes zeroed in on mine and looked as if his coming here was the last thing in the world he wanted to do. Dressed in a black suit, tie and white shirt, he wore a *ghutra* and *agal*. His step was hesitant, and he walked at least three feet away from Yasmin. Yasmin wore a white head scarf that covered her forehead and wrapped around her chin. Otherwise she was dressed in a white, long-sleeved, high-collared blouse and long, black skirt. Salman looked exactly like what he was. A suited-up bodyguard. No *ghutra* or *agal*. The man I'd not met but recognized from his photograph looked like an impeccable Middle-Eastern lawyer. Between fifty and sixty, his hair was jet with silver threads and slicked back. His skin was the color of nutmeg. His black eyes tended to glitter, even at this solemn occasion, and he seemed not to be able to keep them off my face. He wore an expensively tailored, dark-charcoal suit and crisp, white shirt with a dark-maroon tie. The only thing missing was his briefcase. The foursome stopped at the tent and stood at the side. Lake and I moved behind them.

When I turned my attention back to the service, the first priest spoke of Jesus's resurrection and said all who believe in him would have everlasting life.

The congregation said, "Amen."

The second priest recited Psalms 23, "The Lord is my shepherd . . ."

A man stood for Yasmin to take his seat. She shook her head and he sunk back.

Husam and Yasmin stood as though uninvolved in the service as good Muslims would be. Salman and the lawyer stood behind them, looking like they were at an opera and didn't like opera singing.

I didn't take in the words of the liturgy, although I saw the holy water and incense sprinkled over the coffins. I have been to many Catholic burial services and know the rituals. The priest told the mourners if they die with Christ, they will live with him.

"Amen."

The first priest sang a kyrie chant and the second spoke the benediction.

Both priests made the Sign of the Cross over the bodies and spoke together and asked the Lord to grant Donna Lockland Cresley and Lowell Reeve Cresley peace.

"Amen."

Pallbearers lined the coffins and lifted them, and then carried the biers into the marble house—their final resting place. I felt a procession of something like fate creep up my spine as if kismet would be meeting with me soon.

The service over, the cluster of folks under the tent stood and spoke, ignoring the man in the fedora, Lake, as if they knew he was a cop.

Husam turned to us. "Good day."

Yasmin said nothing, but looked at the ground as if everything there was of vast interest to her and nothing above it.

"I'm sorry for your loss," Lake said.

Husam grimaced. "Yes, well, it is a loss, a great loss to the city and the medical profession."

Lake asked, "Are you going to be in Atlanta for a while?"

"No; I shall be returning to New York as soon as possible." With a graceful, backward swing of his hand, he said, "Let me introduce you to my law partner, Jaul Zogby."

Jaul Zogby offered his hand and Lake shook it. I smiled, nodded and said, "Pleased to meet you."

"Same to you," he said, his voice deep. "Circumstances being what they are."

Lake said, "Did you know the Cresleys?"

"I did not know them personally, only by reputation. And, I, of course, have met their lovely daughter, Reeve, and granddaughter, Shara."

Prince Husam said, "It was a gesture of friendship that Jaul accompanied me here. We will do our business later in the day, rest, have a small meal and return to New York late tonight."

"In that case," Lake said, "where can we meet?"

"We are meeting here," Husam said.

"Hardly the place to discuss the case," Lake said.

"Yasmin and I plan to have afternoon tea at the Ritz-Carlton. It is a favorite of hers."

Yasmin raised her head. "Please, Husam, you will go without me. I could not eat a thing."

Very touching. "Do you get to Atlanta often?" I asked Yasmin.

She glanced quickly at her brother, and not at me. "Almost never."

"Yasmin longs for the hot sunshine of Florida," her brother said. "Yes, my pretty sister, you may be excused from tea." He turned to Zogby. "Jaul, would you like to sit to tea?"

Zogby's smile was one of charm and gratitude. "I so appreciate the enticing invitation, but if I may be excused, I shall go over the briefs with a plate of southern fried chicken at hand."

"So be it then," the prince said.

I leaned toward Yasmin and said quietly, "Can we talk?"

"We have talked," she said with a sulk. "I cannot help you."

"What do you know about Lloyd Weatherby?"

She took in air quickly. "Weatherby? From my community?"

"That Weatherby."

"He is a pest. He is after me for some slight he feels. He is disreputable." She backed a step and turned. "I am going for the spa. I need a massage."

"If you're staying at the Ritz in Buckhead, you were lucky to get a room," Lake said to the prince. "The builders are in town."

Yasmin said, scowling, "We do not depend upon luck. We have a condominium at the Atlanta Arms."

Lake, for all his worldliness, looked totally unimpressed. Those places start at two million for a smallish apartment.

The mourners had left the tent area for the crypt, where the pallbearers were lifting the coffins through the door.

Husam's party turned to walk to his limousine. Yasmin and Zogby seemed to be in a hurry and with quick steps arrived at the long car, the doors of which were opened by the chauffeur.

We fell in step with Husam, who walked slowly while he spoke. "It is customary in my land for there to be a gathering of family and friends after a funeral, and I have been to funerals in the United States where that is also the custom, but, in this case, there is not to be a gathering, at least not one to which I have been invited."

Neither Lake nor I responded, although we knew one of Donna's charity associates was holding an open house for funeral goers. Lake and I had planned to drop in, maybe pick up a morsel of gossip.

Husam went on. "That being the case, and the Cresleys are—were—my in-laws, I will respond and invite you to partake with me at the Ritz-Carlton Hotel. They have an excellent tea service and their food offerings are quite wonderful. They are prepared for us at the second seating."

Food always made Lake brighten, even frou-frou food. Before he could say a word, a truck roared up the lane. The driver screeched its brakes behind the prince's limo. I recognized the red truck.

I looked toward the limo. Yasmin had apparently pushed a button and the limo window came down. Her full, white face shone from the open space.

"Janjak Petion," I said.

"Back me up," Lake said, hand on the gun beneath his arm.

I touched the butt of the BUG in its compartment of my handbag.

Janjak popped out of the truck and ran haphazardly toward us. He had nothing in his hands. "Where is the killer?" he cried. "Is he in the ground?"

Lake hurried forward. "Janjak, what the hell are you doing here?"

"I come to spit on grave of my niece's killer." The big man swatted at Lake and ran on toward the abashed crowd standing by the crypt. They scattered just as Lake caught up with Janjak. He grabbed Lake's coat near his shoulder. "Man . . ."

Lake grabbed Petion's wrist and pushed him away while holding the man's gripping arm at the tricep. He pulled the big man toward his chest for a classic arm takedown. Janjak tried to twist away from Lake. Lake kicked his Achilles tendon with the heel of his shoe.

Janjak's eyes popped with fury. Lake locked that arm behind the man's back. "You want the cuffs? Here?"

Janjak snorted outrage, his body jerking. Lake pulled his

other arm down and the man quit moving. He huffed several times and looked at Lake as if he just recognized him. "Let me go; let me spit on the graves. I will leave."

Lake leaned into the man and said words only I and the man could hear. "You can't. Not now. I can't tell you not to come back, but you should *not* come back. You understand me?"

Janjak settled. He looked around at the staring crowd. He said, "They all—they the friends of the murderer? They all just like he, the devil. The devil that took our Astryd." He wailed, "The devil took our Astryd!"

All living souls remained motionless as if ordered to be still for the camera, and then Janjak Petion deflated like a pricked balloon. Lake let go of his arm. Janjak let fall both hands to his sides, a man dejected, a man not given his pound of flesh. Lake nudged him into turning and limping back to his truck.

When Janjak neared Husam, he halted, and, eyes bulging, threw his hands up as if suddenly crazed, then took off at a run toward his truck, jumped in, cranked it and slew gravel backing out.

Lake and I walked up to the prince. "You don't look like the devil," I said.

"I might to that man. I know who he is."

"What?"

"He was the Cresleys' yard man at their old place. Once they moved to the new place, they had a pack of community gardeners and didn't need him."

After extracting all the information Husam could give about the Cresleys' former gardener, Lake said he was sorry to miss tea with the prince—yeah, right—and begged off, either to go to the charity shindig or more likely to find a hamburger joint and then to follow up on the fresh lead regarding Janjak Petion. It made sense. Janjak, the Cresleys' one-time gardener, had contacted Donna Cresley when he learned his niece had a potentially fatal heart condition. He asked Donna to intervene on his niece's behalf with the famous heart doctor. Then it all went wrong. Still, my instinct said Janjak was not a killer. Revenge means different things to different people. Spitting on a grave might have been revenge to him. Practitioners of dark religions take grave desecration, evil spells and assorted voodoo rituals seriously. I hoped for the sake of the rooster in the backyard that there would be no appeasing sacrifice of him.

I looked forward to tea at the Ritz, even though I anticipated the hubbub the prince would bring to the formal meal.

As I drove down Peachtree Street toward the famous hotel, I called Web. "What have you learned about Yasmin Saliba?"

I heard typing and waited for Web to boot up the info. "Here goes," he said. "She is Husam Saliba's half sister by a different mother. He was born of the chief wife, whatever they call them, but not Yasmin. Still, she's a royal princess, courtesy of her father, Hadid al-Saliba. There's nothing about her until the age of seven, when she was sent to a boarding school in Switzerland. She lasted a year on the staff's sufferance, and then went to a public school in England, which is a private school in the US. She learned English easily as well as Spanish, French and Italian—probably so she could cuss out those who wouldn't wait on her hand and foot. She appeared in Parliament to complain about the treatment of Muslims residing in London's ghettoes."

"Hold on, Web, I don't have all day for the yearly tribulations. Paint her with a broader brush."

"Gotcha. She has a degree in Arab Studies from the Sorbonne. That got her into a lot of places when she was in her twenties. She taught at Muslim schools in Paris and went back to Saudi Arabia to get her advanced degree in economics and finance. She is shrewd and well-connected in the Arab-Euro political and financial realms. She has also left debt in her wake. Yasmin does not like to pay her hotel bills, or her jewelers or her clothiers."

"Married?"

"Never. Paul Ardai tells me she's a tyrant and a strong supporter of the king's reforms. She would be. As a woman, she can drive a car in Saudi Arabia, not a small thing. She dresses in Western clothes but wears head scarves. As you know she has a home in Sarasota now, and an apartment in Paris."

"Does she have a job in the US?"

"None that Paul could come up with. Nor Paris, either."

"Seems to me her connections are going to waste."

"She likes living in luxury that someone else pays for."

"Get in touch with Dirk's. I want a shadow on Yasmin Saliba. ASAP. She's at the Atlanta Arms."

"Round-the-clock?"

"Yep. The prince's paying."

"Does he know he's paying for us to watch his sister?"

"Half sister. If he asks I'll tell him why."

"Why would he ask?"

"Exactly."

CHAPTER TWENTY-ONE

The concierge at the Buckhead Ritz, our pal, nodded imperceptibly when he spotted me standing beneath the elaborate, crystal
chandelier with the prince. When we walked into the lobby
lounge heads turned: to him. The mostly women of the
afternoon-tea crowd had obvious admiration and must have
wondered how I got so lucky. A pianist playing classical set the
tone that echoed throughout the fine furnishings.

We were escorted to a table set for four. Afternoon-tea menus
lay on top of the elegant, bone china. From what the prince had
said, Yasmin and he were expected for tea here, but who were
the other place settings for?

Once we were seated, Husam said, "I adore orange jasmine
tea."

"I'll have peach tea," I said, then I looked up.

And who to my wondering eyes should appear but Portia
Devon.

The prince rose and so did I. "Porsh," I said, waving fingers.
"Fancy, and all that."

Crossing his hands on his upper chest, Husam smiled at
Portia. "That is all I'm allowed," he said. "Allah may be watching, my great and wonderful school colleague."

Portia said briskly, "It's good to see you, too, Sammy. Thank
you for inviting me." When she looked at me, she actually
winked. I had a feeling Porsh had managed to invite herself.
She had called a couple of days ago and told me she'd spoken

with him, and that he was disappointed in my lack of progress. He'd told me that in so many words, too. I am an investigator, I remind people, not a magician.

"Darjeeling," Porsh told the waiter.

After I'd poured peach tea from the fancy pot and tasted, I ordered a pot of vanilla bean.

Portia ordered smoked salmon, caviar and asparagus spears—no bread. I chose the smoked salmon and caviar on rye. Husam went with the cucumber dill and lemon ricotta. The three of us shared the cotto d'agnello and melon. Since the others ignored the pimento cheese and chicken salad, it was all mine.

Portia asked after Sammy's family and got the same story he'd told Lake and me.

"What's the king's affliction?" Porsh asked.

"Old age and an illness that he shares with no one, except perhaps the crown prince," Husam said, cutting a portion of prosciutto with the knife in his right hand and putting the food in his mouth with the fork in his left hand, European style. We Americans usually cut and switch. "No one knows his age for certain, but he must be at least ninety, counting the decades that have been documented."

"And how is Princess Yasmin?" she asked, with a hint of emphasis on the *princess*.

"My sister is doing very well," he said.

Armed with knowledge of her degreed resume I wanted to ask if she was thinking about a career in the US when Portia asked, "How long has she lived in the United States?"

"On and off five years," he answered. "She divides her time between Riyadh, Paris and the US."

Hearing the murmur of voices and seeing appraising glances from those seated at adjacent tables, it appeared word had spread to those who didn't know that royalty was present. Apparently becoming aware of the hums, he said, "We will speak of other things."

I expected a blunt retort from Portia, but none came.

When the pastry offerings arrived with a nice champagne, Husam said, "I adore scones and clotted cream and strawberry jam."

I went with the Grand Marnier profiteroles.

When we'd finished our complimentary champagne, Husam asked the bartender if we could continue our champagne repast in the garden. The maitre d' appeared and escorted us over the pavers of the patio.

I declined the champagne and ordered a coffee. So did Portia. The prince ordered a bottle of champagne that must have cost a couple hundred dollars.

The rain had passed and the garden was lovely and fresh with the first blooms of spring. It was still cool but the show-off azaleas allowed me to forget the chill in my bones. I was happy that I'd worn nylon pantyhose and a suit coat. The bamboo chairs, covered in a taupe linen that served to set off the colors of the garden, had been wiped of rain water.

Husam had a smeary smile on his face when he looked from Portia to me. "It was delicious, no?"

"Yes, absolutely, and I thank you for inviting us," I said.

Husam reached into his pocket and brought out a gold cigarette case and offered us one. Portia looked ready to snatch one, but conscience got the best of her. I said no. He lit a cigarette and smiled up into the smoke. "The detective, Lieutenant Lake, he would not have enjoyed this so much, would he?"

"Not so much the cucumber sandwiches. However, he would devour every sweet off the three-tiered stand and ask for more."

A hotel employee came out and Husam quickly put out his cigarette, putting the remains in the gold case. "I observe rules and customs, even if I do not understand the need for them."

The coffee arrived and a server with the champagne. The coffee was delicious. Honestly, the tea had been cloying, so I was thrilled at the robust flavor rolling down my throat.

Prince Husam raised his champagne in a salute and said, "I am ready." As I'd noted before, he drank rather than sipped.

I let Portia begin, "Is there any chance of a coup when your king passes on?"

"You are being delicate and I appreciate that. Today, we were witness to the end of people who were brutally murdered, and a show of grief by one whose child was killed in a terrible accident. My king, if he dies of old age, will have, indeed, *passed on*."

"You didn't answer the question."

"It is a complicated question, but, no, I do not think so. We are experiencing a power struggle, but not like the days of old when the king was killed at *majlis*. That is a place where the king sits and listens to the citizens. That king, my ancestor, had provoked a violent protest when he instituted certain Western reforms. That was long before we three were born. No, I would say we will not have a coup."

"There's still a lot of *religious disagreement*," Portia said, emphasizing the words, "in your country."

"You allude to jihadists, like Al Qaeda. It is not so strong in our country as people believe. Such fanatics will grumble and support those who hate the West, but that is all they can do. They have no chance to overturn our modern reforms." He finished off his champagne and reached for the bottle that stood in a golden ice bucket.

I sat forward. "My question concerns your cousins and the disappearance of Reeve and Shara. Which faction would harm either to get you to return to the kingdom?"

"I cannot believe that any would. It is true that the moderates want me because I am seen as moderate and will keep the country on its slow, transitional progress into this century. The fanatics, because they are disruptors. They want to show that even I had to give up my life in the West to meet their demands."

"Where does Yasmin stand in all this?"

"She is a moderate, like myself, but she is for family, and, therefore, wants me to take Shara and reunite with our family. If that means leaving Reeve behind, so be it. I know you know that, because she told me of your visit."

"I had hoped your sister would be sympathetic to my cause of finding Reeve and Shara."

"Did she say she was not?"

"Our conversation was short."

He set an empty glass on the coaster. "By that, you're telling me that Yasmin was not polite."

"I came away thinking that Yasmin was jealous of Reeve."

He sighed. "It is the way with women."

Portia coughed out her disgust.

I said, "When I left Yasmin's house, Lloyd Weatherby was waiting for me."

"He is a friend of Reeve's. He married a Saudi woman that died. Magda and Reeve were friendly, too." He'd poured himself another glass. A waiter came to refill our coffees.

"I was interested in the name connection. Your man Salman Habibi has the same last name as Magda."

"They are brother and sister."

"Weatherby was at Reeve's last duty station in Boulder."

"That is true, and then he retired to his home in Sarasota. He is an admirable man."

"He seems to think your sister's peddling drugs out of her home."

"That is probably because she is." Portia, like me, seemed mildly shocked, but he laughed like an urbane man of the world would. "She doesn't sell. But she provides and accepts donations."

"That could still spell trouble."

"She has diplomatic immunity. She would be sent home, and that would be a shame for the shops in Sarasota."

"I have no interest in busting Yasmin, but I would like to talk to other Saudis in that community."

"My sister told me you think she's hiding Reeve and Shara."

"I don't think she's hiding Reeve."

"I am certain that Reeve has Shara. They are together."

"Me, too."

He toyed with his nearly empty glass. "I wish for more progress."

"Me, too. In that vein, I met a friend of Reeve's at Boulder when she was there."

"Of course. Thomas Page." He waited for me to speak, and when I didn't he said, "I assume you know the entire story."

"I have talked to Dr. Page, so I know some of the story."

"Then you know he loved her first." His face warped a bit, as if sad, but it didn't make him less smooth.

I said, "They continued to be lovers, on and off, after she met and married you."

Pouring the last of the champagne, he said, "That is so."

"Didn't it bother you?"

"Very much." *Penetrating an armadillo's shell would have been easier.*

"Was it Shara that kept you together?"

"And apart, yes." He sighed.

"Tell me about the trip to New York at Christmas time."

He shrugged, and slowing down on the champagne, he sipped. "What is to tell? Reeve brought Shara to see the windows and the lights and the shows for children her age."

"What did you think of that?"

"The secular Santa Claus I had no objection to. I told Shara he is a fairy tale like *Arabian Nights*. Shara loves those stories."

Portia said, "I recall your narrative ability, Sammy. I recall your telling the frame story where a young king takes a bride. Shortly thereafter he discovers that his wife is unfaithful and had been flagrant about it. The king has her executed and declares, like you, Sammy, that *it is the way with women*."

Husam's smile showed some humility. Then he raised his chin and told the frame story of King Shahryar and the vizier's daughter Shahrazad. He finished with, "So it goes on for a thousand and one nights. Not all of the stories have been published, but I'm familiar with most, particularly those in which I'd hoped to find the true story of my heart."

The prince smiled and lifted his glass of champagne. The ever-hovering waiter brought another bottle and fresh coffee pots for Portia and me.

Portia said, "Tell us a story. One of your favorites, but not the one of the large member."

"I would be embarrassed."

Another bottle of champagne might well cure his embarrassment.

"I know which tale you are thinking of; one that touches upon the subject we have raised. 'The Craft and Malice of Women.' "

"*You* have raised," Portia said. Her lips upturned into a crafty smile.

He tapped his finger against his champagne glass. "It is also called 'The King, His Son and His Concubine.' An old king has one son. He was educated and raised to be king, and, although handsome, he is shy. He meets the king's concubine, who falls for his loveliness. She wants him but he rebuffs her and says that he is going to report this to his father. She gets to the king before he does and has torn her dress and ruffled her hair. She cries that his son has taken advantage of her. The king orders his son's death, but his trusted vizier says, 'O King, it is no light matter to put a son to death on the report of a woman, be she true or be she false; for this may be a lie and a trick of hers against thy son; for indeed, O King, I have heard tell plenty of stories of the malice, the craft and perfidy of women.' Whereupon the king says, 'O Vizier, tell me another story about the craft of women.' "

Portia huffed, "And your vizier is off with another tale against women."

Husam smiled. "And the vizier is off with another *tale* within a *tale* of the *Thousand and One Nights.*" Husam swallowed more of his champagne. He was indeed a good storyteller. His inflections ranged from the softness of the king's one son to the harshness of the king's order.

He smiled. "The tales are stories within stories. The endings are not endings, but beginnings of another tale of suspense."

Portia said in almost a bark, "*Arabian Nights* stories presume the infidelity of women and the subject runs through them all."

The prince sighed. "Not all, exactly, but many."

"While men are excused from infidelity."

I interjected, "Seems to me that the tales are those of powerful men who can do no wrong, including murder on a whim. They are permitted to have multiple wives and concubines so that infidelity is not an issue. Women are depicted as unfaithful or sorcerers and objects of erotica."

Husam shrugged. "Some stories are historical with real people like Abbasaid Caliph Harun al-Rashid and his vizier and court. They lived after the fall of the Sassanid Empire, in which time period Shahrazad is set." He finished that glass of champagne and poured another. "You know, though, they represent Islamic philosophy that still exists in some parts of the region today, particularly the tribal areas. Life was harsh then as it is today. Therefore the laws and punishment had to be harsh."

Portia ruffled her shoulders. "The tales you love so much show a disregard, a serious negative depiction of women that . . ."

"Are you concluding something about Reeve and me in all of this?" As he spoke, he became offended.

"If Reeve could go to Saudi Arabia with you and be a wife in full standing with other royals, would you marry another woman? Have a concubine?"

"I have given this some thought, and I will say most likely yes, because her sons, while royal, could not rule. I would want my sons in line."

Portia said, "Maybe that's what's keeping you from finding the true story of your heart."

"It could be," he said with a sad shrug. "My wife has an intermittent lover, as you know. That I accepted, unlike the husbands in the tales." He spread his hands. "They are just tales hundreds of years old. You do not live like the people in your Bible. Some of those cultural mores have passed into your generations, but many things have changed. It has taken our country longer to change, but it is changing."

I said, "Let me ask you something about Reeve's and Shara's visit to New York."

His head nod was short, but short of put-upon. "Please do."

"You say she was immersed in Santa Claus and the non-religious side of the holiday. Is that exactly true?"

He seemed to spiral downward; maybe it was the champagne. "Shara is schooled with Christians, as well as Muslims and Buddists. You understand what I am saying?" Neither Portia nor I spoke, and he continued, "Her school is not a religious school, and religion is forbidden as a subject from books or songs. Then I heard my daughter, my Arabian daughter, in her room singing a Christian hymn about the birth of the Christ in a manger. I told Reeve that I objected to this sudden blast of Christianity my daughter was seeing and hearing and imitating. Reeve said that Shara was a Christian child. This is the first I heard that she, an atheist, considered Shara a Christian child. I was stunned."

Portia said, "Reeve was raised Catholic. She might be going back to her roots and taking *her* daughter with her."

"It was—is—an abomination to me. You are Christian. I have many Christian friends. You are a good friend. But my daughter, the daughter of a royal prince, cannot be Christian."

I asked, "Did you fear losing Reeve and Shara?"

One of his hands curved tightly around the champagne stem. "I fear losing Shara to Reeve, a woman now unlike the one I married."

"Reeve left Boulder. She was supposed to continue her career in California, but never arrived there. Thomas Page said that she was leaving him as she'd done in the past. She left you in New York. It appears she was leaving her lover *and* her husband."

Approval spread across Portia's features.

Even Husam noticed. "I don't think that is so. There were budget cuts. Her bosses encouraged senior staff to take leave without pay. That is all I know until I speak with her."

I said, "You even suggested that she might have gone somewhere to think about things. Perhaps she feared that you would take Shara to Saudi Arabia—as so many Saudi men do with their American children."

"I would not do that."

Portia said, "You do plan to return to Saudi Arabia, don't you?"

He didn't say anything and, from the look on his face, he wasn't going to.

Portia said, "You know about Dr. Cresley's mistakes, don't you?"

He gulped air, perhaps glad that the subject had changed.

"Yes. Reeve called him the Butcher of Atlanta."

"Do you think these errors led to the Cresleys' deaths?"

"It is something to suppose, but I have no way of knowing."
He picked up his champagne glass.

"I saw a photograph of a couple in a magazine," I said, and
hesitated a tic to see if he'd suddenly react, but he didn't. I
reached into my handbag for a printout of the photo and slid it
across the table to him. "It was taken about three months ago
in Paris. I recognize you, of course, but not the young woman."

He studied it, then sagged back in his seat. "I travel there
often. We have an office there."

"On what passport?"

"What are you asking this for?"

"You didn't travel under your Saudi name."

"I have a French passport under the name Husam S. Saliba."
He reached into his pocket, brought out a wallet and offered a
plastic card. "Here is my American driver's license from DC.
See the name: Husam S. Saliba. It is my name."

"Who is the woman in the photograph?"

His cough was borne on nerves. He covered his mouth with
his hand while trying to look undaunted. Classic stalling
technique. "I have been photographed with many—"

I tapped the photo lying on the table near his champagne
glass. "Who is the woman with you in this photograph?"

He rose to go. "That is Aya."

CHAPTER TWENTY-TWO

I walked down the hall to Webdog's office and stood in the door. Observing his intensity at the computers gave me pause. Rushing back and forth between keyboards and monitors, he appeared frenetic, possessed, so I went into my office to type notes on the day's activities. Where to start?

From the time I rose until I sat down at this computer, the day had been chock-full of much ado—hopefully about things important. It started with Lake coming to make amends for his bad behavior to Thomas Page and me, thus causing an important person in my investigation to leave town. Fortunately, Page had left a solid trail so Web could run him down.

I did a paragraph on the not-so-astounding information from Haskell that Dr. Cresley had other medical blunders, one a death caused by the wrong blood type that left a family member seeking revenge.

I gathered good information at the cop shop when Haskell said that the fingerprint from the wall of the Cresley living room was from the left hand. There was a shadow imprint of the palm which showed the index finger was on the left hand. The analysis contained ash and oil. Muslims clean themselves with their left hands after defecation, but I can't see the prince hiring dirty-handed thugs to kill his in-laws. Maybe I was being naive.

The visit to the Giles and Janjak household maybe put us a few steps ahead when Janjak let us know that because of

Donna's good work and deeds, it was Dr. Cresley who operated on his niece, Astryd. Janjak's emotions, his outrage, that the surgeon tried to cover up the dreadful mistake by injecting her with the proper blood type was overwhelmingly appalling. That it was never reported in the media made it worse because reporters had known about Cresley's horrific mistakes but chose not to report them. I talked to the nurse who supported the Lemmons' claim and she said that she had called the newspaper and the television stations, but never saw a story written or aired.

The Cresleys' graveside service was a kick in the right direction, again owing to Janjak's fury. Were it up to me, I'd have let him go in and spit on the coffins, but, hey, I have several vindictive strands on the old DNA pole. On the other hand, had he gone to spit, he may well have missed seeing Prince Husam, who identified Janjak as a former gardener to the Cresleys. All gods work in mysterious ways.

To depart from facts and slip into hope: I really hoped that neither Giles nor Janjak were killers.

I'd learned more of Yasmin's resume from Web, and it was all I could do to keep quiet about it at afternoon tea with Husam. Yasmin carried herself like a powerful woman, yet sniped like a child thwarted. What was a Sorbonne woman educated in Arab studies—hey, we study English and American history so an Arab can major in Arab studies—and finance in her own country doing lolling like a spoiled princess in a playland paradise? I wondered why she would be allowed such luxury, since her education had to have been paid for by the royal family. Reformers they may be, but that family wasn't noted for educating women for powerful positions.

Portia had said that during her conversation with Husam that afternoon, he'd sounded apprehensive.

I'd been waiting for the right time to spring the woman at the

Paris Ritz on Husam. He had to admit that it was Aya, his cousin, his fiancée. Maybe the anxiety Portia heard in his voice meant he anticipated a hawkish incursion into his privacy. Despite his attempts to appear *haut monde,* I felt he feared me.

Although the day had been a long one, it was not over yet. I rose to go see Webdog. He was still tapping madly and scooting his roller chair back and forth. "Webby, what's with you?"

He looked up, his eyes taking a split second to focus on my face. "Hey, Dru. Yeah, well, it's something I'm working on."

"I can see that. What?"

"Not sure. A notion."

"About?"

"I'm not saying until I get further into it."

"About our case."

"Yes—yes. I can safely say . . ."

"Is it about breaking into . . . ?"

"No—no. Not at all."

"Any news from Dirk's on Yasmin Saliba's moves?"

"She left the Atlanta Arms to meet a man at the International Martini and Cigar Bar. His open tab is with American Express. They both had bacon, lettuce and tomato sandwiches. Two sandwiches, thirty bucks. His name is Jaul Zogby. He's . . ."

"Dirk's works fast. He's the prince's law partner."

"He's Egyptian. Born in Cairo. University of Amsterdam and George Washington in DC."

"Roads the world over lead to George Washington in DC. Married?"

"Yes, two girls and a boy. Wife is a professor of economics at Princeton."

"Stay with him, you and Dirk's."

"You bet. By the way, Princess Aya bint Shah al-Fahid is

listed in the Saudi list of princesses, but she is not listed in the royal house of Saliba. That's all Paul, Dirk's and I could find on her."

CHAPTER TWENTY-THREE

"I've located Thomas Page," Web said.

"Thought you would."

"In New Hampshire."

One of Web's computers dinged and he looked at the monitor. "Pearly Sue Skyping," he said.

"Good; I want to talk to her."

Pearly Sue's face was a bit of a blur because she skyped from her tablet. "Hi y'all!"

"Hi, P.S.," Web said. "You're looking good. What's behind you?"

"Well, I'm here in lovely Central Park. It's cool, but they say it's just the right temperature for this time of year. Want to see Turtle Pond?"

Before I could say no, I'd seen it in person; she was flashing the tablet screen around the place. The images were too poor to show the beauty of the park in spring.

"It's a manmade lake," Pearly Sue said. "And you'll never guess how it got its name."

"Turtles in water?" Web said.

"Yes, but back when they built it, they allowed people in the city who had pet turtles to dump them in the water. Now there's so many they don't want you to do that any more."

"There's a lot to be said for having a dog," Web said.

"Oh Web, there's lots of dogs in the city. Why, I've got Chop-Chop with me now. See him?"

The screen showed the dog sitting at Pearly Sue's feet.

"What brings you to the park?" I asked.

"Oh, the reason I called. You remember me telling you about this homeless man, who seemed to be watching Prince Husam?"

"Yeah," Web and I said together.

"Well, since the prince left for Atlanta, I had nothing to do but wonder about him, and I took to walking Chop-Chop past his bench. That's on the other side of the street from the prince's high-rise. Him and his fake shopping bags take up the whole bench. I got him on the bench on the camcorder."

"How do you know the shopping bags are fake?"

Her big blue eyes flashed on the screen. "All I saw was wadded-up newspaper sticking out."

"I see."

"Well, here's the thing. This morning when I was walking Chop-Chop past him, he said, " 'I know what you're up to.' That's exactly what he said. Clear as day and not in a froggy voice, either."

"Uh oh, made again," I said.

"Well, he moved over and made room for me. I looked around. There were people walking on the sidewalk. I wasn't going to take any chances because I figured he was up to something."

"Why?" Web and I asked together.

"If he knows what I'm up to, it's because he's up to something, too."

"What did he say after that?" I asked, reining in my impatience.

"He said that we needed to talk. I said I didn't need to talk to no one except Chop-Chop. He said I should meet him at the Turtle Pond this afternoon at around four thirty."

"And you did."

"Yes, and he just left here."

"What was it about?"

"Well, I'm sitting on this bench under some lovely birch trees with the camcorder. Lots of people running and walking dogs. We don't get such lovely birch trees in the south like here. Mama says it's because birch trees don't like our hot weather."

"And he came and sat by you under the birch trees," I said.

"Well, yes, and liked to scared me he was so quiet about it. I hardly recognized him at first. He had on a suit and tie, a fedora just like Lake's, and sunglasses. No beard. He looked just like a banker down on Wall Street. I took Chop-Chop there in a cab yesterday because I wanted to see the financial capital of the world. Those buildings, my goodness; like it took all the money in the world to build them."

"Pearly Sue," I said.

"Yes, well, he told me to turn off the video, but before I did I aimed it at him when he sat down. I'll send the file to you. After he made sure the video wasn't running, he told me that he was a federal agent with the Diplomatic Security Service and that he is part of the protection detail for the prince."

"DSS is protecting the prince? From what?" I asked. "The prince has lived in this country for years. I can't believe they've been protecting him that long."

"I don't know about that, and he didn't say how long he's been providing protection for the prince, but I said that sounded like Prince Husam had enemies, and he said something like people in high places make enemies, but not that the prince had any that he knew about, but as an important Saudi and emissary to this country, he was afforded protection by our government." Pearly Sue paused to take a breath. "I wondered about that. I mean, the prince can afford his own bodyguards, and I said so to the agent."

"Did you get his name?"

Web interrupted, "End this chat right now. Send the file to

us, then do a data-wipe and call back on Dru's cell."

Pearly Sue clicked off. Web said that, according to a notorious NSA leaker, Skype's maker had changed its architecture to make it possible to monitor and hand over audio and video calls. Pearly Sue's tablet and cell phone were encrypted by an app but were hardly foolproof. My cell is foolproof because of Web's ingenious encryption methods, which I do not understand, but trust.

When Pearly Sue called on my cell, I switched the call to conference and she asked, "Do you think he wore a wire?"

"Depends on who he is," I answered. "Did he tell you his name?"

"Victor Cartaloma. He said call him Victor, not special agent. He said I shouldn't acknowledge him when the prince comes back and he's acting like a homeless person. He didn't sound American, more like a Brit, but maybe he was from up here. People talk different up here."

"You sound different to them," Web said.

"I said to him, well, Prince Husam is in Atlanta so why aren't you with him? And he said that other agents were in the detail and that's all he could tell me. Then he wanted to know why I was following the prince, and I said how did he know I was following him. He said no use trying to deceive me, I'm an expert at watching people. I hope it's okay that I said I was a private investigator. I also said that was all I was going to tell him until I talked to my boss."

"That's fine," I said. "Describe Cartaloma, besides being groomed like a Wall Street banker."

"He was medium height and slim. He walked kind of like a cat, sneaking up like, on his toes. I couldn't see his eyes because of the sunglasses, but his hair was dark, from what I could see from under the hat. His lips were pouty-like and he had the kind of skin Italians have."

"Thus, his name."

"So, I'm supposed to speak to you today," Pearly Sue said, "which I am right now, and ask what I can tell him about the job. Then I'm supposed to meet him tomorrow at seven o'clock in the morning; me and Chop-Chop at the King Jagiello monument. I Googled that king, since I never heard of him. Jagiello is Ladislaus the second of Lithuania who, with the Poles, won the Battle of Grunwald. He is on a horse holding crossed swords over his head to . . ."

"Pearly Sue, I know the statue. Move on."

"So, should I meet Victor Cartaloma?"

I said, "Make sure there are people around you at that time, otherwise scrap the meet. I want you to tell him to get in touch with me. Have him call the office. Webdog will set up a phone interview. Meantime, Web, you look into Cartaloma's credentials."

"On it," Web said, then spoke to Pearly Sue. "The prince plans to return to New York tonight. He's not listed in any commercial airline manifest, so he may be coming in on a private plane."

Pearly Sue was silent, which meant the wheels in her head were turning. She was scheming at something. I said, "Do not, Miss Ellis, stray from your routine. Do not put yourself in danger. We don't know who this Cartaloma is yet. He may be legit, but maybe not. I share your skepticism, although DSS does guard dignitaries to this country and also our dignitaries abroad."

"But why would they be incognito?"

"That's the question," I said.

"I will walk Chop-Chop at nine thirty this evening, my usual time. I always talk to the night doorman. His name is Jonathan."

Pearly Sue talks to everyone; that's why she gets so much

information, at times critical information subjects don't know they're imparting.

"Good. Take care of yourself and Chop-Chop. By the way, what did the little pooch think of the DSS agent?"

"Chop-Chop is a smart little thing, very observant in my estimation. He knew Victor Cartaloma because he let him pet his head. He turns his head away for strangers."

Webdog had Pearly Sue's video on the screen. She'd been a regular tourist and he cut through those scenes to one that showed the bum on the bench. The bum had watched her video him, but his bench was shielded by trees and shade. At that distance he was indistinct. At the park, Pearly Sue had gotten the man calling himself Cartaloma from the waist up, in profile, as he started to sit beside her. That he wore a hat and sunglasses made the video almost useless. We looked for oddities on his skin and in his movements, but nothing popped out. When he patted the dog's head, the dog wagged its tail.

It didn't take Web long to learn that Victor Cartaloma was indeed a DSS special agent. Dirk's has a complete roster, compiled over the years, of every federal agent of every federal government department, working, retired or deceased. Victor Cartaloma was last stationed in Baghdad at the embassy, but was transferred stateside four months ago. No word of what his new assignment entailed and why he was transferred. That, Web or Lake would have to find out.

CHAPTER TWENTY-FOUR

"I caught up with Heidi Levine today," Lake said through our cell connection. "She was packing for a trip to Miami, to the beach to grieve."

"She look good as a suspect?"

"Clean record. Twenty-five, unmarried, engaged to Lowell Cresley."

"Engaged?"

"He gave her a big diamond, and I mean big. She said she doesn't wear it around the staff. She insisted Lowell was going to divorce Donna and marry her. Then this thing with Reeve disappearing happened, and he put off telling Donna he was filing for divorce. Cresley's attorney knew nothing about an impending divorce."

"Interesting."

"Ready to eat?"

I wasn't hungry but Lake was, and so we met at his place to share dinner and, hopefully, a night together. We'd spent too many nights apart.

Lake had stopped at Celestial Steaks Takeout and brought home two steaks—a small filet in case I developed an appetite, and a thick slab of prime rib for himself—two baked potatoes, a large Cobb salad, and a cherry pie.

I sat across from him at the round, oak table positioned in a corner off the small area called the kitchen of his one-room, two-thousand-square-foot loft. Fancy screens that we've collected over the years partition the former cotton warehouse into smaller rooms.

Lake sliced a hunk of the meat and, changing hands, forked it into his mouth. I told him that I noticed Husam didn't change hands after he'd cut a piece of prosciutto today at tea, maintaining the eating implement—the fork—in his left hand.

"And?" he said, chewing

Lake would not appreciate my talking about Muslim toilet habits at dinner. We could speak of grisly autopsies, but not poop. "Let's just say it goes to the left-hand fingerprint I learned about from Commander Haskell."

He stared. "How 'bout that. Web run down Thomas Page yet?" he asked, swallowing.

"One database purge came up with something promising. There's no paper trail, but there's evidence he might have connections in Woodstock, New Hampshire."

"Database purge?"

"Thomas Page has no phone or address in his name in Woodstock, New Hampshire, but property records show an Anita Page Horne, widow of Clarence Horne, living in Woodstock, as having a son named Thomas Page. She died a year ago. Presumably the Woodstock address was his mother's place, and probably is now his. To be continued."

"Who did the purge?"

"Dirk's. Webdog's too busy with something he won't tell me about."

"If he won't tell you, you probably don't want to know. How goes it with Pearly Sue?"

I brought him up to date on Pearly Sue's grand adventures. "Can you run down Victor Cartaloma's creds with the Diplomatic Security Service?"

"Depends," Lake said, giving me a thoughtful glance. "He commit a crime in Atlanta?"

"Not that I know of."

"Can't help you."

"It's a thread in your murder case. The Cresleys being Husam's in-laws . . ."

"The DSS is very secretive, especially about domestic affairs. State department is like that—very stately. Not at all like the glory hounds at DEA, ATF and FBI. You know the old joke. They all participate in a raid on a house. The DEA dog finds a suitcase full of cocaine. The ATF dog finds a cache of AK-47s. The FBI dog holds a press conference announcing the FBI has just broken up a drug- and gun-smuggling operation."

I grinned at the oft-told joke. "Web told me that DSS has a liaison with local and state cops."

"Mostly they call us for help and pay us when foreign dignitaries come and they're short-staffed."

I remembered that, as a first-year police officer, I was assigned to a detail when the Duke and Duchess of Somewhere came to Atlanta. It was said to be paid for by the feds.

Lake said, "I worked with the resident agent here and a field special agent out of the Houston office last year on the passport/visa murder cases. The resident DSS agent here was awaiting posting overseas. He was a fresh-faced boy wonder longing to get to Rome. Maybe I can run down the ol' boy in Houston; name's David Davis. He owes me a favor. I think you'll find this Cartaloma is what he says he is. Probably being discreet at the prince's request. Remember how this case started with Husam and Portia? Strict secrecy."

"The Cresleys being murdered blew that possibility. How can I find out if Cartaloma is bona fide DSS?"

"My guess is Cartaloma's first stop was DC after Iraq. They get de-briefed and a period of recreation after an assignment in a war zone," Lake said, forking potatoes into his mouth. He chewed, then drank wine. "Four months out of Iraq doesn't seem much time to unwind, does it?"

"That's what I'm thinking." I ran my fork through my Cobb salad. "I'm concerned about Pearly Sue."

A grimace moved across his face. "The girl's good, but unpredictable. That makes her a loose cannon."

"She's shrewd and intelligent, but she takes things to the next step or two without authorization. So far it's worked out."

"That makes her even more vulnerable."

"I never think of her as vulnerable. Maybe over-reaching. I wonder what she's going to do this evening after the doorman tells her what she wants to know. The problem I have with Cartaloma is that he told Pearly Sue he was part of a detail, yet with the prince in Atlanta, he's still on his park bench."

"Get her out of there, Dru. Now."

"I was thinking of sending her to New Hampshire."

"Anywhere," Lake said, beginning on his salad. He prefers to eat salad last in case he's too stuffed from the meat and potatoes. Never happens.

I went for my cell and called Web. "Arrange for one of Dirk's agents to meet Pearly Sue in New Hampshire tomorrow afternoon. And arrange to get a photo of the agent to Pearly Sue by email. She needs to verify his identity."

It wasn't until half past midnight that Pearly Sue answered her cell phone. By then Lake had slept on and off and lovemaking had gone with my panic. Adrenaline, when it comes without real danger, is hard to slough off.

"Where have you been? I've been . . ."

"Sorry, Dru. I couldn't answer," Pearly Sue said, sounding regretful. "I had my cell on vibrate, but . . ."

"Why couldn't you answer?"

"I had dinner with Prince Husam this evening."

"You what?" *I worried for this?*

"I was talking to the night doorman, Jonathan, like I said I would, and here comes Prince Husam's limo—with that Salman driving—pulling up. The prince gets out and sees me and Chop-Chop, and, swear to God, he's happy to see us, because before that, when I looked at him, he looked troubled. Then he sees us, and his troubles are over."

"His troubles are not over. How did this dinner come about?"

"Well, he says to Jonathan to make him a reservation at the Donovan's, then he looks at me and says, 'Are you hungry?' I said I could eat."

"Pearly Sue."

"Well, I could. I can always eat."

Fatigued, I sighed.

Pearly Sue continued, "He tells Jonathan to make it for two and takes Chop-Chop's leash and hands it to his driver, Salman, who looks fit to be tied. Something about *him* I don't like. But, here's the thing: Jonathan told me some very interesting stuff before the prince's limo came along."

"Like?"

"Talk got around to the homeless on the street and in the park." Lake was up on his elbow and I told Pearly Sue to hold on, I was merging the calls so Lake could listen in. Having done that, I said to Pearly Sue, "Who initiated talk about the homeless?"

"I did. I said I was raised in the country and where I come from people who didn't have homes found old, abandoned houses to squat in."

"Did you talk about Victor Cartaloma?"

"His name was never said by Jonathan or me."

"Was Cartaloma on the bench when you were talking to the doorman?"

"No, he wasn't, but there was someone in the park, just off the sidewalk, who was watching us. Gave me the creeps."

"Get a look at the person?"

"No, they stayed in the shadows. Jonathan, a really nice man, said for me to watch myself, being a girl alone and with just a small dog for company. That's when he said there were prying eyes just looking to get a girl alone. Then he said, 'There's a man during the day sits on a bench and watches people coming and going out of this building. He says the residents pay him good tip money to watch what's going on in the neighborhood, even though the building had good security for the rich and famous. I told him I'd noticed the man on the bench myself and asked how long he'd been hanging out there. He said about two weeks. He never leaves the bench, he said, until four in the afternoon. Just picks up his stuff and walks away."

I said, "That would square with Cartaloma meeting you at four thirty today."

"It means," said Lake, "that he lives close by—to have changed clothing so quickly."

"That's what I thought, too," Pearly Sue said. "Did you know that bums have their territories? That's what Jonathan said, anyway. He thinks the man paid the former occupant off to get the bench."

"Now tell us about your dinner with the prince," I said, leery of what her tongue had given away.

"We had wine and steak and some awful coffee. The restaurant is small and not a tourist place. It's a converted brownstone with three floors. The prince eats at Donovan's regularly and has a table he prefers on the top floor. It's a table for four, but from the talk between him and the waiter, I guessed he eats by himself most of the time while he reads. Prince Husam told me it was nice to have someone to talk to for a change."

Reading my thoughts, Lake grinned. Husam probably had more than enough talking to at this dinner.

"What did you talk about?" I asked.

"Nothing about the case. I'm just a country girl filling in for my cousin in China while his dog sitter is sick. I played the role good."

"So what did *he* talk about?" I asked, hoping she'd drawn out some quality info.

"All the things we already know. He's from Saudi Arabia and is part of the royal family, which he said is half the country. He told me to call him Sammy, which is an American nickname for Husam. I asked if he was married and he said he was engaged to a princess in Saudi Arabia. Then he told me a story from the *Arabian Nights.*"

I was too tired to care, but I asked anyway. "Which one?"

"Well, it was one long one that blended into other ones, like Scheherazade does every night so she won't be killed the next morning. Honest to God, I thought we'd never leave that restaurant, but he's good with words and how he says them. He could be an actor." I had to agree and almost said so before Pearly Sue went on. "He compares himself to the stories, like in the haunting of Gherib, the outcast prince. He says the *Nights* is the earliest surviving literature that mentions ghouls."

"What's the story about?"

"Gherib is low-born but powerful in battle. In the end he fights off a family of ghouls, makes them slaves and converts them to Islam."

"I get it."

"Another one is 'The Ruined Man Who Became Rich Again Through a Dream.' The man is told in a dream to leave his city and . . .'"

"Pearly Sue it's late and I'm exhausted."

"Anyway, that's why I couldn't answer your calls. I knew it was you, but I waited for him to finish and then maybe say something important for us. But he didn't."

"Maybe he did," I said. "Maybe it's in the tale. I'll look it up."

CHAPTER TWENTY-FIVE

Since Husam had invited Pearly Sue to a Broadway show—an invitation prompted by her telling him she'd never seen one—she was not happy to leave New York in the morning for New Hampshire. "Two more days," she begged. "We're going to see *Wicked, the Untold Story of the Witches of Oz*. I *so* want to see it."

Lake said, "Dirk's got a man meeting you this afternoon. He'll call you and tell you where to meet him. Web gave him your number."

I thought I heard a growl from her throat. If she didn't like Lake so much, she probably would have told him to go straight to h-e-double l. I don't think I've ever heard Pearly Sue swear.

"Lake is right," I said. "We've yet to vet Victor Cartaloma. I don't much like what I'm hearing from the doorman."

"I don't think I know enough to judge him yet," Pearly Sue said. "Jonathan might be building up worry so he can get more tip money."

"Pearly Sue, that's probably unfair. You're not being professional."

"I—will—go—to—New—Hampshire. Where?"

"Woodstock."

"*The* Woodstock?"

Forget *Witches*, it's *the* Woodstock. But I had to tell her, "That Woodstock was in New York."

"Bother."

"First thing in the morning, call the dog sitter and tell him you need to leave New York. Walk Chop-Chop and tell the day doorman that Chop-Chop's regular sitter is well enough to take over. Don't go to the statue. Wait and see if Cartaloma returns to his bench, then tell him to call me. If he doesn't show an hour after he normally does, get out of there."

"Got it," she said.

So few words.

"Web will be emailing you photos of Thomas Page, Reeve Cresley and her daughter, Shara. Also a photo of Dirk's operative."

"Thanks." *Curt but polite.*

"G'night, P.S. You got a lot to do in the morning."

"Night, boss," she said.

I looked at Lake. "This was one of the most tiring days of my otherwise good-natured life."

"You ready to get back some of that good nature with me? Or are you too tired to get to the best part of the evening?"

"Sorry to disappoint, but evening's gone. It's morning."

He perched on an elbow and twisted his lips. "There's been something missing in my life. Let's see what it's not. For one thing . . ."

"Food."

"Never go without food. It's the fuel that makes life sweet. Let's see what else?"

"Drama."

"The last few days I've been burdened by drama."

"Work."

"Two places at one time; can't beat it for hurrying life along."

"You couldn't mean me?"

"You've been here and there and everywhere, but where you should be, like right now." He leaned over me and flicked his tongue against the seam of my smiling lips. I let my arms flail back onto the pillow, relaxed and ready to be indulged. After the tongue-tease, he pressed his lips into a serious lip join. He eased a little and his tongue met mine in a mating of pleasure and anticipation. We've been together for years now, and he still thrills me with the gentle warmth of his body. Forgotten were my fatigue and the jitters. I put my arms around his, caressed him, lightly rubbing his back ribs. I loved savoring the bouquet of him in the delicate and pleasurable acts of love. Once begun, the rhythm never faltered.

It was after ten in the morning when Pearly Sue called. I was in the office logging in the latest on the investigation and feeling like my wheels were spinning. I put the call on conference in Web's office.

Pearly Sue was on the road, and in tears.

"Chop-Chop, I miss him. He's so sweet. Maybe . . . I've been thinking, maybe I'll get one just like him. He really is a good guard dog. He almost bit some man this morning that ran up and grabbed my arm."

"It wasn't Victor Cartaloma, was it—the man of disguises?"

"No, no disguise. He said that I'm going to ruin their security assignment, and that I should stop before I got pulled in to explain myself."

I mouthed "Husam," and Web turned to his computer.

"Did you see Cartaloma?"

"His bench was empty."

"How about the other street people?"

"They were on their benches. The night folks get up and leave and the day folks take over."

"What did this man look like?"

"He was tall and dressed like a runner—shorts, tee shirt, running shoes. He had on a baseball hat and headphones. He had a scraggly little beard, a billy-goat thing under his chin. After that I packed and the dog walker came. I left in a cab for the rental-car place at quarter to nine. I've just cleared the city."

"What did you say to the man who accosted you?"

"I told him to let go of my arm or I'd scream. I had raised my voice. People were staring and some kid on a bike stopped. The doorman came out and then the man dropped my arm and ran off. Poor Chop-Chop was barking and growling his little head off."

Lake called to say he'd tracked down the Houston field agent he'd worked with on the visa and passport murders that spanned Texas and Georgia. The state department, as usual, was reluctant to reveal where agents were posted, but, after vetting Lake, they divulged that David Davis was at the embassy in Indonesia and advised Lake to visit the website.

Lake said, "I now know everything I need to know about visas if I seek admission into the United States for tourism, business, education, medical treatment, etcetera. Davis's name was not listed among the embassy personnel on the site, not that I'd expected it to be, him being a secret agent and all. I've emailed the Information Resource Center in Jakarta and so far haven't gotten anything back. I asked that Special Agent David Davis email me on a secure hookup, but I'm not holding my breath since we're talking about the state department." It sounded like he gulped air to do just that—hold his breath. "Hang on, I have an incoming email." There was a pause, then Lake came back with an unpleasant sound coming from his nose or mouth. "It's a response to my email. It says, 'Please state the nature of your business with the above named individual.' Signed by the Public Diplomacy Officer in Charge. No name."

"That's it?"

"Yep. Dead end. How can I email that I'm quietly vetting one of their agents in New York? They'll think I'm a global bill collector. One thing they do for their diplomats is shield them from outside tribulations. I can't say it's a case I'm working because the paperwork would overload me. The result probably would be nil. Ergo, dead end."

"Web's got a message in to Paul Ardai. Interpol might be able to tell us something about Victor Cartaloma. I'm trying to reach Husam. Left message, no return call."

"Husam and the state department ought to get together. Say, want to accompany me to interview Janjak Petion? He's in a better mood and agreed to talk about his time with the Cresleys."

"I'd like that."

Chapter Twenty-Six

There was a happy atmosphere this morning in the Caribbean section of Beaver Ruin Road. It was a beautiful spring day and it seemed everyone grew azaleas, and had planted pink and white dogwoods. The cherry blossoms, though, tried to outdo every flower in the neighborhood. And the cock crowed twice, which heralded a welcome. At least I hoped.

I parked behind Lake's unmarked.

Giles Petion opened the door with a jerk. He looked anxious. He said, "We wish to cooperate. We are very sorry about yesterday. Janjak knows he did wrong at the cemetery."

Janjak sat on the sofa as if he were a potted plant. His eyes roamed over us as if we were going to water him before he sighed and hoisted himself up.

Giles said, "Janjak?"

Janjak extended his hand to Lake as he'd been instructed to. "I wish to thank you for your intervention. I have no appetite for spending time in your jails."

"Your grief was understandable," Lake said. "But your emotions got out of hand."

"That is true."

"I won't take up a lot of your time. Running off like you did makes you look guilty of something, particularly since you knew Prince Husam could identify you as his in-laws' gardener."

Giles Petion said, "Let's sit outside in the garden and have coffee."

Janjak was already in motion. We followed him from the front room through a tidy middle room that served as a dining room, with a cot in a corner. In the kitchen, the aroma of rich coffee took hold of my senses. The floor and appliances hadn't been updated since the sixties, but the stove and fridge were spotless in their new yellow paint. A windowsill held a floral extravaganza of orchids. They served as a curtain against the glass panes.

"Wish I could grow orchids," I said.

Janjak said, "They are easier to care for than you think."

"I do okay with African violets on my windowsill, but that's about it."

"You take the orchids outside in summer and put them under the boughs of the trees and they get enough humidity from the air to thrive."

I couldn't argue against Atlanta's humidity.

On the small brick patio, a round table was set with a floral cloth and napkins. Coffee accompaniments were already on the table. The small black woman who had been in the house during our first visit came out of the kitchen with a coffeepot of the old-fashioned, stove-top variety. A rich coffee aroma danced around her.

"This is Auntie," Janjak said. "She did for Mrs. Cresley in the house until her knees gave out."

We greeted her and got seated while I was thinking, *so here we had two people familiar with the Cresley home and inmates.* Could I see Janjak hiding in the study closet with a garrote, standing in wait for the chance to throttle Lowell Cresley, who managed to escape from rather large Janjak, only to be shot down when Auntie and Mrs. Cresley heard the noise and came running? Then one or the other shot Donna for safety's sake? *I don't know . . . People can be so deceptive.*

Giles poured coffee and said, "Have you tasted our Haitian Bleu?"

Lake and I said that we hadn't.

"First taste, then we talk."

The coffee was unlike any I'd experienced. The velvet liquid slid down my throat. It was sweetish and less acidic than coffees I'd brewed and been served in fine coffee shops, and actually tasted like dark chocolate, but maybe that was my imagination. Auntie had brewed it just right. It was neither too hot, nor too cool. Coffee should always taste like this. "Where can I buy this coffee?" I asked.

"Online," Janjak said. "And certain stores now."

Auntie brought out pastries. Giles put an almond-covered one on his plate. Lake helped himself to a cinnamon and ginger bun. He ate a bite and said, "Delicious," and bit into it again.

Janjak fidgeted. He was for getting on with the inevitable interview while Giles played the patient host.

Lake said, "I wish we could sit here and enjoy this meal longer, but I guess we need to get to the reason we're here." He laid his bun on the plate. A sound came from his throat. "It's a sad thing. A good deed, solicited by you, Janjak, of Donna Cresley, ending with your niece dying."

Janjak's chin nearly touched his chest while he shook his head. Then he looked at Lake with large, sad eyes. "I went to Mrs. Cresley when our Astryd was diagnosed by an American doctor in Haiti after the hurricane. He had come to assist doctors from around the world with the sick and dying. Our doctors were overwhelmed by the storm."

"I understand," Lake said, sipping coffee from a delicate cup. "Were you living in Haiti at the time?"

"No, I lived in the United States. I have a visa to work here."

"But, you went back to your homeland when the hurricane struck."

"That is true. I am skilled in hardscape landscaping and gardening. I work with brick and mortar. As such I could help my people rebuild after the flooding."

"Do you use ash in either hardscape or gardening, like for balancing the pH of acidic soils?"

"When we can get it. We burn wood and dung in our cook stoves and use the char as a soil conditioner."

Lake asked, "When did you learn of your niece's heart problem?"

"I know of her problem since her birth, but over time she did not respond to treatments in our country. She was getting worse."

"So you came back to the United States and appealed to Mrs. Cresley."

"Yes, I did, sorry to say."

"It's not your fault or Mrs. Cresley's," Lake said. "How long did you work for the Cresleys?"

"Ten years, on and off, at their old house off East Paces Ferry Road."

"You say 'on and off.' What's that mean?"

"I also worked for a golf course, and when they restructured their landscaping, I told Dr. Cresley that the money was too good to pass up."

"And what did he say?"

"He was angry, as if he owned me."

Auntie piped up in her soft patois. "I had had enough of him. My knees were not so good and I wanted to go home."

"Was that before or after the hurricane?"

"I was there for the hurricane. I come here with little Astryd, for her surgery. Her father and brother got killed in the hurricane. We was all she had."

This story was getting sadder.

I asked Auntie, "What was it like working with Mrs. Cresley?"

"She was a confused soul. She hid herself in her good works until . . ."

"Until what?" I asked.

Auntie, I suspected, was a wise woman, maybe even a *mambo*.

She said, "I do not speak ill of those who I have removed from my protection and favor. They, through their acts, get punished."

"I don't understand," Lake said.

Auntie smiled at something she saw inside herself. "I spoke to the ancestors and my *loa* for her. But she did not heed; she did not tie her body and soul together so that she could love. She was not capable of *kanga*. She did not love."

"Who did she not love?"

"Her daughter's daughter. She turned her back on her family. Your family makes you whole and rids your body and spirit of dishonor."

"Please," Lake said gently, "explain her dishonor."

"I cannot do that. I speak not ill now that she is dead, but I speak with my *loa* that when her soul leaves its resting place, she finds peace wherever her spirit takes her."

Janjak said, "She will find no peace. Neither will her husband. She knew her husband was no good. He wanted money and jezebels, and drink."

"Someone in her family should call out to her," Auntie said. "It will do no good if that man intrudes upon her afterlife."

"Auntie," Giles warned.

"I say no more."

"Please do," I said. "Who is *that man* that you speak of?"

Auntie ruffled her narrow shoulders. "I cannot say."

"Is it Prince Husam, Reeve's husband?"

"He would never be an ancestor. He was not family. He did not worship the deities. He would burn us and curse our ancestors."

Lake said, "What we want here is information—what you can tell us about two people who were murdered, about other people in their lives. I'm not saying they are murderers but they could give us the information that would allow us to find and punish those who have committed the murders. We ask, Miss Dru and I, that you tell us all you know about these people."

Janjak said, "Mrs. Cresley was kind to Auntie. She accepted *Vodou* and listened to Auntie's advice." He looked at his aunt. "But Dr. Cresley, he was not so kind. He worked me like his mule. Always changing the garden. Changing for the sake of changing, not improving. I built beds for the roses. They had to be moved. Then they had to be rebuilt back where they were. Changes always came when he was drinking."

"Did he pay well?"

"That's why he worked me so hard; to get his money's worth."

"When did you finally leave the Cresleys?"

"Right after the hurricane came. He wanted me to move them into their fancy new community, a place where I would have no work."

"Did you have misgivings about leaving your niece's care in the hands of Dr. Cresley?"

"I did not like the man, but he was the best in the city, everyone said."

"Did you later learn that he had settled a multi-million-dollar lawsuit over a botched operation?"

"Yes, but that information had not been in the newspapers or on the television. Why not? The media reports on movie stars. They should instead warn us about evil men like Dr. Cresley."

"How did it come about—your asking Mrs. Cresley to intervene on your niece's behalf?"

Janjak thought a moment. "I wrote to her and she answered right away, inviting us to come for a consultation. I got a medical visa for Astryd and we went to their new home. Mrs. Cresley had a group of women from her clubs there. I felt awkward but Astryd was well enough to eat her food and talk to some of the ladies. They took pictures. The ladies thought Mrs. Cresley was an angel to get Astryd the medical help she needed at no cost to us, except for the hospital charges. We were told the hospital charges would be taken care of by one of her charity agencies. Next day we went to the hospital for tests with Dr. Cresley's associates."

"Did you visit with the doctor?"

"I never saw him at the hospital until the morning of the surgery. I didn't particularly care because I never liked the man. He had a skill that we needed and that was the reason we were there."

"How long until the surgery?"

"It was scheduled a week later. Then it was put off for two weeks. Finally the day came. That's when I saw Dr. Cresley."

"How well did you know Reeve Cresley?"

"Miss Cresley was in schools and away most of the time."

Auntie chimed in, "She wouldn't let me wait on her."

"Good for Reeve," I said.

"A good girl," she murmured. "Her mother dishonored her. A mother should never bring a man love into her household."

Lake and I exchanged glances. Auntie may have been a spiritual mambo, but she was also human. She had the need to tell us about Donna Cresley's lover.

"Did Reeve Cresley know about this man love?" I asked.

"Once I heard them arguing. Miss Reeve was in a rage over the man."

"Who was he? What was his name?"

"I do not know, but the daughter, she knows. She was furious, like a jealous woman. The *loas* that were in the house that day were the wicked ones. I put my hands over my ears and went into my room. I did not want them to invade my soul."

"Were Donna Cresley and this man lovers?"

Auntie looked as if she might demur. "I do not know, but it is what I think. I see with my eyes and my soul and through my *loa* and know that she was not true to her husband."

"But you don't know this man's name?"

"It was never said. I do not read English. I do not listen at doors. But I know."

"Are you aware that Reeve has disappeared with her daughter, Shara?"

"We have recently learned that," Janjak said.

"How did Reeve get along with her father?"

Janjak shrugged. "They did not get along. They argued. Miss Reeve told her father to wake up and smell the coffee."

"No love tied those souls," Auntie said.

That's often the case with a couple of egoists, I thought.

"What was their reaction when Reeve brought a Saudi Arabian prince home?"

"There was a lot of shouting when he wasn't around," Auntie said. "The doctor tell the missus that he would not have a damned Arab in his home."

Janjak said, "It wasn't a happy time. Then the baby came."

Auntie said, "They hated the baby. They hated the foreigner. They hated everyone. They could not tie their bodies and souls together."

"Did you know Thomas Page?"

"Yes," Janjak said. "He came around a few times and Dr. Cresley treated him like he was the prince, not the other man."

"Were you ever in the presence of Yasmin Saliba, the prince's sister, or anyone from Saudi Arabia?"

"If so, I cannot remember," Janjak said.

With Yasmin's ego and behavior, he would have remembered. "Do you have any idea who could have hated the Cresleys enough to kill them in cold blood?"

Giles, Janjak and Auntie shook their heads slowly, side to side.

Lake brought out photographs and handed them to Janjak. "Look at these and tell me if you recognize anyone."

Janjak leafed through them and shook his head. "No one." He handed them to Giles.

Giles shook his head after looking at them. He handed them to Auntie.

"Where would Reeve have taken Shara?" I asked.

"She loved the sea," Auntie said, looking intently at a particular photograph, although I couldn't tell whose it was from across the table.

"Who is that you're looking at?" I asked her.

She shuffled it into the others. "I do not know."

I couldn't persuade her to let me look at the photo because, she said, "I do not accuse so lightly."

I tried until she started reciting in spirit language, then I gave up. I couldn't even get a sense of where in the stack she'd stuck the photo.

Our gracious host, Giles, led us through the house and bid us good luck and farewell. I know he hoped never to see us again.

"Did you see who was in the photo that interested Auntie?"

"No," Lake said.

"I still don't like Janjak for the murders."

He didn't respond.

Chapter Twenty-Seven

I drove behind Lake. It was lunch time. I wasn't that hungry since I had eaten one of Auntie's cloying sugar buns, but I longed to wash the taste from my mouth. Predictably, Lake called and asked if I had a restaurant preference. "Dixie's," I said. "Tuna salad and a Coke."

Lake said, "I'll sacrifice my craving for a steak burger."

I scooted onto a stool next to Lake at the counter. Dixie's is a long narrow diner, an extension of a gas station convenience store. It's my favorite donut and sandwich eatery. The donuts are fried fresh and the sandwiches are hand made. Besides, I needed gas.

I asked, "What do you think we got back there?"

"Besides the obvious?"

"Which is?"

"That they had a score to settle with Dr. and Mrs. Cresley. Janjak's hands had ground-in ash beneath his skin."

"You think Janjak and Auntie plotted their murders?"

"I've been right before."

"Call the media," I said. "Speaking of calling, time to check in with the Webdog."

He hadn't called and that was odd, except that I left him setting himself a frantic pace in front of his computers. I'd told him that if the mysterious DSS agent, Victor Cartaloma, called to find out where I could call him back.

I laid aside my tuna sandwich and called Web.

"No word from Victor Cartaloma," he said. "Paul Ardai called and knows only that Victor Cartaloma was at the Baghdad embassy and was transferred out. There were, he said, some problems with embassy staffers and drugs, but that's not unusual in foreign countries. He said he'd look into it further and get back in touch."

Paul told Web that there was a piece in a French magazine about the turmoil in the Saudi royal family over succession. "Seems the liberal and conservative factions are at war now that the king is about to die. One of the king's many sons told the French reporter 'The liberals want to stay in power and turn us into a western puppet. We want a king that is true to our religious and cultural beliefs.' "

Since Dixie's was ten minutes from Killarney, I rode with Lake. Lake was indulging my inquisitiveness. I wanted information from Carl Langford, like the names of visitors of the male persuasion, come to see Donna Cresley. God knows Atlanta had enough hotels and motels for lovers to while away a lazy afternoon, but, according to her former housekeeper, Auntie, she had entertained at least one man love at her home.

Sonny, at the gate, informed us that Mr. Langford had a lunch meeting with the homeowners' association at the clubhouse. He hesitated about letting us in, something wise I thought.

Lake said, "Mr. Langford said to contact him anytime, anywhere and that's what we're doing, so please let him know we're at the gate."

Not five minutes later, the security car stopped behind the gate. Langford got out. He wore a white shirt, dark suit with a red tie and highly polished, black shoes. He'd met the wealthy landowners in style.

Langford waved us in and swung his arm to where we should

park. We got out and walked toward him. His hazel eyes flashed his uncertainty when he held out his hand. Since it was sunny, sunglasses might have hidden his anxiety. "Hello, detectives."

"Good afternoon," Lake said. "A few questions."

"Let's go to my office."

"Not going to take that long," Lake said. "I know you have a meeting. Can't keep the association people waiting. Security's a big thing with them."

"Sure is," Langford said. "What more can I tell you?"

"Something's come up about the visitors to the Cresley household. I thought maybe you could shed some light on those coming and going."

Langford looked puzzled. "How?"

"Well, if you were living in midtown, you might see a different group of visitors than here in this upper-crust community. There you'd see young people, partying maybe, couples holding hands, gays schmoozing, entrepreneurs with that going-places attitude, older cars, tattoos, people coming home drunk—you get the picture."

"Sure. Not much partying here. Haven't spotted a tattooed individual except for the help. The residents are pretty staid. These people—most are retired now. They made plenty of money and a lot of them want to keep it."

"Where do they go in the evenings?"

By his expression, Langford certainly didn't know where this was going. I wondered if Lake did.

"Like I told you before, I don't man the gates, but I monitor them live and I see the videos. Some of our residents dress up and go out for dinner; others are casual. Some leave looking like they're dressed for a society event or the opera or the ballet. I know a few couples get together and go to the ballet. Is that what you're after?"

"You got it. Where did the Cresleys go when they had a night out?"

"She had her charities and there were events. She went to a lot of charity balls."

"With Lowell, her husband?"

"Not always. He was on call sometimes, at the hospital."

Lake gave him a curious glance that said, *How do you know he was on call?*

Langford hurried into speech. "She was always friendly with the guards. She'd tell them 'I'm baching it tonight. Lowell's on call.' That's what I'd hear on the videos."

"Where did she go during the day?"

"She was always on the run with her work. She was dedicated to childhood education. Lots of charities involving children."

Yet she seemed to hate her grandchild.

"Luncheons?" I asked, and he looked at me like he'd just realized I was there.

"Those, too. Luncheons go with charity work."

"I learned sometimes she had her committees here."

"She'd tell Sonny, or whoever was on duty at the gate, who to let in. And Sonny would advise them where to park so they didn't block the streets. They're narrow."

"Now," Lake began, "I'm going to ask a delicate question and I want a candid answer. I know your job is to keep confidentiality as well as to protect the residents." Langford nodded. "So, that being said, did Donna have male company, day or night?"

Langford didn't know if he should answer or slug Lake. "How would I . . ."

"You *are* the head of *security.*"

"I'm—no—I know of—I know what you're getting at. Mrs. Cresley was a faithful wife as far as I know."

Lake's nod indicated he understood. "I asked because there

are those who say that both Cresleys had affairs. We know about his affair. What can you tell me about that?"

"I don't know of an affair." He squinted against the sun that had popped over the guard house. "That I can recall, no one on the gate let a woman in when he was home alone. You can bet a woman visitor would cause talk. I caution the guards not to gossip, but you can't keep a person from talking. The doctor, he worked late, came home at all hours, went out of town. If he had someone, that would be when he was with her. But Mrs. Cresley, I can't believe she would have affairs. Maybe I'm wrong, but you just don't expect that in a high-society woman, do you?"

Lake said, "It happens."

When Lake paused, Langford jumped at the chance. "Well, I haven't seen or heard anything of that nature."

"You're the eyes and ears of this community. You would know—or not know." Lake turned to go, then turned back. "Thanks, you've helped."

We left Langford with a look of wonder on his face, like *How the hell did I help?*

I didn't have to ask Web to get me a list of Donna Cresley's charities. It was already compiled, along with a list of her longtime friends. My thought was that she might confide in one or two about this man love thing that Auntie brought up. I wondered about her divined knowledge. On the other hand, women can intuit by a word or glance, so I suspect Auntie was right. It seems everyone in the case had an unfaithful bent. Lowell. Donna. Reeve. Husam. Thomas Page. That meant a lot of human entanglements to journey through. The charity list was long, but not necessarily for a society woman. I thought I'd start with the charity that brought Astryd and Auntie to America—Atlanta Med-Air Transport Foundation.

Their website had a contact person and number. I explained in my email the purpose of my call, which was an investigation into the deaths of Dr. and Mrs. Cresley and events leading up to the murders. I gave the contact woman Portia's telephone number and Lake's at the APD, lest she suspect me of being a reporter.

Half an hour later, an Adele Russell called. She told me she'd talked to Portia Devon; that she'd known her from a custody case a couple of years back. She invited me to her house, located off Pharr Road. It was a small cottage, probably built in the 1940s, as were many off that street that were now little shops selling goods and services—flowers, Christmas ornaments, makeup, wine and cheese, nail and hair. All those cute little cottages sat on some of the priciest real estate in Atlanta. I read a piece in the *Buckhead Community Digest* a few years back that the residents-turned-shopkeepers were land-poor. No cash money, especially when it came to taxes. There was even a growing movement to tear out the trendy bars on Pharr Road and environs and build high-rise office buildings, hotels, condominiums and skyline restaurants. I hated to see the old Buckhead go, but, on the other hand, those trendy bars that attracted the metro hustlers and politicians——if there was any difference—had given way to a raucous element that howled and stomped the night away.

Which reminded me that Yasmin might still be in the city and holed up in the Atlanta Arms. There were a few things I wanted to talk to Yasmin about, but she apparently didn't want to talk to me.

When Adele Russell opened the door, I was hit with the smell of coffee and a rueful smile.

After sitting and thanking her, I went over the reason for my visit. She sniffed back emotion, maybe even tears, and said, "It's all so damned awful. Donna got that little girl here. We were so happy to be helping a victim from an impoverished nation. It's god-awful to have a poor nation right off our shores."

I made some encouraging murmurs and she continued.

"That the surgery wasn't successful made us all feel terrible. But that's medicine. As Donna said, her husband was a physician not a magician. Then, of course, we later learned—after his death—we had no idea that he was at fault—*if* he was at fault. You know the Lord works in mysterious ways. He had his own plan for the little girl."

I said, "When was the last time you spoke with Mrs. Cresley?"

"Well, I saw her at church. Oh, my, that was the Sunday before she . . ."

"How did she seem?"

"We just said hello, but I thought she didn't look well. After I heard, I knew why. Her daughter and granddaughter had disappeared. Of course, I learned this after she . . ."

"Mrs. Cresley was going through some trying times," I said. "I was asked by Prince Husam, her son-in-law, and Portia Devon, the judge, to look into her missing daughter and granddaughter. I'd just begun when the Cresleys were murdered. I have an idea that there is a connection and am throwing a net far and wide. I know that the Petions were very angry and planned to sue the estate. There was another problem surgery for Dr. Cresley, probably one that you don't know about."

"Oh, I do. Donna was so terribly upset about that. They were sued, you know. Not many people know that, but Donna and I are good friends."

"She confided a lot?"

"Yes, we were very good friends, from school days."

"Did she tell you anything, give you any hint, that she thought their lives were in danger?"

"No, just like I said, she didn't look happy the last time I saw her. I thought maybe something happened between him and her."

"By him, you mean Dr. Cresley?"

"Well, yes. She had been at her wits' end and then . . ."

"What?"

"You probably found this out, but he was a womanizer."

"We did."

"He took this Heidi woman whenever he went to conventions, especially if they were in Europe or Hawaii."

"Did Mrs. Cresley want a divorce?"

"Oh, no, Catholic and all."

"The Heidi woman was under the impression Cresley was going to leave Donna and marry her."

"Ha. Don't they all believe that crapola. He was a crass egomaniac. I never blamed Donna for her affairs."

"You knew about them?"

"A couple. The men—her being wanted again—put a glow in her eyes and happiness on her face."

"I know you don't want to sic me onto someone and get them subject to police interest, but if you would tell me . . ."

"I talked to one of them before I called you. He flies our planes. He ended with her last year, but he said I could say his name, because, one way or another, you people would find out. He knew he wasn't the only one, but he still liked her a lot. She was a good woman with a bad life."

"His name, please."

"Sean Alvarez. I can give you his telephone number."

"Lieutenant Lake with the Atlanta Police Department will probably be getting in touch with him. Do you know any of her other—lovers?" I almost said man loves.

She hesitated, probably to lie. "Not by name, but I know she had them. She was attractive and enjoyed the company of men. Her life as a doctor's wife was unsatisfactory. Her husband was

225

an ass and a drunk, but she made the best of it. Heidi was pressing Lowell for a divorce to marry her. Why she would want a philanderer is beyond my comprehension. But you can bet, somewhere in all this, someone they knew killed them."

I thought about this. Had that phrase been in the newspapers: that *Someone they knew killed them*? I didn't remember, but it was a good assumption. "You think the Cresleys were murdered over their affairs?"

"You take lust and add it to hate and despair, and yes . . ."

"What about the Haitians? Or the other botched surgery?"

"I knew the girl's uncle from their Paces Ferry house. He worked for the Cresleys. He was a hothead. I could see him seethe when Lowell told him to do something over." She paused. "But, you know, I don't think so. When he wasn't mad at Lowell, he was a nice man."

As if nice men (on the outside) didn't commit murder, for cause or no cause. *Why was I trying to convince myself Janjak had killed them? Because when I found out that he did, I wouldn't feel so let down.*

That was it for Adele. I thanked her, wished her mission well and left thinking she watched too many daytime soaps when she wasn't doing good charity work for the transport foundation.

I was about to call Lake when my cell played Bach.

"Dru," came the voice. "Oh, Dru."

"What, Pearly Sue?"

"There's nobody here. Just a pair of goats."

CHAPTER TWENTY-EIGHT

"Where is Johnson, Dirk's man from Boston?"

Pearly Sue answered, "He never called. I came to the house thinking he'd meet me here because we missed each other and we both know that the house was Page's. I parked at the top of the driveway for fifteen minutes, that's half an hour later than we were to meet up. When he didn't come, I thought maybe he was waiting up the driveway, but there's nobody here but a couple of goats."

Webdog turned to get in touch with Dirk's. I said to Pearly Sue, "Give me the layout."

"I'll do better. I'm getting the camcorder ready to show you. I'll retrace my steps and bring you up to date."

"Do that."

"Call you back."

I called Lake to ask if he could come look at streaming videos from Pearly Sue and gave him a summary of my visit with Adele. I also gave him Sean Alvarez's name and that he flew out of Charlie Brown Airport.

Lake said, "Everybody screwing everybody—literally and figuratively. It's like a tale out of 'Life Styles of the Rich and Famous.' "

"And the *Arabian Nights.*"

"See you in ten."

Web stuck his head in my door. "Dirk's hasn't heard from Johnson. They'll try him. Pearly Sue's hooked up to stream to the computer. Or we could watch on the big HDTV."

My cam was modified by Webdog for two-way audio. It is, like all our electronics, network certified, something Web can explain better than me. The camcorder recordings are data files that allow for the video to be seen directly on the computer by using a memory card in the Mac. It can also stream to my phone or a high-def television.

"Let's hang on until Lake gets here. Make sure we're set to get the video and recording on backup, too." I can't help but worry if something happened to the camcorder, all would be lost.

"If Pearly Sue dumps it in a pond, we're okay," Web said.

I rubbed my crossed arms. "This case—I need more momentum, progress." I was thinking I should be where Pearly Sue was.

I looked up at Web. "Sit."

He turned a straight-back chair around, straddled it and rested his arms on the back, looking ready to help me with the momentum and progress.

I said, "I think Thomas Page is meeting up with Reeve Cresley, or he's intending to. Has he been using his credit card?"

"Dirk's says not since he landed in New York and rented a car."

"He's got himself a kick phone."

"Makes sense. No monthly plan, all cash."

"I'm thinking Page and Reeve have arranged to get in touch in case of emergency. He'd know her cell number. And she his, but they wouldn't use them because of tracking."

"No problem with Fishnet."

"Even if she's got a kick, too?"

"Little more work. All cell phones have to go through a cell tower, even so-called untraceables. You're hiding, but still putting yourself out there on a cell phone; we can set up a fake cell

228

tower to find your number and your location."

"Is the law still on our side?"

"There's a couple of legal challenges, but they will come down in our favor."

Our, meaning PIs and other snoops.

Web explained his rationale. "A fake cell tower is a tracking device, no different than you or me hoofing after a walking, breathing subject. Sure, it scoops in all the numbers in the target area at the time the cell phone is used, but that's no different than when you're following a subject. You see people walking down the same streets as your subject and you might hear their conversations. You might see where they go, even. Fishnet and like devices don't record text messages or emails or listen in. They operate legally because the tracker purges the numbers and locations that don't pertain to his investigation. Since there's no confidential information gathered, there's no invasion of privacy of the others caught in the net."

"Oh, these fine lines in our business." I heard the office door open. "That's Lake. We won't discuss this with him. He's all court orders and subpoenas."

"Aren't you glad you're a PI?"

We met Lake in the hall, walking toward my office.

"Hey, Lieutenant," Web said. "Pearly Sue's ready to stream."

We got settled around the large monitor and Pearly Sue's voice came on clearly. She was in her rental car. "This here's the Daniel Webster Highway in Woodstock, also known as Main Street," she said. I noticed there were no shadows, therefore no sun. It was late in the day. Pearly Sue said, "I'm staying at the Woodstock Manor, a bed and breakfast that had room for me. Cute place with picnic tables by the Pemi River."

Lake rolled his eyes and took his fedora off his knee. He settled back like Pearly Sue was about to take us on a guided tour of the town's wonders.

I said, "Pearly Sue. We get the drift."

She said, "Thought you'd want to get a good look at where I'm at." The camcorder wavered a bit. "It's cloudy here, about to rain."

Lake said, "Johnson ever call?"

"Nope. Maybe he ran into cell-service problems. I'm good, though."

"Go on."

"So, here I'm turning off the main drag heading for the country. You can see by the trees and no houses that the country comes upon you quick after the town ends. This frontage road goes up the mountains where they ski in the winter. But since it's spring, the leaves are coming out. Here now I'm turning into the gravel lane that leads to the Anita Page Horne place."

Pearly Sue got out of the car and held the cam more steadily as it roamed over the house and grounds. The house was a narrow, three-story with a two-story L attachment. She explained, "The longer side of the L is a barn. See here." She panned over the long barn, let the lens slide away until I saw her fumble the door open. I was about to stop her, but she had dashed inside, leaving the door wide open.

She said, "We come to a garage part first. See the small tractor and mower? Wait, I'm slowing the shutter in this low-light environment." Lake told her that the images were better. She continued, "Along the sides and back are pegboards with tools and gardening equipment. You can see it's stuff you'd find in a garage and a barn, but there's no animals, except I spotted a rat when I first came in here. You'd think they'd have cats. We do at home. Keeps the rats away."

Web smiled. No hurrying Pearly Sue.

She walked through a wide door that showed three stalls with mangers. "Over there's a tack room," she said. "Got a bunch of ratty halters and saddles and stuff."

"That's fine, Pearly Sue," I said. "We get the picture."

"There's a ladder to climb up into the hay loft."

"Don't," Lake said. "Hay's hay."

I would have to instruct Pearly Sue about going into ostensibly vacant buildings by herself. She had so much to learn, and I'm not the best teacher. I've come to expect that adults should sense danger. Maybe Pearly Sue hadn't sensed any when she'd been here earlier. She had so many superior qualities given her by country life that, until I saw the risk she was taking, I didn't anticipate her walking into it.

Outside again, she panned the clapboard house. It had been painted white, but successive rains streaked it gray. I guessed it had been built in the late 1800s. It reminded me of a French village house like you see in the north of France. The style had become typically New Englander, though. The third story would be a small attic room. The roof was steep to allow snow to slide off. Like most casement windows, those on this house were soulless eyes. Definitely unlived in.

Pearly Sue said, "I want you to see something." She walked back toward the barn and around it to a chicken-wire fence. Two goats came up *baa*-ing. "Poor fellows," Pearly Sue said, "they're left to starve."

Web said, "Pearly Sue, country girl that you are, you should know that goats will be the last things in this world to starve. They'll eat anything. Those aren't near as skinny as you."

The cam lens passed the goats, a garden gone to seed, a line of grape vines, to slow on a rise in the land that blended into a ridge, which led into a forest of oaks and maples and evergreens. Through the tree trunks and scarce foliage, I could make out a road running parallel above the house, barn and surrounding grounds. The Horne place was a homestead in a small valley.

Pearly Sue walked us around the outside of the house. Three of the four sides were windows. Then I saw that the entrance was off the gravel drive and parking area, tucked in a corner near the barn extension.

Pearly Sue's hand was on the door.

"Wait," Lake said. "Have you been in there?"

"Ah, yes, sir. It was empty."

"Was it locked the first time you opened the door?"

"No, sir. It was unlocked."

"You went in anyway?"

She said, "I called out. Nobody answered."

"And you're sure no one was expecting you?"

She seemed stymied by this for a moment. "I don't understand what you're asking."

"On the way to this house, did you stop and ask directions, say at a convenience store or gas station?"

"I had to get gas. Yes. I did ask if the Anita Page Horne place was very far."

"Your GPS would have told you that."

"I was being polite. He asked me if I was just passing through and I said I was here for a visit."

"Your discussion gave someone a head's-up."

"Gosh, I thought I was to come here and *find* Mr. Page."

Lake said, "You *and* Johnson were to find Mr. Page. You did, and you have now learned that he likely did not want to be found."

Pearly Sue had turned the camera on her own face to glare at Lake. "I figured that out, Lieutenant Lake."

While Lake chastised Pearly Sue—who at first seemed reprimanded before she firmed her spine and defended her actions—I told Web to install his fake tower to the 603 area code towers. That way, whenever Page's prepaid kick phone dialed out, it would swim with many numbers into Web's fishnet in the suspect area code. With Atlanta's many cell towers, assuming Reeve to be in that city, Web would then pinpoint the search by latitude and longitude embedded in the numbers.

Lake was saying, "P.S., don't take this . . ."

A shot echoed through the valley.

I gasped and shouted, "Get down!"

"Above the barn!" Pearly Sue shouted while scrambling behind her car. "Didn't hit nothing!"

"Where did it come from?" Lake shouted.

"Up the hills. There's a road. That shot never came near," she called, jumping up and running for the house door.

"Pearly Sue!" Lake called. "No!"

The cam recorded as she moved into the house, across pine-board floors.

"Pearly Sue," Lake called. "Is there a door from the house into the barn?"

"Yes," she said. "I'm heading for it."

In the garage part of the barn, she sped past an old Mercedes-Benz from the 1950s. My parents had one like it in a peculiar shade of red. She ducked behind the car. I anticipated more shots; but none came through the recorder. Pearly Sue scooted past a refrigerator, a relic from the 1950s, too. Next to it, she panned the cam to a gun rack. A rifle lay across the set of pegs.

"An old Winchester rimfire," Lake said.

Pearly Sue dashed to the back wall. There was a bench and drawers beneath the rack. She pulled open the top drawer. "Twenty-two's, hallelujah!"

I recalled the photo of Pearly Sue on her desk, a shotgun cracked over her shoulder.

"You go, girl," I said.

Lake, the spoiler, said, "P.S., that gun probably hasn't been cleaned or oiled in a long time. Be careful of backfire."

"Guns don't backfire, Lieutenant. They blow up."

Yikes, a gun expert corrected by a girl.

"I know that. I was using a common misnomer so you would

know what I meant."

Apparently Lake hadn't been in Pearly Sue's office to see her collection of gun-toting, snake-handling photos.

Lake was saying, "Check for dirt or carbon buildup in the chamber. Check for a crack in the chamber and an obstruction in the barrel. It hasn't been cased, so it could have rust. Make sure the bolt seats."

"Rimfire's core doesn't get nasty." Then Pearly Sue straightened, alert. "I hear a motor."

Pearly Sue laid aside the cam and said that she was checking the barrel and loading the shell into the chamber. She picked up the cam and it flashed across a table saw and a chain pulley that dangled from the ceiling.

"I hear yelling," Pearly Sue said.

"What kind of yelling?" Lake asked.

"A man yelling for me to come out."

"Careful, Pearly Sue."

She went to an outside door and cracked it. "Who's there?" she called, her southern drawl accentuated.

"Show yourself," the man called back.

"I have a gun," she said.

"So do I."

"What do you want?"

"I want you out of there, and explain yourself."

I breathed out. He didn't sound like a serial killer. I said quietly, but loud enough for Pearly Sue to hear, "Make him throw his gun down."

"Will do," she whispered back. She called to him, "I'll come out when you put your gun down."

"I'm doing it. I just wanted to get your attention, trespassing like you did."

"I'm here to see Mr. Page. Who are you?"

"I'm looking after his house."

"Why did you shoot."

"I told you, to get your nose out of our business. First you went in the house, then you left and then you came back. You just nosy or you selling real estate?"

"I'm coming out, but I'm holding the gun. It's loaded."

"Likely to get hit by blow-by, before hitting me."

She opened the door wide by pushing with her foot. I could see her leg when she brought the cam down. I also saw the long rifle barrel. Then the camcorder flashed to the man's face. Because of the shadows, his age was indeterminate, but he was not old according to his physique, which was muscular and not fat. He had a scratchy beard that was reddish. It looked like he hadn't shaved in a week. Wearing a camo jacket and hunter's cap, he approached her car. Pearly Sue pointed the cam at the gun on the ground, a newer model hunting rifle than the Winchester. The man stepped closer, leaned, reached.

In that instant I saw something—not sure what. Lake took out his cell phone just as it began to mist in New Hampshire.

Back to the cam action, Pearly Sue had stepped back. "Don't come closer."

The man straightened and held out a hand. "You give me that camera or I'll call the sheriff. You can't come on people's property and start filming it. It's illegal. You're trespassing."

"This is my protection. The video is streaming to people in Atlanta."

"I'm not going to hurt you. If I wanted to I wouldn't have fired over the roof."

"I'm here to see Mr. Page. Is he in the woods up there where you shot from?"

"That's none of your business."

"Is he in Woodstock?"

"That's none of your business. That's all I'm saying, so get in your car and leave, and if you leave with that rifle I'll have the

"I don't steal guns. Where's Mr. Page?"

"I told you before, that's none of your business."

"My name's Pearly Sue Ellis. What's yours?"

"That's none of your business, either."

"I'm from Atlanta, here to speak to Mr. Page."

"If he wants to talk to you he'll find you."

"When will he be here?"

"Who says he will?"

She had the cam in one hand, and, whenever she moved it slightly, I saw the barrel of the rifle she carried in the other hand. The cam focused on the man, who stood near the trunk of her car. I couldn't see the gun, but knew she didn't toss it. I looked at Lake; his features creased with alarm. I said to him softly, "I've never shot a rifle with one hand but if anyone can, it's her."

Pearly Sue said to the man, "Step back from my car." He took three steps back. "More." He moved away. She said, "I'll leave the gun at the top of the driveway, against the fence post. Tell Mr. Page I was here."

I didn't see him on the screen, but he said, "Get going."

"You got a good memory, I'll say my phone numbers."

"That's all right. We can find you."

She walked cautiously toward the car. "You're not even going to tell me your name?"

"That's right, I'm not."

"Well," Pearly Sue said, stepping to the driver side of the car, apparently holding the rifle as the camera panned across the car. "I'll wait for Mr. Page's call. Tell him it's important. He knows my boss. She's watching us now."

"Good for her," he said, evidently amused. "Don't speed. There's a trap up the road."

She leveled the camera at him and when he raised his arm,

236

thus parting the sides of his jacket, I signaled Lake. He nodded.

I don't know what she did with the cam, maybe put it under her arm, but I heard the car door click open.

The man said, "A cop is hidden in the trees, so do your forty miles an hour and you won't get into trouble with the law."

Pearly Sue was inside the car. The cam's lens landed on the gun leaning against the passenger seat, the recorder still running. She cranked the motor, and squealed gravel going away.

"Did you get it all?"

Web answered, "Sure did."

"Cut the camcorder," I told Pearly Sue. "Call me on your cell."

We set my cell for conference. Lake answered the call. "Don't get out of your car. Unload the rifle, open your door, and toss it and the bullets in the bushes. Go straight to the cops and stay there. Wait for Dirk's guy, Johnson, wherever he is."

"What's up?" she asked. Her breathing was ragged, but exhilarated. I'd had that feeling, too often.

Lake said to Pearly Sue, "The man had a forty-five inside his jacket. Holstered for a quick hand-over."

Which basically meant for a fast draw.

"Don't I know it," she said. "I kept my eye on his hands. But it's the eyes that give them away when they're going to draw on you."

Lake said, "You can shoot one-armed?"

"Sure can. My daddy taught me growing up. Ride it against your leg, hand in the trigger housing, bring the butt up and anchor it under your arm or by your cheek and fire away."

"Something's going on up there."

"You and Dru coming up?"

"Depends on how it goes," Lake answered. "And what's happened to Johnson."

"On the video, did you see the road running alongside where

I was, up the ridge?" Lake said yes. "I turned on it thinking it was the Horne driveway since country roads here don't have names. I came to some kind of small barn or shed, then I saw the house down the hill and turned around."

Lake said, "Do not, I repeat, do not go back up that road."

Dear God, don't let her do anything stupid. Or anything else stupid. I had a lot to say to that girl when she got back to Atlanta. I'm sure Lake did, too.

"You think something happened to Johnson up there?"

Lake's voice left no room for argument when he said, "Go to the police station. Report what went on, leaving out the camcorder action if you can. It's illegal or might be in that state, depending."

"I didn't make it for court," Pearly Sue said, defiant in letting him know that she was familiar with exclusionary and nonexclusionary disciplines in the private detective's life. She continued, "Certainly the man knew he was being videoed and recorded."

Lake handed my cell to me and answered his own phone.

I told Pearly Sue, "Tell the cops that you are a private investigator from Atlanta, an associate working with the national PI firm of Dirk's Detectives out of Boston, and that you waited for an operative from Boston. When he didn't come, you went to the Horne place to talk to Mr. Page about a case in Atlanta, Georgia, where you are licensed."

"Wait!" she shouted. "A car just turned up that dirt road, the same one I mistook for the Horne driveway."

"Leave it, Pearly Sue."

"It could be Johnson."

"He'll turn around just like you did. If the car doesn't come down, head for the cop house. Lake's on the phone with Dirk's to see where Johnson is. Don't hang up, but if we get disconnected, call me back. And, Pearly Sue, stay on guard."

My nerves were crawling like worms in a bottle. I rubbed my arms.

Lake turned away from his call, and said, "Johnson called in to their dispatch in Boston. He got stalled by a tractor-trailer wreck on the road. He couldn't get cell service and couldn't find Pearly Sue when he got to town."

"Where is Johnson now?" I asked Lake.

"On the way to the Page Horne place." Lake spoke again to Dirk's dispatcher. "Pearly Sue's waiting at the road into the Horne place. After Johnson meets up with her, they need to go to the police station. She needs to report her experience."

Pearly Sue said, "Miss Dru, are you there?"

"Yes."

"Whoever went up the road is coming back down—fast."

Lake signaled to me, and I told Pearly Sue to hold on. This *pas de deux* with cells was getting bizarre.

Lake said that Johnson called Boston and told dispatch that he'd spotted a body in the shed. He didn't touch anything, never got out of his car.

"Holy moly," I breathed out. Harsher epithets came into my head but I wasn't about to spout profanity into Pearly Sue's ears. My eyes started to tear up. Was it Thomas Page who lay dead?

Oh, God. His killer, chatting with Pearly Sue.

Pearly Sue spoke. "Johnson's here. He found a body. A man."

"Call the cops and stay where you are," Lake said.

"You don't need to tell me twice, Lieutenant."

I doubted that.

CHAPTER TWENTY-NINE

"Let's go to your office," Lake said, like my father would have said when he was healthy and vigorous and if he still cared. We sat. Lake looked and acted like this was serious business. "You're going to have to rein Pearly Sue in."

"God knows, I know," I said and pushed hair off my forehead.

"I mean it, Dru."

I sat up. "I said I know."

"No, I don't think you do. I don't think you could put into words what I'm thinking and what I'm going to say."

"I'm holding my breath."

"If anything happened to her, it would destroy you."

His words hit like I'd stopped suddenly on a railroad track and stared at an oncoming train. Because I knew he was right. I could look at the train and visualize the wreck an instant before it rolled over me.

"She's you ten years ago," he said. "Her enthusiasm, her daring, her invincibleness—if that's a word. You're not that fresh-faced girl any longer. You've evolved because you've been trained by the best services in the country. First, you understood your nature and joined the police force. You excelled because you had instructors and expectations *of* you."

"I had you," I said, my voice barely audible.

"And I had you. I learned from you. I'm a guy and a cop. I don't have your instincts. I assess a situation and go for it. You assess and wait to confirm, then you go for it, for all your worth.

Pearly Sue is a long way from that. If she's going to be an asset to you and not something you have to worry about—yes, I saw the worry on your face, the doubt you had about her going into that house alone. I chastised her. But did she really understand what I was saying?"

"Her defenses were up, like mine would have been at her age."

"Besides having the best training in the art of self-defense, you have experience. You'll lay your life on the line for a cause when there is no other alternative. Pearly Sue would do it for the dare, the thrill."

"I couldn't stand it if something happened—if she pulled some of the crazy crap I did, and she didn't survive it."

"After APD training, you were picked for the Yellow Brick Road. How many women were there with you?"

"Three."

"It's a tough go, as you know, but you excelled. I'm not saying this to praise you, although I am and do often, but to say Pearly Sue hasn't had the training, the hand-to-hand, the weapons, distance judged to use them. She an amateur and the reason she's dangerous to herself is she wants to be exactly like you."

He had me in tears.

"Don't get me wrong. She's a fine, tough, consummate southern woman—those heroines who held the South together when their men didn't come back from the war a hundred and fifty years ago. *Gone with the Wind* is an important story, a heroic feminine story, and the reason is because of Scarlett's evolution from spoiled brat to an iron-willed, iron-fisted woman determined to survive and keep her family and way of life together."

I breathed in, trying like hell to stifle the tears.

Lake came around and massaged my shoulders while I sniffled myself quiet. He leaned over and pushed my hair from an ear and kissed it. "While we wait, no sense starving."

"No," I said. "No sense at all."

We sat at our usual table at the steak house. I'd had one martini that scalded all the way to my stomach and ordered another. Lake looked at me like I was going to drink the night away and expect to get up and go to church tomorrow.

"You're squirming," he said, cutting his steak more slowly than usual, although he's always been an elegant diner.

"Waiting."

"Gets to you, but we'll know soon enough who the dead guy is."

"I hate to believe I already know."

"They'll want a positive before they call us. I hope you've forgiven me for Page's defection."

"Of course," I said, not even thinking about the last time we were here. That was when I waltzed in with a good-looking man and expected Lake to smile and be his charming self. No, I was remembering Thomas Page as he was when he wanted to throw me off his property. It's in my DNA. I respect and fall in love with men who are robust, harsh almost, when the times call for it. I don't want men to treat me like a pretty twit who makes them want to prance and show their dimples and wink.

I said, "I was hoping for a call from Pearly Sue. She's not answering."

"Pearly Sue is at the cop house answering for herself."

"She should be okay."

"You never know with small jurisdictions and private detectives. They'll pick her apart."

"My money's on Pearly Sue. She'll pick them apart."

"Amen, sister," he said and started on his salad. "You're not going to eat that salmon?"

"No," I said, pushing it toward him and picking up my martini. I wasn't driving. We would be going to his place.

Buzzed sex is sex on steroids. Before we undressed to the intimacy of touch and talk, to the relishing of the fever in our senses, Lake kissed me with no restraint, having first grasped his arms across my back and butt and landed me on the bedspread. "Now, let's get you out of those clothes."

Since he was so eager, I let him get me out of my clothes himself.

CHAPTER THIRTY

At eight o'clock the next morning, I awoke with a headache and sore muscles. Lake was talking to headquarters while I stood looking out the loft's industrial windows, sighing to the misty day. Pain coupled with rain makes me want to snuggle under the covers, but that wasn't to be. Nor would Lake have this day off. His tensed jawbones told me that. He hadn't had a break in a couple of weeks.

My cell organed out Bach. The display showed my caller to be Prince Husam. So early? His tone was abrupt. "Have you made progress, Miss Dru?"

I told him I was still working to find his wife and daughter.

"I am upset. I had faith that you would have located them by now."

Was he firing me? "The United States is a big country," I said, too weary to care if he told me to quit. I wouldn't because he said to. I'd signed on and would carry on regardless of his pique. "Your wife has not contacted anyone she knows, nor has she used public transportation or her credit cards and money in her accounts. She does not want to be found."

"Maybe she went to France."

"Her passport has not been used."

"You have ways of finding this out?"

"Yes. The police."

"Then if she is in the United States, I don't know where. Somewhere I've never been, I'm sure. Where are you looking?"

"In likely places. Have a little more faith, Husam. Let me ask you something."

"Of course," he snapped.

"Do you think you might be being watched?"

"By whom?"

"Anyone."

"The doormen at my building look out for people like thieves or spies or reporters. I've been photographed when I was unaware of it."

"How long ago?"

"Last year. For that absurd yearly list they concoct."

"Is the United States Diplomatic Security Service protecting you?" I asked.

"Not at present," he said. "They have in the past at the embassies and when I'm acting on behalf of my country."

"But that's not now?"

"No. I have no diplomatic ties at present."

"Do you have private bodyguards?"

"I have my man Salman Habibi."

"Where does he live?"

"He lives where I live."

"Is he the only bodyguard you have?"

"He is all I need. I work for an international firm of lawyers. I do not represent my country in an official capacity. Why are you asking me these questions?"

"It occurs that people could spy on you to get to Reeve and your daughter."

"I am very careful. Since Reeve has been missing, I have curtailed many social activities and obligations. You are asking these questions for a more specific reason, are you not?"

I paced behind the splashing windows. *Rain, go away.* "We've many threads going, all over the map."

"That is not a satisfactory answer. Do you believe a government agency is spying on me?"

"Assume someone is and take extra care. Maybe people from your own country. People connected to this case have been killed."

"I do not forget my in-laws. I do not know why they were killed, but it could be to draw Reeve and Shara out."

"The killers haven't succeeded."

"Nor have you succeeded in finding Reeve and Shara. You send me invoices for expenses, but I get no results."

"What do you want to do?"

"I am at my wits' end. I thought by now . . ."

I let him ramble out his disappointment, then said, "Give me a few more days. I won't charge you, but I must tell you that I will not quit the search, on my own time and dime."

I hung up.

Not fifteen seconds later, my phone played Bach. Husam, of course. "I am sorry for upsetting you. You keep working and I will pay." He sighed. "I must return to work. I'm afraid I haven't been very productive for my firm."

"Take care," I reiterated.

"I will be in Atlanta tomorrow. We should meet."

"Call when you get in."

Was Husam a target? I had no clue. If what Lake said was true, that I assess and wait for confirmation before acting, he was correct in that I was in the process of assessing, but the confirmation seemed a good ways off.

"I will do that."

Shutting the cell, I thought, *Dear God, don't let Page be dead. He's the best thread I have.*

As if God answered my off-the-cuff prayer, Web called and said, "At two a.m. we got a fish in the net. And another at three, and another at four."

Page? Alive? I could only hold my breath.

Lake put away his cell and rose from the bed. He laced his lanyard full of IDs around his neck and grabbed his jacket. All the while listening to my end of the phone call.

I held up a finger that he shouldn't leave. "Is it Page's untraceable?" I asked

Web said, "Could be. I've only gotten the receiver's six-o-three number in Woodstock. Takes longer for the caller's vectors."

I jumped like a kid who hit a home run. Lake's face took on hope. But Web's tone of voice remained lugubrious.

"What?" I asked.

"Looks like she's calling him from her kick to his, but he's not answering. Or I'd get a ping. No ping."

That's because he's dead. No!

Lake was on the move. He grabbed his hat. "I've got to go to the shop. I'm getting company." He headed for the door.

"Who?" He wouldn't be adding the last sentence if it didn't concern me.

"A hotshot from the Diplomatic Security Service. He has a few questions. He'll meet me and Haskell in an hour."

"I'm coming, too."

"You're not dressed."

"I'm right behind you," I said, going to the closet, pulling slacks and blouse out, getting my gun purse off the shelf and laying it on the bed, ready for the day. Things were turning around. Happening. I could feel it.

"Can't guarantee he'll want to speak with you," Lake said. "You know how that goes. Oh, by the way, your eyes need that stuff that gets the red out."

"My brain needs it, too. Listen, I didn't tell you. Paul Ardai reported that Victor Cartaloma was at the Baghdad embassy and was transferred out after just six months deployment. Paul said he'd look into it further and get back in touch. Web called the state department. They weren't cooperative."

Lake's eyebrows rose. "Ah, two inquiries on the same guy, that would tend to raise state's suspicion quotient." He opened the door. "Don't go over the yellow line when you pass me. I'm a cop with blue lights and a mean siren."

I figured I had enough time for Lake to get the DSS guy settled in with coffee and polite comments before the question-and-answer session. They're state, after all, diplomatic and all that.

I love to drive the Bentley, sold cheaply to me by Portia Devon after my Saab was blown up in one of many tragic cases. My fiancé had helped me with the down payment on the car of my dreams those years ago, before he was killed in a drive-by handing out leaflets for a Big Brother campaign in a neighborhood where big brothers were in short supply.

The maudlin feeling returned with a vengeance for any number of reasons. Thinking about the past will do it, but so would the alcohol hangover. So, too, would waiting for news from New Hampshire. What the hell was taking them so long to get an identification? And why hadn't Pearly Sue answered her cell phone? Most likely, the battery was dead—like Thomas Page. *Stop that.*

And what had caused the Diplomatic Security Service to call the APD? I thought I had an idea. Cases at this point can weigh like a yoke across the shoulders. We had collected a lot of information, but what meant anything? Did the Cresleys' infidelity to each other cause their deaths? And what did it have to do with Reeve's and Shara's disappearance? If anything? The *if anything* can race across the playing field of your mind like a hockey game, back and forth with lots of whacks but few goals. What did the botched surgeries mean? If anything? What string threaded through all this, and who held the ends?

My cell played the Bach fugue, reminding me that I'd thought to change it yesterday. Bach, like this case, was weighing heavily. "Yeah, Web, what's up?"

"The dead guy in New Hampshire was the caretaker of the place," he said.

"The caretaker?"

"Can't be the same guy that Pearly Sue yammered with. The caretaker is seventy years old. His name is Joe Clampton. He was shot to death with a heavy caliber. No bullet left in the brain. It all came out the back, bone, bullet and all."

"How's Pearly Sue? I haven't heard from her."

"Tell you in a minute. They found Page in the barn. He'd been drugged and maybe tortured, but he's alive."

I let out a sigh, then squirmed. "Tortured? How?"

"Buckets of water. The water-boarding trick."

And here I thought it an apt way of getting information from the bad guys. But Thomas Page wasn't a bad guy. *Was he?*

"Where is Page?"

"Intensive care."

"He that bad?"

"From what I'm hearing."

"Who called?"

"Dirk, the honcho himself. Johnson's still with Pearly Sue, who's raising hell to see Page."

"That's my girl."

"She and Johnson saw Page when they brought him out of the barn."

"She's probably kicking her own butt for not finding him in that barn when she first surveyed the property."

"He was upstairs in the hayloft, drugged and tied up."

He was up there while Pearly Sue recorded and we watched and listened. "God almighty," I said. "Get hold of Pearly Sue. I'm going to APD and will be out of pocket for a while. Why was she at the barn to see Page brought out?"

"The cops took her there to re-enact her story. That's when they found Page."

Lake met me at the elevator. "I got the report on Page," he said. "Jesus. War torture. And we missed him. Christ. What the hell are we dealing with?"

"Desperate measures for desperate people," I said, an axiom that popped into my aching head. "Where's the DSS chap?"

"Late. Atlanta traffic."

I grinned. "When in Atlanta, it's a good excuse."

My cell played Bach. Lake frowned like he'd like to grab it from me and toss it into the corner. I waved him off. It was Pearly Sue. "I got the report," I said. "Any luck getting in to see Page?"

"No," she said. "He's sedated, but he's okay. He's in a patient room now. Maybe I can get in later. The cops are with him though."

"How did the re-enactment go?"

"Fine. I had to confess about the camcorder. They didn't seem too mad. They have it and let me know that I might not see it for a while. They located the gun."

"They believed you."

"Yes. One cop said I was lucky to have corroborating evidence since the caretaker was dead and Mr. Page was inside the barn, drugged, but alive."

Pearly Sue learns a lesson. People are callous. The world's not all Miss Pecan Pie and Rattlesnake Roundups.

I asked, "Do they have any clue who you talked to on the cam?"

"No one they know, apparently, but they're saying more to Johnson than me. The girl thing."

Not all Miss Annie Oakley, either. "How's Johnson?"

"Nice."

"Stick to him until we get you out of there."

"Won't be long if the cops have their way. But I'm waiting to talk to Mr. Page. I'm owed that much."

"You sure are, baby. And when you get back, we'll talk."

CHAPTER THIRTY-ONE

His name was Gary Scheel and he had flown in from Washington, DC. Lake shook hands with him, as did I. *From the Department of State. All the way from DC.* What had we rumbled forth?

Commander Haskell led the three of us into the conference room on the top floor where the chief and his staff hold meetings. The chief and two staffers were there already.

Gary Scheel made me feel as if I was in a *presence,* like a provincial from the hinterland who wished she hadn't drank three martinis and a jug of wine last night, then topped it off with an all-night sexathon. I'd caught myself in the elevator's polished gold chrome. My eyes didn't look too red, but my thighs yelped when I walked too fast.

"Gentlemen," Scheel began, "Let's get started. I have a plane back to *Washington* at one, and with your traffic, I'll be rushed."

We all nodded. It surely was important that he not miss his plane back to *Washington.*

"You all know what the Diplomatic Security Service is, am I correct."

Heads nodded.

"So that we're on the same page"—a despised phrase—"I'll go over some points so we understand what we're dealing with."

Lake opened his mouth like he was about to ask the same thing I would ask: who is Victor Cartaloma and was he assigned to watch Prince Husam? But a subtle shake of Haskell's head closed Lake's mouth.

Scheel was dead set on a teaching moment. "Diplomatic Security Service agents are federal agents like FBI and Homeland Security. In overseas missions—just like the CIA— DSS agents have the powers of arrest, etcetera. Their primary goal is to protect the secretary of state and foreign dignitaries. As such it is the security and law enforcement arm of the US Department of State."

Scheel orated while I took his measure. Nearly six feet tall, graying, neatly cut hair with a side part, trim, athletic build, navy suit costing upwards of a grand, white, heavily starched shirt, nice, red and gold striped tie. He liked to speak while holding out a hand, palm up. Hand gestures have always interested me. If a person has his palm up, he's being open and honest and wants your trust. But a palm down means he's being dominant. Hitler was a palms-down speaker. That was his salute. Finger-pointing is a belligerent gesture, but making an *O* with thumb and forefinger means no-threat-intended.

Scheel was saying, "We do extremely well in international investigations, cyber security, counterterrorism, and the safeguarding of people, property and information. Agents at domestic field offices are responsible for conducting investigations into passport and visa fraud. Regional Security Officers are charged with the security and law enforcement at US missions, embassies and consular posts." He paused to take a drink of water; and, with a glance around, he seemed to measure our interest quotient before he went on. "We also conduct counterintelligence investigations and oversee—when we can—the activities of foreign intelligence agencies, especially those regarding state department employees." He waved one hand, palm up, while the other was pocketed. "At the request of other law enforcement agencies, we will assist in apprehending fugitives that have fled the United States. You need to know that extensive background investigations are conducted on all employees, applicants and contractors seeking employment with the department." He waved the hand again. "We investigate any and all terrorist incidents that threaten state department employees, missions, embassies, etcetera. There are approximately two thousand Diplomatic Security Service special agents. Unlike other federal law officers, our agents serve multiple-year tours overseas. When they are not overseas, they're in US field offices or headquarters in DC." He was fond of waving his hand. "A small percentage of special agents are members of the state department's civil service and focus on criminal work and dignitary protection within the United States." He paused and drank again. Aside from his thirst, he hadn't uttered one "uh" or had to repeat a word. He asked, "Any questions?"

"Yes," Lake said. "We are seeking information on one of your agents, name of Victor Cartaloma. We understand that he last served in Baghdad before being transferred back to the US."

Scheel raised his chin. "Why and what kind of information are you seeking?"

"In pursuing one of our cases, we learned that he identified himself as being a DSS special agent serving in that capacity while looking like a homeless man and, therefore, in disguise, in New York City. His detail, he told a private investigator, was to keep watch on Prince Husam bin Sayed al-Saliba, a member of the Saudi royal family."

Scheel rubbed the skin between his upper lip and nose with an index finger. "Hmmm. It isn't unlikely that a DSS agent would be incognito in a foreign country as he investigates criminal activity, but just to guard a dignitary like a member of the royal family in the United States, there really would be no reason to go undercover." He looked at the chief of police. "I will look into this, but I would like to know more about the case. Saudi Arabia security details have always been sensitive."

Commander Haskell asked Detective Lieutenant Richard

Lake to bring Scheel up to date on our case. Lake did a thorough job, answering politely questions that had been gone over, but asked again—and again—while reviewing again and again the bench and Turtle Pond video Pearly Sue had shot. In the course of the recitation, Lake produced the New Hampshire video and loaded it into the computer.

While Lake was setting up the video, Scheel asked, "Your operative in New York, this Miss Ellis, is certain that the man categorized himself as a DSS special agent named Victor Cartaloma?"

"She is certain."

"Too bad that didn't get on the recorder."

"Yes," Lake said, not bothering to explain why it was cut short, and Scheel didn't press it.

Sheel raised an eyebrow. "*She* is . . . reliable?"

I rose to her defense. "Of course."

Lake answered evenly, "She is highly intelligent and an excellent investigator."

Sheel studied my face for a second or two. "And she was sent to run surveillance on your client, Prince Husam Saliba of Saudi Arabia. Why did you need surveillance on your client?"

I cleared my froggy throat. "When I take on a case, the client gets vetted along with every individual involved in the case. I've been surprised before. I wanted to know that Prince Husam had no knowledge of the whereabouts of his wife and daughter; and that I wasn't on a fool's errand to smoke out a couple of people who could very well be in danger. Reeve Cresley's parents were murdered right after I agreed to take the case."

Scheel turned to Lake. "Was Prince Husam a suspect or person of interest in their murders by the Atlanta Police Department?"

"We investigated his whereabouts. He was in New York at the time of the murders." Lake paused as if to contemplate.

"There's always a possibility of hired killers. After looking into it, we've not come up with any leads."

"Hmmm," Scheel murmured. "It's known to happen. Have you considered terrorists?"

Terrorism. My aching muscles spasmed.

Lake looked at the chief, who said, "We're keeping watch on two possible cells here, but they're Central European, not Middle Eastern. They're more like gangs of young men."

That was vague; the question unanswered.

Scheel watched the New Hampshire video on the large screen, even cracking a smile from time to time. After it was over, he said, "Your Miss Ellis has an interesting manner—an investigative style that could never be copied or taught."

Or corralled.

Scheel looked at the chief. "May I have copies of the videos made by Miss Ellis, those in Central Park and New Hampshire?"

"I see no reason why you can't."

Scheel smiled. He was *state* of course. He could order anything from any of us in the name of homeland security and terrorism.

"You might wonder at my curiosity," he said, both palms up this time. "This case touches upon foreign nationals that we vet carefully. We vet them ongoingly. The prince, whom I'm aware of, has been in the United States for several years, although he maintains ties with his family and colleagues in the kingdom of Saudi Arabia. What I'd like to do is use our facial recognition software to see if we can learn who the mysterious man is that posed as caretaker on the estate of Thomas Page. The man in Central Park is not a good candidate."

The chief said. "The New Hampshire video is not good quality, either, owing to the weather and light conditions."

"That may be, but we have the best technology in the world."

"Ours is second to none," the chief said, his bulldog face

ready to take on Washington. "Facial recognition relies on the fact the person's image has to be in a database first—like fingerprints or DNA or eye irises that are used for alarm systems."

Scheel appeared set to argue. His palm went down. "The geometric technique looks at individual features. The photometric structure is more precise for identification. Our numerical algorithm distills an image and compresses it to reduce deviation. Mathematical methodology is not without miscalculations, but it is, on the whole, more dependable."

Haskell, who had been fidgeting in his seat, spoke up. "The makers of that kind of software say they can match from profiles, and obstructions on the face like shadows, but not so fast. If a person is standing still and not smiling—you know, full frontal—it works. But as soon as you try to match a profile to a full in a database, there are problems."

I said, "Our New Hampshire caretaker's face was obstructed by a hat, beard hair, poor lighting, dusk and drizzle."

Scheel grinned. "All he needed was sunglasses. Also a big smile and closed eyes. A blur can render any system ineffective." Palms up now. "To your point, in London they've rigged cameras in high crime areas where criminals' full faces and profiles were in the database. In one area ten recidivists were caught on camera; all ten were not recognized by the software. Their failure-to-recognize rate was the same as several police departments surveyed in the United States."

He paused and looked at the chief as if he expected a confirmation from the APD. The chief sat stony. I knew for a fact Scheel was correct. People on the move are hard to pin down facially.

Scheel went on, "We are trying out new, three-D techniques with visa and passport applications while we build our databases. Google and Facebook are useful for building them."

The chief rose. "I'll see you get a copy of the videos. Anything else? Anyone?" His eyes scanned each of us. I shook my head.

Lake said, "Back to Cartaloma. When can we know where he is and what his assignment entails as it applies to Prince Husam?"

"I don't know that you can know that, Lieutenant. You can appreciate the nature of our work, but I will tell you if anyone has been assigned to Prince Husam."

"All right," Lake said.

It was not all right, but that was all we were going to get.

"Want to go with me to talk to the aviator—what's his name? Alvarez?"

I looked at my watch. Although I hadn't had anything in my stomach but coffee, I really didn't want to go to a restaurant. I longed to stop at Dixie Donuts and Sandwiches, grab a ham and egg biscuit and go to the office. I needed to catch up with Pearly Sue and Dirk's on the New Hampshire situation. How was Page? Was he talking? I doubt it would be Pearly Sue who interrogated him first, unless, of course, he asked for her, which would piss off the town and state cops, along with the sheriffs and any federales interested. Oh, the federales were interested all right. Scheel would see to that.

I hate the idea of losing control of an investigation; worse was having it taken away by *superior forces.*

I believe in superior forces when they are superior, but I don't like being the lowly force that brings them up to date.

So I said to Lake, "I'd like to hear what Alvarez has to say about his relationship with Donna Cresley, and what he might know about other lovers of hers, but I'm trusting you can worm that out of him."

"I can and will. First, though . . ."

I knew what he was going to say and turned to go.

"Hey," he called. "Want me to drop a ham, egg and cheese off when I'm finished?"

I glanced back. "You're going to Dixie's? Twice, in less than a week?"

"Dixie makes fabulous hot pastrami on rye, with a perfect dill spear and cole slaw."

"I'm with you, but on the biscuit."

Leaving Dixie's, Lake talked me into going to see Alvarez, which wasn't hard to do because I'd called Webdog and he reported nothing of significance from New Hampshire.

As Lake drove, apparently having fallen into his own mindset, I studied the cityscape, thinking about the case. My thoughts were fragmented like cracks in unbreakable glass. Charlie Brown Airport is a couple of miles out of the city of Atlanta at the junction of two interstates, I-20 and I-285, and a river—the Chattahoochee. The airport is not named after the comic-strip character, but a former Atlanta politician, name of Charles M. Brown. He was on the Atlanta city council in the 1960s.

Lake rolled the car into a lot in front of the modern, glass and white tile building, stopped and turned to me. "And the conclusion is?"

"I was thinking about Adele. She said Donna confided in her, that they were very good friends, from school days."

"But she only gave up Alvarez's name. You said you thought she was lying about not knowing others."

"That's true. Donna may have confided to her men friends. She sounds lonely enough."

"We'll ask Alvarez."

We walked inside the bright office of the Fulton County Airport, aka, Charlie Brown.

Lake stopped at the counter where a pretty, young woman smiled like she'd won the lottery. Lake has that effect.

Lake said, "Here to see Sean Alvarez."

Looking disappointed that she couldn't help Lake, she said, "Sorry, Mr. Alvarez is not here."

"He was to meet me at noon," Lake said, opening his coat so that the gold badge on his belt showed. He also held up his ID that hung on the lanyard. "Right here in the lobby."

A vertical frown line sliced the skin between her eyes. "Sean?"

"That's right," Lake said. "I talked with him earlier."

Her expression was one of intimate concern. *That Alvarez, what a charmer.* She hurried into speech. "Mr. Alvarez is in the air, as we speak."

Lake shrugged as if it were not important. "Guess he got a charter. Work comes first. Where is he headed?"

"I—I," she stammered.

Lake had apparently picked up on her intimate concern, too, because he said, "If Mr. Alvarez has police problems, it's not with me."

She relaxed. "He took a charter to Sarasota, Florida."

I'd begun to turn to leave when I halted. *Sarasota?*

"When will he return?" Lake asked.

"This afternoon. He's on the schedule for a Chattanooga flight. A much shorter one, at five o'clock."

Lake said, "This morning he told me about the Chattanooga flight, but not about the Sarasota flight. It must have been sudden."

"Is there a problem?" she asked, worried again.

"Not that I know of. Who are the passengers?"

"One, sir." She knew she'd slipped up. "For any more information I'll have to get my supervisor."

When she'd disappeared behind a door, Lake said, "Who's your best guess?"

"Yasmin?"

"Not the prince?"

"I talked to him this morning. He said he was coming to Atlanta tomorrow."

A man in shirtsleeves appeared. "Hello, Lake."

I recognized the former cop, now an airfield manager.

Lake said, "Johnny, good to see you."

"You want the name of a passenger?"

"I know, I need a warrant, and a reason."

"You got it."

"Just tell me they're not Middle Easterners."

Johnny's eyes got wider. "He's not, and that's all I can tell you."

"Thanks."

When we were back in the car, I asked, "Charlie Brown wasn't a school for terrorists, was it?"

"Nope. But Venice, near Sarasota, was. That's where two of the Nine-Eleven terrorists got enough training to fly planes into buildings."

That I knew, but hated to let it sink in.

Chapter Thirty-Two

I retrieved the Bentley from the APD's lot and drove to the office. "Page's not talking," Web said, when I stuck my head through his door frame.

"I would have bet that he wasn't talking," I said. "We need to find out if the torturer got any information out of Page—like did he give up Reeve's whereabouts?"

Web shrugged. "Fishnet gave up Reeve's whereabouts, sort of. Took me a while to isolate the number and location, but she was in Woodstock when she was calling Page cell-to-cell and got no answer. I connected the two untraceables from the numbers. They belonged to a block of numbers from a major cell provider. They buy these numbers in block, then sell them as untraceables. There haven't been any other calls between the numbers and there's no GPS embedded in the cells."

"Where is she now, I wonder, and why isn't she still trying to call him?"

"His kick is probably dead. Cheapo batteries."

"But where is the instrument itself?"

"Maybe the fake caretaker. Maybe Page had a chance to get rid of it when he saw what was coming. Maybe the cops found it."

"Get Pearly Sue out of New Hampshire," I said.

"I suggested she come home. The cops won't let her or Johnson near Page. She didn't sound like she would be on a plane anytime soon, so I told her to call you."

"I'll take it from here." Pearly Sue and Web were equals so one couldn't order the other to do anything. I mused, "After Page left us at the steak house the night we flew from Denver to Atlanta, he must have gotten in touch with Reeve. He heads for his late mother's property—now his. So Reeve was physically with him at some point in time."

Web said, "She wasn't on his flight to New York."

"He knew where she was in Atlanta and went to see her. He paid cash for two untraceables, gave her one and then flew to New York."

"She drove," Lake said. "Paying cash for gas and food."

Suddenly a loud ding rattled the air in the room. I knew that was Web's email telling him the e-mailer was someone he urgently wanted to connect with. Web swung his chair toward the keyboard and the monitor. He read the electronic note silently, then leaned back to explain with a grin.

"It's about Victor Cartaloma. When I did fundamental research about the Diplomatic Security Service, I came across a blog where agents and interested people post and comment on a line of inquiry."

"A blog, huh? And a line of inquiry? Sounds very Nero Wolf-ish."

"I've read every book. Love the first ones best."

"You're kind of like him. Sit in an office all day and play with a computer. He read books, but, bottom line, neither of you get off your bottoms to solve the case."

"Nero did once or twice. I can't wait to get into the field."

"Whoa. One at a time. Pearly Sue's already ragged out my last functioning nerve."

Web turned to the computer monitor, and said, "So listen to an answer to my line of inquiry on Victor Cartaloma: '*While in Baghdad VC got cozy with the local cops. Through them, although they're not always reliable, VC learned of a drug operation that involved the embassy. He launched an investigation, even hiring a clandestine service officer—the military version of the CIA—to go undercover. He got photos of exchanges between embassy personnel and drug dealers. Suddenly VC is asked to cease his investigation and close it forthwith and forget it. It's back to the states and training in what to expose and what not to expose. Same the world over. Makes us sick here. Dipshits relieving boredom and our state department covering it up. Stinks. He's somewhere in the promised land is all we know—that being the great U. S. of A.'* "

"Good work, Web," I said. "I have a feeling Gary Scheel could have told us that."

"Maybe he doesn't read the blogs."

I went into my office to get some admin stuff done, including an invoice for expenses. I was taking Husam at his word to continue billing. I wondered why he was coming to Atlanta and then I thought about Yasmin. So far Yasmin had been the princess of rectitude according to the detectives following her. She spends her days at stores like Saks and Neiman Marcus, occasionally having lunch downtown with two women that Dirk's vetted and found to be Americans by birth and bilingual Muslims. They work in the office of Children's Protective Services and deal with people who speak Arabic. After lunch, she returns to the Atlanta Arms condo, where, according to maids who were bribed, she takes a nap, talks on the telephone and spends hours on the computer. In the evening, she drinks vodka, they said, and lots of it.

I needed to discuss a few things with Yasmin. She wouldn't be easy to trip up. Being educated would make it difficult. On the other hand, arrogance often loosens tongues. Educated arrogance was something to sit back and take advantage of when anger shows up, too.

I emailed Prince Husam and asked when he would arrive in Atlanta, and if he and Yasmin would have dinner with me, and

Lake, if Lake was available.

A half an hour later, Husam replied that he and Yasmin would be delighted to be our host and hostess at the restaurant of my choice. I suggested Bacchanalia, an upscale restaurant in an old section of town. The building had once been a meatpacking plant. The menu is prix fixe and the offerings are rack of lamb, prime rib, trout or pheasant. I know of no restaurant that does lamb or prime rib better.

Lake called to say a team of detectives was bringing in a confidential informant and part-time fence in the home-invasion cases and that he would see me when he saw me at his loft. He also told me that Alvarez never came back to Charlie Brown. He stood up his Chattanooga charter.

Chapter Thirty-Three

After a sleepless night, I headed for the office. Lake had tiptoed in at three o'clock. I hummed hello and rolled over, waking again at eight o'clock. Late. I scurried to shower and dress. I was feeling much better. In fact, ready to tackle the world, like if I really thought about it, I could wave my wand and say abracadabra and the case would crack like an eggshell, revealing the yolk of truth. Had I, I wondered, set myself a puzzle to delight in deliciously by taking my time putting it together? No, but it seemed the people involved in the case had conspired to do that for me.

I had made coffee because Webdog was too involved in whatever had captured his fancy during the night to do the usual chore. Once it was finished dripping, I asked Web if he wanted a cup and he was too busy to answer.

Settled in, sipping strong, hot coffee, I looked up to see Web standing in the door frame. I'd seen him like this before. Bags under his young eyes, hair pushed back, shoulders hunched. The remains of another sleepless night. "You look like an intern after three straight days of emergency-room duty," I said.

He had the oddest look on his face, a little sheepish and yet triumphant. "Can we talk?" he asked.

"Sure. Get a cuppa." I handed him my empty cup. "No cream for me. Then we'll sit a spell." I was thinking maybe he had a word or two about Pearly Sue's contrary behavior.

Instead, he said, motioning down the hall, toward his office,

"I need to show you something."

"On a computer?" He nodded yes, and I said, "I'll get the coffees on the way to your office."

I walked into his office and placed his cup of sugary, creamy coffee on a plate he keeps for the occasional drink, when he remembers he's thirsty. He sat in a swivel chair from the 1950s, a collector's item of sorts—not young enough to be called retro nor old enough to be deco.

I sat and looked at his monitor. "What's that?"

"A Tor website."

"Tor, the anonymous server?"

"Tor is a network that provides anonymous networking services."

"Anonymous I like—for me. Pain in the butt in getting info on adversaries."

"Even clients," Web said, raising a blond eyebrow.

"Ah, am I going to be given another lesson in computer techniques that will catch my bad guys?"

"Hope so."

I looked at the monitor. "That website you have up doesn't tell me much."

"It is a hidden website."

"How come I can see it?"

"I know how to find it."

"Is this anything like the Silk Road of a few years ago that was busted for illegal drug selling?"

"Yes."

Silk Road was named for the ancient trade routes across Europe and Asia. Camels, horses and goats carried goods on their backs to trade for other goods, gold or services.

Web said, "The Silk Road website was built on a Tor network. Tor stands for The Onion Router, over which encrypted data passes back and forth."

The onion routers concept, Web explained, was invented by the US Naval Research Lab for sending and receiving sensitive government communications. While onion routing can run on most operating systems, the Tor network is used by journalists and privacy seekers from all occupations and desires because of the thousands of routers it has set up to process traffic all over the world. Naturally, it's used to hide illegal activities.

Web said, "The dark web is vast, let me tell you." Web rattled some keys and a website came up. "You are looking at the new Silk Road Two."

I leaned in. "Interesting. If it's hidden and secret and all that, how come you've got it up on your computer?"

"I use Tor occasionally."

"What for?" I asked. He grinned, and I said, "I don't want to know."

Could my computer wizard be into porn or drugs? I glanced at him. I can't believe it.

I placed my coffee cup on the scarred computer desk. "I guess this is where I ask—how do you route onions?"

He smiled indulgently, and said, "A routing onion is a data package that goes through a succession of routers, also called nodes. A node can either be a modem, a hub or a computer. People volunteer their hardware for onion-routing services."

"How does the router know what to do with the data package?"

"When the package hits the node, an encryption tells it to decrypt the first layer and send it on to the next node. These nodes can be many or few, whatever the sender wants."

"How would I create a package of data?"

"You would write your plaintext message layered with encryption. Each layer would be peeled away like the layers of an onion as it passes through a succession of nodes."

"How do you start an encrypted package down one of these nodes?"

"The sender connects to a designated server, which lists all of the available onion routers. He or she picks a route of three or more nodes to form a circuit."

"Where would I hook up with this designated server?"

"In the case of Tor, you'd have to download Tor and run it on your computer and establish a hidden service."

"What's it cost?"

"Totally free. It's open source." In his spare time, Webdog designs open source software. He explained to this dunderhead, "The data sender connects to the first onion router, and establishes a shared secret key."

I blinked. "Splain-a-me."

"Establishing a secret key allows two entities that have no prior knowledge of each other to establish a shared secret exchange. When your data packet meets the pertinent node and the keys agree, it's called a handshake and the data packet moves on."

"It's a password then?"

"When the data package reaches its destination, the last layer is peeled of decryption to reveal the original message. That's onion routing in a nutshell."

"So all this starts on a Tor network. How are these websites set up?"

"After you install Tor, the network provides directions for setting up hidden services for Linux, Windows, etcetera—whatever your operating system is. Follow directions and you get your dot onion link—the sixteen letter address of your Tor website. Plug this into your address bar and hit ENTER to see your very own onion website. Like the one here I'm showing you."

"Maybe I'll get you to set me up one."

"Then it won't be anonymous. But you can easily do it."

"So that's how Silk Road came into being?"

"Basically."

"So how did the FBI crack Silk Road?"

"You won't stay anonymous on your hidden website if you use unsafe configuring—or behavior, like advertising your site as a market for drugs on public forums. The feds confiscated twenty-five million in bitcoins from the site."

"I like my real money in a real wallet, not virtual money in a virtual one."

"The beauty of bitcoin is there's no tracking the encrypted bitcoin, like you can in a bank account." Web raised a finger. "But anything that is encrypted—like online banking and bit-coin—can be decrypted when the quantum computer is per-fected."

"I'm keeping my money in my mattress," I said. "What's a quantum computer?"

"The principal is based on quantum superposition, where something exists in all states. Binary computers—ones we use today—have to do one calculation at a time, no matter how fast. They use binary bits—zeros and ones consecutively. A quantum computer uses quantum bits—qubits—that are zeros and ones simultaneously."

"Should I worry?"

"Certainly. It will take a decade, probably, to build a computer with enough qubits to decrypt a one-thousand-twenty-four bit encryption, but it will be happen."

"Tech gone wild."

"But we've gotten off-track."

We've?

Web said, "I have proven that onion routing does *not* give sender or receiver anonymity against *all* possible eavesdroppers. It's like with our untraceable cell-phone users—with onion routers there are interception opportunities."

Dare I ask? "How did you do it?"

"I figured if I monitored every onion router in a network, I could trace the path of a message through that network. That's what I've been working on. You see, as I explained to your utter boredom on the prince's law firm's computer system, I got to *see* everything."

"You took it over?"

"Like a remote repairman—only I had to get myself in without the administrator's help. Goes to show, humans are careless, no matter how expert. Their onion router is not set up exclusively for onion routing, which was their first mistake. That means they have to reconfigure their browser settings every time they want to send anonymous data."

"What browser are they using?"

"Doesn't matter. All are susceptible to my charms." His smile was sly, a little devilish. "Most of the time when they finished browsing, they were careful to close any open ports. The list of web pages and cookies was deleted. Tor does not, and by design cannot, encrypt the traffic between an exit node and the target server, so any exit node is in a position to capture any traffic passing through that does not use end-to-end encryption. I wanted protocol data first and that would lead me to the messages."

"You went after the exit node, right?" He nodded. "What about the sender who started it all?"

"If I had the time. But then I got an idea. I ran a rogue-end router and coded the web page to insert Java Script and enable Flash. If they were using a browser with Flash or JavaScript, their browser would signal the exit router and transmit the IP address. Guess what?"

"I couldn't begin to."

"They were using Flash and didn't set up their browser correctly by having it do proper lookups, so the Flash-enabled cookie, GIF, led their computer to do a DNS lookup on a server controlled by me, and sent me the IP address. It then called directly to my rogue-end router without going through the onion layers. It was virtually no better than a proxy server or a virtual private network."

My head, my head, it was about to explode. "Are we getting close to the message?"

"I got the IP host name, services running on the IP, email logins and passwords."

"That sounds like a start."

"Something big's going on, Dru. A load of packet data is heating up the circuit nodes."

"Illegal?"

Web shrugged. "One would expect, else why the ultra secrecy? Before I could get a line on the firm's hidden service, I had to suspect it existed. And what led to that suspicion was me not getting into Prince Husam's email by standard backdoor protocols."

"What do you think? Child porn? Illegal drugs? Guns?"

"Look at the hidden website." He pointed at a blank page on the monitor. "Nothing offered for sale."

"What's the website called?"

"It has an assigned code ending with dot onion, but the name that flashes when the site comes on is Caliphate. Then the site goes white when Caliphate fades away."

"Ah, so."

Web turned back to his computers, and my mind strayed to money—moving it and hiding it. Used to be banking laws in Switzerland made banks a haven for such goings-on, then the Swiss were persuaded to give tax information to their clients' home countries. So, what's a tax cheat or money launderer to do? Well, in this internet-connected world, there came a solution. The bitcoin. Moveable, virtual money through the routers.

My cell rang. I had changed the ring tone to a fast-fingered piano concerto by Mozart, but something in the trills gave me chills. It was Lake. With bad news. Sean Alvarez's plane had gone down near Gainesville in a patch of woods. No one heard an explosion, but the area is sparsely populated, not counting the horses. A rider found the plane and Alvarez dead in the cockpit. Initial inspectors said it appeared he ran out of gas.

"Appearance be damned," I said. "Who was his passenger?"

Lake said, "Unknown at this time. I called Charlie Brown. Apparently, Alvarez was contacted by the client and the charter arranged between them. No name on the flight plan but Alvarez's."

Sarasota. I knew that Yasmin was in Atlanta and was still being tailed by Dirk's operatives. That girl was up to something and I suspect it had to do with Reeve's and Shara's whereabouts.

Lake said, "It was a man whom Alvarez flew to Sarasota. I've sent an officer with photos over there to see if the woman at Charlie B can identify the passenger."

The only other soul I knew from Sarasota was Weatherby. Weatherby and Yasmin in Atlanta, with Husam arriving tomorrow.

I thought of something Web said. *She appeared in Parliament to complain about the treatment of Muslims residing in London's ghettos.* That spells activist.

My thoughts fastened on theories that had been circulated over the years since 9/11. The CIA and FBI were investigating whether the World Trade Center hijackers had help with the planning to crash jets into the trade center. Sarasota was suspected to be the center of a larger network of Saudis who assisted the hijackers. There are so many conspiracy theories floating around, my mind can only handle one. And that one is who fired the shots that killed President John F. Kennedy.

"You still on the line?" Lake's voice sounded odd. "Or am I

talking to myself?"

"I'm thinking to myself," I said.

Lake had spent time on the fraud squad, investigating international criminals and how they moved money in the real world. I asked, "What's the best way to transfer a lot of money overseas these days?"

"Legally," he said, "by international money exchanges, SWIFT and CHIPS. Nope, I'm not going to bite on that, since the cop donuts I had at the crack of dawn are still weighing me down. Here's how it works. SWIFT tells banks when money has been sent and received, and CHIPS tallies and transfers. It takes hours, sometimes days, to complete a transfer because of the bureaucracy, the exchange rate, and it's expensive as hell. Lots of fraud involved with the exchange rates. Our system, here in the US, is ACH and it's almost as complex."

I said, "Bitcoin is made for crooks. According to Web, bitcoin addresses are random characters so no one knows the identity of the owners."

"That is true, but all bitcoins have to go through Block Chain, a federal reserve of sorts. You can go online and Google Block Chain and see the transactions as they are made. You won't know who, by name or account number, but you can see the country of origin. If a user uses the same address, it can be linked to other transactions they've made."

"Change the address."

"Best way, if a user wants anonymity. There's another way using what's called mixing, which is basically a bitcoin laundering scheme. They have mixing services that mix your bitcoins with others to obscure the original source. Like real cash, you've got to trust your mixing service."

"Oh, what a web . . ."

Lake continued, "Regulators are going crazy keeping up with the schemes that pop up regarding money laundering and other illegal transaction. They're devising their own schemes to track huge sums of money. Most normal folks would not exchange Uncle Sam's dollars for money that is math-based and easily lost in the shuffle."

"For me," I said, "unless I can pay taxes with it, I'm sticking to sub cash and check. But terrorists with super computers could act as their own banking system using bitcoin."

"You can bet your butt they're doing it."

Caliphate.

Once I rang off, I consulted Wiki, my favorite know-it-all, besides Web, to find the exact meaning. *A caliphate is an Islamic state led by a supreme religious as well as political leader known as a caliph.* Also, Wiki stated that *the last caliphate was abolished by Kemal Ataturk in 1924.*

Lake called to say that he was going to the Georgia state prison at Reidsville, that a prison snitch said he thought he knew who was doing the prostitutes. Through negotiations, the prisoner would only speak to Lieutenant Lake, the man who had arrested him and put him where he was. Sounded like a very long shot to me, but Lake was on his way to the prison located in the middle of the state.

That meant he would not be having dinner with Husam and Yasmin. I thought I detected a bit of glee in his voice.

Turned out I wasn't having dinner with Husam and Yasmin either. Husam never answered my email on the choice of restaurant and the meeting time. I drove to Bacchanalia, waited and an hour later concluded I had been flat stood up. Too bad; I'd been tasting the prime rib all the way.

CHAPTER THIRTY-FOUR

The new day continued like the old night. Showers and thunder, but I made the most of it by looking between the rain drops on my window and thinking of the coming explosion of May flowers in my backyard. Then the phone rang. Lake, surely. Out with the doldrums, welcome spirit lift.

Until I heard Pearly Sue's news. Thomas Page had dressed and left the hospital in the wee hours without checking out or being seen. *My mama told me nothing good happens in the middle of the night, and I concur. Most of the time.*

Pearly Sue said she was leaving for Atlanta out of the Boston airport, where she would return her rental car. She said Johnson of Dirk's Detectives insisted he follow her every mile to her destination. Which was fine with me.

I called Web and asked that he check the departures from the airports in the New England area, looking for Page and/or Reeve and Shara. Web still had his Fishnet tower set to monitor calls from Reeve's kick number, but I was sure by now she'd ditched it, since I believed she'd met up with Thomas Page after he skipped out of the hospital. Web was also busy with the login and password numbers he collected from the rogue node on Husam's law firm's server. Not exactly the loftiest of uses for his brilliance, but essential to me. What the hell were they up to?

And where the hell was Prince Husam? No email responses or cell-phone call-backs.

The slick streets slowed me, along with the rest of Atlanta, on the move toward downtown. Damn Atlanta traffic.

When I finally reached the office, Web looked worried. He said that the receiver of the decrypted data packets that were coming through the exit node every couple of minutes was Husam himself. The information was passed by way of instant messaging and was about transactions to various clients.

I watched Web, standing over him, arms folded, fascinated with the monitor. His was an impersonal world. His endgame was the successful hacking that led to the recipient.

"Money," Web said, looking up at me. "Money's moving through the tunnels. The traffic coming out of the computers and being funneled into newer encrypted packages, then fed to the onion routers, tells me they are part of the same circuit."

"Where's the money going?"

"All over the globe," Web said. "Pakistan, Cyprus, Belgium, France, Switzerland, Indonesia, London."

"Places with large . . ." I hated to say it. ". . . Muslim populations."

"Terrorism."

"The prince?"

"What better cover?"

"Breaks my heart. Let me call Lake."

"He's on the way here from Reidsville. You must have been in a dead cell zone because he couldn't get you. He told me to tell you he got zippo from the trip, except a threat."

"I must tell him about what you've found."

Web twitched his nose. "Think about this, Dear Boss. The lieutenant will be compelled to tell his superiors at APD and they will be compelled to contact Homeland Security, and a whole lot of other feds, and the case will be taken from us."

"So right," I said, happy that Web had put into words the

same dreads that leapt through my head. "We don't *know* that the law firm is moving money to terrorists."

"Not yet, we don't," Web agreed.

He, like me, hates to let go of a case. The FBI once swiped a case from us, and I'll never forget the agony. The resolution wasn't fatal, but could have been better for the child if everything had been left in our hands.

He said, "I'm still worming through their computer, rooting for hidden truths."

"Can they detect you?"

"A sharp administrator can detect an intruder, but not me. I get in and leave without their ever knowing. I think there's been an admin change since the first time I set off their alarms. They have open ports anyone can walk through now."

"Can they find our ISP or DNS?"

He raised his eyebrows. "We're well-masked, computer-wise, but we may have raised suspicions."

"Our interest in them is apparent through Husam."

"Correct."

"What is the history of their money movement? To whom? What agencies?"

"No history. Wiped. No stored data."

"That doesn't seem likely."

"Probably in some big ledger that is kept in an earthly safe."

"Find out more about that firm. Get Dirk's or Paul at Interpol. If there's been a change, that might mean the prince is on the move."

"To Saudi Arabia, maybe?"

"My thinking. With or without Shara."

"The hell with Reeve, eh?"

"Eh."

I left Web's office and almost walked into Lake. I wondered if he had been listening from the hall. I keep the door into the lobby locked. Visitors and clients know to press a button to enter once the lock is released. Lake, however, has his own key.

He kissed my forehead and rubbed his hand over my arm. "What's going on, Boudicca?"

"See my piercing glare and hear my harsh voice?"

"I do," he grinned.

"So what are you doing sneaking down the hall?"

"Eavesdropping on the battle plan."

"I'll let Tacitus put words in my mouth. *Our cause is just and the deities are on our side. The one Roman legion who dared to face us was destroyed. On my battered body and my daughters' stolen chastity I will win or die; if men want to live in slavery, that's their choice.*"

He clapped. "Bravo. Where'd you park your chariot?"

"Oh, Jeez, I'm double-parked downstairs."

I headed for my office. We often do this thing with history, or comedy, or whatever comes to mind when something off occurs between us.

"You could welcome me back by asking how things went in Reidsville."

"Welcome back. How did things go in Georgia's model prison?"

"It is a model, compared to others and what it used to be. I like the new warden. Other than that, nothing came of the meeting with the scumbag. I think he just wanted to tell me he missed me and what he'd like to do with me once he's out. At least someone misses me."

I made a face, stopping short of sticking out my tongue. "Page is on the move."

"I know. He boarded a flight out of Toronto, to Raleigh, North Carolina."

"You beat Webdog to the info." That was because Web was on the trail of terrorist scumbags. "Too bad you didn't bet me.

Who are Page's connections in Raleigh?"

"None that we know of. But it's a short drive to Atlanta."

"You think?"

"It appears he got a ride to Toronto, walked into the airport and got the first flight to the southern United States."

"Reeve. She was waiting outside the hospital."

"How did they communicate?"

"Computer or smoke signal."

"Same difference."

"She would be on the flight. Check for . . ."

"We did. No women of her description. Four female teenagers traveling to Raleigh, a woman and male child traveling on a French passport, an elderly couple . . ."

"Lordy, lordy. Shara was born in Paris. Betcha anything Reeve has a French passport, too. So would Husam. They were disguised. Shara would have been dressed as a boy."

"Oh, master of disguise, you would think that." I did once successfully pass myself off as a gay man.

"I'll get a man on it. I need to check with the shop now."

He left my office for the hall, where evidently he did his listening.

His call to the shop yielded more information. Things were happening. I could feel the pulse of the case quickening. About time, too. This had been a long slog.

Lake said that, according to the Sarasota police, Weatherby never arrived at his home, if, indeed, he was the passenger that Alvarez flew to Sarasota. He had been gone at least a week, according to his neighbors, who, the SPD officers said, seemed to be happy to be rid of him. "Weatherby doesn't have a rap sheet," Lake said, "but there have been complaints lodged against him and a list of complaints that he's lodged against his neighbors, the gas stations, the shopkeepers and the city officials. Apparently, he and the city manager don't get along. Nor does he get along with the county commissioners. Weatherby's one of those busybodies who goes to every council and commission meeting to gripe."

"Where would this world be without the gripers?"

"Where is Weatherby?" Lake asked the obvious rhetorical question.

"In the wind, evidently," I said.

"The clerk at Charlie Brown didn't recognize him, Husam or Page from the photos my officer showed her. Neither did mechanics."

Web knocked on the door frame.

Lake said, "Hey, Webdog, you look like you just broke into the Pentagon's computer."

"Been there, done that," he said, lazily. "I have some good stuff about Zogby and the law firm."

"Shoot," Lake said.

"First, Zogby seems to be AWOL."

I looked at Lake and thought about the law firm's probable change of computer administrators. Zogby, I guessed, could be the firm's principle administrator and he was absent from the post. I recalled Web's words: *the receiver of the decrypted information packets that were coming every couple of minutes was Husam himself.*

"Go on, Web."

Here's what Webdog told us:

The law firm of Meadows, Wessell and Zogby is a relatively old firm, but not old-old by New York standards. Used to be Meadows and Wessell, and was founded in the early nineteen-fifties by two Princeton graduates. Both men, as you can imagine, came from old-money families and are as liberal as they come. They were into all kinds of law and at one time the firm employed thirty lawyers from all walks of life—Jews, Asians,

Blacks. Oh, they thought they were cock-of-the-walk egalitarians. In the sixties, when blacks were hosed and strung up in the south, they boasted of their belief that all people should enjoy social, political and economic rights and opportunities.

"You know where I'm going with this," Web said.

Along came the Muslims. The partners hired Yemenis and Iranians and Egyptians. Of course it was in their best interest, since they were quickly becoming an international firm specializing in investment and finance.

I interrupted this compelling narrative. "Did they do divorces?"

"How plebian."

One Egyptian in particular was Jaul Zogby's father, Amin. Amin put Jaul through college and then died. Jaul naturally took his father's place in the firm and that was thirty-six years ago. Over the next decades, up until now, the firm had slowly lost lawyers. Attrition, one is led to believe. But lawyers who worked there blamed Zogby.

Specific blame came from a prominent New York lawyer that Web got in touch with through Dirk's data files on attorneys. The lawyer was a Meadows and Wessell dropout back in the nineties. "Jaul Zogby," he told Web, "managed to retire the old guys off to pastures in Connecticut, but before he accomplished that, he was made partner in a firm that vowed the original founders were to be the only partners. Zogby then proceeded to run off the rest of the lawyers so today there are only three, and one is hearing impaired."

Guess Zogby was continuing the tradition of egalitarianism.

I said to Web and Lake, "I read somewhere that attorneys are leaving their firms in droves."

Web said, "Not droves exactly. My lawyer buddy in New York said that the normal attrition rate is twenty percent, even in this rough economy when lawyers should feel lucky to be employed."

"There's always the FBI and other government jobs," Lake said.

"True, but it's more that law firms are bad managers. Their financial structure depends on building a pyramid organization by hiring drones for pittance and working them until they leave. The survivors earn high praise and bonuses. If too many dropped out, the money isn't there for the top earners."

"So how did Zogby manage to stay afloat? Husam al-Saliba?"

"No way. My lawyer informant said Husam is a pain in Zogby's rump. The prince is a poor rich boy. But he's been around for eight or so years."

"So, what are they doing with all those empty offices?"

"They've moved, downsized several times."

"What's Zogby's specialty?"

Web laughed. "I'll give you a hint. What have we been discussing for the past several days."

I looked at Lake. Close your ears and say la-la-la over and over.

Lake grinned.

I said, "Onions."

"Your mama didn't raise no fool."

"And the APD taught her how to reason," Lake said.

Web said, "Zogby's a computer genius. And a financial wizard when it comes to overseas money. And, before you ask, I'll tell you. He's been investigated by the New York attorney general and the feds. So far he's avoided charges."

Lake said, "Which means they don't have enough on him. And that's why DSS or some other fed was watching Husam. They weren't protecting him; they were investigating him and the firm."

"Are the two founders alive still?" I asked.

Web answered, "Meadows died in the seventies, but Wessell is alive and in his nineties. I tracked down his abode. It's a fancy

nursing home in Rhode Island. His nurse says he's lucid at
times and when that happens, he swears and be-damns if he
isn't going back to New York and kick that A-rab out of the firm
and take control again."

I said, "It's enough to make a conservative out of you."

We didn't learn much more that day, and it was puzzling. I'd
felt the buzz of something big happening, but after learning the
history of the prince's law firm, I felt let down. Why? Who knows
when serotonin flows to a low cranny of the brain. Where was
Weatherby? Where was Zogby? Where was Husam? I had been
all pumped up but realized I had nowhere to go.

Lake called and said he needed to eat an early dinner because
he was doing night duty. Although the prison visit wasn't
productive, the fence in the home-invasion cases came through
with a couple of names. They were going to be rounded up and
questioned, hopefully tonight.

Since nothing was happening, I said I'd meet him at his
favorite sushi place on Peachtree.

Arata is a small sushi restaurant tucked between an upscale
antique shop and a hairdresser on West Peachtree Street. Cheap
Japanese statues and wall hangings add to the ambience as
tinny, discordant, Asian music plays. We sat at the bar where the
owner, Arata, makes everything from scratch. Lake went for the
scallops, mango and scallions, with wasabi straight. I ordered
my usual, a sashimi salad with citrus dressing.

Sashimi plates of red snapper and shrimp did a good job of
lifting Lake's mood. After that, came the *oh-toro-nigiri* with lime
juice sprinkled on top. I nibbled on the buttery tuna, but
couldn't conjure an appetite. "You're going to be hungry later,"
Lake said, taking pleasure in his cuisine.

"Don't think so."

"You're going to waste away, and don't forget we're doing

the 10K in the morning. We've been slack lately."

"We need to work less and play more."

He leered. "I'll second that."

Chapter Thirty-Five

I woke up to a sharp report as if a gun had gone off next to my ear. I sat straight up in bed and yelled Lake's name. But Lake wasn't here. He was on duty.

Another vicious crack had me jumping from the bed. In that same instant my bedroom lit up as if a halogen convention were being held here. A boomer rattled the window frames and rain sheeted down the glass. It was dark as pitch and no flashing came from the electronic clock on my nightstand. Switching on the bedside lamp . . . nothing. No power. The cordless phone was dead, and when I'd gotten home, I plugged my cell into the electric outlet. It hadn't gotten enough juice to power on. I sat on the bed and reached for the flashlight, knocked it to the floor and listened as it rolled across the hardwood as if escaping the frightful night to hide under a chair.

I walked to the dresser and peered into the face of a venerable old ticking clock. Lightning struck and showed me the time: three fifteen. No more sleep until the storm abated.

A scorching lightning display branched across the black sky and cracked against windows facing the front yard and street. I shrunk back and waited to hear glass shatter at my feet, it was that close.

A sensation that the intense storm was hell-bent on peeling a layer of skin ran through me. The humidity didn't help the raw feeling, and had me breathing like I had cotton stuck up my nose. I thought of my gun. It was snug in the handbag resting on the island in the kitchen. Damn, I'd meant to take it to my nightstand, where it lay when not on my person. Once in bed, I was too tired to fetch it. *Sloppy, very sloppy.* My holstered backup gun lay on the floor by the chair where I'd taken it off along with my shoes, socks and slacks.

Carrying slippers, I crept to the island in the kitchen and retrieved the Glock from its holster. At least I had a fighting chance if the squall broke through the door and came at me. After that, I moved to the window to look over the backyard. Flickering lightning drove the dark away, but nothing human was in the backyard; nothing animal, either.

I went to the front window and looked out.

A brilliant shaft split through the raging rain. A hooded figure stood on the pavers—just standing there, probably aware of being watched.

As if cued, the figure began to move toward the door while lighting an LED flashlight. *Oh, God, don't let it be an officer having gathered the courage to tell me Lake had been hurt, or worse.*

It climbed the steps to the porch. Came the knock as my heart stopped. Lake? No. I stood to one side of the front door. I would not look out the peephole. People get shot through wooden doors checking out the peephole. I rapped the gun on the wood. I breathed in. "Who's there?"

No answer.

Since my voice competed against thunder, I said louder, "Who is there?"

No answer.

Even a yell now. "Who are you?"

The knock came again.

I turned off the alarm—one that goes to battery juice when the electricity goes out—and clicked the bolt. I took the short chain out of its housing and spoke through the cracked door. "Who's there?"

"Reeve Cresley," the voice said.

Reeve?

The voice was female.

"What do you want?"

"Can I come in?"

"Let me see some identification."

"I have none on me."

"Prove to me who you are."

"I am Donna and Lowell Cresley's daughter. They are dead. I've been hiding and on the run with my daughter, Shara."

"Where is Shara?"

"With a friend."

"What's your friend's name?"

"Thomas Page."

I unhooked the longer chain and trusted she wasn't going to shove a pistol through the crack.

"How is Tom?"

"He's well."

"Did he reveal your whereabouts when he was tortured?"

"No, not even when he was shot full of drugs. He is lucky your girl got there when she did. He would have been shot, like the caretaker. Jesus . . ." She held out imploring arms. "Look, I'm me. You've seen my photograph; I can raise the flashlight to my face." And this she did.

I unhooked the chain and drew the door open. The storm didn't look like it had any intention of lessening. She was inside, pushing the hood off her face, dripping on the hardwood.

Even wet and shivering, I saw by the light she held that Reeve Cresley was a lovely woman. Blond hair strung down the sides of her face. Her blue eyes were filled with trouble. She wore a Burberry and sandals.

Closing the door, I grabbed the flashlight and the back of the coat's collar and pulled it off her. I tossed the wet thing on the floor and got a wool coat from the coat closet. "Put this on and kick those shoes off," I said, picking a pair of sock booties off the closet floor. "Let's go in the kitchen."

Quickly, she did as told, pulling on the booties as she scrambled behind me.

"Tom brought you and Shara food, didn't he?"

She shivered as she said yes.

I followed after her and scooped my handbag off the island where four stools lined one side of the granite-topped structure. "Take a stool," I said, and she scooted onto one. "Pick up your flashlight and aim it at the cabinet above the range. I have candles and a lantern there."

She flashed, and I retrieved my emergency candle supply and the LED lantern.

Having gotten them lit, I asked her, "What brings you here?"

"You're looking for me."

"Did you just learn that?"

"When Tommy came to Atlanta. After you went to Boulder looking for me, Tommy said you told him on the plane why."

"How did he deliver the food and stuff you needed at the Fergusons'?"

"In a van he bought at a company's auction."

"The APD checked. There's been no auctions."

"This was in Boulder, couple years ago."

"He drove it here?"

"Yes. I'd flown to Colorado to get away from my husband, and then Tommy drove us to Atlanta after I talked to my folks and they recommended we stay in the Fergusons' house until we sorted things out. Mama said they wouldn't mind, but she was afraid for us after my husband came looking for us, so we had Tommy bring us supplies."

"What identification did you use to buy plane tickets?"

"My Colorado driver's license is in the same name as my

French passport, if I needed additional ID."

"What name is your French passport in?"

"D. R. Creelay. The French office spelled it wrong and I found it useful for anonymity. Shara has a French passport, too."

"Speaking of fraudulent names, why E. B. White?"

"Shara's favorite story book is *Charlotte's Web.*"

"I'll make us tea."

"Sounds so good," she said, hugging herself to keep from shivering.

I filled the kettle. Thank goodness for a gas stove. I've never gotten around to buying an electric tea maker, because I don't drink that much tea. Out of the corner of my eye I noticed Reeve's head turned toward the living room. She was nervous, maybe second-guessing herself, looking to make a run for it.

"Did Tom tell you someone shot at him, or him and me, while I was at his ranch?"

"Sure."

"I believe he knew who."

"Had to be Lloyd Weatherby. He knows that part of the country."

"Why?"

"He and Yasmin are looking for me. Well, not me—Shara. They'll steal her and give her to Sammy. He'll take her to Saudi Arabia or any place that will have him."

That was a curious statement. Standing across the island, I asked, "Where's Tom now?"

She whirled toward me. "In a place."

"We're all in a place," I said, getting mugs and tea bags ready for the boiling water.

"You know what I mean. I'm not supposed to blab."

I glanced over my shoulder, noting that the thunderstorm

was moving away from my house. "I want to know where Shara is."

"I don't want you to know. I want to pay you twice as much as Sammy to stop looking for us. These things happening so close to home are making me nervous. I want to settle somewhere with people I can trust."

So close to home. While shifting things on the dim counter, my hand went to my purse and felt for my digital voice recorder. "Why should I agree to that?"

"Because you don't know why you're looking for us and what this is really about."

I snapped the record button, and, with sleight of hand, I widened the purse top. I said, "I'll think about it, Reeve, once you tell me what this is really about. I'm not a money hound, so don't dangle coin in front of me." That was a partial lie because I do work for money. Money keeps Mama in her fancy nursing home and me almost guilt-free for her being there.

"I don't have much time. Tommy's coming back for me in half an hour. I stood out there ten minutes getting up the nerve."

I stood across the island from where she sat and folded my arms. "So, let's talk."

In the dusky room with our shadows dancing in the flickering candles and lantern-shaded light, she talked.

"Sammy is not what you think he is."

"We humans never totally reveal ourselves, even to those we love most, but I did figure out he wants to marry his Saudi fiancée, Aya."

The kettle began to whistle, and I turned to it, lest the whistling blot an important piece of her conversation from being recorded. I continued, "I believe he's changed his mind about his political ambitions. I believe he wants to return to Saudi Arabia and take his rightful place."

"Husam al-Saliba will not be fulfilling his dreams of marriage to Aya or kingship."

I poured water onto the mugged tea bags. "Sugar? Substitute? Cream?" She shook her head. I spooned substitute into my mug. "And the reasons are?"

"He can marry anyone he wants to, like he married me. I am not his legal wife in the kingdom, however."

I told her I knew that.

"Once his duplicity is known, Aya will not marry him."

I could believe he was duplicitous.

She said, "Do you understand Saudi royalty and the tenets?"

"Somewhat. You don't have long, so don't keep me guessing." I noticed her rubbing her nose and turned to fetch a tissue.

Against the wired atmosphere of flickering lightning and thunder in the distance, she told me things that completed the riddle of Husam Saliba.

"Sammy is not the son of Hadid al-Saliba as the world thinks." She blew her nose and I retrieved a countertop waste basket. "I've caught a cold." She blew and threw the tissue away.

She continued, "Sammy is Prince Hadid al-Saliba's adopted son. Hadid adopted his cousin's son when Cousin Badru al-Fakeeh died of pneumonia right after Sammy was born. Rana, Husam's adoptive mother and a princess of the royal line, had a baby daughter and so she had milk for him, too. Rana claimed Husam to be her and Hadid's son after Hadid died in a plane crash on his way to Mecca when Husam was eight. I will tell you how I know all of this in a minute."

"I was wondering," I said.

"Hadid was distraught that his favorite cousin, Badru, was dead. He apparently loved the baby boy as much as his cousin and treated him like a son. Hadid married a second wife, another royal princess, brought her into his household and she became pregnant with Yasmin. Rana was also pregnant with another daughter. Hadid had no more sons."

"How could they expect to get away with such a deception?"

"The royal family is huge. Households are huge. More importantly, at the time, Hadid and Rana lived in the Arabian boonies. So did Cousin Badru. Hadid's family moved to Riyadh when Husam was five. I doubt anyone in Riyadh knew about the adoption at the time it occurred."

"But someone from the boonies did and remembered," I said.

She nodded. "The surviving brothers of the kingdom's founder are known to the world. They are old and are dying— but all have many sons, thousands of them, including the sons of those who died a long time ago, like Hadid. Hard to keep track of who belongs to whom." She wiped her nose. "Adoption is different in that country than it is here. Saudis adopt children, especially of kin, all the time." She sipped tea. "Hadid, as the king's brother, was in line for succession. Blood is everything, especially in marriage and leadership."

I started to ask something, but she shook her head.

"Let me finish. I met Rana on my one trip to Saudi Arabia. She was a very forceful woman then, and probably still is. She was ambitious for Husam, and herself. It is about the only thing a woman can brag about in that god-forsaken country. Here's how it works in Saudi law. Since Rana nursed Sammy in infancy, she was a *mehram* to him. He would not be her son, but he would be *like* a son, in that she could not marry him, nor her daughters marry him. He could only be an heir *to his natural family.* However, in the confusion of households, he got away with being a son." She sipped tea again. "Rana dotes on Sammy—the born charmer." Reeve even smiled.

"Did Husam tell you he was adopted?"

"Oh, no." Somewhere in the faint glow of her eyes was victory. "I'm sure that he didn't know it *until I told him.*"

She rose and her shadow moved like spatter paint across the walls. I hurried after her. She looked out the window. "Anyone?" I asked.

"No," she exhaled slowly. She turned to me. "Saudis keep their family's secrets, but I found out."

I urged her back into the kitchen where the recorder was.

She sat and picked out a tissue. "Shara and I were in New York. I hadn't been happy with Sammy for a long time, but I wanted to make it work, if he did. He'd met Aya a few times in Europe, but he said he, too, wanted to make our marriage work. So, I ended it with Tommy, and before I went to work in California, spent my leave on Long Island. This one day, I wanted time to myself and to shop, and so told Sammy that I would be out all day. He hired a nanny who was in the service of a Saudi family. A perfect fit for Shara, the bastard said.

"Come lunch time, I got an idea to go to Sammy's office to surprise him. We would lunch together and start to repair our differences. The law firm is a small office, not like it was a couple of years ago. Jaul Zogby and Sammy were in a conference room, arguing."

I interrupted. "In English?"

She shook her head "no" quickly. "Arabic. I understand it better than I speak it."

"You were saying about them arguing?"

"The door wasn't closed tight. Their law clerk, Mohammed, wasn't at his desk, so I sat and I listened before Sammy came out and saw me. I had heard enough to know what their firm was into. They were arguing about giving a suicide bomber's family money to live out the rest of their lives. The widow of the bomber was to go to a soccer game to avenge her husband's death on those she came in contact with by discharging her body bomb." Reeve's eyes were saucers of disbelief. "Hard to imagine—my husband—talking about funding suicide bomb-ings. Jaul had reservations that the widow could pull it off and wanted to wait before handing over the money. Sammy disagreed with Jaul and came hurrying out of the office before I could get out of my seat.

"He was shocked to see me there, and angry. I got angry. Jaul came out and accused me of snooping. It made me sick to think . . ."

"You were in danger."

"I never thought about that until later. I was sick to learn they manage money for the jihadists through the internet. Do you know about onion routers?" I said that I did. She said, "That day I learned my husband was a terrorist." Her eyes leaked tears. "Husam tried to explain. He said his father's beloved cousin, Badru, was a radical jihadist and studied in Egypt with radical clerics and mullahs. He also said that his father, Prince Hadid, was against the king's reforms and that his mother, Princess Rana, told him that Hadid's plane crash was no accident. Husam tried to make me see how he was born and raised to be a radical. I said I wanted no part of it. Then he said that he would stay in America and do diplomacy in Washington DC and we would all go there and live. He didn't know it at that time, but it was a pipe dream. Wait until he learned of his adoption. The dashing of his dreams would keep him in the arms of the jihadists. I hated admitting it—standing there listening to promises he wouldn't keep—that my marriage was over."

"He made a good spy," I said. "How did you learn of his adoption? Where is his birth mother?"

"She is confined to an asylum. Said to be schizophrenic. That's why Husam was adopted after Badru died."

"Do the many cousins now know about his past?"

"Those who don't know by now, soon will." She coughed,

sounding like a two-pack-a-day smoker, then drank off the last of her tea. "Soon the world will know about Husam al-Saliba. A biographer is writing a family history. Tommy Page told me. Tommy has ties to the Muslim publishing world through his own published books. He shares an editor with the biographer, and the editor confided to Tommy that a book about the prominent royal cousins was in the works. At the time I thought a biography would be a good thing. A biography would make Sammy more than a pretty prince. But a few weeks ago, Tommy told me in confidence what the French author had found out. It must have been a real coup for the biographer when he obtained Sammy's birth certificate and talked to the village people. They may not be scholars, but people know things and they have long memories."

I agreed with her. When a woman brings a baby into a household she hasn't given birth to, and that birth hasn't been witnessed by at least one midwife, people will whisper.

Reeve said, "There has always been infighting in that family, and when the book is released it will ramp up a thousand-fold. The world will know that Husam al-Saliba is not in line for the crown. Nowhere near it. There are other supposed devastating truths about Sammy in the book."

"And they are?"

"His writings in the *madrasa*. He studied English and memorized the *Quran*."

"That doesn't make Prince Husam a jihadist." *Said for the recorder.*

"He is not a royal prince and yes, he is a jihadist."

"How old is Husam?"

"He is forty-one."

Older than I thought, or than he seemed.

"So all this made you flee Long Island with Shara."

She shook her head and looked at me like I was an idiot. "I

have no problem with Sammy's being adopted, or that he can't be crown prince. That day in the office I made him swear that he would give up banking terrorists. But Zogby came in and told Sammy to be straight with me; that they were in too deep and would never be able to stop their work for the jihad. I knew by the look on Sammy's face, Zogby was right. Zogby left and I blurted out my spite. I told Sammy what I knew about his adoption. He was shocked. He hadn't known. He accused me of lying. I was leaving when he stopped me. He begged me not to leave him. He promised to reform, to straighten everything out. But I knew I'd better get out of there. It was hard for him to hold back his rage. He tried to restrain me. The next day, I was driving on Long Island and a car ran me off the road. Six feet farther down the bank, and we'd been in the slough. I saw the silhouette as the driver flashed by me. I'd swear it was Salman. Sammy denied he was behind it, but I left in the middle of the night."

"What were you doing in Montauk?"

She laughed and threw her head back. "Looking at the sea while Shara slept on the backseat. Thinking. I had learned something terrible."

I spoke my thoughts. "His betrayal of you and America."

She thought a moment as if she felt it unwise to comment, but before she made up her mind, headlights flashed through the rain-soaked window panes and slowed, illuminating the gloom of the kitchen. "My ride," Reeve cried, jumping off the stool and running to the door. Once there, she whirled and searched my face. "Yasmin was in New York, too. She came there to oversee Shara's circumcision whenever they got the chance. I got to my daughter just in time. The nanny confessed. They're all extremists."

CHAPTER THIRTY-SIX

"Fishnet is not finished fishing," Web said.

"Oh?" Reeve and Page were together here so no need to phone one another.

Web said, "Something interesting swam into the net during the night. A cell call from the Cresleys' community."

"Is there more?"

"I programmed Fishnet to find matching numbers from phone records at Charlie Brown Airport—the day Alvarez took a passenger to Sarasota."

My heart up-ticked. "That's a lot more."

"Whoever made last night's cell call used the same phone to call Alvarez."

I began to laugh and so did Web. "I did good, boss?"

"Your initiative serves me very well, Webby. I need you to do one more thing."

I hadn't talked to Lake by cell this morning. Yet. That was going to happen as soon as he took a break from his case.

I hopped in the shower to avoid his call—to give me thinking time. I had to tell him about Web's onion router discovery and the visit last night from Reeve. And the cell call to Charlie Brown. The sooner, the better. For me. For our relationship. For our conjoined careers.

Showered, dressed, gun purse loaded, I looked at my mobile phone. Lake had called.

I pressed the number to call back.

"You in transit?" he asked.

"Just got out of the shower."

"What's going on?"

"A lot."

"I'm listening."

"Let's meet at the diner on Fourteenth Street."

"Must be big, you going for Eggs Benedict on a week day."

"I'm going to lose the case, and I will need some salve for my soul."

"To whom?"

"Our favorite feds for starters."

"We figured that, Dru. Long story?"

"Yes."

"Let's roll. Meet you in fifteen."

"Make it twenty."

Web called as I was leaving. "I got an IP linked to an exit router in Buckhead. Yasmin Saliba. The source host is in New York."

So much for Husam swearing off funneling terrorism money. I said, "That's what she was using her brains for."

"Dirk's operatives are still watching her. She's got company in the condo. Weatherby."

"Let me know when she's on the move."

Sometimes I like to keep things to myself, to savor what they represent, especially in victory. But I was keeping Reeve's visit to myself because I was flat-out scared. I hadn't given Reeve an answer when she asked again—right before closing the door and walking into the rain to Tom's car—*Would I take money to quit the case?* I didn't answer her, but rather asked my own question: "Why were your parents killed?"

"Because they were who they were," she said. "They were

right not liking Sammy, but they didn't know why. I'm going to get their killer. Ours was never a happy family, but I have a score to settle with the bastard."

She knew.

"Reeve!" I called as she ran out, into the rain. I was tempted to run after her. In my hesitation—in watching her flee down the path as the car door was opened by the driver inside—I'd let her go purposely.

Because, I, too, knew.

"They're holed up in range of the Cresley condo," I said to Lake after I told him everything—a virtual purge of facts and random thoughts with few interruptions from a man used to asking a lot of questions. *So close to home,* Reeve had said.

He said, "It's a federal case." He didn't look happy. Actually, he put down the bacon he'd picked up when I began talking about money moving all over the world. "How the hell is Webdog going to justify hacking into a law firm's computers?"

"He didn't commit fraud, didn't damage the computers, didn't conspire to overthrow governments, didn't traffic in passwords, codes, commands, IP networks or anything illegal. The government would give him a medal if they ever found out."

"He could be in trouble by affecting interstate and foreign commerce. He involved computers located outside the US. That's our job, and we obtain warrants for reasonable cause."

"Those computers were used to further terrorism, Lieutenant Search Warrant. Webdog knows his boundaries. He was out of there, and he says there's no way anyone can prove he was in there. I don't know how, but he erased his presence."

Lake looked unbelieving. "Where can I look for reasonable cause for us to bust into their computers?"

"Let's go outside."

In his car, I played the digital voice recorder's clear and uncompromising reasonable cause.

"We've still got the murder cases," Lake said, looking mollified. "But if Husam gets out of the country, there will be hell to pay for all of us."

"Do your duty and call your pet feds."

He called headquarters and talked briefly to Commander Haskell's secretary. He told her to run Haskell down and tell him to stick around. "I'll be at the shop in half an hour."

I followed him in my car in case I needed to leave. I may not be allowed into the inner sanctum when the jetsam reached warp speed.

On the way, Web called. "Jaul Zogby was found on his yacht in a bay off Long Island. He'd been beheaded. Qasim and Mohammed were roommates. They were found beheaded in their beds."

I waited in the squad room while Lake took my story and voice recorder into Commander Haskell's office. When the door opened, and the commander summoned me, it was my cue the jetsam had begun to fly and I was to be part of it. I didn't know how I would respond. I was used to being his favorite. Wasn't it he who nominated me for the FBI Academy's training facility in Quantico, Virginia? I go to sleep at night thinking about that six-mile obstacle course laid down by the Marine Corps. It tested my mental and physical strength more than once and saved my life. I would never forget Hogan's Alley, a mock mini-town with a cinema, houses, hotels, used car lots and other businesses, where we were schooled in the use of weapons and vehicle operations. I was there before the era of the terrorists, before the World Trade Center was brought down. I hate secret evil cells and friendly-looking people who turn out to be heartless monsters. I want my foe to be straight up about it. Come at me face-first, armed with a favorite weapon, and we'll fight it out.

When I looked into Commander Haskell's eyes, he nodded as if he knew why I'd looked apprehensive, and why I faced him with an appreciative posture.

"Sit," Haskell said.

I sat on a padded armchair at the antique table in the commander's office.

"I want to hear this from you, Dru."

I could only hope I got the words out right, as in succinct.

"Jaul Zogby took control of an old, liberal New York law firm. As attrition among the white, Asian and Jewish lawyers occurred, he replaced them with Muslims."

"Where are you getting your information?"

"From a former lawyer in the firm. He's Jewish. He talked to Dennis Caldwell and promised to help the APD in their investigation."

"You talking about Webdog?"

"Yes, sir."

"So Zogby hires jihadists."

"I can't swear that they all were. But the firm came down to three people: Zogby, Husam and a hearing-impaired law clerk named Mohammed."

"Okay."

"At some point, the firm got into the business of moving money around to various jihadist organizations, like mosques, cells and charities."

"How did Webdog find this out?"

This was tricky. "Research."

"He's a hacker, isn't he?"

"He's an internet genius who knows his way around the web, yes."

"Thus Webdog." He even made a close-mouthed grin.

I said, "He discovered that the law firm was part of a hidden service network called Tor."

"Know it. We got men monitoring the kiddie-porn sites constantly."

"Well, it's useful for moving virtual money, too."

"Who are the others in the cell?"

"Yasmin Saliba, Salman Habibi, Mohammed, Qasim, who is Husam's trainer. Lloyd Weatherby."

"You know, your computer genius poached on the feds' territory."

"Not intentionally. Who knows where a missing persons case is going to take you? As a member of my staff, and on my authority as a licensed private investigator, he was investigating a missing mother and daughter."

"I hear what you're saying. I think you guys have more leeway sometimes than the Atlanta Police Department when it comes to probing."

"That doesn't mean the feds can't and won't try to bust my chops."

"That goes without saying. Why do you think Saliba *really* hired you?"

"You mean why he picked me above other PI's?"

"He heard you were good, no doubt, but why did he hire a PI?"

"His life was about to crumble. He faced prison, death, deportation, and he couldn't find his wife and daughter. I'll always remember that first dinner, and the afternoon tea at the Ritz, how calm, urbane, charming he was in the face of his impending downfall."

"I wasn't fooled," Lake said. "He was an ass."

Haskell said, "Lot of murderers and thieves put up a good front. But I'm still bumfuckled. Why hire any PI?"

I said, "It began before when Reeve began thinking about divorce. Her life with the prince wasn't satisfying, but his unraveling came when Reeve learned he was a financier for the jihadists. Then when she told him about the release of a book by a French biographer that proved he was adopted—not blooded enough for kingship—he went full panic. He needed to flee, but he wanted his daughter. Putting aside parental affection, Shara would be a bargaining chip in the kingdom or in exile because her grandmother is in the royal line. Husam hired me to do what he needed to get control of Shara. Ultimately, Reeve fled because of his intent to mutilate Shara."

Haskell looked uneasy. "Circumcision of females is a crime."

Lake said, "So is funding terrorists. But ours is a local case, and one we will solve ourselves."

Haskell twisted his lip. "So, Husam killed his in-laws?"

I shook my head. "We've always been dealing with several crimes, including conspiracies and cover-ups. Not all overlap."

"Where's your mother and daughter now?" Haskell asked.

So much of this was rhetorical. Lake had already briefed his commander. I said, "Reeve said she was going after her parents' killer. That presupposes the killer is in this city. We have to find her and Thomas Page. I'm wondering if she didn't give me a clue where they are." *So close to home.*

Haskell said, "I didn't hear it on the voice recorder, if she did. What about you, Lake?"

Shaking his head, Lake said, "Maybe."

Haskell's gray eyes looked into my blues. "You know about Jaul Zogby and the other two?" I nodded. "The New York Police Department has no leads, but even if Husam confesses, there's the diplomatic immunity thing."

"Maybe his king will negate dip immunity?" Lake said.

"Doubt it," Haskell said. "We can't charge, try and convict him on the murders of the Cresleys, even when we prove he is implicated in their deaths." Apparently Haskell still believed Husam had killed his in-laws, or conspired in their murders. "The only thing we can do is kick him home." He looked at me. "When was the last time you talked to Husam and Yasmin Saliba?"

"Three days ago. Husam was in New York and told me he was coming to Atlanta the next day. We arranged to have dinner with Yasmin, but he never showed. I never heard from him again. I haven't seen Yasmin since the Cresleys' funeral."

I should tell him I'm having Yasmin followed, but did he ask?

Haskell said, "Lieutenant Lake, would you fill Dru in on what we've learned from the feds."

Lake looked his official best. "Gary Scheel wrote a report that said, after facial recognition forensic testing, the face on the New Hampshire video is Lloyd Weatherby's. The person in Central Park at the Turtle Pond with Pearly Sue is unrecognizable. So is the man on the bench. Weatherby is wanted for questioning in the death of the Woodstock, New Hampshire, caretaker and the torture-drugging of Thomas Page."

Haskell said, "Scheel called to tell me in confidence that Victor Cartaloma is not assigned to watch Husam. He knew, he said, about the book on the al-Salibas and its revelations. He also said that Victor Cartaloma is dead. That he was killed in Baghdad."

"Was any agency watching Husam and Zogby in New York?" I asked. "Could Pearly Sue have actually been talking to a DSS agent?"

"Yes, to an agency tailing Husam," Haskell said. "They'd been on to that law firm and the cell. Jason Qasim plea-bargained a drug charge and gave up information. The feds were gathering their own facts when you stumbled into their case."

I took exception to *stumbled*. "Which agency?"

"All of them."

Lake said, "How much further can we go?"

"We're out of the terrorist case, whatever it turns out to be, against Husam, his sister, Yasmin, his man, Habibi, his trainer, the late squeal, Qasim, his law partner, the late Jaul Zogby, their associate, the late Mohammad, and the American traitor, Weatherby."

"There must be others involved," I said.

"It's not our watch," he said. "We'd be swatted down quicker than a fly on a picnic hotdog."

I was in my office; it was late, darkness falling, as I wrapped the paperwork on my mother–daughter case. I'd found—sort of— the mother and was assured the daughter was safe. Was that enough to call it a case closed? I'd emailed that information to Husam Saliba, but would he get it? I'd bet his computers were now under the control of some federal agency. I also left a message on his cell phone, which may have suffered the same fate.

Lake called, and, without a *Howdy, how's it going,* said, "It's him. A mechanic at the Sarasota Airport made him. Let's go."

"APD?"

"Yep."

"I'll be waiting outside."

As I was gathering my gun and ammunition, Web stuck his head in the doorway. "Dirk's called. She's on the move with Weatherby."

"Tell the operative don't approach. APD operation."

"You going, too?"

"By invitation."

"You deserve it. Great work."

"You, too, Webby."

CHAPTER THIRTY-SEVEN

A ten-year-old Lexus sedan was parked ten yards from Killarney's entrance—the man within was the shadow from Dirk's. He'd called to report that Yasmin and Weatherby had turned into Killarney Grounds.

When we pulled in, the gate was up and the guard shack empty. "Not good," Lake said. "For the guard."

Lake turned left at the first intersection and drove toward the Cresley house. Last night's net ping sited the building a couple hundred yards right of the gate. Blue flashing lights showed above rooftops from that direction, but we figured the action for us was at the Cresley house.

Driving the winding street, Lake advised, "Watch for the guard." I'd already had my head on a swivel doing just that.

Lake drove around to park at the back of the house where the garages were. It was so quiet the engine's ticking sounded like Lake was rhythmically snapping his fingers—something he does to his inner music. I got out, opening the door easy like when I was a kid and sneaking out to joyride in Portia's mama's Bentley, which was now mine.

We walked side by side to the gate. The spring rains had caused creeping grasses to run rampant over the brick pavers. The back of the house seemed to sag; the swimming pool enclosure had begun to rust. Ivy crawled up the screen like ivy likes to do.

Lake slipped a skeleton key into the lock.

From inside, someone fired a suppressed pistol. It seemed to come from an upper floor. Suppressors, known erroneously as silencers, only suppress the noise from propellant gases. I don't like suppressors. Just as I don't like hearing gunfire in a building I'm about to enter.

Cautious, Lake swung the door in. There was no alarm to be concerned about. The company cut the service before the Cresleys' bodies had cooled. It had come in for some blame, but I'm not sure why. Most likely because the company's honchos didn't like answering questions about letting the Cresleys get killed.

The kitchen was tiled in harlequin black and white. A man's body lay on the tile; his throat had been cut, making him look like he grimaced at the harlequin decor. Salman.

"One we don't have to worry about," Lake said.

I followed Lake around to the hall, past the guest bathroom and the murder study, and up the double-helix staircase. The steps had fancy skid-proof caps on the edge of each marble riser.

We moved quickly to the curve of the helix where it widened before turning away. The last step had us in a small foyer, where a single, floating staircase led to the third floor. In the small foyer, Lake paused and cocked his ear. I stood still and listened. Voices interrupted the silence in the darkness above us. Lake had his Beretta in hand. The Glock was in mine, sighted on tritium dots—the one at the rear notch being a single green dot aligned with a wider front green dot. I brought the pistol up and held it at ear level, the four-inch barrel pointed ceilingward. The reassuring aroma of metal and oil firmed my already solid resolve to get to the end of this case—the aroma of satisfaction and completion.

There was one more choice. Lake held up his pistol and mocked removing the magazine, but shrugged his shoulders, meaning my choice. My Glock was chambered with supersonic cartridges, like his. Even if I had a suppressor, the bullet would make a cracking sound when it broke the sound barrier. Lake was putting subsonics in his Beretta. Subsonics are nearly silent; good for discretion, but not high velocity. The bullets could lodge in a curtain at thirty feet. But who needs fast spurts in a house? I weighed stopping power against stealth. Lake was my guide. He liked stealth in this situation. So did I, because we both believed that a little girl was somewhere in the house.

I hit the magazine release and let it fall into my hand. Slipping it into a designated pocket of my magazine carrier, I then gripped the automatic's slide and pushed back. Quick as that, the chambered round was in my hand and in the same pocket as the magazine holding its supersonic buddies. I retrieved a subsonic magazine, slid it into the butt and locked it into place. I chambered a round and racked the slide. Like cops, I carried my gun at the ready. No racking to give a heads-up to the target.

I gripped the gun with both hands and extended my arms to form a triangle. I moved right and followed Lake, whose footfalls were light as those of a bird-of-paradise. What made me think that, I wondered.

One careful, quiet step at a time took us near the top of the floating stairs. Surely the master bedroom wasn't up there. Floating staircases were not for the clumsy or for drunks. An intersecting hallway went left and right. Lake raised a hand and motioned left. He would go that way. He pushed his palm down twice, meaning I should stay where I was until he signaled with his arm, either to follow him or go the other way.

When my head breached the top of the stairs, I saw a dim streak of light shining beneath a door. I guessed it came from an attic or sitting room. I stared at the light beneath the door to see if any movement crossed it. The voices, once loud, fell faint, barely audible.

Suddenly the silence was shattered by a scream. I took a step back down, my body bent and coiled, muscles tense, prepared as a rattlesnake to strike. The scream was followed by a harsh but controlled voice. One I knew.

I crouched low and moved forward. Looking left, down the hall, I didn't see Lake. Then I glanced right.

There, on the floor, lay a body. Though the hall was dark, I saw it was Husam.

The way the body lay, I figured he'd been shot in the right side of his head and spun ninety degrees before crumpling to the floor. Literally dead before his body hit the floor, his eyes were half-open. With his left hand pinned beneath his chest, one leg was bent and the other straight. He probably didn't have time to register the pain of a piece of lead slamming into the side of his head. If he could have had a flash thought, he'd know who his killer was, and he'd know why he'd been killed, and who killed Zogby and the others. He wouldn't know why the Cresleys were killed or Alvarez, though. Two separate crimes with separate causes.

The raised voices I heard were those of Reeve and Yasmin.

"No need to kill him," Reeve wailed.

"Allah reviles imposters."

"He never killed anyone."

"Shut your vile face."

I crouched, my left hand gripping the banister, my right hand holding the gun. Dim light bordered the bottom of the door, and shadows floated back and forth. I listened to make out the words of two distinct voices. One was louder than the other. A third voice tried to join in but was too indistinct to know if it was man or woman. Reeve shouted. "You bastard. You filthy bastard."

Bastard. A man.

My position was too vulnerable. If someone came running out of the room, hovering in no-man's-land was untenable.

Looking left, I saw the shape of Lake in the darkness. He had his arm raised pointing at the door. It meant we were going in. Standing, I waited no more than three seconds for Lake to give the signal to rush the room. Lake motioned me into the hall.

Just then came a sound from downstairs. It was a slap that only a foot makes on a marble step.

Staying as low as possible I stepped toward Lake and moved behind him. I always had his back in these situations. It was something practiced and maintained since our cop days. Hugging the wall I crept down the corridor a few steps and settled against the companion wall of the room we were about to breach.

Suddenly the door creaked open and a splice of light grazed the corridor. My pistol was up and aimed in half a second. I took three quiet steps back, retreating farther into the darkness, both hands gripping the weapon. The green dots lined up in a perfect row, the pad of my forefinger resting deftly on the trigger.

"We're moving out," a familiar voice from the room said. "Get the girl. She's in the bedroom downstairs at the end of the hall."

"No!" Reeve yelled. "Leave her alone, you traitor."

"Shut up!"

I motioned to Lake that someone was downstairs. He nodded. He'd heard with those supersensitive ears of his.

I moved quickly and quietly to his side. Lake's hand reached out. I leaned slightly forward, the shooter's stance. It would be fast. His right hand went to the door and paused an instant. There was shouting inside the room as Lake flung the door inward. "Slice the bitch!" I heard Yasmin shout.

Lake hugged the frame, his hands and gun filling the open doorway. My gun was locked in a level position. Lake swung his gun right and left at the same time he shifted his weight while hugging the door frame. He leaned just enough into the open doorway so he could take in the entire room while exposing only a fraction of his body. I was behind, keeping his back.

"Wall behind the door," he said. I moved slightly right and still watched the players. Weatherby stood sideways, one hand grasping Reeve's arm, another holding a service knife. Reeve's mouth was twisted with hate and fear. Thomas Page sat bungee-tied in a chair.

I stepped back to see through the door crack at the hinges. I saw the black finish of a gun in the hands of a tall, dark-haired woman.

I moved up to Lake's side, gun leveled. "Yasmin, behind the door."

It seemed a perpetual tableau, a moment in time, of disbelief where everything suspends. Page tied in a chair, Yasmin playing hide-and-seek behind the door. Reeve frozen in Weatherby's grip. Knife near her throat.

Then everyone moved at once.

Page cried out, "They've got Shara in the . . ."

Yasmin stepped from behind the door, raised the silenced pistol. I was ready for her. A martial arts kick to the back of her knees had her crumpling like a knocked-down suit of armor. At the same time, Weatherby made a stupid move. He spun Reeve around to shield himself and throw the knife. He paused an instant too long to take our measures, long enough for Reeve to elbow him in the gut. He regained his balance and grabbed Reeve. He looked at guns held by Lake and me.

Lake's voice was stern. "Don't be stupid, Weatherby. A knife to a gun fight? Put it down. Dru, take the shot."

Weatherby seemed to consider this, then flung the knife at me. Guess he figured I was a prop with a toy gun. Lake had already stepped to Yasmin as I aimed for Weatherby's exposed shoulder. The bullet met the blade in midair and slung the knife back at Weatherby, slicing into his bicep. *I hate it when my aim is off.*

Raising his one good arm, Weatherby pleaded, "Don't kill me. Salman killed the caretaker, not me."

Page said, "You shot at me, but it was her." He glared at Yasmin. "She killed her brother. Ambushed the son-of-a-bitch. What she didn't do, Salman did for her. Then she snuck up behind him and slit his throat. He's dead downstairs."

"Allah disgraces all of you," Yasmin said, raising herself from the floor.

Having regained her composure, Reeve stood tall. "She's a monster. She didn't have to kill him. Her own brother."

Lake's aim was on Yasmin, struggling to her knees. She spewed at Reeve, "I know the evil truth. He's not one with Allah."

Page said, his voice calm despite his words, "She said they were going to hang me. Make it look like suicide."

Yasmin shot to her feet. The pistol that had been under her torso was in her hand. She was quick, I'll say that. She raised the gun, her aim at Page. Because she was in profile, Lake had a shot at her ear—*going for a head takedown.*

"Put it down, Yasmin," Lake commanded.

"Princess!" she yelled, her arm wavering.

In that split second of imperious hubris Lake lunged for her. The suppressed bullet from her gun snicked from the barrel and hit a wall above and behind Weatherby. Lake knocked the gun from her hand and spun her around. She spit at him. He clamped a hand around her mouth. His gun came around and he pressed the barrel under her chin. "Don't move," he said, "or I'll blow your goddamn head off."

At first she was still, her eyes wide in disbelief. Then she began to wriggle away, and squirmed backward. "Stop!" she cried. "I am a woman!"

My gun barrel stayed on Weatherby while he squeezed his arm to keep the blood from flowing.

Lake's hand went to Yasmin's mouth and squeezed her jaws so her mouth made a narrow 0. She fought on. He clamped his fingers on her nose as she struggled. When she gulped air he grabbed her jaws again. "You're a murderer, a crazy Islamic fascist."

She bit down and he moved his hand. She spit. "He died like a lizard."

"You mean Lowell Cresley?"

She hissed. "I shit on you!"

His clamped hand shook her jaws as he said, "Because Lowell scorned Islamists like you scorn America?"

While I watched, I recalled the anger I felt when I learned who had slammed the planes into the World Trade Center. Anger even for Muslims I knew and liked.

She tried to swat at him, and he pressed the barrel of his gun upward, raising her neck and chin until her face was nearly parallel to the ceiling.

"Burn in hell fire, vile pig!"

"How was your bacon sandwich yesterday?"

She spit the word, "Ghoul."

Weatherby seemed amused all of a sudden. Reeve went to where Page was tied and began to unhook the cords. Lake pulled handcuffs from his belt and reached to cuff Yasmin.

At that moment, two men flashed into the room, and passed me.

One said, "We'll take it from here, Lieutenant." I'd heard that accent before. Slightly British, it brought Pearly Sue's face into my mind.

Yasmin screamed, "You can't come in here and take me. You vile son-of-a-mother-bitch."

The backs of their jackets read "Diplomatic Security Service."

The man who talked seemed familiar. I realized by the quick, catlike turn of his body that he was Cartaloma—or the man calling himself Victor Cartaloma—because he was the living image of Pearly Sue's description and his moves caught on the cam at Turtle Pond.

Lake is an expert at cuffing. Despite her rage, spitting and profanity Yasmin was bound in aluminum.

When the DSS agent turned her around, I saw his face from beneath the baseball cap with DSS letters on the front. Yes, he surely was the man at Turtle Pond.

My eyes caught his. "So, we meet, Victor."

Yasmin spat at me.

Cartaloma frowned and gave a short shake of his head. He told Lake that they would take control of Husam's body and the Arab downstairs.

Lake had Weatherby in handcuffs and Cartaloma said, "That bastard goes with us, too." Cuffed behind his back, despite the bleeding slash, Weatherby was led out by the second agent.

I kind of blocked Cartaloma's path, then fell in step in the hall. I whispered away from Yasmin's spitting tirade—definitely not a dry-mouth sufferer, "The reports of your demise were premature."

He smirked-grinned and handed Yasmin to another agent in the hall. We watched her while she was pushed forward to keep from spitting on the agent. Then Cartaloma said, "I liked your agent in New York."

"You were following Husam," I said. "He led you here because he guessed Reeve might be hiding here. It's Reeve's place now that her parents are dead."

"You were following Yasmin," he said. "And here we meet. Wonder what Saliba had in store for his wife and daughter?"

I told him what I thought and knew. "He was after Shara and leaving with Yasmin and Salman. They chartered a private jet out of Nashville bound for Toronto using French passports. Only Yasmin had her own plan and it didn't include the defamed prince or the bodyguard."

"You were thirty seconds ahead of us," Cartaloma said, "because we got the wrong building."

"You got the building where we'll find our murderer," Lake said.

"A dead man's in that building," Cartaloma said. "Your people are there."

That was sobering. I paused a moment to think of Husam's death. Two people I'd gotten to know. One died from love and the other from ideology.

"You want a federal job, we're hiring," Cartaloma said.

Yasmin shouted from the stairs. "I piss for your filthy country. Allah is great!"

"What will happen to them? Trial? Deportation?" I asked.

"Special Agent Scheel will be in touch."

"To tell us when your funeral will be?"

"I was already buried in Baghdad," he said, then winked and walked away.

Reeve and Page came out of the room. I looked at her. "You got the killer."

She shook her head. "He got himself. When he saw us, he knew."

That's when I noticed Thomas Page's empty holster at the small of his back.

Reeve was on the move. "I'm going to get Shara."

I followed her to the floating steps. Tom Page passed me and took hold of Reeve's arm. They got down with a few stumbles, but upright. Reeve dashed down the hall to a room with a closed door. Tom was behind her with Lake and I behind Tom. Lake pushed ahead to Reeve and held out a hand. "Key?" Reeve reached into her jeans and fumbled the key out. Lake cautiously opened the door, peered inside the room, then turned to Reeve and Tom with a smile on his face. "She's fine. We'll need to talk, get your statements."

Reeve started to say something, but Tom took her by the arm and I followed them inside the room. Reeve ran to the play table where a dark-haired girl sat in a chair thumbing at an electronic game. Reeve fell to her knees like a penitent at a healing ritual. "Oh, baby!"

The dark-haired girl smiled at her mother, then she looked at me. She was a beautiful child. Eyes like onyx. I wondered what she would remember about this time.

I said, "Hello, Shara."

She lifted her chin and said smartly, "I want to be called Shahrazad." At least she didn't say *Princess*. She was the image of her father, and I saw that were Lake and I to have a girl child, she would look like Shara—our black hair and Lake's big, dark eyes.

Nope, not going there. We'd gone a whole month without the suggestion of marriage.

When Shara grinned impishly I thought this little girl, this Shahrazad—like her namesake, and with the gift of drama bestowed by her Arabian father—would spin many stories in her lifetime.

We turned for the hall.

I said to Lake, "I looked it up."

"What?"

" 'The Ruined Man Who Became Rich Again Through a Dream.' The man is told in a dream to leave his city and . . ."

"Cut to the chase," he said, walking beside me.

". . . travel to Cairo, where he will discover the whereabouts of some hidden treasure. The man travels there and experiences misfortune, ending up in jail, where he tells his dream to a police officer. The officer mocks the idea of prophetic dreams and tells the traveler that he himself had a dream about a house with a courtyard and fountain in Baghdad where treasure is buried under the fountain. The traveler recognizes the place as his own house and, after he is released from jail, he returns home and digs up the treasure."

Lake thought a moment, then said, "You think Husam hoped his misfortune here would lead to riches in Saudi Arabia when he got home?"

"I do. Like the traveler, Husam lived in a parable world."

"Whatever that means."

"He imagined his life like the romantic fables he told."

"Well, he died in the real world helping kill real people. I see no romance in that."

I thought of our talk at the Ritz, one that touched on the malice of women and the casual murders of adversaries while the man who knew the tales failed to find the true story of his heart therein or there out.

Lake concluded, "If I never hear of the Arabian Nights again, that will be just fine with me."

Me, too. For a while.

Walking toward the security office, we beat the bushes, hoping to not find a knocked-out, not-dead, security guard, and found no one.

We'd passed the gate when I heard a truck behind us. I turned to see a step van turn for the exit and gather speed. Lake glanced my way. "Did I say they could leave?"

"Not that I heard."

"They're gone. No one to stop them."

It was telling that he didn't reach for his radio.

Approaching the security office, in the glare of lights, it looked like a murder of crows—men in black and dark blue outside— some speaking, some smoking, some chewing gum.

Approaching us, Haskell said, "Dead."

"DSS told us," Lake said. "Cartaloma."

We followed Haskell into the security office. A computer monitor showed the gate and the empty guard kiosk. Sitting in a computer chair, facing us, was the body of Carl Langford. A pistol lay in his lap.

"Reeve lied to us," I said.

After studying the dead man, Lake said, "Langford could not have shot himself in the forehead twice."

"No," Haskell said. "They did this. Vengeance, pay back."

"Yes, and they've left the premises."

Haskell nodded. He'd seen the van exit the gate on the monitor. "We'll get them," he said as I watched two APD squad cars roll through the exit, sirens blaring.

Did I hope they got away? Maybe. Oh, justice, you can be a really mean bitch.

"Why'd Langford do it?" Haskell asked. "Kill the Cresleys?"

Lake looked at me. "Dru and I have a difference of opinion."

Haskell gave me his half-benign uncle, half-quizzical expression.

I said, "Donna and Carl Langford plotted Lowell's murder."

"Together?" Haskell said. "She . . ."

"We thought two killers, but we were only half right. Lake, being the cop that he is, wants evidence before he'll go along with my thinking." Haskell looked at his protégé appreciatively. "I'd bet good money that Donna Cresley and Carl Langford conspired to kill her husband and hoped to cover it up by accusing Husam. Reeve's marital trouble and flight gave them the perfect opportunity."

"The fingerprint we recovered isn't Langford's. Military and security man—he'd have prints on file." Lake was shaking his head in agreement.

Despite their negative attitudes, I went on. "The question for me was, who uses a garrote to kill when a gun is handy? The garrote was purposely used to mean that Dr. Cresley was tried, convicted and executed of some cultural shame he'd imposed upon Husam. Had they succeeded and Donna lived, she would have had some handy examples of Husam's boorish behavior and Lowell's replies that would indicate Husam had done the deed. Or had his Saudi pals do it for him. But Langford hadn't a clue how to execute with a garrote. Makes one wonder if he wasn't reading *too* many comics and thrillers."

Looking amused, Lake folded his arms across his chest. "Conjecture."

I continued, "Cresley escaped the attempt, ran to the phone and dialed my number. He may have figured he didn't have much time to escape another attempt. He knew Langford carried a gun. He wanted to tell me who his killer was. Donna heard the commotion in the study and ran to see what was happening. Who knows what went through her mind. Seeing murder being done isn't as pretty as the idea of getting rid of a philandering, embarrassing drunk for a husband while sitting in the parlor drinking a cocktail. Donna screamed at what she witnessed. I heard her through the phone. Langford saw the phone in Cresley's hand, probably heard my voice. He figured he had no choice but to kill Donna."

Haskell's forehead creased with frown lines. "We'll certainly look at the evidence in light of your hypothesis."

"Langford," I went on, "knowing of Alvarez's affair with Donna and her penchant to talk, decided Alvarez had to die. Wouldn't be long, perhaps, police would get around to speaking with Alvarez. Lake was just about to."

"Timing is everything," Haskell said.

"When we came here a second time, Langford panicked and decided some misdirection was called for. He knew of Husam's connection to Sarasota so that's where he'd hire Alvarez to fly him to deflect from himself."

Lake intervened. "I'll add a few facts to the supposition. No one at Charlie Brown saw Langford, but a line man at Sarasota identified him. Alvarez lands the plane, then deplanes and goes inside the hangar office to get a drink. That's fact. Also, he leaves Langford with the plane. We know that for a fact. Here's what we suppose: Langford, thinking he's alone, loosens the gas caps, which will run fuel out fast. A mechanic spotted him walking away to a cab, wiping his hands with a shop rag. Another fact."

Haskell looked at me. "For what it's worth, you make a lot of sense. We'll find the evidence if it's there." He contemplated the dead body of Carl Langford. "We'll have to charge Cresley and Page with him."

"Who fired first?" I asked. "Who fired the shot that killed him?"

Haskell pinched his lips. "We'll start with conspiracy, intent to maim, intent to kill, until we know for sure."

"Good luck with that," I said. "They're in the wind."

Lake and Haskell looked at me like I couldn't be more wrong.

Not ten minutes later, Haskell got a radio call. Officers had found the step van abandoned in Chastain Park, by the golf course. Nothing in it but an ice-cream cone wrapper.

"Cute kid," Lake said, and started the squad car's engine. "She'd be even more gorgeous with big, blue eyes."

When I looked at him, I thought my lungs would never breathe again. He stopped the car and leaned over to touch his gentle lips to my open mouth. Pulling back, he asked, "Nervous?"

I shook my head. "Of course not."

ABOUT THE AUTHOR

Gerrie Ferris Finger is a retired journalist and author of several novels, six published in the Moriah Dru/Richard Lake series: *The End Game, The Last Temptation, The Devil Laughed, Murmurs of Insanity* and *Running with Wild Blood. American Nights* is the fifth in the series published by Five Star. Ms. Finger lives on the coast of Georgia with her husband, Alan, and their standard poodle, Bogey.

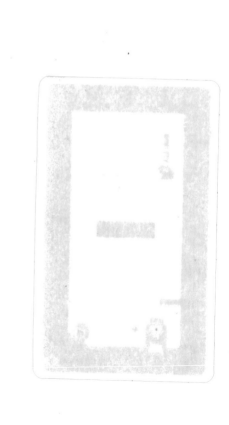